STOR ⸻

When a flash of light⸻ illuminated the bedroom, Dakota's green eyes ran hungrily over Breanna's flawless body. Slowly he pulled her into his arms and tilted her chin so he could claim her lips in a tender-sweet quest that demanded total surrender.

Gasping for breath, Breanna felt as if she had no substance, that he could take her, mold her, and make her into whatever he wanted.

"Breanna, sweet Breanna," he murmured against her lips. "I will take you where no man has ever dared."

She threw her head back and felt his breath on her heated flesh. She quivered while his eyes ran over her. There was no shame in her, because she could tell by his eyes that he found her pleasing.

Dakota pulled her tightly against him. She could feel the rise and fall of his chest, and found that her breathing matched his.

"I fear I am out of control," he whispered. "I need you, Breanna."

"Yes," she murmured. "Yes . . ."

Dakota Dreams

CONSTANCE O'BANYON

ZEBRA BOOKS
KENSINGTON PUBLISHING CORP.

ZEBRA BOOKS

are published by

Kensington Publishing Corp.
475 Park Avenue South
New York, NY 10016

First printing: November, 1988

Printed in the United States of America

This one's for you, JoAnn McCormick. I will never forget how you braved Williamsburg in the rain, and chauffeured me around so I could do research. You are a sister to my husband, and a special friend to me.

Carrie Ledford, researcher extraordinaire, thanks for your help.

Author's note

In 1833, the German Prince Maximilian zu Wied traveled the Missouri River. Although he was one of America's least known explorers, he left a legacy of meticulous logs and records of the daily lives of American Indians. Karl Bodmer, the Swiss-born artist who accompanied Prince Maximilian on his expedition, created some of the finest Indian drawings ever made of that period, as well as invaluable watercolors of the wilderness along the Missouri River. We owe these two men a debt of gratitude for their contribution to our early history. Through their drawings and written accounts we can see and read about America when it was a virgin paradise. They left us an insight to a world we can only reflect on and dream about.

Prologue

November 1833

The icy winds swept down the rock-faced mountain gullies to the valley below. In powerful gusts the wind picked up sheets of snow and whirled them around in a blinding-white blizzard. The small log cabin situated on the banks of the Salmon River was barely visible through the swirling tide of death.

Within the cabin, a woman in her mid-thirties was huddled among soft furs on the makeshift bed, trying to keep warm. A sudden gust of wind hurled its fury down the chimney with such a force that the fire flickered and went out, making the woman's lot even more wretched.

With chills shaking her body, Lady Cillia Remington moved off the bed and knelt in front of the rock fireplace. Tossing the last of the logs on the glowing embers, she waited until the fire ignited. In spite of the cold, Cillia's golden hair lay damp across her forehead, while her strange, jade-green eyes were fever-bright. She had an exquisite beauty that seemed out of place in this crude cabin. Clutching the golden locket that rested against her breast, she pressed the hidden catch, and the locket opened to reveal a miniature of her and her husband. She felt the anguish of loneliness as she stared at the dark-haired man with the finely chiseled face. With a pitiful sigh, she clicked the locket shut, unable to endure the pain of looking upon her beloved's face.

Cillia huddled closer to the blaze, wondering if she would ever be warm again. As her eyes moved around the primitive cabin, the scene took on the feeling of unreality. What was she doing here alone in this vast, uninhabited land? She remembered her father-in-law's impassioned objection to her and Holden joining this expedition to the American wilderness. His parting words now came back to haunt her. She could almost hear his voice raised in anger. *If you go with Holden this time, you will suffer the consequences! The American wilderness is no place for a woman with your delicate nature. You and my son should both stay here in England, where you belong. I am uneasy about this latest folly of Holden's.*

Holden's father, the Marquess of Weatherford, had one burning desire in his life—he wanted an heir who would settle down at Weatherford Hall and be controlled by him. He had come to realize that Holden would never be satisfied under his domination, so the old Marquess yearned for a grandson on whom he could transfer his hopes and expectations.

A tear rolled off the tip of Lady Cillia's lashes and made a trail down her colorless cheek. If she had it to do over again, she would have done no differently. She would follow her husband anywhere he chose to go.

Lord Holden, Viscount of Remington, had been born with an adventurous spirit. Since their marriage,

Cillia had always accompanied him on his travels. They had hunted tigers in India with a maharajah, traveled to a monastery in Tibet, and sailed around Cape Horn. They had stood in the shadows of the great pyramids in Egypt and watched the sunset. They had acquired trophies and valuable art objects, which had been shipped back to England from all over the world. Elephant tusks, tiger heads, and rare and unusual animal skins now graced the walls of the study at Weatherford Hall.

When the German Prince Maximilian zu Wied was planning an expedition down the Missouri River in America, he had invited Holden and Cillia to accompany him, and of course, Holden accepted. Cillia could remember so well Holden's excitement at the prospect of hunting the famed American bison so he could add its skin to his trophies. Her eyes moved to the corner of the room where a large number of buffalo hides were now stacked. Holden had certainly acquired his share of them.

Once more she listened for the sound of his footsteps. Where was he? What could be keeping him? Her hand moved down to her swollen stomach. Holden's father was about to have his wish to be a grandfather fulfilled, because she was heavy with child.

Holden was the only son of Quincy Remington, the ninth Marquess of Weatherford. Father and son were both strong-willed, and Cillia knew this was the reason they had often quarreled. Holden's father could be hard and demanding, and yes, even tyrannical. Few people ever denied the Marquess anything, for he was wealthy, powerful, and influential. When Holden had refused to settle down at Weatherford Hall, his father had tried to bring him back under his control. When the Marquess

11

cut off his son's yearly allowance, Holden had been unaffected and had happily drawn from the substantial trust that had been left to him on his mother's death.

The Marquess had blamed Cillia's childless state on the fact that she and Holden never stayed in one place long enough for her to conceive. The two of them had been married for twelve years, and there had been times when she had despaired, thinking they would never have children. Holden had assured her many times that his happiness was complete and they did not need a child to complicate their lives. But she had often seen the wistfulness in his eyes when he had observed children at play. She had known he had only been trying to spare her feelings, for he had desperately wanted a child.

The expedition had reached Fort McKenzie, on the Upper Missouri, when Cillia had become convinced that she was expecting a child. When she told Holden, he had been overjoyed, and in his concern for her and the baby, he had insisted that they leave the expedition and return to civilization where the child could be born under a doctor's care.

They had started on the long trek back down the Missouri River with only Baxley, Holden's valet, and a scout named Levi Gunther. Levi was a strange man to find in the wilderness. He had obtained a certain amount of fame through several books that had been written on his daring exploits as an Indian scout and buffalo hunter. It was obvious that Levi was well educated and had a good command of the English language — two traits one did not often find in a man who chose the wilderness as his home.

They had hoped to make it all the way to New York

before cold weather overtook them, although Levi had warned them how unpredictable the weather could be this time of year. Even the experienced scout had been unprepared for how swiftly winter had come upon them. After a blue norther had hit with gale-force winds, capsizing their flat-bottom boat, they had been forced to remain in this uninhabited mountain valley until spring.

Cillia and Holden had faced the reality that their baby would be born in this wilderness and that the tents they had rescued from their sinking boat would offer them no protection against the fierce winter that lay ahead. The three men had built a crude one-room cabin. It wasn't until a store of fresh meat had been laid in that Holden decided to send the scout to St. Louis for supplies, while Baxley was sent to make arrangements for their voyage to England before returning to London to inform Holden's father about the forthcoming birth.

In the beginning, Holden and Cillia had looked upon this as just another adventure. With joy in their hearts, they anticipated the birth of their baby and cherished their time alone together.

The wind intensified, making the door rattle on its leather hinges, and Cillia felt the icy drafts that seeped through the cracks in the logs. Shivering, she placed her hand on her swollen stomach, wishing Holden would return. He had only gone in search of firewood and should have come back hours ago.

One glance at the charred logs in the fireplace told Cillia that the fire would soon go out and there were no more logs to build it up again. She stood up and moved to the door, trailing the fur robe that was wrapped about her. Grasping the leather strap that served as a handle, she opened the door a crack, only to have the wind wrench it from her grasp and slam it against the outside wall. She strained her eyes, staring into the swirling white mass, but was unable to see anything that lay more then twenty paces from the cabin.

Panic took over her reasoning. Suppose Holden had gone too far afield in search of firewood and had become lost in the blizzard? Cillia tried to push her anxiety aside. No, Holden could take care of himself. He would never find himself in a situation over which he had no control. Cillia tugged on the door, and after struggling against the wind, finally managed to shut it and slip the latch into place. She moved back to the bed, reminding herself to remain calm while she waited for her husband.

The blizzard continued to howl throughout the day, seeming to throw its cruel fury against the small cabin. While the snow became deeper and deeper, Cillia's fear for her husband's safety intensified. By now the fire had gone out, but so great was her concern for Holden that she did not feel the numbing cold. She realized Holden would never have stayed away so long. Something must have happened to him.

As Cillia stared into the smoldering ashes, she knew she could no longer sit huddled on the bed, shivering. She had to do something or she would lose her mind — she had to search for Holden.

Having decided on a positive action, Cillia quickly pulled on her waterproof, sealskin boots, then wrapped herself in her fur cape. She moved out the door and latched it behind her. Mercifully, it had stopped snowing and the wind had died down, leaving the snowdrifts as high as her boot tops. With difficulty, she made her way toward the river, trying not to give in to her fears. Holden was safe. He was somewhere waiting for the storm to let up, she told herself. At any moment she expected to hear him calling her name. She scanned the nearby foothills, seeing no sign of her beloved, and her heart plummeted. It would be impossible for her to track him since the blizzard would have long ago covered his footprints.

Once Cillia reached the river, she saw chunks of ice floating downstream, and she shivered. What would she do if Holden did not return? If he was dead, she would not want to live either. But what would happen to her baby? A sob arose from somewhere deep inside her.

"Holden, where are you?" she cried. "Please come back to me."

Although there had been no sound that alerted Cillia to the fact that she was not alone, she suddenly felt a strange sensation that prickled along her spine, and she could not control the shudder that shook her body. It was frightening to realize that hostile eyes were staring at her!

She turned around slowly, and a terrified gasp escaped her throat. Not ten paces from her, she saw three mounted Indians, their faces hideously painted, their horses sending frosted breath into the frigid air! Cillia had met many friendly Indians at Fort McKenzie, but these Indians' dark sullen eyes told her that they were not friendly.

Cillia had no time to react to her fear, for when she took a step backward, her feet slipped on the rocks, and she plunged headlong into the icy river! Bitter cold needles of pain stabbed at her skin as the water sucked her under. She was a good swimmer, but she was being dragged down by the weight of her heavy boots and fur cape. Wildly, frantically, she fought to stay afloat and finally managed to reach the surface. She coughed and sputtered when she breathed in a deep gulp of air, expelling the water from her lungs.

Suddenly, a gasp tore from her lips as an agonizing pain ripped through her body. Dear God, she thought wildly, Don't let me have my baby now!

"Holden, help me!" she screamed. Fighting to keep her head above the churning water, Cillia realized that if she did not soon make it to shore she would freeze to death and her baby would never be born. In her fight for survival, she had forgotten all about the Indians.

Now she saw that one of the warriors had dismounted and was standing on the riverbank, looking at her with interest. Her eyes sought his, and she held out her hand in a pleading manner. A strong mother's instinct made her forget about her own safety as she struggled to save her unborn child. All fear of the man was pushed to the back of her mind, and she reached out to the Indian as one human being to another, beseeching him for help.

"Help me. Please help save my baby," she whimpered.

Two Moons, war chief of the Arapaho, stared at the white woman, observing her struggle for life. Although he could not understand her words, she reached a place of pity in his heart. With a strong grasp, he took her hand and pulled her from the icy jaws of death. When he lifted her into his arms, he saw the roundness of her stomach and felt her stiffen with pain. He knew she was heavy with child, and he thought of his own wife who was about to give birth.

Turning to his companions, Two Moons spoke. "I will help this white woman deliver her baby, though it is doubtful that she or the child will live. You will ride back to the camp and wait for me there." Leaving his friends to wonder at his strange behavior, Two Moons carried the woman into the cabin and closed the door.

He quickly stripped off her wet clothing and placed her among the furs on the bed. Cillia did not cry out, nor did she feel afraid as rough hands rested on her swollen stomach, feeling the contraction that knotted her muscles. The kindness in Two Moons' eyes belayed any apprehension Cillia might have. She knew she had nothing to fear from this Indian. He was going to help her.

It was long after sunset, and still Cillia labored to bring forth her baby. No words passed between her and the Indian, but they experienced a strange bond, a bond to save the child. Two Moons held a jug of water to Cillia's mouth so she could wet her dry lips, and she read compassion in his dark eyes. He left her only once, and that was to get firewood so he could lay a fire.

Cillia did not know at what moment she realized she was going to die. Death beckoned to her like a kind friend, offering her sanctuary from pain of body and spirit. Deep inside, she felt that Holden was dead, and she only wanted death to hasten her to his side. Agonizing pain ripped through her body, and she caught the Indian's hand, her nails digging into his skin. Too weak to scream, her body arched with the building pressure. With a gasp, she felt the child issue from her body, giving her peace, glorious peace.

The only light in the cabin came from the roaring fire. Cillia watched the Indian lift her baby in his arms; she heard the feeble cry. He turned the baby to her, and she saw that she had a son! How proud Holden would have been.

"Please," she whispered weakly, pushing the baby more firmly into his arms, "take my baby . . . do not let him die here with me." Suddenly it became important to her that the child have something that belonged to her. With her last bit of strength, she reached up and unclasped the gold locket she wore about her neck, and with trembling hands, held it out to the Indian. "Please keep this for the child . . . so he will have something of mine."

Two Moons took the gold locket from the woman and watched as her eyes closed and her last breath came out in a soft hiss. Lady Cillia Remington now walked among the spirits!

He glanced down at the infant boy in his arms, doubting the child would survive the night. Two Moons could not have said why, but it suddenly became important to him that this white baby live.

Wrapping the infant in warm robes, the Indian moved to the door. He would take the baby to his village and away from this scene of tragedy. If the Spirit willed it, perhaps he would cheat death at least once this day.

Lord Holden Remington gritted his teeth in pain while he dragged himself along the frozen ground. The rag that was tied about his leg was blood soaked. He tried not to look at the protruding bone, or think about the fall over the cliff that had broken his leg. He was half-frozen and near death after having limped for over five miles with a broken leg. He was in agony, and would have given up long ago, but knowing that Cillia needed him gave him the strength to continue against impossible odds.

It was after the midnight hour when he at last reached the cabin. With determination that came from his love for his wife, he pushed himself forward.

A bright moon on the new snow gave the appearance of day, and his heart froze in fear when he saw the moccasin footprints that were deeply imbedded in the snow. Fear for his wife and unborn baby gave him renewed strength. Gritting his teeth against the pain, he hefted himself up and pushed the door open.

It was as cold as a tomb inside the cabin, and it took a moment for Holden's eyes to adjust to the darkness. With the bright moon streaming through the doorway, he saw his wife lying on the bed, and he knew before he approached Cillia that she was dead!

Wild, unbridled grief took over his thinking, and he eased himself down beside his wife. At first he thought she had been killed by Indians, but a quick examination told him there was no sign of violence. When his hand moved to her stomach, he saw that she had died in childbirth. As his eyes ran frantically over the cabin, he realized the baby was not there.

His mind worked fast, and he realized that the Indian tracks outside the cabin now had a greater significance. The Indian had taken his baby! Holden's mind cleared as he reached for his journal and, with his last bit of strength, began to write. His hand shook so badly that he hoped his writing would be legible. He had to leave this written evidence so his father would begin a search for the baby. Holden felt at peace, knowing his father would not rest until he had located the child.

On this day, the first day of November, in the year of Our Lord, 1833, Cillia died, delivering our child while I was away. It is my belief that the child lives and has been taken by Indians. It is my hope that every effort will be made to find the baby so it can be sent to my father in England. It is my wish that my wife and I be buried in a common grave so we might spend eternity together.

The journal slipped from Holden's hands. There was an ominous rattle in his chest, and he felt numb all over. Ignoring his pain, he lay down beside his beloved Cillia, whom he thought beautiful even in death. Gathering her cold body to him, he waited for death to speed him to her side. Thus the Viscount drew his last breath, making his newborn son the Viscount of Remington!

The sun had set in the Arapaho village as the three warriors made their way past the laughing children and welcoming smiles of the tribe.

The war chief's wife, White Wing, was seated before the fire suckling her newborn infant, when she heard her husband's moccasin footsteps outside the tepee. Two Moons had been away for many days, and she had joyous news to share with him. Two Moons would be so pleased and proud that he had a son! There was much love in Two Moons' lodge, but White Wing and her war chief husband had been childless for many years. The two of them were no longer young, and their happiness had been boundless when they learned they were going to have this child.

The lodge flap was pushed aside, and she watched her husband enter. Elation danced in her dark eyes as he knelt beside her.

"You have a son, my husband," she said with pride.

Two Moons looked on his dark-skinned child with wonder. "The Spirits are good, my wife, for where we once had no sons, we now have two." White Wing noticed for the first time that her husband carried a fur robe. She watched in amazement as he folded it back to reveal a sickly white-skinned baby.

When Two Moons told his wife about the white woman who had died giving birth to the child, White Wing's heart melted and her eyes filled with sadness for the orphan child. She took him in her arms and held him to her breast, where he suckled hungrily.

Her bright eyes sought her husband's. "Can we keep this baby?"

Two Moons nodded. "His mother gave him into my care. I believe it was meant that this baby should come to us. If he lives, we will call him Dakota."

"Yes, Dakota is a good name." She thought of its meaning, "feeling affection for."

Two Moons took his own dark-skinned son in his arms and held him above his head while the child cried loud and lustily. "Our two sons will learn to walk as one. They will grow to manhood together, and bless this lodge twice over."

"If the white child . . . lives, my husband."

Two Moons' dark eyes saddened when they rested on the sickly Dakota, whose pallor was more yellow than white. He knew it was unlikely that the infant would live past another week. It was a miracle that he had lived this long. "Yes, if he lives," he agreed.

Chapter One

June 1839

Levi Gunther adjusted his spyglass and aimed it at the Arapaho Village across the Wind River. He had been watching the village for two days, and had not as yet seen what he was looking for. Levi had been corresponding with Lord Holden's father, the Marquess of Weatherford, for five years. The Marquess had hired him to find his grandchild, and the hunter had dedicated his life to that aim. It wasn't so much the money, although the Marquess was paying him very well. Finding the child, if it was still alive, had become an obsession with him. At times he would get discouraged and want to give up, but he kept going, hoping one day to find the missing child.

He had spent the last five years running down leads, checking out rumors, and chasing shadows. He had been to over fifty Indian villages without succeeding in his quest. Three weeks ago he had come upon a bit of information that had caused him to hope his search was nearing its conclusion. George Murphy, at the Murphy Trading Post, had told him about a white boy who was living with the Arapaho tribe that made their home across the Wind River. Levi's excitement had mounted when Murphy had informed him the boy had green eyes! He remembered vividly Lady Cillia Remington's emerald-green eyes.

Levi watched a large body of Arapaho warriors cross the river. He hunched down behind a tree, praying they wouldn't find his horse that was grazing nearby. After they disappeared from view, he renewed his vigil. He was unfamiliar with this branch of the Arapaho tribe. Murphy had told him that they kept very much to themselves and were not nomads, as were many other Arapaho tribes.

He scanned the village, noting that there were mostly women and children, busily going about their daily tasks. He pushed his spyglass shut, shoved it in his leather satchel, and went in search of his mount. Now was as good a time as any to cross the river. Tying his leather satchel onto the back of his horse, he pulled out a roll of jerky, deciding that if he were going to die today, it would not be on an empty stomach.

With more determination than courage, he mounted his horse and rode down the slope, entering the shallow part of the river. The Arapaho had chosen the perfect place for their village, because the Wind River circled them on two sides, making it impossible for anyone to come upon them from this direction without being seen. Thus, Levi was spotted just as his horse entered the river. Word of his approach spread throughout the village, and when he rode up the riverbank, a dozen warriors were there to greet him, bows drawn, and hostility and suspicion gleaming in their dark eyes.

"I come as a friend," he said, speaking in the tongue of the Arapaho.

"Dismount," one of the warriors ordered, his arrow drawn and aimed at Levi's chest, his dark eyes probing and cold. Levi had always liked to think of himself as a brave man, but at that moment, his body quivered with fear, and he felt a sickening churning in his stomach.

Levi held his arms in the air, crossed his leg over the saddle, and slid to the ground. He felt the sharp point of a spear in his back, and he knew that the Indian would not hesitate to ram it into his body if Levi made one wrong move. "I come in peace," he said past the bile rising in his throat.

It was at that moment that a tall Indian walked toward him. Levi knew this was no ordinary Indian, but one of great importance. He wore three eagle feathers in his gray-laced dark hair. Tall and proud, the man's dark gaze was probing and searching.

"What . . . are you . . . called?" Two Moons said in halting English.

"I am called Levi Gunther," he answered in perfect Arapaho.

Two Moons' dark eyes moved over Levi from head to foot. "I have heard of you. It is said you are a very brave man and have always respected the Indian and our customs. I have also heard it said that you can enter the territory of my brother, the Blackfoot, unmolested."

Levi began to hope he would not die. "I have lived with the Blackfoot and Arapaho and am proud to call

all Indians my brother. May I know who you are?"

"I am Two Moons, war chief of the Arapaho."

Levi nodded. "I have also heard of you, although not in detail. It is said you keep your own counsel."

"Why have you come among us, Levi Gunther?"

The time of truth had arrived, and Levi hesitated, knowing he could meet his death in earnest when this chief learned of the reason for his intrusion. "I am looking for a white child," he blurted out, deciding he had come this far, he might as well challenge death. "The child would be in its fifth year."

The dark eyes became piercing. "I knew why you had come. I have known for years that you were searching for a white child. You are foolhardy, Levi Gunther, to have come among us alone and uninvited."

Levi tensed and then continued. "I have been searching for this child because there is a grandfather in England who is very powerful and wants his grandchild with him."

"No grandfather, no matter how powerful he is elsewhere, has any power here," Two Moons reminded Levi.

"This is true, but the grandfather is also very wealthy and will give many horses and blankets to those who return his grandchild."

Two Moons stared at the famed hunter, feeling different emotions. It had always been his wish to meet this man who had shown great friendship for the Indian. Levi Gunther was a great hunter, and it was said he was fearless in battle. "If the boy were here, he would not be for sale, no matter how many horses were offered for him."

Levi's eyes narrowed just a fraction. He could feel the turmoil in this man. "I did not say the child was a boy. But if he is here, many horses can mean great prosperity for this tribe," Levi suggested.

Levi was never to know what Two Moons would have replied, for at that moment two young Indian boys came running out of the woods and drew the war chief's attention. Levi watched the boys come closer, and he sensed Two Moons' anxiety.

Although both boys had black hair, Levi noticed that one of them was lighter-skinned than the other. As they reached Two Moons, the lighter-skinned boy grabbed the Indian's leg and laughed up at him. "I won, Father. I won the race."

Levi stared at the young boy and then into green eyes that were reminiscent of other green eyes — Lady Cillia Remington's! He did not need to be told that this was her son and that his long search was over at last.

The other boy drew Levi's attention as he kicked at the dirt, his face sullen. "I am the fastest, Father. I could have outrun Dakota if he had not had a head start."

Two Moons grasped the arm of each boy and shoved them away, speaking sharply to them. "Go, and bother me no more today."

The young Dakota turned to Levi and looked at him with interest. "Why does this man have hair on his face?" the young boy asked, apparently unafraid of his father's reprimand, leaving Levi to surmise that Two Moons was not a strong disciplinarian with the boys.

"This man has hair on his face because he is a white man," the father explained. He then turned to Levi.

27

"These are my two sons, Black Otter and Dakota."

Levi knew his life was in real danger now that he had discovered the war chief's secret. He also realized that Two Moons would never let the boy go. He could see the love and pride in the war chief's eyes when he looked upon the boy he called Dakota.

Levi's and Two Moons' eyes met and locked, both knowing that the child Levi had searched for stood between them. "Until I decide what to do, Levi Gunther, you will not leave this village. I would not want to shame a man such as yourself by confining you with ropes. Will you give me your word that you will not try to leave the village?"

"You have my word," Levi readily agreed.

Two Moons smiled. "Your word is good, hunter. But"—now he grinned openly—"there will be two guards outside your tepee tonight."

Levi returned his smile. "I accept your hospitality, and I thank you."

The young Dakota had never seen a white man before, though he had heard of them, and he stared at Levi with open curiosity. "Are you really a white man?" he asked.

Levi looked into green eyes made more prominent by the little tanned face. Yes, he thought, those were Lady Cillia's green eyes. He bent down to answer the boy's question. "Yes, I am a white man."

"Your eyes are a funny color."

"Yes, they are blue. Your eyes are most unusual also, Dakota."

The young boy gazed in awe at the ivory-handled knife that stuck out of Levi's sheath. "Can I touch your

28

hunting knife?" he asked with rounded eyes.

"If your father says it is all right, I will give it to you."

"No!" Two Moons growled. "The boy is too young to have such a knife." He pulled Dakota away from Levi. "Go and play with your brother."

"When I am older, I will have such a knife," Dakota declared.

"When you are older, perhaps your father will allow you to have this one," Levi suggested.

"Dakota!" Two Moons said in a warning voice. "Go with your brother at once."

With a last curious glance at Levi, Dakota dashed away and was soon halfway to the river.

"This is the boy I have been searching for," Levi said, glancing up at the war chief. "Can you tell me how he came to be in your care?"

Two Moons stared with pride after Dakota. "I have two fine sons, Levi Gunther. One is the child of my loins, while the other is the child of my heart. One would be foolish to ask a father to give up his son."

Levi nodded. "Pity, because Dakota would have a wonderful life waiting for him in England."

"Will this grandfather love him more than I? Will he fill his belly fuller with food, care more about him when he is ill, or have more pride in him when he succeeds at something? I do not think so. I was with Dakota's white mother when she gave him life. Before she died, she gave him over to my keeping. He is mine, and I will not give him up."

Levi shook his head. "I can see that the boy is happy, but will the others allow him to forget he is white? Will he not be better off with his own kind?"

29

Two Moons held out his hand for Levi to precede him into the tepee. "We shall talk no more on this. Dakota is my son, and I will never give him up!"

London, England

Levi was seated across from Dakota's grandfather feeling uncomfortable and out of place in the elegant salon. The Marquess did little to put the hunter at ease as his gnarled hands tightened on the gold-handled cane. Levi had just informed the Marquess that he had found his grandson alive. Either the man was a good actor or had little feelings for the boy, because the eyes that stared back at Levi were cold and unfeeling.

"I have paid you good money, Levi, why did you not bring my grandson back with you?"

"As I explained, Two Moons looks on Dakota as his own son. He will not give him up."

The Marquess poked his cane at Levi's chest, but stopped short of touching him. "Then you must take my grandson by force. I expect you to use whatever means you deem necessary to obtain his freedom. It is imperative that you bring him to me."

"I am afraid that will be impossible, Marquess. Even with an army of men you couldn't get Dakota away from Two Moons."

The old man shook his head. "Dakota. That is a hell of a name for the next Marquess of Weatherford."

"He may never be the next Marquess. You do not know the Arapaho. No one takes from them unless they are willing to give. You must understand Two Moons is not willing to give Dakota to me or anyone else."

"Is the boy well treated?"

For the first time Levi saw something akin to concern in the old man's eyes. "He is treated with love and respect."

The Marquess's eyes locked with Levi's. "I have heard from reliable sources that you are a good man to deal with, Levi Gunther. I was also told if anyone could obtain my grandson's freedom, it would be you. Did you not say you were on friendly terms with this Two Moons?"

"I don't know that you would exactly call us friends. But I faced the war chief and still live—that in itself in a accomplishment."

"Are you willing to do everything in your power to bring my grandson to me?"

"I am willing to try and convince Two Moons that Dakota has a future here in England. But as I said, I cannot, and will not, take the boy away by force."

The Marquess nodded. "Then stay near him, look over him. If at all possible, teach him English. Tell him about me and the life he has waiting for him here in England. Entice him with promises of wealth and anything he wants."

"I will stay near him if Two Moons allows it. I will teach him English and even teach him to read, but you must understand nothing I could promise the boy would lure him away from a father he loves. Take my word for it, Dakota does love Two Moons as any boy would love his own father. The young boy I met in that Indian village has no conception of wealth. He is happy and content, he thinks like an Indian and even looks like one."

There was dullness in the Marquess's eyes. "I could send a hundred men to bring my grandson to me, but I have a feeling you could do more to gain his freedom than anyone else I could send. Go to him and stay nearby. Keep me informed on his progress."

Levi stood up, knowing the interview was ended. "I will do what I can for Dakota. He is a fine-looking boy, and you can believe that Two Moons will teach him to walk as a man."

The Marquess suddenly looked sad. "Yes, he will be taught to become an Indian, while I shall be cheated of his childhood." His eyes became cold. "But mark this, Levi Gunther, I will not be cheated out of an heir to my titles and lands. I want my grandson back. I don't care how you do it—just do it!"

November 1843

It was Dakota's tenth birthday, and he walked beside the river with Levi. A smile lit his eager young face as he ran his finger over the ivory-handled knife. With the joy of possession in his eyes, he slipped the knife into his leather scabbard. "I have wanted this ever since that day I first saw it, Levi," he admitted. "Are you sure my father will allow me to have it?"

"When we are alone, I want to speak in English, Dakota," Levi reminded him, "and yes, your father has agreed that I could give the knife to you." Levi spoke English with a clipped New England accent. His grammar was good since his father had been a schoolmaster, and he was even more careful with his pronunciation when he was with Dakota so the boy would learn proper English.

Levi had been a frequent visitor at the Arapaho village for years. He and Two Moons had become good friends, and he was allowed to spend time with Dakota to teach him of his heritage. Levi had been teaching Dakota to read and write English, and he was grateful that his own father had been a stern disciplinarian and had insisted Levi study his lessons six hours every day. Levi had been just fifteen when he had been struck with what his father had termed "itchy feet." He had left New England and had never returned. The mountains and prairies of the vast wilderness had called to him, and he soon found himself a respected guide and hunter. Civilization was still of no interest to him.

"Did you bring more books for me to read, Levi?" Dakota asked hopefully.

"Of course I did, you young scamp. I can't order them from St. Louis fast enough to suit you." Levi glanced at the black hair that hung about Dakota's shoulders. The boy's skin was so dark from the sun that it was hard to tell from a distance that he was not an Indian. He was sturdily built, his young body flexible and healthy.

Levi saw the golden locket Dakota wore about his neck. He remembered seeing it around Lady Cillia's neck. "Where did you get that?"

"My father gave it to me yesterday. He said it belonged to my white mother."

"That it did."

"Tell me about the white woman who was my

33

mother. What was she like, Levi?"

"Well, why don't you open the locket and see for yourself? Your mother once showed me the likenesses of herself and your father inside."

Young Dakota looked bewildered. Turning the golden oval over in his hands, he shook his head. "I cannot see that it will open."

Levi reached out and touched the small catch, and the locket sprung open. "Now," he said, "look upon the faces of your real mother and father."

Dakota stared at the miniatures, his face almost reverent. He had never seen anyone as lovely as the woman. Her white skin only added to her fragile beauty. Her green eyes, so like his own, gave her a fanciful look. He stared at the man who was supposed to be his father, suddenly feeling resentment for him.

"Two Moons and White Wing are my real mother and father." He would have jerked the locket from around his neck, but Levi stopped him.

"I understand your feelings. You want to rebel against your real parents because you do not want to be white. Do not destroy the only link you have with Cillia and Holden Remington, because you may one day regret it."

"I do not want to be their son."

"I know, I know," Levi said, realizing it was time to change the subject. "Come and help me unload my packhorse so we can find your books."

Dakota closed the locket, determined never to look upon the faces of his true parents again. But he did. As time passed, he would often stare at the two images that haunted him and left him feeling very unsettled.

July 1846

Dakota was in his thirteenth summer when his life changed dramatically. It had rained earlier in the day, washing the land with a clean, fresh aroma. A warm sun beat down on the village when White Wing decided to take her two sons and cross the river to pick blackberries. On their way through the village, they encountered the chief's daughter, Running Deer, who begged to be allowed to go with them. Now a party of four waded their mounts into the water and up the grassy slopes on the other side.

Black Otter kept insisting the whole time they rode along that this was woman's work and he should be hunting with the men, while Dakota only smiled, finding no shame in accompanying his mother.

White Wing and Running Deer were picking berries while Dakota and Black Otter sat nearby on a slope, keeping watch. White Wing was the first to hear the rustling in the bushes. Knowing that bears were drawn to blackberries, she listened intently. Now there was a loud thrashing sound joined with bellowing and growling. She grabbed Running Deer's hand and urgently took a step backward—another—and still another. White Wing knew they had disturbed a bear.

Black Otter jumped to his feet, his dark eyes bright with fear. "We will all be killed," he yelled out. "Flee, Mother, run."

By now the horses had picked up the bear's scent and were rearing and shying away until they finally broke loose from their constraints. Without stopping to consider his actions, Black Otter grabbed one of the horses, jumped on its back, and rode toward the river, hoping to put the safety of the river between him and the bear.

Dakota watched helplessly as his mother, in her haste to escape the animal, tripped and fell backward, dragging Running Deer to the ground with her. Now the bear emerged from the thicket, sniffing the air. Then, angry and crazed, he charged his fallen prey. Dakota knew that if he didn't do something, his mother and Running Deer would die!

Grasping the handle of his knife, he raced forward with no plan in mind, knowing only that he had to do something to save his mother.

"No, Dakota, no!" his mother cried, scrambling to her feet and clutching the frightened Running Deer to her. "Save yourself, my son."

Dakota was on a rise above the bear now, and his mother was no more than ten paces away from the hideous killer. He felt fear knot his stomach, but pushed it aside, knowing his father would expect him to act as a warrior. Leaping down the embankment, he landed in front of the bear. For an instant, the animal paused, distracted by his new quarry.

"Run, Mother. Run toward the river!" Dakota cried, poising his knife in front of him, even though he knew the flimsy blade would do little to deter the bear.

Black Otter was halfway across the river when he saw his father and several other warriors riding toward him at breakneck speed. Evidently they had heard the commotion. "Mother—a bear!" Black Otter cried when his father drew even with him. He watched as the warriors rode in the direction he had indicated, but he could not bring himself to follow them. Fear was coiled inside him like a snake and his young body trembled. When he reached the opposite bank, he jumped from his horse, but his knees were too weak to hold him and he fell to the ground, ashamed of his cowardice.

Women and children gathered about him, and when he could catch his breath, he told them what had occurred. "I rode for help," he said, trying to convince himself, as well as the villagers, that he had acted bravely.

The bear swiped at Dakota, and he felt the heavy blow that sent him reeling backward. With pain so intense he could hardly catch his breath, he somehow managed to scramble to his feet. Now, he had the bear's full attention, and the animal had forgotten about his mother. Dakota leaped backward, finding his route of escape blocked by the embankment. Now he had no choice but to fight, for the bear stood between him and freedom. He realized he had little chance of winning against the bear, but he would die as a warrior so his father would be proud of him.

He still clutched his knife, and with a forward thrust, Dakota buried it to the hilt in the bear's shaggy chest. A mighty roar went up that echoed around the valley, and the bear attacked Dakota, his claws tearing across the young boy's chest and laying the skin open to the bone.

As Dakota fell to his knees, his last conscious sight was of the advancing bear!

Two Moons and his warriors topped the embankment just as the bear reached Dakota. With bow drawn, Two Moons aimed at the animal's heart and released the arrow, praying it would hit the target. The bear stopped, his foam-flecked mouth now red with blood. The other warriors released their arrows and the savage killer toppled to the ground—dead!

White Wing ran to her wounded son, falling on her knees and pulling him into her arms. Soon her husband joined her, and he lifted the limp body in his arms.

"He was the bravest warrior I have ever seen," Running Deer said, her eyes brimming with tears. "He did not think about his own safety, but only of saving our lives."

White Wing's eyes held an urgency. "Will he live, my husband?"

Two Moons glanced down at the wound that had been laid open by the bear's claws. There was blood on Dakota's face, and his arm appeared to be broken. "He will live," his father said with assurance. "This brave little one has come too far to die now."

Dakota was unconscious and did not know that he rode in triumph in front of his father's war horse while all the village came out to pay homage to him for saving the life of the chief's daughter. The story was told and retold about Dakota's bravery.

Black Otter stood on the outside of his father's tepee, his eyes flashing with jealousy, his heart filled with anger and a growing hatred. When Running Deer came up beside him, he turned angry eyes on her. "I do not want to hear from you how wonderful Dakota is. I am sick of hearing about his bravery. If I had not ridden for help, you would all be dead now."

Running Deer's eyes were soft and luminous. "He is truly touched by the Great One. I have never seen anyone so brave as your brother."

Black Otter felt rage eating away at him because he had always wanted the chief's daughter, Running Deer, to look upon him with favor. He now knew that she favored Dakota. She did not try to hide her admiration or her feelings. "He is not my brother," Black Otter said through clinched teeth. "He is white, and has no right to be called 'son' by my father and mother."

Running Deer's eyes saddened. "He has earned that right today, because he saved your mother's life, as well as my own. He is so grievously wounded that I fear for his life. It would seem that you should be proud to call Dakota your brother. He is a great warrior, and it does not matter what color his skin is. He will always be honored among the Arapaho."

Black Otter turned away, needing to be alone. Though no one said anything, he knew they were thinking he had behaved as a coward today. He envisioned himself in Dakota's place, the medicine man fighting to save his life, the tribal members gathered outside the tepee, waiting for word of his condition, his mother and father in fear of his life. He, Black Otter, was all but forgotten while everyone sang praises to Dakota.

"I hate him," Black Otter cried aloud. "I wish he would die!"

39

Dakota was still weak from his wounds, but he was proudly seated in the circle of honor, his father on his left, the chief on his right. The warriors of the tribe were paying homage to one of their own. In the background, the women and children pressed forward to watch the solemn ritual.

Two Moons stood up, motioning for Dakota to do likewise. "From today forward, you shall be known as a warrior for your brave deed." He reached into a pouch and removed a necklace of bear claws and placed it around the young boy's neck. "White Wing and Running Deer have made this from the claws of the bear which threatened their lives, to honor you for your bravery. I, as War Chief, honor you and welcome you to the ranks of warriors of the Arapaho." His dark eyes told of his pride in Dakota, his son.

"But, my father," Dakota said in an awed voice, reverently fingering the bear-claw necklace, "it was not my hand that killed the bear."

His father smiled. "Yours was the first blow that was delivered to the bear. Who is to say it was not your knife that finally brought about his death? Inside your body there beats the heart of a true Arapaho warrior, my son."

The young boy's eyes shone with pride, and his heart swelled with the honor that was being paid to him. In his joy, he glanced at his brother, Black Otter, wanting to share this moment with him, since they had always shared everything. He was puzzled that his brother was not also being honored. That was when he saw the anger and resentment on Black Otter's face.

"What I did was not any more important than what my brother did. Without Black Otter summoning help, I would not be alive to receive this. I wish to honor him." Walking forward, Dakota removed the treasured bear-claw necklace and placed it around his brother's neck.

Black Otter's dark eyes narrowed, and he jerked the necklace from his neck and flung it away. "I do not want this, no more than I want you for my brother." He stalked away, leaving Dakota staring after him in concern.

White Wing touched her husband's arm. "One son does us honor, while the other shames us before the whole village."

Chapter Two

March 1857

Levi Gunther halted his horse on the banks of the Wind River, noticing it was running swiftly because of the spring runoff. Across the river, looking peaceful in the noonday sun, lay the Arapaho village. When he nudged his horse into the shallow part of the river, he knew his coming would attract little attention since he was a frequent visitor. It was well known that he was a friend of the war chief, Two Moons, so he passed among the people unmolested.

As his horse moved past the tepees, he was haunted by old memories. Had it been twenty-three years since he had returned to the cabin by the Salmon River to find the decomposed bodies of Holden and Cillia Remington? He remembered reading Lord Holden's last thoughts and carrying out his wishes to be buried with his wife.

Levi had watched Dakota grow to manhood, and he

knew the Remingtons would be proud of the man their son had become, even though it appeared his destiny was to become a great war chief of the Arapaho, not a titled lord in England.

The years had deepened the respect Levi and Two Moons had for each other. Levi and Dakota had become close, and by now Dakota could read and speak English as well as Levi. The hunter used every opportunity to tell the young warrior about England and his grandfather who wanted him to take his rightful place as Viscount of Remington. Dakota, though unimpressed by his illustrious grandfather, had always been fascinated by England.

Throughout the years, Levi had made two more trips to England to meet with the Marquess and advise him of the fate of his grandson. The fiery old man often demanded that Levi take his grandson by force if need be and bring him to London, a feat that Levi tried to convince him was impossible. Dakota was devoted to his Arapaho family. Dakota's skin might be white, but inside him beat the heart of an Indian.

As Levi's mount moved slowly through the village, he received many warm smiles. Suddenly his eyes met and locked with the dark, hostile eyes of Two Moons' blood son, Black Otter. The young warrior had always been jealous of his adopted brother, Dakota. Levi had seen the jealousy in Black Otter's eyes long before it developed into open hatred, and he had always been fearful that Black Otter would one day do Dakota harm. Once Levi had even warned Dakota about Black Otter, but Dakota had only laughed and told him he was becoming suspicious like an old woman.

Bringing his thoughts back to the present, Levi halted his horse before Two Moons' tepee. He was mystified as to why the War Chief had sent for him. Levi adjusted his buckskin shirt and smoothed his white beard before he called out to be admitted.

The flap was immediately pushed aside by the medicine man, who beckoned Levi to enter. The heat was oppressive as Levi stepped inside. Even though the day was warm, a fire had been laid, making it even more unbearable. Levi knew something was wrong when he saw Two Moons lying on his robe in the middle of the day. He was stunned when he saw how frail and ill Two Moons appeared.

"You have been gone from us for a very long time, Levi Gunther," the war chief said, beckoning him closer. "I began to think you would not return unless I sent for you." Two Moons' voice was so faint that Levi could hardly catch his words. Raising on his elbow, Two Moons gave the hunter a slight smile. "I would not want to pass from this world without you to disturb the tranquillity of my last hours, my old friend."

Levi dropped down on a reed mat and crossed his legs, while a worried frown creased his wrinkled face. As always, he spoke to the chief in the Arapaho tongue. "I can see that you are ailing, Two Moons. It is hoped you will soon recover."

The war chief fell back on his buffalo robe, his face plainly showing the agony he felt. "It is the sickness in my breast that festers and worsens. I will not recover, old friend." His eyes turned sad. "One of the things I will miss of this world is matching wits with you, Levi Gunther. You have become a friend to me and to my son Dakota."

"It saddens me to see you thus, Two Moons, but I know you will recover from this affliction and match wits with me for many years to come."

"That cannot be, my friend." This was spoken without remorse. "I have not felt at home in this world since White Wing left me to walk with the spirits." His eyes darkened with desperation. "She has sent me a vision, and I must tell you about it."

Levi knew the Indians placed great importance in visions. "You are talking nonsense, my friend. Death will never find you on your pallet," he said, feeling sadness in his heart that such a strong and valiant man should weaken. "A warrior as great as you is destined to meet death in battle."

The medicine man came forward and raised Two Moons' head and gave him a drink of some foul-smelling liquid. After a fit of coughing, Two Moons waved the man away. He then turned his attention back to Levi. "It is because of what my wife reveals to me in the vision that I have asked you here. She has told me that Dakota must be with his own people. She has asked me to send him to his white grandfather across the great water."

Levi could not believe he was hearing correctly. For years he had been trying to convince Two Moons that Dakota belonged with his own people; now perhaps it was too late. "I do not know if Dakota will be content in the white man's world, Two Moons. He is twenty-three summers, and no longer young and impressionable. He is as much an Arapaho as you are."

"Yes, he is an Arapaho," Two Moons said with pride shining in his dark eyes. "He has a love for this land and her people." Two Moons shook his head. "Still, I want him to know his own people. That is not the only reason. When I am gone, there will be a power struggle, and the tribe will be divided. Many warriors and most of the elders will be on Dakota's side, but there will be those who will join Black Otter, and there might be war among the Arapaho. This I do not want. You must take Dakota away."

"Dakota will fight me on this, Two Moons," Levi said pointedly, knowing the young warrior would not want to leave.

"Dakota will not fight you, Levi Gunther, because I will tell him that it is my dying wish that he go to his own people. He will do as I ask. He has always been an obedient son," Two Moons assured Levi.

"Yes, it is well known that Dakota has been the son of your heart. He will go with me if you ask it of him," Levi concurred.

Two Moons tried to rise, but his strength failed him. "Give me your word that you will remain here until my death and that immediately afterward, you will take him away. There is danger for him here, and I cannot protect him after I am dead. I will leave that to you."

The two men stared at each other with understanding. Levi put into words what Two Moons could not. "You think Black Otter will try to harm Dakota if you are not here to prevent it."

"There will be no lies between us, Levi Gunther. We both know that my son, Black Otter, will strive to be war chief after I am gone. If this happens, he will destroy Dakota, something he has not dared do while I live."

"Have you told this to Dakota?"

"No. He has been hunting in the north land for many of your weeks. I chose not to send word to him that I had taken ill. Word has come to me that he will be returning today, and I will tell him. From no one but me will Dakota believe the malice toward him that lies in his brother's heart."

At that moment, the tepee flap was thrown aside and Black Otter entered. He was lean, of average height, and walked with a swagger. When his black eyes rested on Levi, his face twisted with anger. "Why do you worry my father, white man? Can you not see he is ill?"

Levi's eyes were unfaltering as he stared back at the young warrior. Before he could answer, Two Moons spoke in a voice of anger. "You will not insult Levi Gunther in my tepee. I am still war chief, and I give the orders here. My friend is here because I sent for him."

Black Otter's eyes narrowed, and he spat toward Levi. "Why would you send for this white man? He is not worthy to watch a great war chief prepare to leave this world."

"It is not for you to question who I choose to attend my death. I told you that you are not yet war chief."

Black Otter's anger distorted his face. "If you had your way, Dakota would be war chief after you die. It is a pity his skin is white, or he would stand in your

47

moccasins instead of me, the true son of your body."

Two Moons struggled to rise, and finally succeeded on sitting up with Levi's help. "You will never walk in my moccasins, Black Otter, because there is anger in your heart toward your brother."

"Dakota is not my brother! If you pierce his skin, he will bleed like any white man. He has always tried to take what I wanted. When she was alive, my mother loved him well. The woman I love turns her face away from me, but looks upon him with love. Even my own father prefers him to me."

Two Moons did not deny his son's accusations. Sadly he breathed in a ragged breath. "I will charge you not to harm your brother after I am gone. He will be leaving this land to journey across the great water. You will not raise a hand against him."

Black Otter looked doubtful and suspicious for a moment. He had not expected this from his father. "Dakota will not leave this land. He lies to himself by pretending he is Indian. He believes he belongs to the Arapaho tribe."

The chief slumped back against the buffalo robe, too weary to argue with his son. "Dakota will leave if I ask it of him, and I will ask it of him. I feel shame in my heart that the son of my body harbors distrust and anger toward his brother."

Black Otter's face was again distorted with anger. His eyes were poisonous as they rested on Levi. "I will be glad to see Dakota gone from my life. I will not harm him, because if he is dead, the woman I love will mourn him. But if he leaves, she will always know that he abandoned her. Then she will turn to me. No, I will not harm him if he leaves." Turning away, he stomped out, leaving a feeling of uneasiness behind him.

"Black Otter is dangerous, Two Moons. I do not trust him," Levi said.

"He is . . . a disappointment to me," Two Moons said sadly.

Two Moons glanced at the opening at the top of the tepee where smoke was mingling with a clear blue sky. He, himself, felt as if he were no more than smoke that dissipated and disappeared without leaving a trace. He wondered if after his death he would have left nothing behind to remind others that he had once walked this land. Trying to push his troubled thoughts aside, he spoke. "Remember, you are to take Dakota away as soon as you hear I am dead. I would ask you to take him sooner, but he will never leave while there is breath in my body." He glanced at Levi and saw sorrow in the pale gray eyes. "Leave me now. I want to be alone when Dakota arrives if I am to convince him to believe in White Wing's vision."

The buffalo grass rippled in the strong wind, resembling waves upon a troubled sea. Beyond the grasslands, rising suddenly from the plains, stood the majestic mountains, their highest point still snowcapped, presenting an impregnable barrier to the west. In sharp contrast to the mountains, a green valley with multicolored windflowers dotted the land as far as the pine forest to the north. Spring had come early to

Shadow Valley and already the afternoon sun beat down with a punishing force. This pristine wilderness was a land of harsh survival—a land where rivers were born, where the faint at heart dared not journey—it was Indian land—Arapaho land!

In the distance, the thundering sound of approaching riders broke the silence. Two Indian warriors topped the hill and reigned in their mounts. One of the warriors was dark, but the other, though he had shoulder-length black hair, looked strangely out of place because his eyes were emerald green and his skin was not bronze like his companion's, but golden from the sun.

Dakota had not thought much about his appearance in several years. There had been a time, when he was younger, that he questioned the difference between him and the other members of his tribe. But now he was a proven warrior, and he no longer thought about those differences. Inside, his heart beat as one with the Arapaho.

Gazing down at the Wind River, Dakota easily controlled his powerful war horse with just the merest pressure from his muscled legs. The giant beast snorted and pranced about, tossing his shiny mane while his hooves plowed up the soft ground along the riverbank. Dakota glanced across the shimmering water, noting the peacefulness that settled over the Arapaho village that he called home. His heart was light because he had been away for a long time, and he was eager to see his father.

Dakota turned to his boyhood friend, Shadow Walker. "It is good to be home," he observed in Arapaho.

Shadow Walker stared at Dakota, his eyes resting momentarily on his black shoulder-length hair which was circled with a rawhide band. In profile Dakota's face was boldly outlined with haughty features. He carried himself proudly, arrogantly. His green eyes were fearless, penetrating, and their color rivaled the grasses in high summer. Shadow Walker looked into those eyes that now seemed clouded and troubled.

"Do you think of Running Deer and the love you have for her, my friend?" Shadow Walker asked.

"No. It is useless to think of her when my brother desires her. I would never stand between him and the woman he wants. I have told this to Running Deer, and I will tell this to my brother if he asks."

Shadow Walker's eyes clouded with anger. "Must you always give Black Otter what he wants? Will you never stand up and say 'enough'? Too many times I have seen you step aside to allow him to have his way. As your friend, *I* say 'enough.' "

Dakota reached out and clasped his friend's arm. "Do not be distressed for me, Shadow Walker. If I thought I could make Running Deer happy, I would not step aside for my brother. Although I love her, there is something missing between us."

"Can it be that your heart is not as one with Running Deer? Do you not feel a man's love for her?"

"How can I know if I love her? I have desired her, and I know of no maiden who has her beauty, but how can a man know if he loves a woman? Sometimes I think only of her, and at other times, I cannot even recall her face."

51

"If you have this doubt, then you do not love Running Deer. When a man loves a woman, she is in his heart night and day. Her face haunts him, and he could never forget her image."

Dakota smiled. "When did you learn so much about a man's feelings for a woman?"

Shadow Walker looked embarrassed for a moment, and then he, too, smiled. "Since I began to love Running Deer's younger sister."

Dakota's eyes clouded over once more. "Come, let us ride to the village with haste. I have an uneasy feeling that something is not right."

The two horses bound into the river, stirring up mud and causing ripples to reach the opposite shore. Dakota rode through the village, his eyes searching, wondering why his father had not joined the others who welcomed him home. Why was everyone looking at him with such sorrow? His eyes met Running Deer's and he read pain in their dark depths.

With heart beating in fear, he reached his father's tepee, and was surprised to see Levi Gunther waiting for him outside the entrance. The sadness and disbelief he saw on the old hunter's face wiped out any happiness Dakota felt at seeing his friend. He did not need to be told that something was wrong with his father; he could see the truth in Levi's eyes. He experienced grief so strong it tore at his heart. Raising his head, Dakota glanced into the dark eyes of Black Otter, wishing his brother would assure him that nothing had happened to their father in his absence.

Black Otter's eyes were cold. "Welcome home, Dakota. You have returned to watch my father die before you leave this village forever!"

Chapter Three

Dakota took a step toward the tepee, still unable to believe his father was dying. Black Otter moved to block the entrance and poised his lance against Dakota's broad chest. "You will not be at my father's side when he draws his last breath. You have taken everything else away from me, and I will not allow you to rob me of my father's last hours."

Levi Gunther, and more than a dozen warriors, tensely stood by, knowing the trouble that had been brewing between the two brothers for years was about to come to a head. Everyone knew by the stubborn set of Dakota's jaw that they were about to witness a long overdue confrontation.

"Move out of my way, Black Otter. I will see my father if I have to go through you to do it." Dakota had spoken softly, but the glint in his eyes caused Black Otter to drop his own gaze and move aside. He was humiliated that Dakota had made him back down, and he swore to himself that he would find the means to humble his father's favorite.

Dakota quickly entered the tepee and went down on his knees beside his father. Two Moons opened his eyes, and the sadness Dakota saw there tore at his heart. The old war chief reached out a shaky hand and placed it on Dakota's.

"I began to fear that you would not come in time, my son. I am weak and have fought to hold on to the breath of life until I could see you once more." Two Moons' voice was surprisingly strong.

"I will not listen to such talk," Dakota said, unwilling to accept that his father was dying. "You will live to see many grandchildren."

"No, my son," Two Moons said sadly. "Before the sun sets today, I will join your mother."

Dakota, looking at his father's sunken, lusterless eyes, and the skin that was stretched taut across his face like fragile old parchment, could not hide the shadow of grief that came into his eyes.

"Why did you not send word for me to come home, my father? Did you not know that I would want to be with you to lend you my strength?"

"I knew you would arrive before I passed on." Two Moons looked upon Dakota's face. He remembered the sickly white baby that had grown to manhood and earned the respect and friendship of his adopted tribe. He remembered the pride he had felt for Dakota as he developed a sense of honor and became a fearless warrior. "You have brought joy and pride to my tepee, Dakota. I have always known you to be an obedient son."

"It was not difficult to obey you, my father. The tasks you have set for me have been tempered with fairness, and I have learned by watching you."

Two Moons grasped Dakota's hand. "Do you know that I have loved you well?" he questioned, his voice now weak.

"I have known this."

"Then know what I asked of you is done out of love."

"Yes, I will know."

Two Moons' eyes brightened feverishly. "After I am gone—"

"I will not hear this," Dakota interrupted.

Two Moons held up his hand, his voice insistent. "Hear what I have to say. After I am gone, I want you to go away with Levi Gunther."

"But—"

"Hear me, Dakota. There is danger for you here. I want you to go to your grandfather and learn the ways of the white man. It was selfish of me to keep you when you belong to a great and powerful family that needs your strength and wisdom."

Dakota was bewildered. "I do not like the white man's ways. I am Indian and will walk in the Arapaho way."

"I have seen a vision from your mother, and she has told me that you must leave the Arapaho. It is my wish that you return to the family of your birth."

Dakota felt a chill pass over him, and he was thrown into confusion. "This is the only home I have ever known. How can I leave?"

"Dakota, you are aware that your brother is jealous

of you."

The young warrior dropped his eyes. "I did not know you saw this."

"I saw. What you do not know is that when I am no longer here to hold the peace, Black Otter will cause a division between the people. Some will follow him, more will follow you, but in the end it is the Arapaho who will lose, because they will fight among themselves. I would not rest easy knowing my sons were tearing the Arapaho apart."

"I will never fight against my brother, nor will I raise a hand against any Arapaho."

"You would fight because it would be forced upon you." A spasm of coughing shook Two Moons, and he fought to catch his breath. Helplessly, Dakota watched his father weaken before his eyes. Now Two Moons' voice was faint as he spoke. "Promise me that you will leave with Levi Gunther. Give me your word that you will do this for me." There was desperation in his father's words. "Promise me, Dakota, that no blood will spill between you and your brother."

Dakota knew his father was begging for his assurance. He fought against the tears behind his eyes and the tightening in his throat. When he spoke, his voice came out in a painful whisper. "You have my word that I will leave with Levi Gunther, if that is your wish. If the tribe becomes divided, it will not be because of me. If my brother's blood is spilled, it will not be by my hand."

Relief eased the suffering on the old war chief's face and love was shining in his dark eyes. "It is good, my

57

son. Now leave me and send in Black Otter. I must charge him with keeping the peace for our people."

Dakota hesitantly rose to his feet, knowing grief in the very depths of his soul. He looked upon his father for the last time, and turned away, fearing the weakness of tears would shame him. His voice broke as he said, "I have loved you well, my father."

"I have loved you since you drew your first breath, my son." Two Moons looked long on Dakota's face. "From the time I drew you from your white mother's body, you have belonged to me. No father has ever had a finer son. Know that whatever else you do, you have brought pride and joy to me and your mother. No matter where your destiny takes you, remember in your heart that you are the son of Two Moons."

By the light of the moon, Dakota tied his meager belongings to the back of his horse while the death chant for Two Moons filled the night air. Heavy of heart, he turned to Levi, who stood beside him. "I am going with you to honor my father's wishes, Levi, but nothing will ever make me think as a white man."

Levi nodded as he watched Running Deer approach Dakota. The young maiden's eyes were bright with tears, so Levi moved away to allow her and Dakota to say their good-byes.

Dakota took Running Deer's hand in his, wishing he could absorb her into his body. She represented everything he was leaving behind, and his heart was heavy. "I will often think of you and hope that you find happiness," he said.

"Take me with you," she cried, throwing her arms about his neck. "I do not want to live without you."

Dakota had no time to react because Black Otter rushed forward and tore Running Deer out of his arms and flung her away.

"You will leave now, Dakota. You are not wanted here," he said in a voice that throbbed with anger.

Remembering the promise he had made to their dying father, Dakota resisted the urge to challenge Black Otter. "I will go, but only because I gave my word to our father. I do not wish you ill, Black Otter, for I have looked upon you as a brother. I hope you will one day know this."

Black Otter thrust his lance forward and rested the point against Dakota's neck, causing Running Deer to cry out in alarm. Levi cursed the fact that he would not be able to reach his rifle in time to help Dakota, while several members of the tribe gathered around, watching the two warriors confront each other.

"I want to forget all you were to my family, Dakota. Your skin is white, no matter how many times you would deny it. If I were to end your life, you would merely be one less white man the Arapaho have to worry about."

Dakota's green eyes bore witness to his anger. There was no fear in his heart as Dakota jerked the lance from Black Otter and thrust it against his throat. "You are no credit to the Arapaho or the father and mother that loved us both."

Black Otter took a step backward. "Would you have

my blood on your hands?" he asked angrily, knowing Dakota had once more gained the advantage.

So tight was the restraint that Dakota was keeping on his anger that the muscles on his arms bulged and his hands trembled. With great effort, he remembered his promise to his father and broke the lance over his knee, tossing it aside. "No, your blood will not be on my hands."

Running Deer rushed forward and threw herself into Dakota's arms. "You must take me with you, for I love only you, and want to be with you always."

Dakota looked into her face, noting the way her dark eyes glistened with tears. With a heavy heart, he laid his cheek against hers, knowing he could never take Running Deer with him, even though to leave her would be one more pain he must endure.

Suddenly he heard a gasp from the crowd, and he felt Running Deer stiffen. A soft moan escaped her lips, and she went limp in his arms.

In his confusion, it took Dakota several moments to realize that Black Otter had picked up the broken lance and had plunged the sharp end into Running Deer's back! With an anguished cry, Dakota jerked the lance out of her back and gently picked her up in his arms, cuddling her next to his heart.

Murmurs of anger and disapproval rumbled through the tribe. Black Otter realized what he had done when he looked into the hostile eyes of his chief. He reached a pleading hand toward Running Deer's father. The chief drew and armed his bow. The flying arrow of vengeance struck Black Otter in the chest, and he slumped to the ground.

"Help me, my brother," he cried, reaching out to Dakota. "Don't allow them to kill me. You owe my father this."

Everything happened so quickly that Dakota was left dazed. He felt a heavy hand on his shoulder as Levi took Running Deer's body from him and gave her over to her mother and sister.

Dakota was aware of the hostile crowd that had gathered around Black Otter, for not only had Running Deer been the chief's daughter, but she had been well loved. Uncontrollable rage burned in his heart as he pushed his way through the crowd to get to Black Otter. He stared at the man he had loved as a brother, for the first time seeing him as he really was. Bending down, Dakota grasped the arrow that protruded from Black Otter's chest and yanked it free, unmindful of the scream of pain that issued from his brother's lips. With trembling hands, Dakota poised the bloody arrow above Black Otter's head, ready to plunge it into his heart.

All reason was gone, and Dakota was driven only by hatred and anger. "You die, Black Otter," he hissed. "I will enjoy watching your blood spill for what you did to Running Deer. I will feed your dead flesh to the dogs!"

Black Otter weakly grasped Dakota's arm. "Are we not brothers? Would our father want you to spill my blood, Dakota?"

"Now, when it pleases you, we are brothers," Dakota ground out between clenched teeth. "The brother I once loved would not take a woman's life. You are a coward, and you deserve to die like a dog."

Levi rushed forward and grabbed Dakota's hand, forcing him to release the arrow. "Allow Arapaho justice to punish this crime. I do not ask this because of Black Otter, for he deserves to die. Rather, I remind you of your promise to your father. Let justice be done by Running Deer's father. Let no blood flow between you and Black Otter."

Slowly, Dakota's mind cleared. In his anger and grief, he had forgotten his promise to his father. Standing up, he glared at Black Otter. "As the old hunter said, I will leave your punishment to our chief."

Black Otter's face froze in anger, and he spat out at Dakota. "You had better kill me now, because if you do not, I will one day slay you."

"A shallow boast from one who will not live past the morning sunrise," Dakota hissed, stepping over Black Otter's prone body. For a moment he hesitated. That which his father had feared had come to pass. Blood had been shed and a life had been lost. The innocent Running Deer's life had been forfeit, and her only crime had been in loving him. "I do not fear a ghost, Black Otter. Before the sun sets again, you will walk in the shadows, but not with our father. You have shamed Two Moons' memory."

Black Otter pressed his hand against his wound, trying to stem the flow of blood. "I will not die tonight, Dakota. One day, you will know that nothing can stay my hand from killing you. I made no promise to my father."

Dakota had not known until today that his brother

harbored so much hatred for him. With a last look at the Arapaho people he loved so well, he turned to Levi. "I am ready to go. Let us leave this place that I once called home."

There was sadness in many dark eyes as the Arapaho watched Dakota mount his horse and ride away beside Levi through the village, and across the river. Not once did Dakota look back at what he was leaving behind. Everything he loved was gone. Not one Arapaho tried to stop his departure, not even his friend Shadow Walker. They all knew that his destiny lay in a different direction.

He did not see Black Otter being dragged through the village. He did not dwell on what punishment would be wrought on the murderer of the chief's beloved daughter. His heart was too full of grief, his mind unable to accept the losses he had suffered today.

That night there was no moon. Dakota stood alone beneath a star-sprinkled sky, feeling as if someone had ripped out his insides. Even though he knew a warrior should not cry, tears washed down his cheeks, for no one was around to see.

With his keen hearing, he picked up the sound of Levi's footsteps. Levi's voice broke the silence. "I know what you are feeling, Dakota. Grief is something that will only lessen with the passing of time."

For a long moment Dakota did not answer, and then he said, "Levi, I do not want you to think I will not honor my word to my father. I will go to England with

63

you, but I need some time alone, to reflect on my grief."

"Yes, I can see that."

"Will you wait for me at Murphy's Trading Post?"

"Yes, I will wait. And I will send word to your grandfather that you are coming. How much time do you think you will need?"

"I do not know. All my life I have been an Arapaho; it will not be easy to make the change. I will come to you when I am ready to enter the white man's world."

Chapter Four

England, June 1857

Lady Breanna Kenton lifted the front of her faded green gown and descended the rickety stairs. As always, when she viewed the disrepair that had befallen her ancestral home, she felt pain in her heart. She tried not to see the dust of neglect that had gathered on the mahogany banisters, the threadbare rug runner at the foot of the stairs, or the chipped marble in the entry hall. Since there was no money to retain servants to manage this huge manor house, it was up to Breanna and her sister-in-law, Sophie, to keep it clean, a task that had at one time required a full staff of servants. Many of the rooms had been boarded up, and the once proud mansion had fallen on hard times since her father's death.

It was well known that Breanna's brother, Fielding, the Fifth Earl of Kenton, was a compulsive gambler and had squandered the fortune that had come to him on his father's death. He had impoverished his family, and they were in dire straits. Valuable paintings, furniture, and jewels had long since been sold to pay Fielding's gambling debts.

Once this house had rung with laughter and happiness; now it was crumbling with decay and neglect. Breanna remembered when her mother and father had been alive and the house had gleamed and smelled of lemon wax, full of treasures acquired by preceding generations.

Breanna sighed. She had often wished that she had been born a male. If she had been, she would have left long ago. Her days were spent in hard work, and she had by now abandoned her dreams of a season in London. The only good part of her life was her friendship with Sophie, and the joy she had in watching her three nephews grow.

"Breanna, could you come in here for a moment?" Her sister-in-law stood in the doorway that led to the morning room, looking as if there were something troubling her. "I would like to . . . talk to you," Sophie said hesitantly.

Looking at Sophie, it was hard to believe she had once been considered a beauty. Her brown hair was now white at the temples, and her soft gray eyes had lost much of their luster. In spite of the adversity, Sophie's spirit was uncrushable. She had the rare ability to always look on the bright side in almost every situation, a trait Breanna admired, since there had been so few bright sides in their lives of late.

On entering the morning room, Breanna was surprised to see that tea and finger cakes had been arranged on a table near the fireplace where a crackling flame chased the chilling dampness from the room. "Are we expecting visitors, Sophie?" she asked, knowing that tea was a luxury they could ill afford. What little money they had must be spent on essentials for them and luxuries for Fielding.

Sophie's eyes were downcast, and she seemed to be having trouble deciding what to do with her hands, so she clasped them behind her. "No, the tea is for you." She raised her head, and sadness as sharp as a knife brightened her eyes. "I have something to talk to you about."

Breanna was puzzled. Why was her sister-in-law acting so strangely? Suddenly she was afraid. "Please, tell me nothing is wrong with Fielding or the children."

Sophie gave a small shake of her head and motioned for Breanna to be seated. For a moment, she allowed her eyes to move over Breanna critically. For the first time, she became aware how lovely Fielding's young sister had become. The sunlight poured through the window, making Breanna's hair sometimes appear red, and other times it would come alive with streaks of golden highlights. Loveliness was molded into every soft feature on her face. Her eyes, golden with brown flecks, always seemed to be dancing with humor and merriment. She was outgoing, and she had a kind and loving temperament. Yes, Breanna was a beauty, but her looks had been wasted in this remote corner of England. Sophie hoped that after today Breanna would have the kind of life she deserved.

Before Sophie spoke, she poured a cup of steaming tea and handed it to Breanna. "I hardly know where to begin. Fielding wanted to tell you himself, but knowing his gruff manner, I insisted on being the one to relate the events of this morning to you."

Breanna was in the process of raising the teacup to her lips, but she set it down with a clatter. Something was definitely wrong. She looked at Sophie suspiciously, trying to imagine what it could be. "Tell me what is wrong, Sophie," she insisted, unable to stand the suspense.

Sophie clasped her hands in her lap, looking older than her thirty years. "You know it has been a joy for your brother and me having you live with us, Breanna. Since I never had a sister of my own, you became like my younger sister."

"Yes, I have always thought of you as my sister also, Sophie." Breanna was bewildered. Why was Sophie acting so strangely? Had she finally decided to leave Fielding? Had she grown weary of doing without and sacrificing for Fielding's obsession with gambling— tired of his squandering his inheritance and that of his sons? In the last two years it had taken Breanna's and Sophie's combined efforts to keep the creditors from taking the house and lands. "What are you trying to tell me, Sophie?"

"Were you aware that the Marquess of Weatherford's solicitor was closeted with your brother all morning?"

Breanna's face registered her surprise at the twist the conversation had taken. She, like everyone else in England, knew of the Marquess of Weatherford. He was one of the most powerful and influential men in the country. "No, I was not aware that Fielding was even at home. Why would the Marquess of Weatherford's solicitor call upon our humble home?" Her hand went to her mouth. "Surely Fielding does not owe the Marquess a gambling debt."

"No—nothing like that." Sophie looked befuddled for a moment. "Breanna, this happened long before you were even born, but do you recall hearing accounts of how the Marquess's son and daughter-in-law disappeared while on an expedition in the wilds of America?"

Breanna was still mystified, but she searched her mind, trying to remember what she had heard about the death of the Marquess's son and his wife. "I vaguely recall that they were lost and it was believed they had met with a mysterious end, leaving the old Marquess with no heir."

"That's right, but it seems that before the daughter-in-law, Cillia, died, she gave birth to a son."

"How ironic. Why have I never heard this?"

"Because the Marquess has been working for years to locate and bring his grandson to England."

"Where is this child?"

"He is not a child, but a man in his twenties. I don't know the particulars, but it seems the grandson was raised by a tribe of Indians. As extraordinary as it sounds, he is now on his way to England."

"What a remarkable tale." Breanna smiled. "Even though I am not acquainted with the Marquess, I am glad that his story has a happy ending. Of course, one can only speculate on what the grandson will be like. He will be uneducated, of course, and I should think something of a . . . primitive."

Sophie's face whitened. "The story is not ended yet,

Breanna." She took her sister-in-law's hand and clasped it tightly. "Can you imagine the happiness the old Marquess felt, knowing his line had not died out? He had lost his only son, and his title and fortunes were to pass to a distant cousin. Just think of his elation at finding his long-lost grandson."

Breanna was beginning to feel a prickle of apprehension, though she could not say why. "Yes, I can see that he would be happy . . . but how does that concern us?"

"You have to understand, Breanna, that Fielding has your best interests at heart. For years we have taken unfair advantage of you. I have always been grieved that you could not have a season in London. I fancy you wearing lovely gowns and making new acquaintances with others of your own age and social standing. The only people you ever see here are villagers and tradesmen."

Breanna felt her heart beating loudly, and she shook her head. "I have not been unhappy with my life—"

In spite of the fact that Sophie squeezed her eyes shut, a tear escaped and rolled down her cheek. "Oh, Breanna, I do not know any other way to say it. You have been chosen to marry the Marquess's grandson!"

Breanna jerked her hands free of Sophie's clasp and jumped to her feet. The words were ripped from her throat, and anguish sparkled in her eyes while the color drained from her face. "What are you saying? Dear God, the Marquess's grandson was raised by Indians. He is a . . . savage! No, I will not do this. Fielding cannot make me."

Sophie stood and held her hand out to her sister-in-law, but Breanna backed away. "How can you and

Fielding even consider such a prospect? I thought you loved me."

Tears ran freely down Sophie's face. "We do, Breanna. It is tearing my heart out to . . . I cannot bear to think of . . ." She took a deep breath and wiped her tears from her face with the back of her hand. "Fielding has pointed out to me the advantages to such a marriage. You will be marrying into one of the oldest, most prestigious families in England. I am told that the Marquess is wealthy beyond anything we can imagine. He has promised that you can have anything your heart desires."

Breanna felt the helplessness of her situation weigh heavily on her young shoulders. She was the sister of an impoverished Earl. She was in her nineteenth year, and as of yet, no one had offered for her hand, or even sought to court her. She was not what her brother termed a "marriageable advantage." The Kenton family had fallen so far into disgrace because of Fielding's gambling that friends had ceased visiting years ago. Breanna raised her head and looked into the tear-filled eyes of her sister-in-law. She knew this was none of Sophie's doing. She also knew her brother would not have given her hand to anyone unless it had gained him some sort of advantage.

"What did the Marquess offer my brother in exchange for me?"

Sophie shook her head. "No, no, you must not think like that. Try to understand why your brother agreed to this marriage. He is truly interested in your future. He is aware that we have ill used you. You have been little more than a servant in this house. You have found joy

71

in loving our children, but I want you to have children of your own."

"Children by an . . . Indian?"

A sob expanded Sophie's chest. "Breanna, please—"

"What did the Marquess offer Fielding?" Breanna asked again, this time more pointedly.

Seeing there was nothing to be gained by withholding the truth from Breanna, Sophie spread her hands in a hopeless gesture. "He offered to pay off all Fielding's debts and to transfer fifty thousand pounds to him on the day you are married to his grandson."

Breanna took a deep breath. She was hurt—she was angry, but most of all, she was frightened. "I will honor my brother's bargain, but only because the money may make life easier for you and the children. If you are wise, you will insist that Fielding allow you to handle the finances, lest the money find its way onto a gambling table."

Sophie loyally defended her husband. "Fielding has changed. He has not gambled in over three months. I have never known you to be cruel about your brother's shortcomings, Breanna. This attitude does not become you."

"You will have to forgive me, but you see, my brother just sold me as if I were nothing but a chattel, and I am not feeling very charitable toward him at the moment."

"I hope in time you will find that your brother has done well by you. You have been wasting your life here, Breanna—this is no way for you to live. You are lovely and sweet, but as the years passed, they would have taken their toll on you. They would have taken your looks and your sweetness."

Breanna walked to the window and stared out at the garden that was choked with weeds. "Can you tell me anything more about the man who is to be my . . . husband?"

"No, I'm sorry, but you see, the solicitor knew little to tell us. He did tell Fielding that the Marquess was not overly concerned that his grandson had been raised by Indians."

"No, of course not, why should he be? An heir is an heir by birth, no matter what his character is or how he was fostered."

"Breanna," Sophie spoke hurriedly. "The solicitor intimated to Fielding that if you were to have a son from this union, the old Marquess would lay the world at your feet." Sophie caught Breanna's hand. "Perhaps it won't be so bad. The act of marriage is one that must be endured by all women no matter who they marry. But children are such a blessing, they make it all worthwhile."

Breanna knew that Sophie was trying to comfort her, but she had succeeded only in making her more apprehensive. She trembled when she tried to imagine what the man she was to marry would look like. The vision that came to mind was a ghastly painted face and a half-naked body. "Dear God, how can my own brother treat me with such small regard? How can he banish me from everything I hold dear and cast me into a life of . . . of . . ." Words failed Breanna. She could not imagine what kind of life she would be leading once she left Kenton.

"Try to think about the wonderful adventure that

awaits you, Breanna. First, of course, you will travel to London, where you will meet the Marquess and be fitted for your trousseau. Then you will be going to Weatherford Hall in Cornwall. It is one of the largest and most impressive estates in Great Britain. I am told that the house is extraordinary, as are the farms and villages that surround it."

Breanna remembered the time last winter when she had come upon a rabbit that had been caught in a trap. The snow surrounding the trap had been bloody because the poor creature was tugging and pulling, trying to extricate itself from the trap. Breanna had quickly released the poor animal, but shortly thereafter it had died. She now knew how that rabbit must have felt, because she was in a trap and there was no escape. Her fate was sealed. How could she think of being a wife to a man she had never met — a man who in all probability could not even speak her language. Was this some nightmare that she would awaken from? She felt the trap closing around her tighter and tighter.

"Is there anything more that you haven't told me, Sophie? I prefer to hear everything here and now. I don't want any more surprises."

"There is one other th—thing." Sophie stuttered. "You are to be married by proxy once you reach London."

"What is that supposed to mean?"

"The Marquess has insisted that you and his grandson be married with all haste. I believe his grandson will be married to you as soon as the ship bringing him to England clears American waters."

"Then the wedding will not be valid?"

74

"I can assure you it will be. The Marquess will have someone to stand in for his grandson. The marriage will be lawful; however, there will be a more formal ceremony after you and the Marquess's grandson arrive at Weatherford Hall. Apparently the Marquess wants no doubt in anyone's mind that the marriage is legal and binding."

"I do not understand why the Marquess has chosen me for his grandson."

"The way the solicitor. explained it, the Marquess wanted a woman from a good family, who had not been to Court and corrupted by frivolous ways."

Now an angry sparkle shone in Breanna's eyes. "What he meant was he could not find a woman of good breeding whose family would sell her to a savage." Breanna shook her head, unable to understand the web that was closing in around her. With a sob building up from deep inside, she ran from the room and up the stairs to her bedroom, where she could be alone.

Sophie wished she had the words to comfort Breanna. With a steady gaze, she left the morning room in search of her husband. She would try one more time to dissuade Fielding from this folly, but she knew she would have no effect on his decision. He had convinced himself that he was doing what was best for his sister. In reality Breanna had been sold the Marquess, and there was nothing Sophie could do to stop the marriage. Breanna had been right in her assessment of her predicament — she was being used as a chattel by her brother as well as by the Marquess.

Breanna's heart was shattered, and she was feeling very alone and frightened. There was no one to turn to, no one who would sympathize with her plight. Her life had taken an unexpected twist, and there was nothing she could do to free herself. When she entered her bedroom, she threw herself onto the bed and stared at the ceiling. She may have been sold to some savage, but the man would never crush her spirit. She shivered, feeling the hopelessness of her situation.

Chapter Five

The coach jostled over the rough roads as Breanna stared out the window at the passing scenery. Her brother, uncomfortable and ill-at-ease, sat beside her, avoiding eye contact. She was still too hurt and angry to make it easy for Fielding, and she hoped his conscience was bothering him for his blatant disregard for her welfare. How could her own brother have sacrificed her for money?

"Breanna," Fielding said at last. "We are but an hour from London. I need to explain some things to you."

She turned to meet his eyes, which were golden in color, like her own. Breanna had once thought Fielding had all the charm in the family, but she had not found him charming for a very long time. His eyes were dull and red-rimmed from indulging in too much rum. His complexion was blotchy. Now his hand shook as he held it out to her.

She ignored his hand, so he stuffed it in his pocket. "You have nothing to say that I want to hear, Fielding."

Her eyes sparkled with unshed tears. "Right now, I do not even want to be in this coach with you."

He cleared his throat nervously. "Now, Breanna, you are taking entirely the wrong attitude. Deciding about your future has weighed heavily on me for several years. It was a tremendous responsibility to me. Whether you believe it or not, I have set your future on a firm foundation."

"No, what you have done is to cast me aside, and in doing so, have made your own future more assured. But rest easy in your mind, for I am no longer your responsibility."

Fielding's eyes shifted away from her steady gaze. "You are an ungrateful chit, Breanna. I don't know why you are acting this way. I hope that with the passing of time, you will be thanking me for making this advantageous match on your behalf. You cannot possibly conceive the power you will wield once the old Marquess dies and you become the Marchioness of Weatherford."

She ran her gloved hand down the frayed seam of her gray velvet traveling gown, hating this rift between her and Fielding. "You will pardon me if I don't show my appreciation, but you see, I am fresh out of gratitude. Perhaps with the passing of time, your conscience will bother you less, and you will be able to forgive yourself for what you have done to me—but I shan't."

Fielding's jaw tightened. He was angry because she was making him feel guilty. "Well, missy, whether or not you approve of the plans I have made for your future, you will never have to worry about money. You will never have creditors knocking at your front door.

With my agreeing to this marriage, I have assured you of wealth beyond your wildest dreams."

"Yes, and you have managed to profit also, have you not?" she asked accusingly, her words laced with sarcasm.

He reached forward and gripped her hand. "Breanna, you are my sister. Let us put these bitter feelings aside."

Tender feelings tugged at her heart, and she could see some of his old charm shining through his smile. "Yes, I *am* your sister, and that is why you have wounded me so deeply. Did you think this arrangement would bring me everlasting happiness?"

His eyes cleared. "Wealth can go a long way toward taking the edge off your unhappiness. I have been both poor and well off, and I can assure you I prefer the latter. I really do believe that this marriage will be best for you in the end, or I never would have given my consent."

She shook her head. "How can you believe that? I am to be married to a . . . words escape me . . . I don't know what I will be married to!"

His hold on her hand tightened. "Listen to me, Breanna. You only have to stay with this man until you beget a son. After that, you can go your own way, and he can go his, and you will never have to worry about finances."

"Has it occurred to you that I might not be driven by the same obsession with money that you have? I always thought the man I married . . . I always hoped . . ." She tried to steady her voice. "I cannot bear to think of . . . of this stranger . . . this savage touching me."

Fielding seemed completely indifferent to her apprehension and dismissed it with a shrug. "As I see it, you will only have to endure this man's presence for a few weeks, several months at the most. Then you are free to do as you choose." He looked uncomfortable again. "I hope Sophie talked to you about your marital duties. You will be expected to produce an heir."

Her golden eyes flashed. "Will you receive any money if I produce a daughter?"

He did not reply, but stared out the window — what could he say? The solicitor had made some remark about the Marquess's generosity, but only if his sister produced a son.

By now they were entering London and Breanna stared out the window. She had never been to London, and under other circumstances would have enjoyed the sights and sounds around her. "What is our destination, Fielding?" she asked at last, not that it really mattered. Nothing mattered now.

"You will be staying at the Remington townhouse, which I understand is most impressive."

"Is this where I am to meet . . . the Marquess's grandson?"

"No, but you will be married to him by proxy tomorrow. While you are staying at the townhouse, you will be fitted with clothing appropriate to your new position." Fielding's eyes were now bright with enthusiasm. "Think of it, you have but to say what you want, and it is to be given you."

"What I want is to go home."

His lips twitched nervously. "Hardly a request that will be granted. I hope you will not embarrass me by being discourteous to the Marquess and ungrateful for all his generosity. Consider our family honor before you say anything you may later regret."

"Our family has no honor," she stated flatly.

Fielding's face whitened. "Make no mistake about it, Breanna, the Kenton name is still respected in England, which was one of the reasons the Marquess chose you for his grandson's bride. If he is displeased with you, he could still find another to take your place."

Breanna understood Fielding's concern. He was afraid that she would displease the Marquess and he would send her packing and insist that Fielding return the money that had been advanced to him. "Have no worry on my account. As distasteful as it is, I shall honor your agreement. But I want it understood that I do this for Sophie and the children. My only hope is that you will not squander the thirty pieces of silver you received for selling your own sister."

His eyes sparked with anger. "You go too far, Breanna. Remember this one thing: If the Marquess tosses you out on your ear, don't come crying to me."

She sighed heavily, knowing it was useless to argue with Fielding. She remembered how her brother had been her childhood hero—how she had always admired and loved him then. Her respect for him had lessened as she had grown older and become aware of his selfishness. Too many times she had seen Sophie with tears in her eyes because of Fielding's shortcomings as a husband and provider.

"I can promise you this, Fielding, I will never again live with you—not after what you have done to me."

His features were grim. "Now we begin to understand one another. Listen to me, because we are almost there, and I have a few things that I want to explain to you."

She stared straight ahead. "Such as?"

"I want to tell you something about the old Marquess so you will have some notion of the kind of man you will be dealing with."

"I am not marrying the grandfather."

"No, but you may as well know he is the one who will be ruling your life until you give him a great-grandson."

She became resigned. "All right, Fielding, tell me about the formidable Marquess of Weatherford."

"First of all, he is not a well man, and from what I understand, he is confined to his room most of the time. He has been a recluse for some years, and it is said that the driving ambition in his life is to have an heir to survive him. Give him that heir, Breanna, and he will deny you nothing."

"Have you ever met him?"

"No. He sees no one." Fielding reached for Breanna's hand, but she jerked it away from him. With sadness etched on his face, he realized that he probably merited his sister's scorn. "As you wish, Breanna. Perhaps the time will come when you will look on me with a little more tolerance."

Before she could answer, the coach turned through an iron gateway which led to a circular, tree-lined driveway. In a flurry of activity, the carriage door was wrenched open and several liveried servants lined the steps leading to the huge double doors. A footman bowed before Breanna and offered his arm. "I am instructed to welcome you, my lady," he said with a warm smile of greeting.

After Breanna stepped to the ground, she noticed that her brother made no attempt to follow suit. Her eyes were wide and questioning when she looked into his.

"One of the Marquess's stipulations was that I was not to accompany you any further than the front door. You see how it is, Breanna?"

Suddenly, she felt more alone and frightened than she ever had in her life. Even though she was angry with her brother, his presence had lent her a degree of comfort. "Will you abandon me completely?" she asked, shivering at the thought of facing the Marquess alone.

"I must," he replied, leaning forward and closing the carriage door. "As I said, that was the agreement. Just remember that you are a Kenton and don't allow anyone to intimidate you, Breanna." With those parting words, Fielding tapped his cane on the roof, signaling to the coachman to drive on.

Breanna stared after the departing coach, knowing she had just been deposited in a world where she would have to fend for herself. Feeling the servants' curious stares, she raised her chin and faced the twenty steps that would take her up to the front door. Her whole future awaited her on the other side of that door, and she trembled in fear at what she might find there. She recalled her brother's words, and oddly enough, they did give her courage. Yes, she was a Kenton, and she would face her adversary with dignity and pride in who she was. No one would make her cower in a corner, not the Marquess, and certainly not the unknown man who was to be her husband.

From the top of the steps there appeared an elderly woman whom Breanna decided must be the head housekeeper. With a disdainful glance at Breanna's threadbare appearance, the woman smiled tightly. "I am the housekeeper, Mrs. Crowder. The Marquess has asked that you be brought to him immediately upon arrival."

Breanna was oblivious to her surroundings as she was ushered up twisting stairs to the second floor. She was vaguely aware that the huge green vase she passed was from the Ming Dynasty, and that the paintings on the wall were masterpieces, finer than any that had hung at Kenton, even in its more prosperous days. When Mrs. Crowder stopped before a door, Breanna was overcome with dread. She was about to meet the great man himself, and she hoped she could hold her own with him. Something told her that if she did not establish her independence on this first meeting, she would be lost forever.

The housekeeper opened the door and stepped back so Breanna could precede her inside. Breanna's nostrils were immediately assaulted with the nauseating smell of strong medicines and other unidentifiable sickroom odors. The room was so stuffy that Breanna could scarcely breathe. She could see no more than a vague outline of the man who was reclined on a big mahogany canopy bed. Even so, she felt her confidence evaporate at the thought of meeting him.

"Lady Breanna Kenton, my lord," the housekeeper announced without warmth or feeling.

"Come closer, girl," a raspy voice ordered with irritation. "Why do you dawdle in the middle of the room?"

Breanna took as many hesitant steps as it required to bring her before the white-haired gentleman. At first, until her eyes became accustomed to the shadows cast by the hanging canopy, all Breanna could see was a gnarled hand, one finger circled with a crested ring. "Closer, girl. How can I see you when you hang back like a frightened rabbit? I want to find out if I got my money's worth in you."

His whole manner incensed Breanna. She did not appreciate his high-handed, insulting attitude. "You will find, my lord, when you come to know me better, that I in no way resemble a frightened rabbit. As to whether or not you got your money's worth, you will have to judge that for yourself."

There was silence as the gnarled hand reached out and lit a candle on the bedside table. The candle glow chased the darkened shadows away, and her eyes met with the lightest blue eyes she had ever seen. Bushy eyebrows arched over a wide nose. The Marquess's cheeks were sunken, and his pallor had a yellow cast to it, leaving little doubt in Breanna's mind that Lord Quincy was seriously ill. Steely blue eyes ran over her from the tip of her red-gold curls to the toe of her worn black slippers.

"I take it from your tone of voice that you are not happy about the arrangement between your brother and myself."

She gave a proud toss of her head. "That's correct."

"Did your brother tell you about the wealth I will bestow on you?"

"Yes," she said dully, staring into his probing eyes. "If

you think to impress me with your wealth, you are wasting your time and mine."

He snorted. "I was told you were a beauty, but I've seen prettier than you. I can't say much for your manners. You are not as easily humbled as your brother was."

"I'm glad you realize that at the onset, because it will save us both a lot of time." She tossed her red-gold mane. "While we are on the subject of what we have been told about one another, I must point out that I was informed you would be unreasonable and domineering. I find that was not an exaggeration," she countered.

Crackling laughter filled the room until it turned into a spasm of coughing. After the Marquess caught his breath, he motioned for Breanna to seat herself near his bed. She obeyed, demurely tucking her hands in her lap.

"I'm glad you aren't one of those silly women who cringe every time a man speaks sharply to them." His eyes bored into her as if he were assessing her hidden qualities. "You could be really incomparable with the right finery. I never cared much for redheaded women, but your hair wouldn't be too bad if it was fashionably dressed. Your skin's nice. I don't know about the rest of you since you are covered with that hideous gown that a scullery maid wouldn't be caught dead wearing."

For the first time, Breanna smiled. "It's your fault, my lord, if you do not like what you see. One should never buy anything without first judging its merit for oneself. It would serve you right if you find me unacceptable."

There was no mistaking the amusement in the old man's eyes. "I know more about you than you know about yourself, Breanna Kenton. I had my solicitor look long and hard before I decided that you had the perfect qualities to be my grandson's bride."

"What qualities are those?" she boldly asked.

"You have an impeccable bloodline," he admitted. "Despite your brother's attempt to drag your family name through the mire, you are well respected in your village. You are an unsullied maiden, virginal, without worldly wisdom, stubborn, but with a good head on your shoulders. As I said, you are not bad to look upon. We will do something about your clothing and polish you up a bit so my grandson will be attracted to you. The rest is up to you."

"I am surprised you haven't asked to see my teeth," she remarked in disgust.

His eyes danced with amusement. "I don't have to. I already know you have perfect teeth," he answered, smiling. "Yes," he said, turning his head and staring into space. "You will do very nicely." His attention was drawn back to Breanna when she came to her feet.

"By the way," she asked, "what is wrong with your grandson that you have to buy a wife for him?"

"If you can curb that tongue of yours, you will make an admirable wife," he replied, ignoring her question. "I imagine that my grandson is accustomed to Indian maidens who are subservient to their men. I hope you will remember this."

Breanna's eyes sparkled with a dangerous glint. "I will be subservient to no man. Not even if that man is my husband."

A strange light came into the Marquess's eyes. "Perhaps therein will lie your true charm, Breanna Kenton. It seems I have chosen well. You may be worthy to mother the next Marquess of Weatherford."

She was puzzled for a moment. "Haven't you skipped a generation, My Lord? By right of succession, should not your grandson be your next heir?"

His eyes clouded with sadness. "My grandson will be unfit to rule since he knows nothing of our ways. No, I will have him make his mark on paper renouncing the title in favor of his son."

Breanna felt a chill in her heart. "Knowing your grandson is unworthy to inherit your lands and title, knowing him to be uncivilized, strikes terror in my heart!" she admitted.

The Marquess's heavily-lidded eyes blinked. "I believe very few things in life would strike terror in your heart. I have little doubt that you will deal well with my grandson. I will admit to you that I have very little interest in my grandson other than his ability to produce a son." His eyes narrowed in on her. "Do we understand one another?"

She stared back at him unflinchingly. "Yes, perfectly, my lord. You are using me and your grandson as breeders."

"Crudely put, but accurate. Now leave me. I have instructed Mrs. Crowder to see to your comfort. Starting tomorrow, my cousin, Harriet Milford, will see that you are properly attired. Tomorrow night you will be married to my grandson by proxy."

Breanna bobbed a quick curtsy and moved across the room when his voice stopped her. "Breanna, if a son is born to you from this union, then I will deny you nothing."

She didn't bother to reply, but hurried out the door. The meeting with the Marquess was most unsettling and had ended so abruptly that it left her confused and unsure. She had found him to be a hateful, domineering old man who was accustomed to manipulating people with no thought as to what they might be suffering.

Outside the room she was met by the unsmiling housekeeper, who led her to a door at the other end of the long hallway.

"This will be your room while you are here, my lady," the woman announced, showing Breanna inside and leaving abruptly.

Breanna had told herself that she wasn't going to be impressed by anything she saw here. In spite of that resolve, she gasped in disbelief at the huge bedchamber. The walls were pale pink and the furnishings, rugs, and window hangings were all white. It was so magnificent it took her breath away.

She was caught up in admiring her surroundings and did not see the tiny woman who rose from the chair near the window and approached her from behind. "I am Harriet Milford, my lady, his lordship's cousin. I am very glad to welcome you."

Breanna turned to stare into soft brown eyes. "Yes," Harriet Milford said, walking around Breanna. "You have potential." Her eyes shone with anticipation. "We shall make a great beauty out of you."

The next day Breanna was tucked, pinched, and prodded. Dressmakers, couturiers, jewelers, and shoemakers paraded through her bedchamber. She was draped in silks, and her hair was washed, scented, and pulled away from her face to fall down her back in long ringlets.

As night fell, and the time for the wedding approached, Breanna was dressed in a white satin gown and led to the Marquess's bedchamber. Harriet Milford's son, a sober man in his late fifties, stood in for the Marquess's missing grandson as a bishop performed the marriage by proxy. Breanna made the proper responses as terror waged a war inside her. She heard the name of the Marquess's grandson for the first time. The Bishop had called him Lord Dakota Remington. What kind of name was Dakota? Of course it was an Indian name, she reminded herself.

There was no celebration after the ceremony was over, but the shine in the Marquess's eyes showed he was delighted.

Feeling sick inside, Breanna excused herself and returned to her bedchamber. Dark terror filled her mind as she thought of the uncivilized man, Dakota, who had just become her legal husband! She could not imagine what the future held for her. The most that she could hope for was that this Dakota would find her undesirable. Perhaps, since he was accustomed to Indian maidens with their dark coloring, he would find her unattractive. She hoped that would be the case.

Breanna could not help thinking over all she had heard about Indians. It was said that no white woman was safe with them, that they were murderers and thieves who couldn't drink liquor because it made them crazed. She wondered if this Dakota had ever taken a human scalp.

She tried not to think about her new husband. After all, anything could happen to Dakota Remington before he reached England. Storms frequently came up at sea and ships were lost without a trace, she told herself, not feeling in the least guilty for taking comfort in that fact.

Chapter Six

For two weeks Levi and Dakota had been traveling, and in that time, Dakota remained silent and brooding. Levi kept his thoughts to himself, realizing that Dakota was still grieving over the deaths of Two Moons and Running Deer.

Even at night, when they set up camp, few words would pass between them. So far, Levi had avoided most of the white settlements, but when they reached Indianapolis, he knew they could no longer avoid civilization.

As the old hunter and Dakota walked down the main street, Levi became aware of the curious glances Dakota was receiving. Therefore, their first stop was the general store, where Levi attempted to purchase clothing for Dakota. But Dakota stubbornly refused to exchange his buckskins for the white man's attire.

Levi noticed that Dakota was beginning to take an interest in his surroundings. Everything was strange to -the young man, since Two Moons had kept his adopted son isolated from white settlements, fearing someone would try to spirit him away.

With an amused smile on his face, Levi watched Dakota's eyes follow a young lady down the street, whose wide hoop skirt swayed gently as she walked. With amazement, he turned to the hunter. "How can it be that the white woman has such a strange shape to her body?" he asked in Arapaho, bewilderment and disbelief etched on his face.

Levi laughed. "Speak in English, Dakota, and to answer your question, the white woman in many respects is little different from the young maidens of the Arapaho tribe. You see, they have this contraption under their gowns that make them stick out all funny like. Don't ask me why they do it. It seems damn foolish to me, but then I never did understand women, whether they be white or Indian."

At that moment, a pretty young woman passed by and Dakota followed her with his eyes as he spoke to Levi. "I like better the way the Indian woman dresses. A man should not have to marry a woman and not know the shape of her body until it is too late."

Levi smiled and scratched his beard, amused at Dakota's observation. "I'd never thought of it that way. You could be right."

Levi spent the day introducing an astonished Dakota to civilization. Instead of sleeping in a hotel, they spent their last night beneath the stars. The campfire had gone out, and Levi was drifting off to sleep when Dakota spoke.

"I feel as though I am leaving behind all that I love and am going into a deep void, Levi. My heart hurts because of the death of my father, and my soul cannot find peace because my brother killed Running Deer. I know that by now, Black Otter will have been put to death, and even though it was not by my hand, in some ways I feel responsible. I am tormented with the thought that my father's spirit may not be able to find peace."

Levi had been waiting for the day Dakota would decide to confide in him.

"Do not blame yourself in any way for what happened to Black Otter. If he met Arapaho justice, he got what he deserved."

"Where do I belong?" Dakota questioned, in a plea for understanding.

"I know you are feeling misplaced at the moment. Sometimes I wonder if I am doing right by taking you away from the life you have become accustomed to. I don't know where you belong, Dakota, I just don't have all the answers."

"If it had not been my father's wish for me to accompany you, I would have stayed with . . . my people . . . with the Arapaho. My father knew that if I remained, Black Otter and I would have to face one another. He knew one of us would die."

"Yes, Two Moons knew."

"Levi," Dakota said, changing the subject, "you have told me many things about England. You have brought me many books, which I have read. Will England be a settlement such as we saw today?" Dakota asked in Arapaho.

"Speak English, Dakota," Levi reprimanded mildly. "And yes, there are some similarities. But in many ways they are very different."

"Which is no answer at all," Dakota observed.

Levi smiled at Dakota's quick mind. "I suspect you will just have to judge for yourself."

"Will you remain in England with me?"

"I will not abandon you."

"Levi, tell me more about the man and woman whose likenesses are in this locket. I know they are my father and mother, but you have told me very little else about them."

"I don't know much. I was their guide, but since I was not on the same social level with them, they did not confide their personal life to me."

"What does this mean, social level?"

"Well . . ." Levi said thoughtfully, "they were of the gentry—the nobility of England. They are likened to chiefs in their own land."

"Does this make them superior to you?"

"In the white world, it does. You may as well realize, Dakota, that you are one of the nobility. If you want to be happy, you will have to put your old life behind you and look to the future."

"No, never. I will not forget the father that raised me. I never want to forget my mother, White Wing."

"I would not want you to forget the two people who gave you love and made you their son. I'm just saying that if you brood on the past, you will be wasting the future."

After that, Dakota fell asleep, but Levi remained awake pondering the fruit of his labors. Was he doing the right thing in taking Dakota to England? The old Marquess was a hard man who was steeped in family tradition and would not be welcoming his grandson out of love, but from duty. No, the Marquess of Weatherford's only concern was to have an heir. Many thoughts plagued Levi. He was fond of Dakota, and hoped he hadn't been instrumental in adding to the young man's

95

confusion and unhappiness.

It was a hot, sultry afternoon when they arrived in New York. Dakota accompanied Levi into the Blue Horse Inn, where the Marquess's solicitor had arranged for them to stay until they sailed for England. Levi was aware that Dakota was attracting attention, especially from three well-dressed young gentlemen who were seated at a table playing cards. He had given up trying to convince Dakota to change his buckskins for the more conventional apparel of the white men.

John Donegal had been instructed by his great-uncle, the Marquess of Weatherford, to wait at the Blue Horse Inn for the arrival the Marquess's grandson, and teach him the rudiments of social graces so he would not be an embarrassment to his grandfather. John had been waiting for weeks, and had just about exhausted all the enjoyable activities this provincial town had to offer. He had counted himself fortunate when he became acquainted with two fellow countrymen, Alec and Tate Henley, who were the sons of a wealthy tradesman. In England, he would never have spoken to the Henley brothers, but here, in America, it seemed the sensible thing to do. Together they had passed the time playing cards, and John had won a great deal of money from them.

Now his eyes moved across the features of the old hunter, and then on to the tall, dark Indian who stood at his side. So, John thought, this was his cousin, the Viscount of Remington, future Marquess of Weatherford. John, who was wearing a dark green frock coat and trousers along with a bright yellow waistcoat, regarded the buckskins his cousin wore with distaste. How in the hell was he expected to teach this man enough manners so he could function in polite society? As John glanced at the buckskin moccasins Dakota wore, he wondered how he would ever get him into a pair of fine English boots.

Rising to his feet, John threw his cards on the table. "It seems we shall be parting company, gentlemen. Unless I am badly mistaken, my cousin has arrived."

Alec Henley, the oldest brother, dabbed at his brow with a lace handkerchief while staring at Dakota in disbelief. "Surely you are mistaken. That is an Indian savage! Your uncle has set you an impossible task. You will never be able to introduce him into polite society. I wager he will never be accepted by the gentry. He will be made sport of the moment he steps on English soil."

John Donegal's eyes lit up with humor. He had dusted the pockets of Alec and Tate Henley, and saw a way to extract even more money from them. "I say you are wrong. How much are you willing to wager?"

Tate poked Alec in the ribs. "Make it high, we are about to get the money back that John won from us." He cast a sly glance toward Dakota, who was following the old hunter up the stairs to the second floor. "No one could make that uncivilized person into a gentleman."

John reached into his breast pocket, withdrew a leather bag, and tossed it on the table. "Here's two hundred pounds, which is every cent I have in the world. I'll wager it all to prove that I will present Lord Dakota Remington to you by the time we reach England, polished and primed for his role as heir apparent to the Remington fortunes."

"You wouldn't have that money if you hadn't won it

from us," Alec Henley stated. "But yes, done."

"Done," his brother parroted.

With the wager still ringing in his ears, John made his way up the stairs to present himself to his cousin and the old buffalo hunter. He knew the task he had set before himself would not be an easy one, but he had never been one to disregard a challenge! Still, the odds had rarely been so much in favor of his opponent.

Not liking to be closed in, Dakota left open the bedroom door that led to the hallway. He moved restlessly around the room, examining the porcelain water pitcher, the soft material of the window covering, the mirror on the wall. He sat on the edge of the bed, sinking into its soft, feathery depth. "I have seen many wonders since starting out with you, Levi—but this place—this place you call New York, is beyond anything I could have imagined."

"This is nothing compared to what you will see, Dakota. Wait until you get to England and observe wonders that will make you question your own eyes."

"You always say this to me, Levi, but I find your knowledge of England severely limited."

The hunter smiled. "Although I have traveled there twice at your grandfather's request, I have little knowledge of the English, especially the titled ones. You're the one who read all the books on England—you should be the one telling me what it's like. I wish it was in my power to make you feel less lost when we arrive, but your needs go beyond anything I can teach you."

At that moment a voice spoke up from the doorway. "If you are Lord Dakota Remington and a hunter

called Levi Gunther, perhaps I could be of assistance."
John Donegal smiled jauntily.

"That's who we are, but who are you?" Levi asked,
looking the stranger over, noting his fashionable mode
of dress and the fine way he had of speaking. He gathered this would be someone who had been sent by the
Marquess.

John gave an exaggerated bow. "Allow me to present
myself. I am John Donegal, from the Scottish branch of
the Remington Family." His eyes twinkled. "Actually,
we are the poor side of the family — good bloodline, but
no money."

So far Dakota had not spoken, and John wasn't sure
he understood English; therefore, he did not know how
huge a task he had set himself. "I am Lord Dakota's
cousin," he added.

Dakota came to his feet, his eyes moving over the
fancily dressed gentlemen who claimed to be his
cousin. "How is it that you are my cousin?" he asked.

"Well, I'll be damned!" John exclaimed, breathing a
sigh of relief. At least he wouldn't have to teach Dakota
English, though he would have to polish his accent.
"Actually, my grandmother was your grandfather's sister, so you can see I am no threat to you as far as
inheriting from my uncle."

"I do not understand," Dakota said. "What do you
mean by inherit, and why do you call me Lord Dakota?"

"All will become clear to you in good time, cousin,"
John answered. "Right now, I want to take you to a
good tailor so you can be fitted with the proper attire."

Dakota was not certain if he liked this man who
admitted to being his cousin. "I will not wear clothing

such as yours," Dakota stated obstinately, reminding John of the Marquess. "I do not want to look like you."

John chuckled. "We will try to dress you more conventionally. I have instructions from your grandfather to see that you are attired as befits an Englishman of your rank. Of course, we shall find you the proper tailor once we reach England."

Dakota's eyes flamed, and his chin clamped shut in an inflexible line. Levi smiled to himself. John Donegal was not going to have an easy task trying to make Dakota conform to his expectations.

Chapter Seven

The frigate *Durham* was two days out of New York, and a fair wind caught her sails while the morning sunlight bathed them in a golden glow.

Still dressed in his buckskins, and having refused to cut his hair, Dakota drew many astonished glances as he and John moved about the deck. John talked to him about England, and since Dakota had been curious about England since boyhood, he was fascinated by what his cousin was telling him. They were forming a warm bond of friendship and mutual respect. Dakota found John entertaining as well as informative.

"Why do you sometimes call me 'my lord'?" Dakota wanted to know.

John looked astounded. "Surely you know that you are the Viscount of Remington?"

"So you tell me, John. I have read many books about the peerage in England, and of course Levi has told me that my grandfather is a marquess, which is like being a chief of the Arapaho, but I do not understand why I would have a title; I have done nothing in the white world to deserve it."

John threw his hands up in exasperation. "That's the wonderful thing about it, you don't have to deserve it, Dakota. You title is inherited because of what one of our ancestors did, and I fear you can do nothing to dissociate yourself from it."

"Who was this ancestor, and what did he do to deserve such an honor?"

"His name was Alexander Remington. In Queen Elizabeth's time, he sailed Spanish waters, captured Spanish galleons, and brought back to England nine shiploads of Inca gold for the royal treasury. A grateful queen bestowed the title of Marquess of Weatherford on him, and gave him lands and palaces, which remain in the family to this day."

"I have read about such men as he. They were called pirates, were they not?"

John's mouth fell open and he quickly looked around to see if anyone had overheard Dakota. A grin curved his lips. "If I were you, I wouldn't make that observation when you are with your grandfather. He's rather proud of the . . . old pirate."

"This is all very confusing, John. A man should not be born a chief, he should earn that right."

John nodded. "I cannot disagree with your logic, Dakota, but that is not the way it is done in England. The moment your father died, you became Viscount of Remington; should your grandfather die, you would become the Marquess of Weatherford, a title which commands great respect."

"What does a peer do?" Dakota asked, still looking bewildered.

"If he is wealthy, as you are, he doesn't have to do anything unless he so desires. In fact, I know several members of the nobility who have lived their whole lives without doing anything useful. This will be a good time to inform you that you have inherited a sizable fortune from your father's estate. We will not go into what you will one day inherit from your grandfather."

"It is important that a man have money?" Dakota questioned. "I have never thought you could measure a man's worth by his worldly possessions."

"That should be the case, but too often it isn't," John agreed, smiling. "Take me for instance. I am too honest to make money by ill-gotten means, and in my position, I could never make my fortune in trade." He spread his hands in a helpless gesture. "Thus I am forced to live by my wits. I was most desperate when my great-uncle asked me to take ship to America and meet you."

"So my grandfather is very wealthy?"

"That's correct. He has mines in Cornwall, farms and townships outside of London. Hell, he even owns whole counties in Ireland."

"What will I be expected to do when we reach England, John?" Dakota asked with growing concern.

"Well, first of all, your grandfather wants me to take you to one of the finest tailors in England and have you brought up to snuff."

"What does this mean?"

John chuckled delightedly, amazed at Dakota's insatiable thirst for knowledge. "That means you must be dressed in a manner befitting a viscount."

A shadow fell across Dakota's face and he glanced up to find two fashionably attired gentlemen approaching them from across the deck.

John leaned forward and quickly whispered to Dakota. "Those are the Henley brothers. Do me a courtesy, and pretend you do not understand English. I have a wager with these two gentlemen, and I may even be able to increase my winnings."

Dakota nodded, thinking that white men certainly had a strange sense of humor.

While Alec and Tate Henley conversed with John, they kept staring at Dakota, but he pretended not to understand them. After a few moments, they walked away smiling, positive that they would recoup their losses. John Donegal would never turn the white Indian into a gentleman, they thought smugly, no matter how noble his ancestors.

Dakota stood on deck, allowing the sea spray to hit him in the face. Every passing moment, the *Durham* was taking him farther and farther away from the only home he had ever known. When he closed his eyes, he pictured all the faces that had been a part of his world. He could still see his mother's sweet smile. He tried not to think of his father as he had looked the last day of his life, ill and wasted away. How vividly he could picture Running Deer as she had looked in death. He tried to push his troubled thoughts aside, because his memories were still too painful to dwell upon.

"There you are, Dakota, I have been searching below deck for you." John came up beside him, and they both watched the dying sun tint the western sky in a blanket of amber.

"I will hear no more lessons about England today," Dakota announced.

Levi had described to John the troubles Dakota had faced, and John felt sympathy for his young cousin, even though he did not understand why Dakota was reluctant to leave behind the life in which fate had placed him. John vowed to do everything to help Dakota fit into his rightful place. He would do this not merely because his uncle had asked it of him, but because he was growing fond of his cousin and knew he would have a difficult time when they reached England.

"No, no more lessons today. You have progressed splendidly, Dakota. Have you noticed how your accent has improved? If I don't watch myself, you will surpass the teacher."

"At first all English sounded alike to me, but since you have been teaching me, I can see that there is a difference."

"That's right. Levi did well in teaching you English. I have merely refined your speech. Your progress is remarkable. Tomorrow, we start on table manners."

Dakota's eyes flickered with disdain. "You have already taught me how to hold a fork."

"Yes, but there is more to eating than merely holding a fork. Good manners are what separate us from the commoners."

Dakota smiled to himself, remembering the times he had eaten meat with his fingers, and wondering if anything he would eat with a fork would taste half so good.

John glanced out to sea, a worried frown on his face. "I have something else to tell you now, and I know of no way to say it other than to say it right out."

"I am listening."

"Do you know what proxy means?"

"No."

John gripped the railing, not knowing how Dakota was going to respond to his grandfather's order. "Proxy means to have a substitute, someone who will stand in the place of another."

Dakota glanced at John with a puzzled expression on his face. "I do not understand."

John sighed, wishing this task had not fallen to him, for he found it very distasteful. "Dakota, it is your grandfather's wish that you be married tonight. The captain has been instructed to perform the ceremony."

Dakota was baffled. "I have met no one on this ship that I would wish to marry. There are only two women on the ship. One is the captain's wife, and the other his daughter. The wife is married, and the daughter is long past her prime."

John squared his shoulders, knowing there was trouble ahead. "That's where the proxy comes in, Dakota. The captain's daughter will stand in for your true bride."

Dakota's eyes blazed. "No, I will not marry that woman. I do not know her, and she is not the woman I would choose as a wife."

"She will not *be* your wife," John explained patiently. "Your grandfather has already chosen a bride for you — she is Lady Breanna Kenton, and she is in England, awaiting your arrival. The captain's daughter, Rose, will only represent her tonight. In England, Lady Breanna will also be married to you by proxy with someone to stand in for you."

Dakota was trying to understand. He had been taught to respect the elders of his tribe, and he was willing to transfer that respect to his grandfather, but marry a woman he had never seen? No! "This kind of marriage does not appeal to me, John. If I am being married to someone I have never seen, she must be extremely repulsive, and my grandfather knows that if I see her, I would not be her husband."

John glanced up at the sky in a gesture of helplessness. "That's not the way it is at all, Dakota. This kind of marriage is not uncommon with the nobility."

"I want to respect my grandfather, but I will not bond with a woman I have never seen," Dakota said stubbornly.

"It is your grandfather's command, and you don't have a choice."

Dakota was still trying to understand. "If I do as my grandfather asks, will it be a real marriage?"

"I am told it is legal."

"John, have you ever seen the woman who is to be my wife?"

"No, I haven't," John answered honestly. "All I know about her is that she was chosen because of her blood-line and because of her chastity."

Dakota frowned, wishing he could understand the white man's peculiarities. "I have known of many chaste women in my village. Some of them were virginal because no man wished to take them to his mat."

John suppressed a smile. "We have all known this kind of woman. Let us hope it will not be so with your wife. If fate is kind, she will be a real beauty."

"I can see by your eyes that you do not believe this. Would you not have heard of her if she were a great beauty?"

"Well . . . perhaps she will have an admirable personality."

Dakota did not find this humorous. "I will do this thing, but only because it is my grandfather's wish. But . . . if I do not like the woman, I will not take her to my bed, and I will not hesitate to put her aside."

John quickly nodded, not daring to explain to Dakota that in polite society, it was not so easy to rid oneself of an unwanted wife.

Suddenly Dakota's face whitened beneath his tan. "John, just how far am I expected to go with the captain's daughter tonight?"

John's lips twitched in humor. "You are not expected to sleep with her, if that's what you are afraid of."

"I will not be husband to that woman," Dakota said in a voice that deepened with determination.

"Rest easy, my friend. You will be required to do no more than go through the ceremony with the captain's daughter." He smiled. "The joys of your wedding night will be saved for the Lady Breanna."

That night, in the captain's cabin, with John and Levi in attendance, Dakota Remington, Viscount of Remington, was married to some faceless woman in England. Her substitute, a horse-faced woman in her early thirties, with a nervous giggle, did not serve to dispel Dakota's concerns. As soon as the ceremony was over, Dakota left abruptly, still not convinced that he would not be expected to take the captain's daughter to his bed.

His thoughts were even more troubled as he wondered about the wife awaiting his arrival in England. He was determined that no one would force him to couple with a woman he found distasteful.

Breanna's new wardrobe was being packed in trunks for her journey to Weatherford Hall at the end of the week. There she would be expected to await her new husband.

Harriet Milford rapped on the door and breezed into the room, without waiting to be invited. "Well, my dear," she exclaimed, her eyes shining with delight. "My cousin, the Marquess, is most pleased with you. He is smug because he has made a wise selection in a bride for his dear grandson."

Breanna did not much care for the woman, who seemed to take everything the Marquess said as a reverent statement of fact. "Will you be coming with me to Weatherford Hall, Harriet?" Breanna wanted to know.

"No, you will not need me from here on out. I will be

leaving in the morning for a holiday in Bath with my husband."

Breanna was glad she would not have to endure this woman's company for much longer. She had no liking for the two members of this family that she had met thus far.

Harriet looked uncomfortable for a moment. "Breanna, my cousin has asked me to . . . he was wondering if you have any notion . . . of . . ."

Breanna fingered the lovely diamond brooch that the Marquess had given her, knowing why the woman was feeling uncomfortable. "My sister-in-law has told me a little of what my duties are as a wife, if that is what you are asking. The Marquess has been less discreet, and has made his views quite clear on the subject. He has arranged everything but the rope to tie me in bed with his grandson."

Harriet gasped in disbelief. "What you are implying is shameful. My cousin would not—"

Breanna was glad she had shocked the woman. She was angry with all the pretenses of trying to make this appear like a normal marriage. The Marquess had bought her for his grandson, and no amount of pretending otherwise would change that fact. "Your cousin has been vociferous in voicing his demands. You see, Harriet, the Marquess has pointed out, in no uncertain terms, that I am to be a breeder, and his grandson a stud."

Harriet's eyes widened in shock. "I am sure he knows what he is doing," she sputtered, looking at Breanna as if she were shameless. "I will say good-bye to you now," she said, hurrying across the room to the door.

Breanna smiled to herself. Let the woman report their conversation to her cousin. She hoped the Marquess would be very displeased with her — her face stiffened — she hoped the Marquess's grandson would find her totally unacceptable!

Chapter Eight

When the coach conveying Breanna to Weatherford Hall came to a halt before the great house, she was quickly assisted to the ground by a smiling footman. As she ascended the steps, she glanced back at the three coaches that carried her belongings and had to admit that the Marquess had not exaggerated when he'd told her that she would be showered with beautiful possessions. Eleven trunks were bulging with gowns, shoes, and bonnets for every occasion. The jewels he had bestowed upon her were worth a king's ransom and were locked away in six velvet-lined chests.

Breanna would gladly have returned everything in exchange for her freedom. She realized that she had somehow lost control of her own destiny.

A column of servants stood on the steps awaiting her pleasure, while she glanced out at the rugged Cornwall countryside. Weatherford Hall was a red brick Tudor-style palace which had been built in the reign of Elizabeth. Built by the first Marquess of Weatherford, after he tore down the original Norman castle that had stood on the site, it was perched high on a cliff overlooking the rock-strewn shoreline of the Atlantic Ocean. Although Breanna could not see the ocean from the front of the house, she could hear the breaking waves splash against the cliff.

Harriet Milford had informed Breanna about the picturesque little village of Weatherford which was an important fishing port. Breanna looked forward to exploring the village and meeting the people who lived there.

Here, in this alien land, with no friend or family member to stand at her side, she was forced to await her husband's pleasure, and deep inside she was terrified.

The coach rattled down the London street. Levi pulled his hat low over his forehead, studying Dakota, who was seated across from him. He had to admit that John Donegal had transformed Dakota's outward appearance. The buckskins had been exchanged for elegantly cut blue-gray trousers and coat. The Indian moccasins had been replaced with a fine pair of black leather boots.

The three men were now on their way to the Davenshire Hotel, where they would be residing until such time as John decided Dakota was ready to be presented to his grandfather.

Dakota had been hesitant to give up his buckskins, for he knew with them went his old way of life. He flexed his shoulders, feeling the confinement of the garments he wore. He had the urge to rip the cravat from his neck so he could breathe properly. Why did the white men put on so many trappings? he wondered. The Indian way was better, where one's body was not constrained beneath heavy clothing.

With mild curiosity, Dakota stared out the window of the moving coach. This was the London he had read about. To the west, he could see a view of London Bridge. Then his eyes moved on to the mass of humanity pressed together on the crowded street. Women were ladened with heavy bundles and children dashed about in a game of tag. There were apple stalls, vegetable vendors, and fishmongers selling their wares. The chimney sweep walked unimpeded beside the tradesmen. The singsong voice of a woman selling lavender could be heard above the crowd. "Lavender, buy my sweet lavender."

The coach turned off the main thoroughfare and onto a quiet, tree-lined avenue. They had reached the hotel, and John ushered Dakota inside. As of yet, Dakota had refused to have his hair cut, and John was wondering how he would get around this final obstacle. He realized that each new accomplishment Dakota mastered brought him one step closer to the day he could be presented to his grandfather. John had discovered that Dakota could not be coerced into doing something he didn't want to, so he would have to make Dakota want his hair cut.

When they reached the suite of rooms that had been reserved for them, Dakota paced the room like a caged animal, while they waited for their trunks to be delivered and unpacked.

Levi watched Dakota with amusement. John may have made him look like a young lord, but he was finding the confines and rules of the nobility somewhat constraining.

"How soon can I meet my grandfather?" Dakota asked, stopping behind John, who was standing before a mirror and straightening his cravat.

"I don't know," he said easily. "That depends on you." He turned away from the mirror, pretending to be indifferent to Dakota's inquiry.

"How does it depend on me?"

"It's very simple. After your hair has been cut, I shall take you to meet your grandfather."

Dakota was quiet for a moment, and Levi knew he was pondering the dilemma. "I will have my hair cut now," Dakota said at last. "I do not like it, but I have seen that it is the way everyone else wears their hair."

John stood up, ready to act before Dakota changed his mind. "You wait right here while I send for Sidney Cox, who is the best hairdresser in London."

Dakota observed the stranger in the mirror, with the neatly clipped hair, feeling as if he had lost his identity. Now he was just one of many, looking like the mass of humanity that occupied London.

"Dakota," John said, breaking into his thoughts. "Do you recall I told you that I made a wager with the Henley brothers?"

A muscle twitched next to Dakota's lips as he tried not to smile. "Yes, I believe you wanted to prove to them that you could turn a savage into a gentleman."

115

"Yes, well something like that. I believe the time is right to collect my wager. When that is accomplished, I will take you to meet your grandfather."

"Just where do you expect this meeting to take place so you can show off your successful attempt to civilize me, John?" This was asked with humor dancing in Dakota's eyes.

John realized that only a man with great inner strength could jest about the situation. "Now, this is the tricky part. As you know, the Henley brothers are not on the same social level as you and I, and it is most unseemly that we should invite them here."

Dakota's lips eased into a smile. "No, perish the thought. That would never do for it to become known that we associate with the likes of them."

John ignored the insinuated jab at his snobbery. "Would you consider coming to their club with me?"

Dakota picked up one of his prized books and thumbed through the pages. "I suppose that is the least I can do for you, after all you have done for me; however, this is the one and only time I will make a spectacle of myself for your gain."

John nodded, grinning. "This is the last time I ask it of you. It pains me to admit it, but I have used the fact that you feel indebted to me to obtain your consent."

Dakota laughed at his cousin's humor. "Indebted? Perhaps."

John rubbed his hands together, anticipating the conclusion of his wager. "This will be the easiest money I have ever earned."

"Are you saying it was easy to make me an Englishman?" Dakota's eyes were seeking and probing as if

John's answer was important to him.

The teasing light left John's eyes, and he became serious. "It was easy because of the man you are. I have to be honest with you. When my uncle first assigned this task to me, I had little hope I would succeed. I taught you a few manners, took you to a tailor and boot maker, and changed your mode of dress. But you were already a gentleman by birth. I thought I would find an uneducated man once I reached America; instead, I found a man who had read more books than I will read in a lifetime. I found you to be truthful and honorable, and I am proud of our kinship." Thinking he was becoming too serious, John smiled. "You know, you could ruin me if you decided to be Dakota the Indian when we meet the Henley brothers."

Devilment danced in Dakota's eyes. "Yes, I could, could I not? That's something you should think about, John. If I turn savage on you, what will you do?"

As the brougham turned onto St. James Street, John reached forward and straightened Dakota's elaborately tied cravat. He quickly assessed his cousin, taking in the single-breasted black jacket which reached to Dakota's thighs. The black trousers hugged his legs, and were pulled taut by the strap that fit beneath the short, black boots. The green silk embroidered waistcoat gave just the right finishing touch, and brought out the color of Dakota's green eyes. Dakota's hair had been clipped in the latest style, his sideburns tapered almost to his chin, but Dakota had adamantly refused to grow a mustache; his Indian upbringing was still too much

117

ingrained in his mind.

John's eyes gleamed with a light of triumph. "Damn if I don't think I'll pull this off, Dakota. Now remember, act aloof, and don't say anything until just the right moment."

Dakota's lips twitched in amusement. "I suppose it does not matter to you that I am to be paraded before your friends as your creation, your successful transformation of a savage into a gentleman?"

John rubbed his gloved hands together with glee. "First of all, you have to understand the Henley brothers are not my friends. They are simply acquaintances, whom I enjoy taking money from. Secondly, I promise you will not be paraded, because I intend to fleece the brothers with the utmost decorum. This will be my finest hour; it had better be your finest hour, too, Dakota."

They came to a halt before the Broadrick Club, one of the exclusive men's clubs in London, but not one John had ever frequented, or ever would after today. "Remember, Dakota, follow my lead," John instructed as the coachman jumped to the ground and whisked the door open.

Dakota stepped out, and John looked him over one last time. Yes, Dakota had an air of dignity about him that had nothing to do with his fashionable attire. He somehow represented a nobility that went beyond his rank, John thought, gaining a fresh insight into the inner man.

John could already feel the money warming his pocket. He clapped Dakota on the back. "Come, the brothers Henley will be waiting for us. Shall we honor the peasants with our presence?"

Dakota filled his lungs with air, pulled on his white gloves, and smiled at his cousin. "You are a pompous ass, John."

"Yes, admittedly," John acknowledged. "When one is light in the pocket, sometimes all he has to fall back on is his arrogance."

By now they had approached the doorman, who bowed, knowing from their mode of dress and their lofty airs that these men were of import. "Your names, sirs?" he asked politely.

"I am John Donegal, and this is Sir Geoffrey Spaulding. One of your members, Alec Henley, is expecting us."

The man checked his list before glancing back to John. "Sir, I have your name on my list"—he hesitated, feeling embarrassed—"but I do not show your companion."

"It's of no importance," John said, lazily tapping the man on the shoulder, and with practiced snobbery, stepped around him. "Don't bother announcing us. We shall find our own way in."

"What was that all about?" Dakota asked as they walked down the gold rug runner to the gaming room beyond.

"The memberships of these clubs are jealously guarded, and they strive to keep out undesirables. However, I am sure this one has never before had any-one of your rank cross the threshold. The club you will later join will consist of your peers, and not tradesmen."

Dakota's hid his amused smile. He would never grow accustomed to the class distinction and snobbery the

English leveled at their fellow man. "Oh, I see. I keep forgetting how important I am." Suddenly his laughter rang out. "Would you consider Levi beneath me? He has sold animal skins; would he be considered a tradesman?"

"Well," John considered seriously, "he is a friend, and that goes beyond social classes . . . I suppose."

"You relieve my mind. I feared I would have to rid myself of him," Dakota said, his words laced with irony.

John spotted the Henley brothers at one of the gaming tables. When Tate Henley glanced up and saw him, he caught his brother's attention. Both men threw in their cards and advanced on John and Dakota.

"By the way, I am about to give you a demotion. I am going to introduce you as a baron. Get ready," he mumbled under his breath. In a louder voice, he remarked, "My dear Alec and Tate, how are you?"

"You are late. We had decided you weren't coming."

"Sorry for the tardiness, but you see, I ran into a friend of mine, and we got to talking—you know how it is—anyway, I decided to bring my friend along with me. I hope you don't mind."

Alec glanced at John's companion, who was looking down his very aristocratic nose at him. "Of course not, you are both welcome."

"Good. Now may I introduce you to my friend? Sir Geoffrey, may I present Alec and Tate Henley?" Dakota acknowledged the introduction with a slight nod.

John was definitely enjoying himself. "Alec and Tate, meet Sir Geoffrey Spaulding, the Baron of Cheltworthy."

Alec and Tate both looked at the stranger suspiciously at first, thinking this might be John's cousin. But when the gentleman's eyes moved over them with bored indifference, they dismissed the possibility as ludicrous. This man was not John's cousin; this was a lord born to the manor.

"Where is your cousin?" Tate asked, glancing over John's shoulder.

"I thought you were bringing him," Alec said smugly.

"I regret to inform you gentlemen that my cousin is elsewise occupied."

Alec smiled. "What you mean is, you couldn't turn that savage into a gentleman, so you forfeit the wager."

"As you wish," John said airily.

"Come," Tate cajoled, the smile of triumph on his face. "Don't take it so hard. Let's have a drink, and toast our victory." He held up his hand, signaling to the servant that he wanted four brandies.

John put on a hangdog expression. "Would you humble me in my defeat?"

"Nonsense," Alec spoke up. "It is considered a great triumph to win over a man with your reputation. It is said that you live by your wits and have rarely been bested at any game . . . until now."

"I modestly admit to all charges," John said, smiling to himself.

"What do you think about the wager, my lord?" Alec asked, turning his attention to their illustrious visitor. It had been only on rare occasions that he had been in the company of a titled gentleman.

"I care not for wagering myself," Dakota replied, his eyes piercing and cold, with the aloofness of the highborn when conversing with someone beneath his station. "I find it all a trivial waste of time."

"Surely your lordship turns a card or wagers on a phaeton or horse race?"

"True, I have placed a small wager on horse racing in the past," Dakota admitted.

"Then you must not belong to a club?"

"No, not I."

Alec's eyes gleamed, thinking how it would be a feather in his cap if he could bring a baron to the Broadrick Club. "I wonder if you would allow me to be your sponsor for membership in this club?" he asked hopefully, putting his thoughts into words.

"I think not," Dakota replied, glancing around with a distasteful curl to his lip, acting, to the hilt, the part John had handed him.

By now the waiter had appeared with the drinks. Tate raised his glass to John. "Let us drink to your failure and our success. I knew you could not win in this."

"Before I concede defeat," John interrupted, "let me ask you why you were so sure I would lose."

Tate leaned in close and whispered, "Your cousin may be highborn, but he will never fit into the aristocracy."

"Don't feel too bad, John," Alec piped up. "Scratch the surface of us all and you'll probably find a savage lurking there."

"You would know this?"

"Well, of course, neither my brother nor myself are members of the aristocracy, but we do know that they are a tight group and will not accept outsiders. And you can be sure they would consider your cousin an outsider, no matter how noble his blood."

"Are you saying," John asked, "that my cousin would never be accepted into a club like — he glanced around — say this one, for instance?"

"Never!" Alec spoke up. "The fact that he is of noble birth would not help his chances of getting in here. No, it's unthinkable."

"Would you be willing to wager on that?" John asked, his eyes gleaming with hidden lights.

Alec caught his brother's eyes, and they both roared with laughter. "You just don't know when to lie down and say 'enough,' John. I would only be taking your money if I accepted this new wager."

"I'll chance it."

Tate and Alec put their heads together and whispered among themselves. Finally Alec spoke, "How much more time would you need before presenting him to the club members?"

"Time is not important. Do you accept the wager?" he reiterated.

"Yes," Tate answered. "My brother and I have decided to be generous." He grinned. "How would you like to go for double or nothing? This will give you a chance to get your money back."

"Done," John agreed, offering Tate his hand.

"Do you want to pay up now?" Alec asked, a satisfied grin on his face.

"No, but I'll take your money. Let's see," John said as if he were calculating the terms. "You owe me two hundred pounds for our original wager; add this, and it will come to four hundred pounds. Of course, if you split it between the two of you, it will only be two hundred pounds each. You see, I was not quite truthful with you gentlemen. I'm afraid I deceived you when I introduced you to this man. May I present you to my cousin, Lord Dakota Remington?"

"What!" Alec exclaimed.

Tate glanced at Dakota, his eyes disbelieving.

"Did you not yourself just ask my cousin if you could propose his membership to this club, Alec?"

"But—"

"Well, did you?"

Alec looked aghast. He stared closely at the green eyes and saw not arrogance, but humor dancing there. Now he recognized the man as John's cousin. "I'll be damned," he said, a slow grin spreading on his face. "You foxed me, John, you did it!" Suddenly Alec Henley realized the unflattering remarks he had made about Dakota. "Your lordship, I hope you will not take offense to anything I said. I never meant . . . I never thought . . ."

Dakota merely smiled as he worked his fingers out of the white gloves. "I take no offense, Mr. Henley. After all, scratch the surface of us all, and you may find a savage lurking there."

"You may send the money around to my hotel," John informed the brothers. "This afternoon will be soon enough," he said with the light of victory shining in his eyes. "Or will you need time to come up with it? Your credit is always good with me."

Alec raised his glass to John. "One would think I would quit gaming with you, John. I have yet to best you."

John smiled at Dakota. "It was not I who won here

today, but my cousin, Lord Dakota."

Dakota had often enjoyed a jest with his Arapaho friends, and he could see the humor in this situation, but deep inside, he felt he had gained nothing by the exchange.

Dakota's thoughts moved ahead to tomorrow when he would meet with his grandfather. It was becoming clear to him that his grandfather had not sent for him out of any affection he felt for him, or else he would have asked to see him the moment he landed in England. Why, then, had he been brought here?

The sound of John's laughter brought Dakota's mind back to the present. All his questions would be answered tomorrow.

Chapter Nine

As the carriage with the Marquess's crest on the door moved down the streets, John gave Dakota a quick assessment. Dakota wore his elegant apparel with the flair of one born to it.

"I must say, Dakota, your grandfather is going to be impressed," John stated, glancing at Levi, who nodded in concurrence.

"Don't think, just because I agreed to wear this confining clothing while I am in London, that I will continue to dress this way."

John chuckled, settling back against the cushioned seat. "I don't care what you do with the clothing afterward, just as long as you wear it when you meet my uncle."

"Underneath, I am no different than I ever was," Dakota reminded John. "You might want to remember that when you present me to my grandfather today. I have already come to realize that my grandfather does not care for me as a person, else he would have seen me the moment I came ashore in England."

John could not deny the truth of that, and he was

glad that further conversation was impossible because they had reached the Marquess's townhouse.

Dakota stared at the house, torn with emotions he could not understand. Since he had been a small boy, Levi had filled his head with the idea that he had an obligation to this man who was his grandfather. He knew his grandfather had spent years, as well as a fortune, trying to get him to England, so surely he must want him.

Doubt and uncertainty nagged Dakota's mind. This man he was about to meet had always been bigger than life to him. Would the reality of the man be overshadowed by the picture Dakota had drawn in his mind?

"Dakota," Levi said, breaking into his thoughts. "There's something I want to say before we take you in. I don't know your grandfather very well, but after you have met him, if you do not wish to remain in this country, I will see you back to America."

John had become fond of his cousin, and he nodded at Levi's statement. "And I'll help you get there also. We have never really talked about your grandfather in detail, Dakota. I should have told you that he is a hard man, driven by family pride and family traditions. I have not found him to be a loving man, but then I have watched his struggle over the years to bring you here, so he must feel something for you," John said doubtfully.

"I will see him now," Dakota announced, wondering why he should feel so unsure of himself. While growing up with the Arapaho, his father had instilled in him a confidence and assurance that had dwindled as he became more deeply ingrained in the white world.

The doors of the mansion were whisked open and a

liveried servant watched the three men advance up the steps. "His Lordship is expecting you," he said politely to John, but his eyes were on Dakota. "May I say, my lord, that all of us are delighted that you have come to England."

For a moment, Dakota thought the man was addressing someone else. His brow furrowed when he realized the servant had been speaking to him.

John indicated that Dakota should enter the house, and Dakota stood in the entryway, awed at the grandeur that met his eyes. He immediately noticed a portrait which hung on the wall above a gilded table. He walked over to the portrait of a white-haired man who looked dignified and stern. "Is this my grandfather?" he wanted to know.

"Yes," John answered. "Of course, your grandfather was considerably younger when he sat for this."

Dakota turned to the only two friends he had in the white world. "Stay by me," he whispered, staring up at the portrait of the man he had never known and to whom he felt no bond. The eyes held no warmth, the mouth was set in a thin line with no hint of humor. "Don't allow me to make any mistake. I have a strange feeling my grandfather will expect more from me than I will be able to give."

"We shan't desert you," John said, feeling the close ties of kinship and loyalty for Dakota.

The old hunter stood to Dakota's right, knowing what the young man was feeling. "We'll stay with you as long as you need us," Levi assured him.

The housekeeper, Mrs. Crowder, appeared from the top of the massive staircase, her eyes on Dakota as she descended. Her gaze was respectful, her manner warm, when she saw the green eyes that reminded her of Lady Cillia. "My Lord, your grandfather has asked that you attend him at once." — she glanced at John and Levi, — "and you are to come alone."

The moment had come, and Dakota, who had faced a hundred foes in battle, had faced a bear when he had been only a boy, now felt fear at facing a frail old man.

He followed Mrs. Crowder up the stairs, his back straight, looking neither to the left nor the right.

When the housekeeper stopped before a door and opened it, she stepped back. "You will not need me to announce you; his lordship is expecting you."

The room was ablaze with candles as Dakota stepped inside. It was stifling hot, and a smell of medicine lingered in the air. His eyes moved to the red velvet chair, where a white-haired gentleman was seated, a lap robe covering his lower body.

"Come closer, boy. Don't just stand there," the aged voice crackled out. "How can we talk if I have to yell across the room at you?"

Dakota moved closer, knowing the shrewd eyes watched his progress. When his eyes locked with the old man's, Dakota saw no light of welcome there. "Your hair is dark like your father's, but you have Cillia's eyes." A smile touched the Marquess's lips. "I'll bet the young Indian maidens hankered after you, because you are a handsome devil, just like your father. He could have had any woman he wanted, and he got the best of the lot when he married your mother."

Was this the only greeting he was to have? Dakota wondered. "I am pleased to meet you, Grandfather," he said, glancing at the gnarled hands that rested atop the lap robe, and wondering if this weak old man could

129

understand what he was feeling.

"Sit down," came the command as the Marquess pounded the chair across from him with his cane. "It strains my neck to have to look up at you."

Dakota did as he was asked, knowing all the time his grandfather's eyes were assessing him.

"John told me that you speak English remarkably well, and I see that he is right. I am willing to bet that if no one knew your upbringing, they would assume you had been born into society."

Something about this man brought out the anger in Dakota. He had not expected his grandfather to fall on his neck and weep with joy, but neither had he expected this cold indifferent assessment. "I have little liking for your society," Dakota remarked haughtily.

The old man smiled. "Yes, I can see that. You hate us all, don't you?"

"I do not hate you."

"I don't care if you do or not. What we think of each other is not important. All I want from you is a great-grandson, and then you are free to go your own way."

Dakota felt the coldness of the Marquess's words in the depths of his soul. If he had expected any affection from this man, he had deluded himself. "Am I to be a breeder then?" The words were spoken coldly.

"Hump, that's what your bride wanted to know. Now that I have seen you, I can imagine you and she will not have too much trouble producing a child."

Dakota raised his head, feeling as if all the life had drained out of him. "Is this all you require of me?"

"It is." The old man's head sank to his chest. "Leave me now; you have an anxious bride waiting for you at Weatherford Hall."

Breanna counted off the days as they passed. Although she was surrounded by an army of servants, whose only concern was to make her happy, she was lonely.

Now it was the end of summer, and she had not heard from her new husband, although she had been informed that he had landed in England weeks ago. His was an acquaintance she was not anxious to make.

She was grateful for the fine horseflesh that was kept in the stables at Weatherford Hall, because when she was riding, it helped her pass the time, and she could put aside her loneliness for a time and try to forget that somewhere she had a husband who would one day appear and probably demand that she fulfill her wifely duties.

Since Breanna had never had a personal maid, and she felt she didn't need one to cater to her every whim, she chose Etta, one of the downstairs maids, to attend her. Etta, a tall big-boned Scottish girl, was delighted with her elevated position.

Now, Etta was fastening the back of Breanna's yellow riding habit. Placing the yellow hat on her head, Breanna patted it in place. As she rushed down the stairs, she pulled on her black leather gloves.

On the way to the stables, she noticed that it was a warm, cloudless morning. The stiff breeze from the ocean was tinged with salt, and she found it invigorating and her spirits soared.

Frazier, the head groom, smiled as he led the spirited white mare forward. "She'll be needing a good run this morning, my lady. I could hardly keep her still whilst I

131

saddled her."

Breanna had inspected all the horseflesh in the stables and had selected a magnificent Arabian named Joya as her own. Joya could be a bit skittish at times, but Breanna was a good horsewoman and could easily control the mare.

She patted the sleek neck. "We both need a run, don't we, Joya?" The horse nodded, as if she had understood, and both Breanna and Frazier laughed at the animal's antics.

Once in the saddle, Breanna felt all her troubles melt away. With the wind in her face, she galloped across the meadow, scattering a herd of cattle in the wake of Joya's thundering hooves. She was miles from the house before she slowed the horse's pace to a canter.

Her mind wandered as she cantered past the jagged wall, all that remained of an old Roman ruin. She tried to envision the daily lives of the ancient people who had left their mark on this land.

So deep in thought was she that Breanna didn't see the flock of seabirds that had made their nest in the ruins until it was too late. The frantic fluttering of wings spooked Joya, and the horse reared up on her hind legs. Breanna clung to the reins, but the frightened animal shied to the right, and Breanna went sailing through the air to land with a thud on the ground. Her head struck a sharp rock, and she felt exploding pain just before she lost consciousness.

Dakota glanced out the coach window, still feeling unsettled by his meeting with his grandfather. Although Dakota knew John and Levi had been curious about what had transpired between him and his grandfather, they had refrained from asking questions, and he did not feel inclined to enlighten them.

As the coach left London, with its crowded streets and mass of humanity, Dakota began to feel more at ease. As they traveled across Cornwall toward Weatherford Hall, he became aware of a beauty that touched his heart. He had been told that this was the land of his ancestors, and he could almost feel the pull of the land, as if long dead Remingtons were welcoming him home.

As if Levi could sense what the young Viscount was feeling, he spoke. "If I was to live in England, this would be the place I'd choose."

"I agree with you, Levi. This is always what I think of as home," John said.

Dakota rested a tan hand on his black boot. "One thing that has been bothersome to me is being called 'my lord.' I was not comfortable with the attention from the servants at my grandfather's house. It does not suit me to have people cater to me."

John chuckled. "You may not like it, but that's your lot in life. There are many who would gladly exchange places with you. Besides, you look the way a young viscount should look. I did a hell of a job smoothing off your rough edges, don't you agree, Levi?"

A teasing light danced in the old hunter's eyes. "You had a lot to work with, John, but yes, he does fit the picture to me. Lordly, aloof . . . well dressed."

Dakota frowned, not the least amused by their light banter. "It's easy for the two of you to laugh. You don't have to deal with a wife you have never seen. You don't have to worry whether she is . . . uncomely . . . old . . . of a quarrelsome nature. When I try to picture her

133

in my mind, she always seems to resemble the captain's daughter."

"Whatever she's like, you'll find out today," John observed lazily.

At this point John called out to the coachman. "Pull off the road here." To Dakota he said, "I want you to see Weatherford Hall from this vantage point."

The coachman readily complied. John opened the door and stepped out, motioning for Dakota to follow him. "This is a sight you will never forget. There can be no more beautiful spot in the world."

Dakota allowed his eyes to run along the rugged coastline. Huge waves slapped against the cliffs, and at the highest ridge he saw the house gleaming like a red jewel in the sun. Green meadows with flocks of grazing sheep and frolicking horses lent a tranquillity to the landscape.

Dakota was reminded of the contrast between Weatherford Hall and the tepee he had grown up in. At the moment he was caught between both worlds, feeling like he belonged to neither. "It is different than I thought it would be," he murmured. "I never imagined it would be so magnificent."

"It will all be yours one day," John told him. "As far as you can see in any direction, the land belongs to your grandfather. While you were meeting with him, I was talking to his solicitor, who assured me there is conclusive proof that you are the legal heir to the title and estates. No one will ever challenge that you are the Viscount of Remington."

Dakota shook his head. "I feel the responsibility will be great. I have not been trained for this. Besides, I am not sure I want to remain in England."

"It's in your blood. You can manage it," John said with confidence. "Already you know that this is where you belong."

Dakota surveyed the beauty around him and in some hidden corner of his mind, he felt as if he had truly come home. He did not know what the future would hold, but for the moment, he belonged to this land as surely as if he had been born here.

"People die—brothers might turn on one—but land endures, and Weatherford Hall is forever," John said solemnly.

When the carriage pulled through the arched, vine-covered gateway, it was apparent there was some kind of commotion in front of the house. Several servants were milling about, some of them were mounted on horseback. John stepped out of the carriage, followed by Dakota and Levi.

"What's the trouble?" John asked the head groomsman.

"Oh, sir, it's glad I am that you are here," Frazier declared. "The Lady Breanna's horse returned without her. We was about to ride out and search for her ladyship."

"This is the Viscount," John introduced Dakota hurriedly. "Give us three horses, and we will begin the search."

Frazier bowed to Dakota. "I'm sorry that you should arrive to such disturbing news, my lord. Her ladyship is a good horsewoman, and I never considered she'd take a tumble."

Dakota glanced at John. "Are they saying that the woman who is my wife fell from her horse?"

"Yes," John confirmed. "We had better hurry; she

might be injured."

A horse was led forward, and Dakota quickly swung himself into the saddle. "In which direction did your lady ride?" he asked Frazier.

"She rode in that direction, my lord." The groomsman pointed toward the meadow.

Before the others could mount their horses, Dakota's sprang forward. Racing over the meadow, he easily followed the fresh tracks that Breanna's horse had left. Dakota outdistanced the others and was soon out of sight.

Chapter Ten

Dakota saw the woman lying on the ground, and concluded that she was unconscious. Leaping from his horse, he knelt beside her.

A strange emotion took hold of him as he looked for the first time upon the face of his wife. Red-gold hair was tumbled about her porcelain face, a face that was almost too perfect to be real. Her long lashes fluttered open, and he stared into eyes that were golden like the autumn leaves of Arapaho land.

Breanna opened her eyes, momentarily blinded by the sun streaming through the branches of a tree. She felt someone beside her, and when she could focus her eyes, she stared into a pair of the greenest eyes she had ever seen.

Breanna was frightened at first. She tried to move away from the stranger, but he held her firm. "Do not move," he cautioned. "You have been thrown from your horse and may be injured."

She could tell by his voice that he was not from England, but she could not place his accent. Perhaps he was Italian, or even Russian, she thought. He was certainly the darkest man she had ever seen.

His eyes swept her face, and she saw concern there. "I remember falling," she said. "I must have been knocked unconscious."

"Sit up slowly," he urged, while he supported her back. "Do you hurt anywhere? Your arms—your legs?"

"No, I . . . my head aches, but other than that, I do not believe I am hurt."

Dakota tenderly brushed her silky hair from her forehead and saw a slight discoloring of the skin and a pebble-size bump. "Yes, I see that you have hit your head. Do you think you could stand with my assistance?"

John and several of the riders topped the rise, with Levi in the lead. When the hunter saw Dakota with his new bride, he knew that they were not needed. "The lady is in capable hands," he said to the others, motioning for them to ride on and leave the two young people alone. "He certainly doesn't need us to complicate his first meeting with his wife."

Breanna leaned heavily on the handsome stranger. Her head was swimming, and she clutched his shirtfront. "I am sorry to be such a bother, but I feel weak as a kitten."

Dakota looked into her soft eyes, and a feeling not unlike drowning shook him. "You are not a bother. Would you like to sit down for a moment?"

"Yes, perhaps that would be best," she said, wanting to distance herself from this disturbing stranger.

He led her to a smooth rock and eased her down gently. Kneeling down beside her, Dakota watched as she twisted her long hair up and secured it to the back of her head.

"I fear I have lost my hat," she said, feeling strange under the man's close scrutiny.

He glanced around until he spotted an object the same color of her gown, which he judged to be her missing hat. Standing, Dakota walked in that direction.

Breanna watched the man move away, thinking he must be someone of extreme importance. His coat fit snugly across his broad shoulders. He was tall and carried himself with an air of assurance. He was perhaps the handsomest man she had ever met, but his green eyes were the most unusual thing about him. They were probing, searching, startlingly open and honest eyes. She felt drawn to him, and it frightened her. She touched the bump on her head and decided her reaction to the man was caused by her confused state. Yes, that's what it was. After today, she would never see or think about him again.

When Dakota returned, he held her hat out to her and watched her place it atop her red-gold head. Could she tell that his heart was beating fast? he wondered. Could she sense the turmoil that was going on inside him? She was so lovely it unsettled him. He realized he should tell her who he was, but how could he tell this lovely creature that he was her husband?

"Perhaps it would be good if you walk about for a bit," he said, offering her his hand.

Hesitantly, she placed her small hand in his, and he eased her to her feet. "I should return to the house," she said only half-convincingly. The mere touch of his hand sent a thrill through her body, and she moved away from him, her heart throbbing. Over the rise, Breanna could hear the surf pounding, and she hurried in that direction. What was the matter with her? she wondered frantically. The bump on her head must surely have unsettled her mind.

Breanna breathed in the sea air in deep gulps. She turned so the salty spray would hit her in the face, hoping it would have a calming effect on her emotions. She felt the stranger beside her, and she glanced up at him. Their eyes met, and for what seemed an eternity, they stared into each other's eyes.

Dakota was the first one to move. He reached forward and lightly touched her cheek, which was moist with beads from the salty spray. When she swayed on her feet, his strong arms went about her waist.

"Allow me to support you. You are still too weak to stand alone." Suddenly he feared this lovely woman might not be his wife. He had to know if she belonged to him. "I do not know your name. Will you tell it to me?"

"Breanna," she answered breathlessly. "Breanna K— Remington," she said, remembering she was a married woman. "Lady Breanna Remington."

"Breanna," he repeated in a deep voice, as joy sang in his heart.

She quickly glanced up at him. "You must not call me by my first name. We have not been introduced. I shouldn't even be speaking to you!" She moved to put some distance between the two of them, but he held her to him.

"I apologize if I have committed an offense. I am unfamiliar with many of your English customs."

She drew in a cleansing breath. "I am grateful for your assistance, sir, but you see, I am a married woman, and I must go now. It would not be suitable for me to be alone with a man who is not my husband."

His eyes softened. "This man, your husband, is a very fortunate man. What is he like?"

"I . . . don't know." She gazed at the distant horizon. "He is from America."

Dakota sensed in her a bewilderment that was tinged with fear. He wanted to tell her that he was her husband, but he was silenced by the thought that she might reject him.

"I have the feeling you are troubled about something," he said, wondering how she felt about being married to a man she had never met. "I am a good listener if you want to talk."

Breanna experienced a tide of feelings that she did not want to examine. This sympathetic stranger was tugging at her heart and drawing out all her secrets. She had been alone for so long with no one to confide in, and the words poured from her mouth.

"I am troubled because I have never met my husband." She turned her face up to him. "You see, we were married by proxy."

"And this disturbs you?"

"Yes," she admitted. Raw feelings riveted through her mind—feelings of being used by her brother for his personal gain, anger that she had been sent to the country and abandoned to her fate by the old Marquess. Too many nights she had lain in her lonely bed, fearing the noises she heard were her new husband, and that he would demand his husbandly rights.

There was a tightening in Dakota's chest, and he could feel Breanna's unhappiness. He had never considered that his bride might be as much against the marriage as he had been.

"You did not wish to be married to a stranger?"

141

"It's not even that . . . it's . . . it's, that he was raised by Indians, and I am frightened of him. I think he must be uncivilized and I don't even know if he can speak English. I have a horror that he will eat with his fingers and have no social graces. I am afraid he will hurt me."

Dakota's jaw clamped tightly together. "Why should you think him uncivilized?"

"Are the Indians not savages?" She lowered her eyes to avoid his brilliant gaze. "I should not have confided in you, but it seemed so easy since we are strangers and I shall never see you again. No one seems to understand my fears. I suppose I am foolish, but I always thought I would marry a man who . . . who . . ."

"A man who is your peer?"

"Yes, and a man who—"

"Whom you can love?"

Her eyes glistened because of her embarrassment. "I know it sounds fanciful, but yes."

Dakota's eyes flamed. "What will you do when your husband arrives?"

"I don't know. I have considered running away, but I have given my word that I shall honor this marriage. I have never gone back on my word."

"So, you will submit to this man out of duty?" Dakota asked with interest.

Fear clouded her eyes. "I cannot allow myself to think about that. I pray that someone will come to my rescue and spirit me away before my . . . husband arrives." She looked embarrassed. "But of course, that is a childish dream. When my husband comes, I will do what is expected of me."

"A moment ago, you said you had given your word that you would honor this marriage. What do you mean?"

Breanna knew she was revealing too much to this stranger, but it somehow comforted her to tell someone about her problems. "It's not actually *my* word that was given. You see, my brother, Fielding, was deeply in debt. He is a gambler, and he lost all the family fortune." She blushed and ducked her head. "I cannot believe I am telling a complete stranger such intimate details about my life." She smiled. "I suppose the solitary existence I have been living has unhinged my mind."

He raised her chin. "I want to know what your brother's gambling had to do with your marriage to the American."

"Fielding and the Marquess of Weatherford made an agreement, that I was to marry his grandson and he would pay Fielding's debts and give him additional money to live on."

"Why did you not protest?"

"You said you are not accustomed to English traditions. In this country, a girl cannot always choose whom she will marry. Often that decision is made for her."

"That is not a good custom."

"No, but I am bound by it."

"So you wait for the man who is your husband?"

"Yes, I wait for him, and I dread the time when he actually arrives." Breanna finally realized she had said too much. "I should not have told you about my situation. I pray you will forget all I have said. Please, if you are going in the direction of Weatherford Hall, would you send someone for me," she said, dismissing him.

"That will not be necessary."

Before she could protest, he scooped her into his arms and carried her back up the hill. When he reached his horse, he hooked his boot in the stirrup and mounted with Breanna in his arms. "I will take you home," he said, pulling her securely against his body so her head fit against his shoulder. He felt her stiffen, and he smiled down at her with tenderness. "Rest easy, I will see you safely home."

Breanna had never been this close to a man before. She knew she should insist that he put her down, but she didn't want to. She felt safe for the first time in many years. Her eyes moved up to his face. There was something about him that was different from other men. It was . . . it was as if he was from another time, a time when knights roamed the land slaying dragons and rescuing young maidens. Yet there was something almost primitive about him, as if he was uncomfortable with the role of gentleman.

She raised her eyes and found him looking at her. With a maidenly blush, she turned her face into the rough material of his coat. She became conscious of the strong arms that encircled her waist, and she was very aware of him as a man. She wondered what he would be like if he loved a woman. Perhaps he even had a wife, she thought, and then pushed that thought aside.

Closing her eyes, Breanna listened to the drumming of his heart against her ear. What was the matter with her? she wondered. Why was she feeling so strange? She had certainly not been herself since the bump on her head.

"Are you comfortable?" he inquired in a deep voice that seemed to vibrate through her whole body.

"Yes. Are you married?" The words seemed to have

come out of their own accord, and she blushed at her daring.

He smiled slightly. "Yes, I am."

To hide her embarrassment, she quickly stated. "I hope your wife will not mind that I have confided in you, but you have been so understanding."

"I am not sure how my wife will react," he admitted ruefully.

"What is your wife like?"

He was reflective. "She is lovely." He was thoughtful again. "I suspect she can be obstinate at times, and probably has a temper," he said, eyeing the red highlights in Breanna's hair. "Beyond that, I cannot say what she is like. Does any man ever truly know a woman?"

Breanna felt the pain of disappointment as he spoke so lovingly of his wife. Why should she care that this man was married? He was a stranger to her. Besides, she was a married woman and had no right to be having such unsettling feelings about any man other than her husband.

She stared at his sun-browned hand as he easily controlled the horse. They were strong hands, sensitive, yet masterful. Did he control his wife with the same strength with which he controlled his horse? she wondered, and then blushed, hoping he could not imagine her thoughts.

Breanna saw that they were nearing Weatherford Hall, and she sat up. "Please let me down here, and I will walk the rest of the way. I do not want to have to answer a lot of needless questions."

"Are you sure you feel well enough to walk? I would not mind taking you right up to the house."

"No, that would cause me to have to answer too many questions. I feel fine now. Please, let me down."

Gently Dakota set Breanna on her feet and gave her a warm smile. Before she could thank him for his kindness, he nudged his mount forward and rode away.

She stared after him, wondering if their paths would ever cross again. She was sorry she hadn't even asked his name.

Now she was feeling even more alone than before, and she had the sensation that her only friend was riding out of her life forever.

Chapter Eleven

Slipping in the side door, Breanna went directly to her room, where she found Etta anxiously awaiting her return.

"My lady, we was frightened half out of our wits, fearing you was injured. Were you hurt? Do you want me to send for the doctor?"

"Don't fuss, Etta. I just want to lie down for a while and be left alone. If you really want to be helpful, bring a cool cloth for my head."

"But, my lady, don't you know his lordship, your husband, has arrived?" Etta questioned in an excited voice.

Breanna was peeling off her glove and she tensed; every nerve in her body seemed to throb with fear. "He's here?"

"Yes, my lady. Everyone is so curious about him, but we have yet to catch a glimpse of him. "

Breanna stared at the streak of light, from the dying sun, that filtered between the draperies. So, that which she had been dreading had come to pass. She felt numb until she realized what this could mean for her, and then she felt pure panic. She tossed her gloves on the dressing table and spoke to Etta.

"Prepare my bath and lay out my orchid gown," she said, knowing she needed to look her best to build up her confidence and control her fear. Her first instinct was to flee, to get away from the man whose very presence struck terror in her heart!

The candles burned low in the wall sconce as Breanna descended the stairs. At the bottom of the long winding staircase, she gripped the railing, then forced one foot in front of the other. She had been informed by Etta that her husband and two other men awaited her pleasure in the formal sitting room. Closing her eyes, she tried not to form a mental picture of her husband, knowing her imagination had caused her terror on numerous occasions.

Her footsteps lagged as she approached the open door. Drawing in a deep breath, she called upon all her courage to face what she must.

As Breanna crossed the room, she saw three gentlemen standing near the fireplace. On hearing her, they all turned in her direction.

Breanna glanced first at the older man with white hair, who looked strangely out of place and uncomfortable in his black suit. She dismissed him, knowing he was not young enough to be her husband.

Next her eyes went to the man with light brown hair. His soft blue eyes held a wealth of warmth as he smiled at her. Suddenly she was flooded with relief—all this time she had been expecting her husband to look like an Indian, and of course he wouldn't, since he was English.

"Lord Remington," she said, dipping into a quick curtsy.

John laughed and shook his head. "I am indeed sorry that I am not he, my lady. I am John Donegal, your husband's cousin. This gentleman," he said, indicating the hunter, "is Levi Gunther, and this," he said, indicating the man who stood to his left, "is your husband."

Breanna nodded politely to the old hunter before her eyes moved reluctantly to the man who stood in the shadows. Her heart stopped beating as he stepped forward and she felt the room spinning. Dear Lord, it was the same man who had aided her after her fall this afternoon! She shook her head to clear it, her muddled mind not accepting that this man she had been attracted to was her husband.

Dakota had watched Breanna advance across the room, knowing the dread she was feeling. When she drew near, he could hear the whisper of her silk gown. He gloried in the way the candlelight played on her red-gold hair. It was difficult for him to comprehend that this exquisite creature belonged to him. Now, seeing her confusion, he was sorry that he hadn't confessed to her earlier that he was her husband.

In a graceful movement that showed her long arched neck, Breanna dipped in a curtsy. "My lord, I believe we met this afternoon, although you failed to properly introduce yourself."

He took her hand, holding it in a firm clasp, not

149

missing the proud tilt of her head. "I feared the shock would be too great for you in your condition. As you began to tell me about your husband's shortcomings, I did not think it wise to interrupt you. You did not seem inclined to meet . . . what did you call your husband? A . . . what?"

Her golden eyes sparkled with anger. "I believe I referred to you as a savage, my lord."

John chuckled, and Levi turned away to hide his smile.

"Don't let my cousin bait you, my lady," John said with humor. "I am glad to make your acquaintance, and I look forward to being of service to you."

Breanna was angry and tried to control the urge to walk out of the room. How could she be expected to make polite conversation when what she really wanted to do was strike out at the man whom she believed had humiliated her? How dare his lordship play such an unchivalrous trick on her!

Dakota watched Breanna, realizing what she was feeling. He wished he had the words to make Breanna smile and forget their first meeting. Inside he was tied up in knots, knowing he had deceived her.

At that moment, dinner was announced, and John offered Breanna his arm. "I claim the right to escort my new cousin to dinner."

Dakota felt a pang of jealousy, an emotion new to him, and one that he did not welcome. This was his wife, his woman.

Over dinner, John did most of the talking. Several times Breanna would feel Dakota's probing glance and look up to catch him watching her.

Once, Dakota spread his napkin on his lap and picked up his fork. Through lowered lashes, his eyes challenged Breanna to remember their conversation earlier in the afternoon.

Breanna's face flushed, and she felt the sting of embarrassment as she remembered telling him that her husband would probably eat with his fingers. With deep humiliation, she lowered her head, wishing the earth would open and swallow her.

Somehow she managed to get through dinner, but she didn't taste the food. After the dessert had been served, they all adjourned to the sitting room, and Breanna sat in the chair nearest the fire, her hands folded demurely in her lap. She knew the situation would have been awkward had not John Donegal kept the conversation flowing. As it was, she could not bring herself to meet her husband's eyes.

"Why is it that I never met you in London, Lady Breanna?" John inquired. "Surely you had a London season?"

"No, I had never been in London until the Marquess sent for me." Her eyes finally met Dakota's. "How is your grandfather's health, my lord?"

"He is in ill health."

Tension was thick in the room.

"Well," John said, nudging Levi. "It's been a long day for me. I believe I'll take my leave of you. How about you, Levi?"

"Yep. It has been a long day." Levi stood up and stretched his arms over his head. "Be seeing you tomorrow, Mrs. Remington—er, my lady."

Breanna helplessly watched the two men depart, feel-

151

ing trapped. She turned frightened eyes to her husband, wondering what he would expect of her now that they were alone.

Her anger came to her rescue. "I am not happy with you, my lord. How could you take advantage of me and encourage my confidences this afternoon? It was not a chivalrous action."

"My lady, at first my intention was not to deceive you. I was concerned about your fall. I admit I took unfair advantage of you since I knew who you were and you had no knowledge of my identity. Will you forgive me?"

"Well, I . . . yes, I suppose."

Dakota stood up slowly and moved to the fireplace, where he towered above Breanna. Resting his arm on the mantel, he glanced down at her. "You need have no fear of me. I have never harmed a woman, nor is that my intention with you."

"I . . . what do you expect of me?" she had the courage to ask.

"I don't know. Like you, this marriage was thrust upon me. We are strangers that just happen to be tied together by the whim of a desperate old man."

"Yes," she agreed, still not trusting him.

He searched her face. "Forgive me for not asking sooner, but do you suffer from your fall today?"

"No, my head hurts only when I touch it." She watched him move to the chair across from her and sit down. As she had earlier in the day, when he held her on the horse in front of him, Breanna felt drawn to this man in some mysterious way. He was nothing like the man she had expected.

"I don't know what to say to you . . . Breanna." He looked at her questioningly. "May I call you Breanna?"

"Of course, you have that right."

His green eyes were almost hypnotic, and Breanna felt herself being drawn even closer to him. "You are my husband," she reminded him.

He toyed with the cuff of his shirt. "I don't feel like your husband, Breanna. After our conversation this afternoon, I realized that you were frightened of me." His eyes flashed. "I also recall you said some very unflattering things about me."

She sat forward, now on the defensive. "That was your own fault, my lord. You should have announced who you were. You took unfair advantage of me and deserved what you heard," she said with spirit.

He smiled slightly. "I assume you were pleased to discover I know how to eat with a fork."

"You are not a gentleman, or you would not remind me of that."

His eyes darkened. "You may as well know this from the start, Breanna, I am not like the gentlemen of your acquaintance. If you strip off this fancy wearing apparel, you will find a man who would fit your description of a savage. I make no apologies for what I am. But I do understand your reluctance to this marriage. Like you, I had little say in the matter."

Breanna was still suspicious of him. "This afternoon, when you told me you were married, you said your wife probably had a temper. Would you mind explaining that?" she asked defiantly.

He smiled. "I was referring to the fire in your hair, and I thought you might have a temper to match. It

153

was said in jest."

"I warn you, I do have a temper. And I do not take kindly to a jest when it is aimed at me."

He resumed a serious expression, while controlling the twitch of his lips. "I shall certainly bear that in mind for future reference."

She sighed heavily. "Your grandfather has us both trapped in a situation over which we have no control. What shall we do?"

"For the moment, nothing. I have many things to learn and many other responsibilities to assume. Perhaps you and I could start off by becoming friends, Breanna."

She could hardly believe her ears. "Do you mean that we . . . that you and I . . ."

"Yes, you and I shall sleep apart. I would find no joy in taking a frightened woman to my bed, and even less pleasure in knowing she was forced to be there."

Relief washed over her. "My lord, I believe that is a very sensible solution."

His lip curled. "Would you say it was a civilized decision?"

"Please, my lord, do not remind me of my uncharitable remarks this afternoon. They were made out of fear."

He stood up, took her hand, and assisted her to her feet. "You have had a disturbing and emotional day, Breanna. I suggest you go to bed and get a good night's sleep."

She felt her hand tremble in his. Suddenly she wondered if he found her unattractive. Was that why he didn't wish to share her bed?

"Yes, my lord," she murmured, freeing her hand and making a hasty retreat. What was the matter with her? She should be happy that he had given her a period of grace—but she wasn't—she definitely was not. The troubling emotion she felt was one of being rejected!

Dakota watched Breanna move gracefully across the room. The sweet haunting aroma of some strange perfume lingered, and he could still feel the softness of her skin. He realized how far apart they were. They should have been born into the same environment, but circumstances had placed them an ocean apart. He couldn't analyze his feelings, but the thought of her sent his head reeling and sent a trembling thrill through his body. In giving her time to adjust to him as her husband, he was also allowing himself time to discover what she expected of him.

He walked across the room and almost bumped into an old man who was lingering in the hallway. The man's eyes were alive and searching, and were glowing with respect. "I'm Baxley, my lord. I was valet to your father, his lordship, and would feel honored if you would allow me to serve you as well."

Dakota nodded absently, since his mind was still filled with visions of his young bride.

"I accompanied his lordship and her ladyship to America, my lord. Are there any questions I could answer for you since I was in their service for so long?"

Dakota looked into the man's eager eyes. "I know next to nothing about my parents." He reached in his pocket and withdrew the golden locket that held the miniature of them both. "I have always kept this with me, I don't even know why."

155

"If your lordship will accompany me, I will show you."

Dakota agreed with a stiff nod, and followed the old retainer down the hallway past the stairs.

Baxley pushed the door open and Dakota stepped into the room with its smell of leather and dust. It was a library where shelves of leather-bound books lined the wall. A warm fire was glowing in the fireplace.

"I prepared the room for you just as I once did for his lordship. When he was at Weatherford Hall, this was his favorite room. He and her ladyship spent most of their time here. The animal heads on the wall came from their many expeditions around the world."

Dakota stared at the two life-size portraits that hung behind the huge desk—he realized the miniatures in the locket had been painted from those portraits.

He spoke softly. "It's ironic, Baxley, I had to become acquainted with my heritage through portraits and secondhand information. It is difficult to feel that I am their son, since I never knew them."

"I knew you would be feeling confused, my lord. If I can help you feel a little more like you belong here, I would consider it a privilege. It is the least I can do for his lordship's son."

"What was she like, Baxley?" Dakota asked, staring at the image of the lovely young woman who had borne him and given him into Two Moons' keeping.

"She was kind and generous, my lord. I never heard her say an unkind word to anyone. She even got on with the old Marquess, which was no easy task." Baxley looked uncomfortable for a moment. "Begging your pardon, my lord, if it seemed I was speaking ill of your

156

grandfather. With his lordship, I always spoke my mind; I fear he permitted me great liberties."

"I hope you will feel the same way with me, Baxley."

"It would be my honor, my lord."

"My father, what was he like?"

"He was what the London clubs called a man's man. He was a fearless hunter, a loyal friend, and a good husband to her ladyship. His only regret was that he was not close to his own father. Had he lived, he would have been proud of you, my lord. I can remember how joyful his lordship and her ladyship were when they learned they were going to have a baby."

The old man's eyes turned sad. "I was devastated when the tragedy struck."

Dakota tried to comfort the old man. "I wish I could have known them, as you did, Baxley."

Baxley smiled, blinking back tears. "Were you aware his lordship kept a daily journal, my lord?"

"No. I was not aware there was a journal."

"I thought not. I took the liberty of placing it on the desk should you wish to read it."

Dakota nodded, anxious to read words written by his father. "Very good, Baxley. I will not be needing you any longer tonight."

The valet's eyes gleamed with happiness. It felt good to be serving a Remington again. "I shall lay your things out in the bedchamber, my lord."

Dakota sat down at the desk, running a finger over the leather journal with the gold lettering. He was grateful that Levi had taught him to read, because now perhaps he could gain some insight into his father's mind.

Opening the pages that were yellowed with age, he began to read about his parents' exciting exploits. Holden and Cillia's life unfolded on the pages, and Dakota found the writing witty, amusing, and informative. He came to know his parents as he read about the deep love they had for one another. He could feel the joy his father had experienced when he discovered his wife was going to have a baby. Dakota felt heartbreak and a deep loss when he read the last entry in his father's journal.

On this day, the first day of November, in the year of Our Lord, 1833, Cillia died, delivering our child while I was away. It is my belief that the child lives and has been taken by Indians. It is my hope that every effort will be made to find the baby so it can be sent to my father in England. It is my wish that my wife and I be buried in a common grave so we might spend eternity together.

The candle had burned low when Dakota closed his father's journal. It was as if he had come to know his mother and father and had lost them in the same day.

He clutched the journal and moved out of the room. Pausing in the doorway, he turned and looked back at the portraits of his parents. He wished he could cry out to them to help him find his way. He found himself in a world that he did not understand, forced to live a life that he had not been trained for. How would he face each day and do what was expected of him?

Wearily, Dakota climbed the stairs, trying to make

his mind a blank. He didn't want to think about his young bride because he didn't know what to do where she was concerned. He almost wished she had been homely as he had feared she would be, then he would have no trouble moving her to the back of his mind.

Entering his bedchamber, he discovered Baxley had unpacked for him and that the bed had been turned back. Blowing out the candle, he lay down fully clothed, wondering if this was the room his father had used.

"Breanna," he whispered softly. "What am I going to do with you?"

Chapter Twelve

Breanna awoke to the sound of shutters banging back and forth. Sitting up in bed, she saw that rain was peppering through the half-opened window and soaking the bedroom rug.

Jumping up, she hurried across the room to close and bolt the window. Grabbing a cloth, she went down on her knees and began wiping up the water.

"Here, my lady," Etta cried, coming into the room and seeing her mistress down on her knees. "You'll catch your death. Let me do that."

Breanna relinquished her task and stood staring out at the bleak landscape. On this side of the house the ocean was visible, and Breanna saw that a thick fog was rolling in, shrouding the view.

"Has his lordship arisen yet?" she asked the maid, hoping he would not send for her.

"Yes, my lady. He was about long before dawn. I was told that he and the other two gentlemen rode out with the intentions of inspecting the estate."

Breanna wondered why Dakota would choose such a dreary day to ride abroad. She was glad, however, that she did not have to face him at breakfast.

"If I may say so, my lady, the house is fairly buzzing with activity. It's exciting the way Weatherford Hall is coming to life. Is it true there may be a ball? Mrs. Hopkins says there will be no slacking from the servants any longer. As head housekeeper, she's cracking the whip over everyone. She's getting old, hard-of-hearing, and she can be somewhat churlish at times."

"Don't gossip, Etta," Breanna reprimanded. "I will take my breakfast in the morning room. Ask Mrs. Hopkins to bring the menu to me there in one hour."

"Yes, my lady. Will you dress now?"

"Yes. Lay out my gray-and-white candy-striped gown." Breanna was not accustomed to having a personal maid, so she moved to the dressing table and seated herself before the mirror while quickly running the boar bristle brush through her hair. She parted it in the middle and wrapped it around in a tight chignon.

In a flurry of tight lacings, petticoats, and a whalebone crinoline, Etta helped her mistress dress.

A short time later, Breanna made her way downstairs. She had chosen the morning room as the place to handle her correspondence and to run the household, since the magnificent floor-to-ceiling windows faced the ocean, giving her a tranquil view.

After eating a light breakfast of poached eggs, Breanna met with Mrs. Hopkins. The elderly housekeeper sat on the edge of her chair, her eyes lively and bright, her round rosy face drawn up in an apprehensive frown. "Will you be approving the menu each morning, my lady?"

"Yes. Since my husband has arrived, I will see to the running of the house, supervise the menus, and visit

161

the kitchens at least once a week."

"My lady, let me say I know about the gossip that's going around about me. There are those that complain that I work them too hard. Some even say I am too old to be head of such a large house." She looked as if she would like to cry. "I admit I do work everyone hard, but I don't ask anything out of them that I'm not willing to do myself. As for getting old . . . we all either have to age or die. That's the only choices we have."

"Do you feel that the work is too much for you?"

The little woman rose to her feet. "No, my lady." She hesitated before she spoke again. "Is Your Ladyship pleased with my running of the house, or would you prefer to bring in a younger housekeeper?"

Breanna saw the anxiety in the older woman's eyes. "I have seldom seen a more organized household, and I attribute this to your ability. Are you pleased to serve this house?" she asked.

Mrs. Hopkins's face gleamed from the compliment. "Oh, yes, my lady. I was born at Weatherford Hall, and it has been my pleasure to be in service here for forty years, the last twenty as head housekeeper."

"Then you will continue with your duties as long as it pleases you. I have no intentions of interfering with a well-run house; I merely wish to incorporate your ideas and mine for our mutual benefit."

Mrs. Hopkins's eyes shone with relief, but she had been well trained not to show any emotion when speaking to the mistress of the house. "Very good, my lady. I will do the best I can for you and his lordship. It's glad we all are to be having members of the family living with us once more. It's been many years since we have been called upon to serve the family."

"Did not my husband's grandfather live here at Weatherford Hall?"

"Not in over ten years, my lady."

Breanna found that odd. "You may go, Mrs. Hopkins."

"Will you be wanting anything else, my lady?"

"No, not now."

Mrs. Hopkins bustled out, almost colliding with John Donegal in the doorway.

Dakota's cousin smiled at Breanna as he moved into the room. "I can see that you have things well in hand, Lady Breanna. One can tell that you have been trained in running a large household."

Her eyes challenged him. "I am sure you are aware that I helped run my brother's household because we could not afford servants."

He chose not to comment on what he knew about her brother. "This has always been my favorite room. As a lad I liked to come here when it was storming and watch the waves pound against the cliff. If the storm was severe, the waves would crash against the windows. Once they hit with such a force that all the windows in this room were smashed."

"May I offer you a cup of tea?" she asked, reaching for a china cup that rested on the silver tray.

"Yes, if it's no imposition, and I take mine with milk. This will give us a chance to get to know one another."

"I thought you rode out with my husband."

"No, not me. Few things could induce me to ride out on a day like this."

Breanna smiled as she handed him a steaming cup of tea that had been laced with milk. "I have been alone

163

for so long, I fear I may have lost the art of conversation."

John tried not to stare at the lovely angel, but he couldn't help noticing how her skin resembled the petal of a blushing rose. He assumed that her severe, matronly hairstyle was worn in an effort to make her appear older, but it had failed. She looked young and defenseless.

"Tell me about yourself," he implored. "I had heard of your brother, in fact I met him on several occasions, but he never said anything about you. I know nothing about you save the fact you are married to my cousin."

She leaned back in the chair, looking misplaced for a moment. When she smiled, John sucked in his breath at her ethereal beauty. "To talk about myself would only bore you, Mr. Donegal. Nothing untoward has happened in my life that would make interesting conversation."

"Not so. I would be interested in anything you could tell me."

She was beginning to like John Donegal. His soft blue eyes held an earnest light, and she had the feeling he was a good friend to her husband. "My life was spent on my family estate, and I had never been to London until your uncle sent for me." Again she gave him a smile that melted his heart and made him envy Dakota's good fortune.

"I can see why your brother kept you in the country, Lady Breanna. You are far too pretty to flaunt before the whole of London."

Her golden eyes were radiant. "I believe you mean to flatter me, Mr. Donegal. And please call me Breanna. I don't believe there is any great need for us to stand on ceremony here in the country."

"Breanna," he repeated. "I suppose cousins should call one another by their given names. Will you call me John?"

"Of course, John."

John and Breanna found it easy to talk to one another, and they were soon conversing like old friends. Breanna was laughing at John's tale of a certain gentlewoman whose belled gown had caught a gust of wind and the poor woman had tumbled end-over-end down Percy Street in London.

Mrs. Hopkins had directed Dakota and Levi to the morning room. As they advanced down the hallway, Dakota heard the tinkling sound of Breanna's laughter joined by John's deep chortle.

"You should have seen the poor woman, Breanna. It took two men to halt her downhill roll," John said, laughing heartily.

Breanna covered her mouth, trying not to laugh. "I know it isn't kind to find humor in the unfortunate woman's misadventure, but you tell it so entertainingly, John, I can almost see it as it happened."

"Gentlemanly decorum prevents me from revealing the poor woman's name, but I can tell you that since that incident, she never goes abroad on a windy day."

Levi saw the muscle tighten in Dakota's jaw as he stood in the doorway watching his wife and his cousin laughing together. To relieve the tension, the hunter moved into the room. "I wouldn't say no to a cup of that tea, Lady Remington, and I like mine best with three lumps of sugar." He plopped down in a chair and smiled at John. "It's not a fit day out for man or beast. You were wise not to come with us."

165

Breanna could feel her husband's gaze, and her hand trembled when she held a steaming cup of tea out to Levi. "Would you also like a cup of tea, my lord?" she asked, wondering why Dakota's green eyes were glimmering with anger.

He moved over to stand at the window before he answered. "No. I have never acquired a taste for the white man's bitter brew."

His back was to her, and she stared at him, looking confused. "Why should you call it white man's brew?"

He turned and his eyes swept her face. "You will do well to remember that I do not consider myself white; therefore, I am not inclined to waste time sitting on a satin chair, making polite conversation."

John, seeing more than Breanna did, knew Dakota was feeling pangs of husbandly jealousy. "If you will all excuse me, I have taken up enough of Breanna's time. Levi, how would you like to take me on in a game of cards?"

Levi chuckled. "Not if money's involved. I have no desire to be skinned alive by you."

Breanna watched both men depart, wishing she could also leave. Dakota was staring at her, and she felt her throat close off. "Is there anything I can do for you, my lord?" she asked in a small voice.

For a moment he stared down at his mud-splattered black boots, feeling very unsure of himself where Breanna was concerned. With pride as his shield, his face did not show how vulnerable he was. "I believe we should get to know one another. Would this be satisfactory with you?" His voice was formal and stiff, to cover up for his uncertainty.

Breanna thrilled at the sound of his deep voice. His

speech was cultured with just the slightest hint of an accent. The thought of spending time with him made her tremble with some unknown anticipation. "If that is your pleasure, my lord," she replied with anticipation of the unknown tugging at her heart.

Dakota realized that he must allow her to get to know him slowly. She was so beautiful, it made him feel good just to look at her. It was beyond his conception that this lovely delicate creature belonged to him. He had been appalled at the way the fashionable hoop skirts looked on other women, but on Breanna they swayed gracefully as she walked, and he found it a most pleasing sight.

He stood staring at her for so long that she began to feel uncomfortable. "Can I help you with something, my lord?" she asked at last.

"No," he said, unable to think what to say to her next. "If you will excuse me, I want to talk to John."

"Yes, my lord," she said stiffly. Breanna watched him leave the room, wondering what went on in his mind. She had a feeling that he found her displeasing, and it was most unsettling to her.

Dakota found John and Levi in the library playing a game of cards. "What are you doing here when you have that beautiful wife to pass your time with?" John wanted to know.

Dakota sat down in a leather wing-back chair, his thoughts troubled. "I don't know how to talk to her, John. Shall I tell her about a buffalo hunt, or would she rather hear about the rites of a young warrior coming of age? What do English ladies like to talk about?"

John smiled to himself and exchanged glances with Levi. "Well, I guess she would like to hear about how pretty she is. Tell her you like her eyes."

"Mention her hair," Levi piped up. "Women are always doing something about their hair."

"Yes, that's good," John agreed. "And you might want to ask her opinion on something. Women like to think they are helping a man find his way."

"Yep," Levi agreed. "I once had me an Indian woman that wanted to reform me. It took two years for me to untangle myself from her." Levi smiled. "Course she had other advantages that made me stay around so long."

Dakota frowned. "Breanna is different. I have a feeling she would not like flowery compliments."

John shook his head. "I never met a woman who didn't like to be told she was beautiful."

Dakota closed his eyes for a moment, and Levi realized the turmoil that was going on inside him. "You have always had women hanging on to you, Dakota, and you were never at a loss on how to handle them before. I always say every woman is the same underneath."

Dakota stood up. "I have never been near a woman like Breanna. She ties my tongue in knots, and I don't know what to say to her. When I'm alone with her, I can feel that she is frightened of me." He looked at John for direction. "What am I to do to win her confidence?"

"She needs time to get to know you. Do things together, like riding, talking, or just take a walk by the ocean. In time, you will both feel more at ease in each other's company."

Dakota was contemplative for a moment. "Yes, I will do that. I will give her time to know me."

* * *

After dinner that night, John and Levi excused themselves, leaving Breanna and Dakota alone in the salon. For a long moment there was silence between the two of them.

Breanna wore a gown of white, with green ribbons on the sleeves and skirt. Her hair was pulled away from her face with a green velvet ribbon and fell in curls down her back. She moved about the room, examining different objects, pretending interest. She picked up a delicate white porcelain vase, softly touching the tiny yellow roses interwoven on the smooth surface. In truth, she could hardly breathe because Dakota's eyes were on her, watching her every move.

"Breanna," he said at last. "The night is warm. Would you care to walk with me in the garden?"

"Yes, my lord," she said, quickly moving across the room like a dutiful wife, knowing he was following her into the garden.

It was a beautiful night. A bright moon was suspended in the ebony sky, and stars twinkled like thousands of fireflies.

Dakota stood beside her, taking care not to touch her. He decided to make polite conversation.

"Breanna, I read in a book that when it is night here, it is daytime where I come from."

"Can you read?" She hadn't meant to ask that, and wished she could take the words back when his jaw tightened.

"Yes, I can read. I have been reading books since I was a child."

"It is astonishing, is it not? I mean—the part about it being nighttime here while it's daytime in America."

He smiled. "Yes, it is astonishing. It means that

before I came here, while you were awake, I was asleep."

"Do all Indians read?" she asked, hoping she hadn't offended him.

"I cannot speak for others. Levi always brought me books. I have come to appreciate that since it prepared me for this time in my life."

Breanna glanced at his handsome profile in the moonlight, wishing she could know all about him. She could tell he was a complex man, and she found herself wanting to please him.

"I have read very little. I suppose there was never enough time."

Dakota turned to her. He watched the soft moonlight play across her face and felt his throat tighten. He had not been with a woman in a very long time, and this one was so desirable, and she was his wife. He wanted to say something to show how he felt about her beauty, and John's suggestions came to mind.

"Your eyes are beautiful," he blurted out. "Your hair is lovely." It sounded rehearsed, even to his ears.

She smiled. "Did you read that in a book?"

A smile curved his lips. "No, actually on asking advise on how to please a woman, John and Levi offered me those choice suggestions." His voice deepened with sincerity, and his eyes plundered her face. "However, I hasten to add that your eyes and hair truly are extraordinarily beautiful."

Breanna stared into his eyes, feeling the magnetic pull of them. She knew she was swaying toward him. Her hand came up against his hard chest, and she jerked it away quickly. She could scarcely catch her breath. "I . . . feel chilled. Would you mind if I go in now?"

"No, of course not," he said, hiding his disappointment and wondering what he had done wrong. "Forgive me for keeping you out in the night air."

She searched his face, wondering if he would allow her to go to her room alone. "I will bid you good night, my lord," she said nervously.

"Yes, sleep well," he told her, wondering if he would ever breach the wide gap that separated the two of them and join their two worlds together.

Chapter Thirteen

For two days it had been raining, and Breanna's spirits were dampened. She saw Dakota only at dinner. Immediately thereafter, he would excuse himself, and she would not see him again until the next day.

Breanna wondered what she had done to offend him, and why he was trying to avoid her. She was hurt and disheartened, thinking he did not find her pleasing.

She often stood before the mirror, trying to find what might be displeasing to her husband. Even John appeared to be avoiding her company. The only one who seemed to tolerate her presence was Levi, and she thought Dakota might have encouraged the hunter to be her companion, so it would free him from the task.

She liked Levi, and found his tales on America fascinating. So far, however, they had avoided talking about the one person who dominated Breanna's thinking—her husband.

* * *

172

It was a cloudless morning as Levi accompanied Breanna into the garden to cut fresh flowers. She was dressed in a blue taffeta gown that rustled as she moved down the garden path, gathering flowers that were in full bloom. She had to smile at the picture of the rough hunter following behind her, carrying an armful of red roses.

It was a glorious day, and she slowly felt her cares melt away beneath the clear blue skies. Breanna was unaware of her fragile beauty, but Levi was very aware of it. He smiled, knowing this little girl had Dakota in a spin.

Raising a delicate rosebud to her nose, she filled her lungs with its sweet scent. "Isn't it wondrous weather?" she said, reaching out her arms as if she were embracing the day.

Levi's heart was filled with her beauty. He was grateful that Breanna was young in spirit and mind so she would infect Dakota with some of her enthusiasm for life. Dakota was far too serious for his own good.

Levi was beginning to admire this young woman, and to realize how fortunate Dakota would be if he ever decided to overcome her maidenly resistance and take her to his bed.

"Yep," Levi agreed. "It's a right nice day. Of course, I find this island of yours too confining for my taste."

"Island? I never thought of England as an island."

"Well, it is to me. I have a hankering for home."

"Where do you call home, Levi?" she asked, realizing that she had never thought of him as living anywhere in particular.

"Most anywhere there's not many people about. I'm

partial to the mountains, though."

"I would love to one day see your country, Levi. I can only imagine how magnificent it must be."

"If you don't mind me saying so, Breanna, I saw a mite more of your country than I wanted to. I want to go where I can breathe the mountain air, and where a man can ride for days without meeting another human being."

"You are staying in England for . . . Dakota's sake, aren't you, Levi?"

"Yes. And if he goes back, I'll go with him."

Her heart sank. "If he goes back?"

Levi realized he had spoken out of turn. "I don't suppose he'll ever go back home, now that he has a wife."

"Has he no one in America he cares about?"

"He has friends. But me and him is kinda like family." He gave her a bright smile. "You are family too," he added generously.

Breanna laughed delightedly, knowing the old hunter had just paid her a high compliment. She had a feeling he didn't give his friendship easily. "Thank you," she said, laying her hand on his. "I can use all the family I can get."

"Breanna," Levi said, and the way his eyes shifted away, she knew he was about to say something that made him feel uncomfortable. "We are just getting to know one another, but still I feel like I can talk to you."

"I'm glad, Levi."

"You mustn't think Dakota is ignoring you. He's very aware of you at all times. He has had a lot of grief in his life lately, and is only learning to handle it. Here, everything is new to him, and you might say he's kinda finding his way."

"Why is he grieving?"

"He lost someone who was very close to him," Levi said, unwilling to go into detail. If Dakota wanted Breanna to know about Two Moons and Running Deer, he would tell her himself.

"I sense that he is troubled."

"He don't show his feelings like other people, but I can always tell what he's feeling."

"Is he feeling trapped in this marriage with me, Levi?"

"It's not my place to convince you of Dakota's feelings. I just want to say this. It's like when he met you, he got a fox by the tail and he don't know what to do with it. The fox might be a beautiful animal, but it takes lot of guessing to know what its next move will be and how to handle it just the right way."

She smiled. "Do you think me a beautiful animal, Levi?"

His eyes danced. "I surely do."

Breanna's laughter danced merrily on the wind. "It's a novel idea being compared to a fox. Do you Americans always compare people with animals?"

Levi looked embarrassed. "I didn't mean to offend you none, Breanna."

"Oh, Levi, you didn't. Are you saying Dakota is afraid of me?"

"Somewhat. But I reckon it will be best if you find out about that for yourself. I was trying to explain Dakota to you, but that takes a mite of explaining. I'll just say this and nothing more. He is the most honorable and noble man I know. His Indian father instilled in him a gentlemanly code that you won't find on the pages of a book, in the drawing rooms of London, or Washington, for that matter. If he tells you something, you can take it for the truth."

"You admire him, don't you, Levi?"

"Yes, I do. If I'd had a son, I wouldn't want him to be any different from Dakota."

"I wish I had an understanding of him, Levi. I find him very complex. Also, I must admit I am afraid of him."

"In what way? He would never harm a woman. He is a gentle and caring man."

"Well, we come from different worlds. He is different from all the men I have known. . . . I have to admit I haven't known that many."

Levi chuckled. "You don't need to fear him, he's afraid of you enough for the both of you. He wants so badly to be the man he thinks you expect him to be."

"I have not seen this, Levi."

"Sometimes we can't see what we are standing too close to. I probably shouldn't be telling you this, but do you ever wonder what he does with his nights?"

She gave Levi a guarded look, since they both knew Dakota didn't spend his nights with her. "It had crossed my mind to wonder where he rushes off to each night."

"Don't ever let on that I told you, but he reads— book, after book, after book. He has a thirst for knowl- edge that can never be satisfied. Since he met you, he has driven himself even harder wanting to please you."

"I don't understand."

"One day you will. You got a good head on your

176

shoulders, so one day you will know what goes on inside of Dakota. For now, it is enough for you to know that he is trying to better himself, so he can stand even with you."

Before Breanna could make a comment, she saw Dakota walking down the garden path toward them. He was dressed in dark blue trousers, black boots, and a light blue shirt. His dark hair glistened in the sunlight, and Breanna found her heart pounding rapidly. As always, he seemed remote and cold. Only his emerald eyes held a hint of warmth.

As Dakota drew even with her, a slight smile curved his lips. "My lady, may I ask a favor of you?"

"Yes, of course."

"Is it possible that you play chess?"

She was so taken aback by his question that it took her a moment to answer. "Why, yes, I am a very good chess player, if I don't sound too overconfident."

"I have been studying the chessboard in the library, and I have read a book on chess that tells all the moves. I believe I understand the game, but I have no one to play with. John says he does not know the game."

Breanna caught Levi's eye and his look as much as said, "I told you so." "I would be delighted to play with you, Dakota. But I warn you, I can be a ruthless opponent, and I will give you no quarter merely because you are a beginner."

Dakota's eyes sparkled as he realized she had called him by his name for the first time. "I will chance it," he said, taking her arm and leading her toward the house, while Levi's eyes followed them.

Levi knew if the two young people spent much time

in each other's company, nature and human feelings would take care of all the rest.

For the next three days Breanna and Dakota spent the afternoons playing chess.

With the chessboard between them, Breanna sat on a cushion on the floor, her chin resting on her hand, her mind searching for a way to get out of the trap Dakota had laid for her. She reached out and touched her bishop—but no—if she made that move, she would lose her bishop to Dakota's rook. A smile curved her soft lips. She remembered one of the rules her brother had taught her in playing chess. The best way to protect yourself, he had told her, is to launch a strong attack.

Her eyes met Dakota's, and with renewed confidence, she slid her queen across the board to confront his king. "Check!" she said with arrogant satisfaction.

Dakota arched an eyebrow at her. "You fell into my trap, Breanna. I applied an old Indian strategy to the play. I allowed you to surround me so I could pick you off."

She glanced quickly at the board. "I don't see . . . oh . . ."

He smiled, shaking his head. "This really pains me, Breanna . . . but, such is war and chess." He slid his knight forward, took her queen, and announced without an ounce of smugness, "Checkmate, madame!"

She slumped forward in a flurry of petticoats, her smile impish. "You have me. Never have I seen anyone play chess the way you do. I haven't won a game since the first three we played."

She glanced up at him, meeting his steady gaze and remembering what Levi had said about him wanting to please her. Breanna was sure Dakota was a man like no other, and she was astounded by his ability. "I am amazed at your proficiency in everything you do, Dakota. I am considered a more than fair chess player, yet you, who learned to play from a book, have totally destroyed my game." She touched her head in a salute. "To the victor goes the spoils."

His eyes softened. "May I consider you the spoils of war?" he asked, his eyes probing and searching.

In a move that took her totally by surprise, he grabbed her wrist, pulled her across the chessboard, scattering the game pieces in every direction. She gasped when he held her against him. "It is a wonder I could concentrate on anything with you sitting across from me, looking so adorable and tempting," he admitted.

Breanna lay in his arms, looking up at him and watching the darkening of his eyes. She knew that she had seen that look before, and it made her tremble with some unknown anticipation. She realized she should twist away from him, because she knew what he had in mind, but she lay there, unwilling, or unable, to move. Now his eyes were focused on her parted lips as she waited, aching for the touch of his kiss.

Softly his lips touched the corner of her mouth, but when she turned her head to meet his mouth, he raised his head and looked deeply into her eyes. "I took your queen—shall I now take my Viscountess?"

She looked confused. "I . . . no, please."

His eyes closed for a moment while he brought his

labored breath under control. "You are free to go," he said, standing up and offering her his hand. "Flee, while you can, my lady. The day will come when I shall checkmate you."

With her heart pounding, Breanna gathered up her gown and fled from the room. On her way upstairs, she wondered what would have happened if she had not run away.

Chapter Fourteen

The mounting tension between Breanna and Dakota was becoming unbearable. Each day, she would feel his eyes pulling at her, and she had to fight to keep from falling into his arms, his willing slave. Levi noticed that when Breanna was around, Dakota would follow her with naked yearning reflected in his eyes. He could also see that Breanna was affected by Dakota. Once when Dakota chanced to touch her hand, she took a deep intake of breath. It was clear to Levi that she was an innocent and did not know how to deal with the feelings her young husband awakened in her body. Fate may have thrown them together, but they were obviously drawn to one another.

Although Breanna was alarmed at the thought that her relationship with Dakota might deepen, she waited for him to show some sign that he wanted to consummate their marriage.

When Levi saw that matters were not progressing, he decided to give human nature a helping hand. He

181

found Dakota standing on a bluff, staring down at the churning water below.

Levi seated himself on a boulder, took out his knife, and began whittling. "Is this all you can think of to do with your time, Dakota?" he said offhandedly.

"What should I do?" the young man bit out. "Play chess? That didn't work out too well."

"Why not?"

"Because all I could think about was the color of Breanna's eyes, or the softness of her. . . . Do you have a reason for seeking me out, Levi?" he snarled.

"Yep. I wanted to ask you how long you intend to play the frustrated lover?"

"I cannot see that it is any concern of yours."

Levi was unaffected by Dakota's heated remark. "You are worse off than I thought. Has it ever occurred to you that there are too many people around for you and Breanna to get to know one another?"

"It has occurred to me," Dakota said stiffly.

Levi sighed gustily. "I guess someone has to do your thinking for you in matters of the heart."

Dakota glared at his old friend. "You have never been married, Levi. What makes you such an expert?"

"Common sense. Do you remember that hunting lodge that we saw the other day while out riding? If you were to instruct the servants to have it made ready, I wager it would make an excellent honeymoon retreat."

Dakota was thoughtful while he pondered Levi's words. Suddenly he smiled. "I am ashamed that you had to be the one to point this out to me." Suddenly he looked troubled. "Do you think Breanna would go with me?"

"I know how you can find out. Why don't you ask her and see?"

That evening after dinner, Levi and John excused themselves as usual, leaving Breanna and Dakota alone. Dakota was seated beside Breanna on the cream-colored settee. He tried several times to tell her what was on his mind, but he was finding it difficult to express himself. Finally in exasperation, he blurted out:

"I have a proposition to offer you, Breanna. One day while Levi and I were riding over the Weatherford estates we chanced upon a cottage in the woods. I was told by my grandfather's gamekeeper that it is a hunting lodge. How would you like to spend a few days there . . . with me so we can become better acquainted?"

She did not see the eagerness in his green eyes, but he saw the fear and uncertainty in hers. "Do you mean just the two of us alone?"

"Not exactly. We would have someone to clean and serve the food. Of course they wouldn't stay at the lodge at night."

Breanna felt her body tingle with excitement. "I am your wife, my lord. I will go wherever you say."

He turned back to the window, watching pearls of moisture roll down the glass surface. "I only want you to accompany me if this is what you want," he said.

Breanna moved to Dakota's side and glanced out the

window. "I want to go . . . but it's just that . . . I . . ."

"We will maintain separate bedchambers, if that is what troubles you. I will not insist that you come to me until it is right for you."

She suddenly became aware of a great sadness and bewilderment in her husband. But certainly she was mistaken. He appeared so sure of himself, so masterful and in command of every situation. Why did she sense this turmoil going on inside him? "I will go with you, my lord."

A slight smile tugged at his lips, and he turned to face her. "I have many things to discover here in England, Breanna, and you are first and foremost."

Thrill after thrill moved through her body as she considered what that might entail. "When will we leave, my lord?"

"Do you think you could manage to call me Dakota, and drop the 'my lord'? And we shall leave tomorrow if this is agreeable with you. In anticipating that your answer might be yes, I have had the hunting lodge made ready."

"I will go up and instruct Etta to pack what I will need, my . . . Dakota."

Turning back to the window, he listened to the soft rustle of her gown and the sound of her footsteps fade away. With her, he felt somewhat like a man who was reaching for a brilliant star. Would he ever hold her warmth in his hand, or would he find her cold and unobtainable? Perhaps her brilliance would be the light he needed to guide him through the baffling times ahead.

Could he possess her, make her his own? If she had been an Indian maiden, he would have taken her to his bed the first night, but she was different from the women he had known. Dakota could not imagine Breanna being acquiescent. He wanted her more than anything he had ever wanted in his life, but she had to come to him freely. He did not know if it was love he felt for her, or if he merely wanted to possess her and burn his brand on her so all would know she was Dakota's woman.

While Breanna supervised Etta's packing, her heart fairly sang. She looked forward to becoming better acquainted with her husband. She found him fascinating and intriguing. He was kind and understanding to allow her this time to get to know him. She did not believe there were many men who would demonstrate so much forbearance. In Breanna's eagerness to be with Dakota, she looked forward with great anticipation to the next day.

A dispute had arisen between two of the tenants, and Dakota had sent word to Breanna that he would meet her at the lodge as soon as he had made peace between the two men.

The day was bright and sunny as the groomsman, Frazier, accompanied Breanna to the hunting lodge. She felt the sun on her face as Joya galloped down the well-worn path, and she had a feeling of well-being. It was good to be alive.

Later, after Breanna had unpacked, she walked through the hunting lodge, examining every nook and cranny. There were five bedrooms, a common room, and a kitchen. She almost felt like an intruder because this was definitely a man's domain with its unpolished wooden floors, stiff rugs, and leather furnishings. Guns hung on the wall, and the large windows allowed sunlight to illuminate each room. The lodge had been built on an isolated spot, inaccessible except by boat or horseback. Dense woods were located fifty paces from the back door, while the front of the lodge faced a steep incline that descended to the ocean.

Suddenly she felt a desire to be out in the sunlight. Feeling young and carefree, she grabbed her shawl and moved out the front door and down the rocky path toward the sound of the roaring surf.

Breanna walked along the jagged shoreline, glancing out to sea. She tried to picture the land that had fostered her husband. Was America as wild and unpredictable as Dakota? Would he ever feel that England was his home?

Dakota had come up behind Breanna so silently that she was startled when he touched her shoulder. "I would have announced myself, but your thoughts seemed far away, Breanna."

She smiled up at him. "Actually, I was wondering about America. What is it like?"

"I cannot say. I only know about the land which belongs to the Arapaho."

"The Arapaho, that is the name of the Indian tribe

186

that raised you?"

He watched as sunbeams played across her hair, making it flame, almost as if it were on fire. "Yes, that is the name of the tribe, but I was raised by the war chief, Two Moons. I was proud to call him father. I would challenge any man to produce a more patient and loving parent."

Her eyes glowed softly. "Tell me about your Indian mother, what was she like?"

"Her name was White Wing. I suppose she was little different from most mothers. She worried about my health, saw that I ate properly, and she kept a pleasant home to which the men in her family were always eager to return."

"I don't remember much about my parents, Dakota. Do you ever wish you had known your real mother and father?"

"You will have to understand that I have some very confused feelings about that just now. I have known from an early age that I was white, but inside I felt like an Indian — I still do." Suddenly he remembered Breanna referring to him as a savage, and he gripped her shoulders, forcing her to look into his green eyes. "You must understand that I do not apologize for who I am. I am just as proud of Two Moons and White Wing as you are of your parents."

Unexpectedly, her eyes softened. "I am glad you feel that way," she said, deeply moved by his devotion to his Indian mother and father. "I would be disappointed in you if you had nothing good to say about two people who loved you and gave you a home."

He released his hold on her, but still held her gaze. "Were you happy growing up in your brother's home?" he wanted to know.

"Most of the time. It was a strange life in a way because we were considered nobility, yet we were very poor. Sophie always told me that one is never poor unless one feels poor, and I found this to be true."

"I think I would like this Sophie. Who is she?"

"She is my brother's wife. I would like to be the kind of wife that Sophie is to Fielding."

She tried to hide her blush, but Dakota saw it and smiled. "Would you, Breanna?"

"Yes. She is patient and understanding. Only once have I heard her voice raised in anger, and that was done in staunch defense of my brother when I pointed out his shortcomings." Her eyes were troubled as she continued. "I fear I am neither patient nor understanding. I have been told I am obstinate, and as you surmised that first day we met, I sometimes have an explosive temper." She shook her head while pain throbbed in her every word. "I have always attempted to be better, but I fear I will never be like Sophie."

His eyes danced across her face, and she reminded him of an endearing child. "It is not Sophie I am married to. I like a woman who stands up for her beliefs. If you are angry with me about something, tell me. I would not want a timid wife who only agreed with me out of loyalty or devotion."

"Truly?" she asked innocently.

"Truly," he answered in a deep voice.

"I am amazed at how quickly you seem to adjust to

your new life, Dakota."

"Breanna, this is a confusing time for me. I am no longer a member of the Arapaho tribe, I am not an American, and I do not feel like an Englishman. I cannot decide just what and who I am."

Once more her heart went out to him because she was aware of his vulnerability. "You are English by birth, and will one day be the Marquess of Weatherford. That is your birthright, my lord. No amount of uncertainty and introspection will change that. It is the law, and no one can deny you that heritage."

"What you say is true. But I want to be honest with you from the first. If I decide that I do not fit into the mold of an English gentleman, I may return to what I consider my real home."

She searched his eyes. "Would you ask me to go with you?"

He hesitantly reached out and touched her face. "No, Breanna, you are an English rose that would never bloom anywhere but in England." He was silent for a moment, as if trying to decide how to tell her what was on his mind. "What I want to say is, if you do not wish to be married to me, I will free you. We were never married in a proper ceremony, and I am told that we could petition for a document of annulment because our marriage has not been consummated."

Something akin to pain stabbed at her heart. "Do you wish to have our marriage dissolved?"

"It is not my wish that must be considered, Breanna. I want no wife that comes to me out of duty or fear."

"What are you saying?"

"I am saying that you can walk away right now and I will give you your freedom. I will also endow you with a generous settlement, so you can have your own household and would not be forced to return to your brother's house where you were unhappy."

Dakota hoped his eyes did not betray how desperately he wanted her to choose to remain with him and become his wife in every way. He had given the matter much thought before making Breanna this offer of freedom. In all fairness, Dakota felt he could not consummate their marriage unless he gave her the opportunity to leave if she so desired.

Breanna had an urge to throw herself into his arms and beg him to hold on to her. She wondered how she had ever felt alive before he came into her life. "I still don't know what you expect of me, Dakota."

"You can do one of two things. If you want to leave, I will see that you are transported to the destination of your choice. But if you want to see if we can have a life together, remain here with me until we come to know one another."

"And if you decide to return to America?"

His heart sank. "Then we would both be free to do as we chose."

"What if I agree to stay with you?"

He took her hand. "Then I will strive to woo you with patience and understanding. You have my word that I will not force my attentions on you. If, and when, you decide to consummate our marriage, it will be when you come to me."

A blush tinged her cheeks and her heart throbbed.

"For now, I choose to remain with you," she said through trembling lips.

His laughter was infectious as he hugged her to him, and Breanna felt happiness surge through her body. "Today we begin to know one another. You can ask any question of me, and I will endeavor to answer it as honestly as I can, Breanna. But the same must be true of you. Will you answer all my questions honestly also so we might get to know one another?"

"I will," she said with determination.

"Good." Taking her hand, he led her toward the water's edge. "Can you imagine how wide this ocean is, Breanna?" He glanced down at her, awaiting her answer.

"I know it would take many days to cross to America."

"That is true, and that is how wide the gap is between you and me. We were both forced to wed against our will. Do you think we can close that gap?"

"I don't know, Dakota, but we can try." She glanced up into his handsome face, wishing she could bridge that gap. A moment ago when he had held her in his arms, she had felt safe and secure, as if nothing could harm her. She felt that if he let her go, she would flounder like the restless waves that now washed upon the shore.

"Let me take you back to the lodge, Breanna. I have to call on another tenant who claims his house will fall down around his head if he doesn't get a new roof. It seems that since I arrived, the tenants expect me to take control just because I am a Remington."

"You will not be here to dine with me?" she asked, disappointed.

"No, not tonight. But we shall spend tomorrow together."

As they moved up the path, he assisted her. Later, as she watched him ride away, she realized she had never wanted anything as much as she wanted to be a wife to this complex man who was her husband.

Chapter Fifteen

The clouds moved away from the moon and a beam of light fell across Breanna's face, waking her from a troubled sleep. Hearing the waves crashing upon the cliffs, she climbed out of bed and moved out of her bedroom.

The night was warm, and she could feel the ocean calling to her. Glancing down at her filmy white nightgown, she decided no one would be about, so she opened the front door and made her way down the path to the ocean.

She was delighted that the hunting lodge was located in a secluded bay and surrounded by rock-face cliffs that offered complete privacy.

She hadn't heard Dakota returning to the lodge, so she concluded that she was alone. Wading out into the foamy water, she felt it swirl about her bare feet. This was something she had wanted to do since she had first arrived at Weatherford Hall.

Kenton Estate, where Breanna had grown up, was located far from the coast; therefore she had never seen the ocean before coming to Cornwall.

She found the restless waves invigorating, and joyfully she moved backward as if being chased ashore by the waves. She became so caught up in her childish play that she did not see Dakota on the cliff above her. Her foot became entangled in her gown and she tumbled into the water. Laughing at her own misfortune, Breanna scrambled to her feet.

Dakota stared at his wife as she weaved in and out with the waves. Her filmy nightgown clung to her soft curves, and the bright moonlight made it seem as if she wore nothing at all. He moved silently down the slope to stand just behind her.

Breanna whirled around, attempting to miss an advancing wave. She was startled when she slammed into someone, and stared up at her husband. The smile froze on her face, and she ducked her head to hide her embarrassment for being caught behaving in such a childish manner.

"Is the game for just one, or may I join in?" he asked, raising her chin and smiling down at her.

"I fear I got carried away, my lord. I do not usually give in to such childish antics. Am I disgraced?"

"On the contrary," he said, slipping off his boots and flinging his shirt down on the sand. "I beg to be allowed to join your game."

She smiled at him with uncertainty, while her eyes avoided his bare chest. "I should go back to the lodge," she said, only half-convincingly.

He caught her arm. "I wish you wouldn't."

Breanna looked at him through silken lashes. "You will surely think you married a child."

His laughter was warm. "Believe me, Breanna, you do not look like any child I have ever seen." His eyes ran

194

over her soft curves, and she felt a tingling all the way down her body. She became aware that her wet gown clung to her, and she crossed her arms over her breasts.

Dakota saw the blush on her face and quickly spoke, hoping to take her mind off her embarrassment. "How would you like to go for a swim?"

"I do not know how to swim," she confessed ruefully.

"Then you must learn. An Indian maiden learns to swim almost as soon as she learns to walk."

"I . . . have always wanted to learn, but it is immodest for an English girl to—"

"Nonsense." He took her hand, slowly leading her to waist-deep water. "Everyone, even properly brought up English girls, should know how to swim."

She was frightened of deep water, and yet she wanted very much to please Dakota. Even more, she wanted to be with him, to come to know him . . . to become his wife. . .

When a wave splashed against her body and salt water stung her eyes, Breanna gasped to catch her breath, clinging to Dakota's neck as if it were a lifeline.

"Easy," he said soothingly. "I am going to turn you on your back so you can float. You trust me, don't you?"

"Yes, but—"

He eased her onto her back, noting the fear in her eyes. "Relax, Breanna. I can assure you I am a very good swimmer and I would never allow anything to happen to you. Do you believe this?"

". . . Yes." She willed her body to relax and finally succeeded because she could feel his firm grip about her waist.

Dakota needed to concentrate on what he was doing, so he tore his eyes away from her soft curves that were visible through the transparent nightgown. His deep voice lulled her into a state of tranquillity. "Close your eyes, Breanna, and think of something very pleasant. You are floating, floating on a peaceful sea of dreams."

Cradled by the warm water, and soothed by the sound of his voice, she was unaware of when he released her, and she remained afloat on her own.

"I knew you could do it, Breanna. Now open your eyes slowly." When she did as he instructed, she saw she was indeed riding the waves without his aid.

"Don't panic," he urged. "I am going to turn you over on your stomach, and I want you to relax as you are doing now. I warn you that you will be submerged, but remain calm and you will not sink."

With ease, he rolled her over. For a moment, Breanna felt panic, but his hands were firm on her waist, and she began to relax again, her desire to please Dakota giving her the courage to follow his instructions.

"You are doing well, Breanna." He lifted her out of the water. "Now I want you to continue to float, but this time kick your feet and use your arms." He demonstrated by moving her legs and showing her what to do with her arms. "Now you are ready. I will stand right here and you can swim toward the shore."

She nodded eagerly, and before he could give her further instructions, she went underwater. When Breanna kicked her feet, she lunged forward feeling a surge of accomplishment. She giggled to herself, knowing how a fish must feel. When the water became too shallow for her to swim, she stood up and glanced back at Dakota.

"You did it," he called out. "You learn quickly. Now

swim back to me."

Warmed by his praise, she dove under water and paddled toward him. Now she was able to raise her face out of the water. When she reached Dakota, she was so overcome with joy that she jumped up and threw herself into his arms. "I did it! I can swim!" she cried.

His laughter was warm against her cheek as he drew her tighter against him. "Yes, you did it. If you aren't careful, someone will mistake you for a mermaid."

She tossed back her wet hair and smiled up at him. Suddenly their eyes locked, and she no longer thought about her accomplishments. She became aware of the hard muscles that were pressed against her and the way his eyes drew all the strength from her body, making her feel like a limp rag. Surely if he had not been supporting her, she would have sunk to the bottom of the ocean.

Primitive feelings of ownership shook Dakota. He held the world in his arms and the law said she belonged to him. Dare he take her? He could easily break down her defenses—she was ripe and so ready for a man to love, her eyes told him that. Shaken by a feeling of protectiveness, he crushed her against his body, molding her curves so they fit against his hard frame. Breathless with wanting and needing her, he ran his hand down her back, pressing her tighter against him.

Breanna felt Dakota's warm breath against her cheek and she arched her neck back, as new and unexplored feelings moved through her body like waves advancing on the shore. The moon and stars merged with the silvery water of the sea and she wasn't sure which way was up, and which was down. Shaken to the very core of her being, she felt his lips move down her arched

197

neck to plant feathery kisses in the hollow of her shoulders.

A whimper escaped her lips when he moved her wet nightgown aside and pressed soft kisses on the tips of her exposed breasts. Her hand slid through his ebony hair and she arched to get closer to the heat of his body. Yes, his body was promising her fulfillment and oneness. She ached to be possessed by him completely.

Breanna had not been aware that Dakota was carrying them both toward the shore until he walked out of the water with her in his arms. Blinded by starlight, she felt him lay her on his shirt that he had earlier thrown on the sand. As he hovered above her, water from his wet hair dripped onto her face and she tasted the saltiness on her tongue. His eyes were asking her a question and her body was begging to respond.

Dakota's hand trembled as he pushed her gown off her shoulders. "Breanna, I gave my word I would not take you against your will. Are you willing now?" he asked in a tight whisper.

"I . . . I . . . surely not here!" Her throat was dry, and she was having difficulty breathing.

With a smile of understanding, he traced a pattern down her neck, across her shoulder to circle a throbbing breast. "There is no one about save the two of us, Breanna. All the servants left hours ago." Shivers of delight danced across her skin when he moved his finger around her nipple.

"Breanna," he murmured, stirred by her sweetness. "Breanna. . ."

Caught up in earth-shattering emotions, she moved forward and clasped her hands behind his neck. With the offer of her parted lips, she felt his mouth touch hers, while her body exploded with urgent needs.

Dakota lips were soft and firm, and his hands moved along her leg and thigh, pushing her wet gown upward. When he pulled away from her to lift her gown over her head, she watched his eyes darken with desire as he stared at her nakedness.

His green eyes reflected the moon as they moved over her body, taking in the long legs, the rounded hips, the tiny waist. Breanna felt no shame as she saw appreciation in his glance.

He watched her firm young breasts sway with her every movement. This time when he lowered his head, his lips parted and he took the rosy tip in his mouth.

"No, Dakota, no," she whispered, beginning to be frightened, not of him, but of the wild abandoned feelings she was experiencing.

Dakota immediately released her and sat up. Taking a deep steadying breath, he wrapped his shirt around her and helped her stand. "I am sorry, Breanna. It would appear I got carried away by my little mermaid."

She stared into his eyes, wishing she could explain how she felt, but unable to reason out her feelings even to herself. "I should go in now," she said in a trembling voice, not really wanting to leave him but needing to be alone to think about what had happened to her tonight.

Dakota tried to beat back his passion and stepped back from her. He stooped to pick up her wet gown and held it out to her.

She had thought he might be angry with her, but he looked at her with a half-smile. "I gather from your reaction to me that you have never before been with a man, Breanna."

"Of course I haven't. You should know that."

"I thought not, but as I told you before, I am unfamiliar with your English customs." He was gladdened by her words because he would be the first with her. Oh, he would have her, he knew that now. Nothing could stop this aching hunger in his body but her.

He realized it would be easy to overcome her resistance tonight, but the time was wrong. He would not take her in the sand. He would wait until she was driven out of her mind by desire as he was. Their coming together would be like an explosion, and neither of them would have any doubts or hesitations.

Holding her dripping gown in her hands, and trying to look dignified with nothing but his shirt draped about her, Breanna had an answer for him. "Surely you did not think that your grandfather had chosen a woman of soiled reputation to be your wife?"

He turned her toward the house, and as they walked along, he tried to clear his mind. "I had hoped not, but I couldn't be sure until tonight."

She stopped, glancing at him questioningly. "Would it have mattered to you if I had been . . . ?"

"Soiled?" he supplied. "Yes, and no. I would not have abandoned you had you been with another man, but I must confess that I will be honored to be the first to be with you."

Her legs went weak at his sensuous words, and she clung to his arm. She watched the moon trace patterns across his face, and Breanna knew she had to ask the question that was on her mind. "Have you ever loved a woman, Dakota?"

He thought before he answered. "I told you that I would answer all your questions, so you must not be offended by the answers, since the questions are yours.

If you are asking if I have been with a woman, the answer is, of course. But if you are asking if my heart has been engaged, I have to answer that I am not sure what love between a man and a woman feels like. I will tell you that I have not been with a woman since I became your husband."

Breanna didn't want to think about him holding another woman the way he had held her tonight. To keep her hands from trembling, she pulled the shirt across her breasts. Warm color stained her cheeks when she discovered he was watching her with amusement dancing in his eyes.

"Do not distress yourself, Breanna. You have done nothing wrong."

She had the strangest urge to bury her face against his wide chest and have him hold her until her tilted world righted itself. "I know I am your wife, and I am aware of what is expected of me, but I . . . I . . ."

"Do not torment yourself, Breanna. Remember, we struck a bargain, and you have my word that I shall honor that bargain."

As he helped her up the path, she stopped on the edge of the cliff and asked him the question that had bothered her since she discovered he was her husband. "I have not stopped wondering why you did not tell me you were my husband that first afternoon we met?"

He smiled and pushed a damp curl from her forehead. "You said some very unflattering things about your husband that afternoon. I would have been a fool to admit I was he."

A smile lit her eyes. "Yes, I was dreadful, and I hope you have forgiven me for my blunder."

He raised her hand to his lips and placed a warm kiss

there. "You are forgiven, my lady."

They continued on to the lodge, and when they reached the front steps, Breanna hesitated again, unwilling to end their conversation. "Were you surprised to find that I was your wife?"

He laughed aloud, remembering the image he'd had of his wife. "I can say in all honesty that I was overcome with immediate relief when I discovered you were my wife. I had pictured you quite differently."

"Had you?"

"Yes, I can assure you that I had."

He reached around her and opened the door. "After you, my lady wife."

She moved inside, not wanting to go to her room but knowing it was expected of her. "Shall I see you in the morning, Dakota?"

"It's already morning. You swam the night away, Breanna."

"Yes, I suppose I did."

"If you like, we will go riding, say about seven? We can pack a lunch to take along with us."

Excitement laced her words. "Oh, yes. I would like that very much."

He steered her to her bedroom door and opened it for her. "Try to get some sleep. I will see that you are awakened in plenty of time to get ready for our adventure."

Breanna entered her room and closed the door behind her. Leaning against the door, she smiled happily. She wondered if there had ever been a man such as Dakota. He was everything she had ever dreamed of in a husband, and more. She lay on the bed, wrapped in his shirt because she was reluctant to part with it, feeling his nearness in every part of her body.

"Dakota," she whispered, "I know what love feels like, because I believe I love you!"

Chapter Sixteen

Breanna rode through the thundering waves, her pulse racing, her heart pounding, her red-gold hair flying in the wind.

Dakota pulled up his mount and watched her from a distance. He had never seen a more beautiful sight. There were so many sides to Breanna. He had seen the innocent child, the reluctant wife, and now a bewitching siren.

Nudging his horse in the flanks, he shot forward to join her. For several moments they rode along the shoreline until they came to a cliff that jutted out into the ocean, blocking their forward progress.

Breanna smiled at Dakota. "It would seem our excursion is at an end."

"If we can't go forward, we will go back. How would you like to explore those caves we saw just beyond the bend?"

"Oh, could we?"

"Yes, but only if we do not venture too far into the interior, and we must retreat before high tide. John told me that people have drowned in those caves."

"We still have several hours until high tide," Breanna reminded him.

He could read the eagerness in her eyes and smiled to himself as they galloped back the way they had come.

Breanna slid from her horse and ran to the mouth of the cavern while Dakota secured their horses.

He took her hand and ushered her inside. They had to step from stone to stone so they wouldn't get their feet wet. Like shining crystal chandeliers, the icicle-shaped stalactites caught the light and shot out brilliant rainbow colors on the cave wall. Several shallow ponds had been formed in the limestone and she could see tiny minnows swimming about.

"This is magnificent," Breanna declared, turning around in a circle. "I have never seen anything like this, have you?"

"I have been in mountain caves, but nothing like these caverns. However, I have read books that tell of such wonders as this."

She sat down on a limestone rock, pondering his words. "It would seem that you have read books on almost every subject."

He dropped down beside her, his clear gaze probing her eyes. "I hope that does not make me a bore."

Breanna picked up a smooth pebble and skipped it across the pond. "I have not found you to be a bore, Dakota. In fact, I find you—" Her face reddened.

"Yes," he said, smiling.

"Was . . . was it very confusing for you having two sets of parents?" she stammered, changing the subject abruptly.

He smiled. "You cannot imagine. But you must understand that I always wanted to be an Arapaho. There

205

was a time when I rebelled against everything that reminded me that I was white."

"Was there an Indian girl you were interested in?"

Long lashes swept over his eyes, and she sensed a hesitation in him. "Yes. Her name was Running Deer. She died in my arms, killed by my Indian brother, Black Otter."

She saw pain in his eyes as he spoke about a tragedy such as she could only imagine. "How awful for you. Did you love her very much?" She dreaded hearing his answer, but she had to know.

"Love wears many different faces, Breanna. There is the love you had for your parents, your brother and his family. There is the love I hope you will have for your husband, and eventually your children. I have always found it difficult to measure love. The Arapaho have a saying. You can fill a jug with love — give a handful to this person — a handful to that person and two handfuls to someone else. Yet when you gaze into the jug, you will find it is still full to the brim with love."

She thought about what he said, realizing he had not answered her at all. She still had no idea how he had felt about Running Deer. Did he suffer because his love had been killed? Did he still grieve because she died in his arms? Breanna wished she had never asked him about the Indian girl, because now she would always wonder if she had to compete with the ghost of a lost love.

"What became of Black Otter?" she asked, moving on to what she thought would be a less painful subject.

"Black Otter was put to death for his crime. You see, Running Deer was the daughter of the chief of my tribe, and she was well loved by all."

"Look," Breanna said, standing up suddenly, not wanting to hear any more about Running Deer. "I believe the tide is rising."

Dakota came to his feet and took Breanna's hand. "Come, it is time for us to leave. In another hour, this cave will be filled with water."

The water was ankle deep by the time Breanna stepped out into the bright sunlight. She moved over to Joya and patted the white mare. "We have not eaten our lunch, Dakota. I have had such a wonderful time that I did not realize it was well after the noon hour."

"Have you enjoyed yourself?"

"Yes, very much."

"How would you like to ride into the village after we have eaten?"

"I would love it."

While they ate, Breanna told Dakota about her life at Kenton. She did not hesitate to explain about her brother's gambling or how he had lost the family fortune.

Dakota's back was braced against a big boulder. "I am told that I have more money and holdings than a family could spend in three generations. Would it please you if I gave your brother enough money so he and his family could live comfortably?"

Breanna was wiping her mouth on a soft white napkin. "No! That is the one thing you must not do. If Fielding is ever to learn a lesson, he must not have things made easy for him."

"Your reasoning is sound. But if the time should come when you wish to help your brother, you have only to ask it of me."

Breanna felt her heart swell with love for this man.

He was so caring and thoughtful of others; she only hoped she would one day be worthy to be his wife.

She watched Dakota gain his feet with the agility of a feline. As he flexed his muscles, Breanna felt hot and cold at the same time. Here was a man of sensitivity, yet she knew that he was only a hair's breadth away from reverting to his primitive instincts. She had the feeling that if you took away his gentlemanly garments, his manner would change, and Dakota would become as untamed as the wild land where he had been born, and as fierce and unpredictable as the Indian tribe that had fostered him into manhood.

Dakota offered Breanna his hand and pulled her to her feet. "Shall we ride into the village now?"

"Yes, I'd like that," she said, almost sorry that she would now have to share him with others. She was fascinated by this man. She could listen to him talk all day. She thanked the lucky star that had cast her in the role of Dakota Remington's wife.

Breanna could feel the turmoil in the very air she breathed as they entered the small fishing village of Weatherford. At first the only sound that could be heard was their horses' hooves clattering on the cobblestone streets. Old salts stopped mending their nets, women and children came out of their houses, silently staring at Dakota and Breanna.

She was astonished that the whole village was soon following along behind them, but there were no smiles on the villagers' faces.

Breanna and Dakota halted their mounts in front of an old Norman church with its gray steeples and six bell towers. When Dakota helped Breanna to the ground, the crowd closed in around them.

One man, bolder than the others, stepped forward. "Be you the new lord and lady up at the big house?" He spoke in a heavy accent, his dark eyes searching and suspicious.

"Yes," Dakota answered. "I am the Viscount of Remington and this is my Viscountess."

"We heard you was here, my lord. The village's been too long without guidance. We got trouble, and we was wondering if you plan to do anything about it?"

Dakota stared at the man. "What kind of trouble? Tell me what it is, so I'll know if I can help."

The man's lip curled. "That's what your grandfather always said, and he didn't do nothing for us. He hasn't even been here in over ten years."

"Tell me about your trouble," Dakota said again.

"Well it's from the village of Saffron down the way. Since we had no lord to take our part, the Saffron fishermen and their lord forced us out of our private fishing waters and the magistrate won't hear our grievances. Some of our villagers have even been killed trying to get back what belongs to us."

Dakota moved closer to the fisherman and was soon the center of twenty-odd men, while the women moved around Breanna, their bold glances hostile and cold.

Breanna noticed the gaunt faces of the children, the suspicion on the women's faces, and the hostility in the men's eyes.

One of the women, who was wearing a sober black gown, unrelieved except for a narrow white collar, spoke up boldly. "I'm Mary Ouster, the vicar's wife. You aren't from around these parts, are you, my lady?"

209

"No, I am not from Cornwall," Breanna answered, moving a step closer to Dakota.

"I thought not," Mary Ouster replied. "You look like London born to me." By the tone of her voice, Breanna knew the woman was not paying her a compliment.

Breanna looked to Dakota for guidance, but he seemed to be engrossed in what the men were telling him. She could feel the animosity from the villagers and wondered if Dakota was aware of it also.

After a few moments of conversing with the men, Dakota moved toward Breanna. "Stay at my side," he whispered. "Act as if you aren't afraid."

"But why should—"

"Do as I say," he demanded. Then he lifted Breanna onto her horse and mounted his own. "You will hear from me," he said in a voice that was loud enough to carry to all the men. "Do nothing until then."

Breanna saw the embittered glances cast their way. She heard their mumbled words. "Why should we trust him? We trusted his grandfather, and he did nothing to help us."

Breanna breathed a sigh of relief as they rode out of the village. "What was that all about?" she asked. The day had been so perfect, and now a cloud hung over her happiness.

"I had no idea what being the Viscount of Remington entailed. I am ashamed to say my grandfather has neglected the villagers for years. They have been left to fend for themselves, with no one to champion their cause. As a result, I am afraid they have fallen upon hard times. Did you notice how hungry the children looked, Breanna? No child should ever go hungry."

He was quiet for a moment, remembering the past. "Never, not even in the Arapahos' leanest years, have I seen such suffering."

Breanna's heart softened even more toward him. Never had she known anyone to feel others' pain as Dakota did.

She frowned. "They did not look like they would welcome any help from you or me, Dakota. Still I cannot imagine eating until something is done about their hunger."

Dakota was glad that Breanna had sympathy for the villagers. "I will see that food is taken to the village tonight," he assured her. "You are not to worry about the problem. Tomorrow I will exercise my rights as lord, and see how much power that wields. I can only hope that the villagers of Saffron and their lord consider me as important as John always tells me I am," he said with an attempt at humor.

He was silent during the remainder of their ride back to the hunting lodge, and Breanna felt him shutting her out. She wanted to be a part of his plan to help the villagers, but apparently his plans did not include her.

Dark clouds were gathering on the horizon as they reached the hunting lodge. Even the weather seemed ready to dishearten Breanna's spirit.

She wondered if Dakota would use his power to bring prosperity back to the village that was under his protection. Beneath the hostility she had felt in the village, Breanna had also sensed that the people were like children who looked to Dakota for guidance. She thought it had been wrong of the old Marquess to abandon his responsibilities and leave the village to flounder on its own.

"You have heavy obligations, Dakota," she said in a throaty voice.

He nodded in agreement. "I am only beginning to understand that." He then dismounted and swung her to the ground. "You go inside, Breanna, while I ride to Weatherford Hall to make arrangements for food to be transported to the village."

She frowned. "Don't go to the village alone, Dakota. I was frightened while we were there today. Why should they feel such loathing for you and me when they don't even know us?"

His green eyes narrowed. "That wasn't loathing you saw in their faces, Breanna, it was disillusionment." He gave her a slight smile. "I should be back in time to dine with you."

She watched him wheel his mount and ride away, wishing he had asked her to accompany him.

That night, as Breanna and Dakota dined in the small alcove behind the hunting lodge, he assured her that food had been delivered to the villagers.

As they finished their meal, the first drops of rain began to fall, and before they made the dash to the lodge, they were both soaked to the skin.

As Dakota tenderly brushed beads of water from her face, Breanna was glad that he had sent the servants back to the main house and they were alone.

She stood before the big window, watching the rain pelt against the pane. The wind came up in great gusts, and the waves splashed high against the cliff. Breanna turned fever-bright eyes to Dakota, who had been watching the way her wet gown clung to her upper body, outlining her firm, young breasts.

She did not resist when he came up behind her and pulled her to him so that her head rested against his shoulder.

"I enjoyed our time together, Breanna."

She felt all warm inside. "So did I, Dakota."

Thunder struck, and lightning flashed across the sky. Now the waves reached high into the air and splashed against the window.

Breanna's heart was drumming a loud tempo, but it wasn't from fear. She turned to her husband, her golden eyes soft with the light of surrender. "I want to be your wife in every way, Dakota."

His breath came out in a hiss. "Are you sure?"

She stood on tiptoes and pressed her cheek against his. "I have never been more sure of anything in my life."

The tenderness that came into his eyes stopped the beating of her heart. Gently, he touched her cheek. "I have wanted to hear this from you since the first day I saw you. I knew that I had to be the most fortunate of men to have you for a wife. When I discovered you were afraid of me, I knew I would have to woo you slowly." A rakish smile crossed his face. "It took far less time than I anticipated, however."

She clasped his hand and raised it to her cheek, loving him in the very depths of her soul. "That's because you didn't know the power of your own charm."

With a quick intake of breath, he pulled her tightly against him. His lips were hot as they settled on hers, and her head spun drunkenly so she had to cling to him. Releasing her lips, he nibbled on her ear. "I hate to admit this, Breanna," he whispered hotly in her ear, "but I haven't the slightest notion how to get this contraption off you."

She laughed as he gazed down at her wide skirt that covered the crinoline. "Come, my lord, and I will give you your first lesson."

She felt bold, beginning to enjoy playing a seductress. She tingled at the thought of surrendering herself to her husband.

The storm intensified, charging the atmosphere with electricity. Dakota could hear the waves crashing against the window as he lifted Breanna into his arms and carried her into his bedroom.

She was trembling as he took her hand, and he didn't know if she was frightened of him or the storm. But he would calm her fears, he thought, glancing at her lovely face.

Red-hot passion shook his body as he glanced down at her. "There is nothing for you to fear, Breanna. Neither the storm nor I will harm you."

Chapter Seventeen

Breanna's whalebone crinoline lay in a heap at her feet. When a flash of lightning illuminated the bedroom, Dakota's green eyes ran hungrily over her flawless body. Slowly he pulled her into his arms and tilted her chin so he would have access to her lips. His tongue probed and parted her mouth in a tender-sweet quest that demanding total surrender. She clung to him, pressing tighter against his hard strength, aching for the fulfillment his body promised her.

Slowly and sensuously, Dakota's hands moved down her satiny skin while her firm young breasts were crushed against his chest. He moved ever so slightly, and she could feel the hair on his chest brush against her nipples.

Gasping for breath, Breanna felt as if she had no substance, that he could take her, mold her, and make her into whatever he wanted.

"Breanna, sweet Breanna," he murmured against her lips. "I will take you where no man has ever dared.

Together we will discover the real meaning of touching and feeling."

Breanna threw her head back and felt his breath on her breasts. She quivered while his eyes ran over her from the crown of her red-gold hair, to the arch of her delicate foot. There was no shame in her, because she could tell by looking into his eyes that he found her pleasing.

She watched him kneel before her, then she felt herself sinking to her knees, and didn't know if it was under her own power, or if Dakota had brought her down with him. All her feelings were heightened as his hand ran down her thigh to trace a pattern around her navel.

She could hear the waves crashing against the cliffs, the rain peppering against the roof, the thunder rumbling in the distance—or was that her heart beating a wild tempo?

Dakota's breath caught in his throat. He was on fire with a passion that threatened to burn out of control.

Breanna's pale skin looked like silver when a streak of lightning flashed across the sky. Gently he laid her on the rug, then he lay down beside her.

"Breanna," he whispered past the lump in his throat. "I am smoke, I will fill your body, satisfy your deepest need, teach you about love." His lips played with her nipples until they hardened and a moan passed her lips. His voice trembled. "If I am smoke, Breanna, you are fire. Your fire ignites a flame in my body, a flame that burns day and night. I will have no rest until I possess you, but in doing so, I risk being consumed by your fire."

216

His beautiful words touched her heart, and she reached out to him.

This time, when lightning brightened the room, Breanna allowed herself to look at his body. The shadow of black hair covered his chest. He was beautiful to behold. His bronzed nakedness was lightened at the spot where he had worn a breechcloth. His legs were long and powerful. In the shimmering reflection of the lightning, she saw the dark hair in the shape of a vee and gasped when she saw his swollen need.

Dakota's breath hissed, and he pulled her tightly against him. With bruising strength, his mouth crushed hers.

She could feel the rise and fall of his chest, and found that her breathing matched his.

He laced his hands through her tumbled hair, pressing her even closer to him.

"I fear I am out of control," he whispered in a husky voice. "I need you, Breanna. I need all of you."

"Yes," she murmured. "Yes, Dakota."

Gently his hand moved down to part her thighs. Slowly, at first, he circled her pulsating opening. Breanna groaned when he slipped his finger into her hot core. Deeper and deeper he penetrated, until he found the barrier of her maidenhood. With a quick jab, he broke the skin and smothered her mouth with a hot kiss when she moaned with pain.

"The pain is over," he promised. "Now there will be only pleasure."

The intensity of his passion electrified Breanna. She ached for fulfillment. When he was positioned above her, she was unable to speak. Blinded by desire, she

217

arched her hips, inviting him to enter her body.

His body trembled as he slowly moved forward, penetrating just inside her. "My blood sings," he murmured, thrusting deeper and feeling the heat of her close around his throbbing shaft.

The rhythm of the waves pounding against the cliffs set the tempo for their lovemaking. The electricity in the air heightened their pleasure, and Breanna was gently introduced to a new side of her husband. Dakota's tempered strength merged with Breanna's softness, and their bodies were in tune with the age-old song of love, fulfillment, hearts beating as one, and life being renewed.

Erupting, shattering fulfillment fused them together, and Breanna's eyes were soft with wonder when Dakota held her tightly to him.

"I never knew about such feelings," she said, raking her fingers through the mat of curly black hair on his chest. "Will it always be like this?"

A red-gold curl drifted across Dakota's cheek, and he closed his eyes, too moved to answer right away. When he found his voice, it came out in a whisper. "I never knew about such feelings myself, Breanna. This is as new to me as it is to you."

She raised up on her elbow. "But I thought you said—"

He smiled and placed a finger over her lips. "I said I never felt anything like what just happened to us."

". . . Oh."

He brought her head to rest on his shoulder. "You have me completely under your spell, little mermaid. I wonder if you know that?" he murmured.

She smiled. "I am glad."

Breanna noticed the jagged scar that ran from Dakota's shoulder to his ribcage, and she traced it with her finger. "How did you get this scar?" she asked.

"When I was but a boy, I came face-to-face with something that was bigger and stronger than myself."

"But who? This must have been very serious."

"It was. I came up against a bear."

She was horrified. "What happened?"

"Let us not talk about the past," he said, brushing his lips across her cheek.

Deciding not to press him further, Breanna curled up in his arms and, for the first time in her life, felt as if she belonged to someone. "I owe my brother an apology," she said, thinking aloud.

"Why is that?" Dakota asked, smiling down at her.

"Oh, he did me a tremendous favor, and I want to tell him so one day." She remembered Fielding telling her the day might come when she would thank him for the arrangement he had made for her marriage. She laughed and placed her ear against Dakota's chest, comforted by the steady beating of his heart. "Yes, I shall indeed thank Fielding for his foresight."

"Do you care to share your humor with me?"

"No, you wouldn't understand." She was reflective. "What shall we do tomorrow, Dakota?"

"I cannot be with you tomorrow, Breanna. I have important business to attend to. I believe I shall call upon the Earl of Saffron, to see if the two of us can come to an amicable arrangement concerning the villagers."

"I see." There was disappointment in her tone. "I

219

have overheard the servants talking, and they say the Earl is mean and vindictive. You will be careful?"

"I can assure you that I will. And don't fret, my lovely. I will rush to your side the moment I am able." He laughed and hugged her to him. "I promise you that I will spend every moment with you that I can."

Breanna, warmed by his words, felt herself drifting off to sleep. How right it felt to be curled up in Dakota's arms. How wonderful it was to be alive.

It was still dark when Dakota eased himself out of bed so he wouldn't awaken Breanna. While he dressed, he stared down at her, loving the way her glorious hair was spread across the pillow. In sleep, she looked more child than woman. He watched the rise and fall of her breasts, caused by her deep breathing. He had the urge to climb back in bed beside her, but he had to see if he could do something about the fishermen's plight.

He stopped and kissed Breanna softly on the lips. She stirred, rolled over, and sighed contentedly without waking.

Regretfully, Dakota pulled on his boots, slung his coat over his shoulders, and left the bedroom. Hearing the sound of pots and pans banging in the kitchen, he stuck his head in and spoke to the cook. "Allow your mistress to sleep. When she awakens, remind her that I will be gone most of the day."

Dakota had been told by his gamekeeper that the Earl of Saffron had encouraged his villagers to fish in

Weatherford waters. Dakota decided it was best to attempt to talk with the Earl first, then if that did not bring satisfactory results, he had other means with which to deal with the man.

Dakota dismounted and handed the reins of his horse to one of the Earl's servants. Climbing the steps, he rapped at the front door, noticing that the gray stone house was small in comparison to Weatherford Hall, but impressive nonetheless.

The door was immediately opened by a stoic-faced butler who bowed stiffly to Dakota. "Good morning to you, sir, how may I be of help to you?" the man asked, his words coming out wooden and formal.

Dakota remembered that Two Moons had often told him to look an antagonist straight in the eyes. With an air of arrogant indifference, he replied, "Please inform your master that the Viscount of Remington wishes to see him on a matter of great import."

The man's whole attitude changed. A forced smile curved his lips, and his eyes shone with respect. "Please step in, my lord. I will inform his lordship that you are here. Would you care to wait in the formal sitting room?"

Dakota nodded stiffly and followed the butler across the entryway. While he was waiting for the Earl, he stood at the window, thinking it was a pity that this house did not have the magnificent ocean view that he enjoyed at Weatherford Hall.

His keen hearing picked up the sound of rustling silk, and he turned to watch a woman dressed in a pale yellow gown enter the room. Her black hair was pulled away from her face, and her soft brown eyes struck a cord of painful memories, because something about her reminded him of Running Deer.

"Lord Remington, this is such a pleasure. I am Lady Rye Saffron, my brother is the Earl of Saffron." Her eyes widened when they moved over the handsome stranger. The fact that he was tall and broad shouldered was not lost on her. His raven-wing black hair glistened in the sunlight that streamed in the window, and his eyes were a most unusual color of green.

Dakota bowed from the waist, not in the best of moods for being kept waiting. "I am honored to meet you, my lady, but my business is with your brother and not with you."

She moved around Dakota, smiling. "I like a man who speaks his mind. You are a tall one, aren't you?" When Dakota did not answer, she continued, "We had heard that the old Marquess's grandson had arrived at Weatherford Hall, but I never thought you would be so young and handsome."

Dakota returned her smile. "Are you trying to flirt with me, my lady?"

She threw back her head and laughed, showing perfect white teeth. "Of course I am. It's not often we have a man with your connections come for a visit. I would be a fool not to take advantage of the situation."

Dakota was amused by her honesty. "I am flattered, but I really must insist on talking to your brother. You see, my time is limited."

Her hooped gown swayed gracefully as she came up beside him. "Martin knows you are here. He sent me to entertain you until he can come himself." Her hand moved up the arm of his coat. "London made. I so

222

seldom get to London these days." She placed her arm through Dakota's. "Perhaps you would like to tell me all about the balls, parties, and masquerades of last season."

His voice showed his irritation. "I know nothing of such things."

"I have heard it said that you are from America and were raised by Indians. Can that be true?"

"Yes, it is true."

She toyed with the button on his coat, and looked up at him through lowered lashes. "Then you must be very fierce."

Laughter came from the man who stood in the doorway. "You will have to forgive my sister, Lord Remington. You see, she is always so susceptible to a handsome face."

Rye did not seem to take exception to her brother's words. "As you have probably concluded, my lord, that is my brother, Martin."

The Earl was of the same dark coloring as his sister, of medium height, and handsome in an ostentatious manner.

Lord Saffron's dark eyes held no humor. "Leave us, Rye. If I'm not mistaken, Lord Remington and I have business to discuss."

She released Dakota's arm and gave him a soft smile before turning to her brother. "Be nice to him, Martin, and don't scare him away. Heaven knows there are too few real men around here as it is."

Dakota stared at the Earl of Saffron. Green eyes and brown eyes met in mortal combat, and they both knew there would be trouble between them.

Martin moved over to the sideboard and poured two glasses of bourbon and handed one to his guest.

"No, thank you, but please feel free to drink yourself. I have never acquired a taste for liquor."

Martin looked astounded. He had heard of the Viscount's background with the American Indians, so he hadn't expected a man of such high intellect and refinement. "My, God, man, where were you raised — in a monastery? I don't trust a man who won't drink with his friends."

"It remains to be seen whether or not you and I will be friends. The matter I have come to discuss with you may very well cast us as enemies."

Martin saw cold strength in Dakota's green eyes. He quickly downed his glass of bourbon before he spoke. "If you have come to discuss fishing rights, you may be correct."

"I have."

Martin pointed to a chair. "You may as well sit down, this could take a while."

"No, thank you, I prefer to stand. What I have to say to you won't take very long."

Martin plopped down in a chair and smiled. "I'm listening."

"It's very simple. The fishermen from your village are encroaching on the territory of the fishermen from my village. If you will intercede and put a stop to the encroachment, then there will be nothing further for us to discuss."

"And if I don't?"

"Then you will suffer the consequences." The threat was spoken softly, but it held a ring of truth.

Martin laughed. "Do you think I fear a threat coming from you? Your people have been left too long to survive on their own. I am willing to bet you couldn't rally enough loyal men to follow you if you offered them all the fishing rights in Cornwall. I believe that if it comes to a fight, you will discover you stand alone."

"I thought to go to the magistrate, but I discovered you have the man in your pocket."

"Yes, he's a fool, and easy to manipulate. He sees only what I want him to see."

"Am I to take it that you do not intend to restrain your fishermen?"

"Restrain them, hell, I'm encouraging them to fish wherever they please. The waters belong to no one."

Dakota's voice was like tempered steel. "That's where you are wrong. I have seen an old document that was signed by my great-grandfather and your uncle. I know the contract is binding, because I consulted a solicitor before I came here."

Martin traced the cut-glass pattern on his glass. "I do not feel compelled to honor a document that was signed before I was born."

"May I ask you a question?"

"Of course."

"Why will you not cooperate on this? I warn you, if you don't, the day will come when you will regret your actions here today."

The Earl exhibited a pompous air. "I doubt it. You see, our waters are fished out, while your waters are brimming with fish." Martin's laughter was insulting. "It looks like a fight, and I relish a good contest of wills."

Dakota nodded grimly. "I had hoped to avoid a confrontation, but you leave me little choice. As of today, I am warning you, keep your fishermen out of our waters, or be prepared to suffer the consequences."

Martin lazily flicked a piece of lint from his coat. "You know the way to the door; you can show yourself out."

Dakota saw the challenge in the man's eyes. "So be it, Lord Saffron." Dakota walked to the door and paused. "What happens now will be on your head, not mine."

Chapter Eighteen

Dakota made his way through Weatherford Village with a resolute gleam in his eyes. Women watched his progress from their windows with hope in their hearts. Would the young lord champion their cause? Or would he turn a deaf ear to their plight as his grandfather had?

Dakota walked past the old Norman church toward the sandy shore where several small fishing boats had been beached. His eyes moved over the men who were watching him skeptically.

When Dakota spotted an old fisherman, sitting alone mending his net, he walked in his direction.

The old man looked up at the young lord with little interest, dropped his eyes, and continued mending his net. Dakota seated himself on the edge of a beached boat, watching the gnarled hands aptly perform the age-old task.

The fisherman took a draw on his pipe. "Be you not feared that you'll muss those fancy britches you're wearing?" the old man asked with obvious scorn.

Dakota ignored the fisherman's pointed remark.

"You know who I am?"

The old man took another draw on his pipe, his faded gray eyes seeming to look right through Dakota. "I know. I was told you came into our village yesterday and pretended to be interested in our troubles. I saw the wagon load of food you sent last evening. If you think to appease us and dismiss your obligations by handing out food, then you are no different from your grandfather."

Dakota allowed the old man to have his say, then he asked, "Who might you be?"

"Name's Will Simonton."

"Do you mind if I call you Will?"

The old man didn't bother to look up, but kept on with his labor. "It's your right."

"Who is the oldest man in the village, Will?"

Now he had the man's attention. "That would be me. I turned ninety-one this past spring."

"Then you are the one I want to talk to. In the Indian village where I grew up, the wisest and most esteemed men were the elders. The young warriors often went to them for advice. That is why I have sought you out. I need your wisdom."

Will looked at Dakota with interest, but he was still leery of him. The gentry were a race apart from the common people and Will had often found them self-serving and deceptive. He surely didn't trust this one who hadn't even been born in England. "What could I tell you that would be of interest to you?"

"You could tell me from the beginning about the feud between this village and Saffron Village."

The old salt dropped his net, his eyes reflective as he tried to recall the day the trouble had begun. "It started with small things at first. I think the Earl was testing us, wanting to see if his lordship, the Marquess, had any interest in us. When the Marquess didn't come to our rescue, the incidents grew bolder, until finally they had us shore-bound. Course, when we complained, we was told by the Marquess that we could always fish in deep water. But our boats aren't built for deep-water fishing."

The old man looked at Dakota slyly. "Then the Marquess sent us a wagon load of food, and we ain't heard from him since."

Dakota's lips twitched. "I see. Tell me, did any of you try to regain your fishing rights on your own?"

Will drew himself up with dignity. "Course we did, but it weren't no good. We were too few, and they had their lord to stand with them." Will's eyes took on a sadness. "I had me a boat, she weren't nothing fancy, but I built her myself and she was a fine boat. I carved her name deep so it would last as long as the boat stayed afloat." The old man's eyes became misty. "Named her the *Annie,* after my long dead missus."

"Where is the *Annie,* Will?"

Anger twisted the old fisherman's face. "She was took from me. They came boldly up on shore and took her. When me and my grandson tried to get her back—he . . . Rob was shot dead!"

"I take it you did not get the boat back?"

"No, but I see her sometimes. They never even bothered to change her name. It's almost as if they was flaunting her in my face. It eats at my guts that I can't have what rightly belongs to me." He held up his hands in a hopeless gesture. "I'm an old man. I tried to tell the younger men that if we fight to get our fishing rights

229

back, even if we lost, we would get back our self-worth." He shook his head sadly, looking pensive. "But they don't listen to an old man like me. I don't know that I blame them."

Anger pulsed through Dakota's mind. He felt a kinship with this man and the other villagers, who had been neglected by the Marquess. Dakota didn't understand why his grandfather had not stood behind these people. His Arapaho background had taught him that every member of the tribe was a part of a family. His feeling of kinship and responsibility now extended to every man, woman, and child of this village. In Dakota's mind, it was as if he were the chief, and the village was under his protection. He would not rest until everything was put to rights.

"I'm listening to you, Will. What do you think we should do?"

The old man's eyes projected hope. "Did you say *we?* Are ye going to help us?"

"Will, you have my word that if it is in my power, you will once more stand master of the *Annie*. It's time someone taught the Earl and his underlings a lesson in manners."

Dakota glanced across the water, knowing that their foe's village lay just out of sight. "Surely there are some good men in Saffron Village. They can't all be under the Earl's heel."

"Well, you see, he has this strange hold over them. I've known some men that had this same uncanny ability to make men do what they wanted them to. You can't beat the Earl until you best him at his own game."

Dakota noticed movement out of the corner of his eye. Glancing up, he saw the other fishermen of the village walking toward him, and they did not look as if they were coming to pass pleasantries.

Will shook his head. "They be bound for trouble, Your Lordship," he said respectfully. "Let me do the talking."

Dakota stood up, waiting for the men to reach him. "No, Will, they have grievances to air, and it's time someone listened to them. Yesterday they were vague in their demands. Perhaps today, they will be more inclined to tell me what is on their minds."

The men's faces were surly as they circled Dakota. Hubert Clowes, a thickset redheaded man, who had appointed himself spokesman for the group, expressed their complaints. "We're here to have some answers, my lord. We heard that you was putting new roofs on the tenant farmers' huts. What are you going to do for us? We got pride, and we don't want handouts or wagons of food. We just want what's rightfully ours."

Dakota crossed his arms over his chest, and silence fell as he looked at each man in turn. "How badly do you want your fishing grounds back?" he asked pointedly. "How far are you willing to go to settle the wrong that has been done to you?"

There was mumbling among the crowd. "We can't do nothing by ourselves — we already tried that. We got six widows in this village to moan the ones that died to prove that — my sister lost her man in the last tiff. There's not a man here who didn't lose someone or something because of the Earl."

Dakota nodded in understanding. "I intend to be in this with you, but only if you are committed to take the fight all the way. I cannot do this alone. We will have to work together if we are to succeed."

Astonishment and disbelief mingled with hope on the men's rugged faces. They had stood alone for so long, been beaten into the dust, ignored by Dakota's grandfather, and it was difficult to believe that someone was willing to help them. Acceptance came hard to them.

"How do we know we can trust you?" Hubert wanted to know.

"After what you have all been through, I don't expect you to take me on faith. I realize I'll have to prove myself to you."

Each man looked into clear, earnest green eyes and saw the truth. "Will you make our fight yours?" Hubert asked.

"I will."

Several shouts went up, and the leather-faced fishermen smiled and patted each other on the backs. They had found a champion! They no longer stood alone; they had hope in their hearts.

"The Earl is a strong one, my lord," Hubert warned. "You will have to look to your back and your front."

Will Simonton grinned, and his faded old eyes sparkled. "The Earl won't be so strong when he comes up against us now. I got this feeling that Saffron Village is about to pay homage to our Viscount."

"What do we do?" Hubert asked, his eyes bright, his chest heaving with excitement. "When do we go to Saffron Village and take them on?"

"We don't go to them, we make them come to us," Dakota said in a voice that carried to every man. "Then we ambush them. I know several Indian tricks that just may turn the tide of battle in our favor."

The men gathered in closer as Dakota explained the

meaning of ambush as the Arapaho had taught it to him.

Breanna heard the sound of a rider, so she ran to the front of the house, hoping it would be Dakota. When she wrenched open the door and saw it was Levi, the welcoming smile froze on her face.

Levi chuckled. "Sorry to disappoint you, my lady, but it's just me and bearing ill tidings at that. Dakota sent me to tell you he wouldn't be back for several days, and he asked me to escort you back to the big house."

Disappointment showed on Breanna's face. "What has happened, Levi?"

"Well, you know about the trouble with the neighboring villagers? Dakota don't aim to stop until he gets our villagers' fishing rights back."

Breanna smiled because the old hunter had included himself in the feud. "Come in, Levi. I had a special dinner prepared for Dakota, but since he isn't here, will you share it with me?"

Levi's eyes lit up. "I'd be proud to be your guest. Besides, I haven't had a jealous husband mad at me for nigh on to twenty years."

Breanna felt some of her disappoinment fade as Levi charmed her with his crusty wit. "We shan't tell my husband that I sent all the servants home and it was just the two of us for dinner."

"Now that sounds right nice, my lady."

"It always sounds like 'my lady' sticks on your tongue, Levi. Why don't you call me Breanna?"

He flashed her a smile that made his faded blue eyes shine. "Dakota will surely be jealous now. Already his wife wants me to call her by her intimate name."

Over dinner, Levi charmed Breanna with tales of the American wilderness. She was spellbound as he talked of Dakota's life in the Arapaho village. But she noticed he avoided mentioning Running Deer, and she could not bring herself to ask him about the dead Indian maiden.

As the afternoon sun streaked low on the horizon, Levi and Breanna walked in the woods.

"Levi, I have heard many stories about trappers and hunters in the American wilderness, and you do not fit the picture I have painted in my mind."

He chuckled. "Are you referring to my manner of speech?"

"Well . . . yes. While you don't sound like an Englishman, your speech is refined at times."

"It's very simple. My papa was a schoolmaster, and I learned at his knee."

"How ever did you end up trapping. Levi?"

"There's no mystery about that. I had itchy feet and didn't like being confined to a town." He squinted his eyes up at the sun. "There can't be more than three hours of daylight left. I'd better get you over to the big house."

"I'm not going, Levi. I intend to wait right here for Dakota."

"He won't like it."

"My mind is made up. When you see him, you can tell him where to find me."

Levi saw the stubborn tilt of her chin and the determined look in her eyes, and he knew it would do no good to try and dissuade her. "At least let me take you back to the lodge, Breanna."

"No, I want to stay here in the woods for a while." She smiled at him. "I'm glad we had this time to get to know one another better. I can see why Dakota counts you his best friend."

He grinned. "I can tell he's going to be mighty partial to you, too. I wasn't too sure how you two would get on when I first heard he was marrying a real lady by birth; now I couldn't think of a better match than you and Dakota."

The teasing light left Levi's eyes and he became serious. "Dakota deserves happiness in his life. He's had more than his share of unhappiness."

Levi realized he was being too serious, and he grinned. "Of course, he wears unhappiness well. I never knew him to complain. Now I best be off, we got things to do tonight. If Dakota's plan works, the fishermen from Weatherford will soon be back in their own fishing grounds."

"Will there be danger?"

"Not so as you'd notice it. Don't go worrying that pretty head of yours."

Breanna raised an arched eyebrow. "Do all men from your America cut their women out of their lives and try to pacify them by telling them not to worry?" she asked.

Levi winked at her. "It doesn't always work with the American woman, and I have a feeling it isn't going to work with you." He tipped his cap. "I'll tell your husband that you decided to stay here instead of returning to the big house. Might as well let him know right off that he might suggest something to you but he can't give you orders."

Breanna watched Levi move down the path, his head held high while he whistled a merry tune. What a strange man he was, but she liked him. The old hunter was a crafty man, for she realized that while he had shared many things with her about Dakota's life, he had actually told her very little.

Between waking and sleeping, Breanna heard the wind blowing through the tree branches, its powerful gusts making an eerie sound. She came fully awake now, her senses alert to a different noise. Someone was in the house with her!

Sitting up straight, she strained her ears. She had sent all the servants away and was alone in the lodge. Why hadn't she thought to bolt the doors?

A floorboard creaked in the hallway, and she leaped out of bed and moved quickly into a shadow, her heart pounding, her breathing labored. Someone was definitely in the house with her and was taking pains not to awaken her.

Reaching forward in the dark, she felt around on the dressing table until her fingers closed around her hairbrush. Drawing on all her courage, she stood motionless, waiting for the intruder to show himself. The door opened a crack, and she saw the shadowy form of a man move into the room and stand over her bed.

Breanna flew at the man and was quickly caught in a viselike grip and flung over his head, landing on the bed. She quickly rolled over and came to her knees, ready to do battle with the intruder.

Dakota grabbed her wrist and brought Breanna forward against his body. He felt her tense body relax when she saw it was him. Prying the hairbrush from her fingers, he tossed it on the bed. "How did you plan

236

to defend yourself with a hairbrush, Breanna?" he asked with an amused smile.

Now that her fear had ebbed, a feeling of irritation took its place. "Why did you come sneaking up on me? What did you expect me to do . . . run?"

"Running would have been far wiser than staying to take on an intruder with such a flimsy weapon. What I expected of you was that you be at Weatherford Hall. When Levi told me that you had disobeyed my orders, I came here to find out why."

He could see her face clearly now, and he watched the red-golden curtain of hair swirl around her face.

"I wasn't aware that you had issued a command, Dakota. Don't expect me to behave like one of your Indian women and obey all your orders unquestioningly."

"If you were an Indian woman, then there would be no question that you would do as I said."

Dakota had never spoken to Breanna in such a sharp tone, and her lips trembled. "How fortunate for me that I am English. You can just leave, because I don't want you here if you are going to be like this."

She held herself rigid as he pulled her into his arms. "Don't send me away, Breanna. I would much rather spend what remains of the night here with you." She could feel him shake with laughter. "Besides, I may need you to protect me with your hairbrush."

Breanna tried to remember that she was incensed with Dakota, but his warm breath stirring her hair made her forget everything but his presence.

"Say I can remain with you," he whispered in a deep voice.

Her arms went around his neck, and she nestled her

cheek to his. "Please stay," she answered. "I don't want you to leave."

Before she could say more, his mouth came down on hers. Like a spear, his tongue darted between her lips, probing and arousing her deepest feelings.

He laid her back on the bed and joined her there. While his mouth ravaged hers, his hands grew bolder in their quest.

Pleasurable feelings took over Breanna's reasoning when she felt him quickly dispose of his clothing.

With a tug, Dakota moved her nightgown up over her head and tossed it onto the floor with his own clothing. Shyly she went into his opened arms and he crushed her to him.

"Breanna, Breanna," he breathed in her ear. "You are in my blood, and I need you."

Like a delicate rosebud, she opened herself to him, and he again took her on a voyage of sensuous feelings. Time and time again, he took her body to the brink of surrender, until at last she lay exhausted in his arms, her heart pounding in her ears.

Clasping her hand in his, Dakota raised it to his lips and kissed each finger. "It gets better every time I am with you, Breanna. I can hardly wait to discover some new joy with you."

She nestled her face against his neck, feeling sleepy and fulfilled, and warmed by his beautiful words. With a soft yawn, she sighed contentedly and felt herself drifting off to sleep.

Long after Breanna had fallen asleep, Dakota lay awake, holding her and staring into the night. Some of the confusion he had felt when he first came to England had dissipated, but he was still confused about his fiery-haired wife. Yes, he had drawn an answering fire from her body when he had made love to her, but then he knew what women liked, and she was such an innocent.

A pang of guilt settled on his shoulders as he tried to recall Running Deer's features. All he could remember was a pair of soft brown eyes and a ready laugh. He thought of Rye Saffron and how she had somehow reminded him of Running Deer.

Glancing down at Breanna, Dakota stared at the dark lashes resting against her pale cheek. He pressed his lips against her cheek, knowing the ache in his heart was caused by his need for this woman. She was life to him. She was his world. He wondered if he would ever reach her heart.

Dakota knew he faced danger tomorrow when the clash between the two neighboring villages came to a head. Before, he had never thought of the dangers of battle. But now, he had so much to live for.

Chapter Nineteen

When Breanna awoke the next morning, Dakota was not beside her. The only evidence of his presence the night before was the impression his head had made in the pillow. She touched her lips and smiled. How wonderful it was to be his wife.

While Breanna fastened her gown up the front, she hummed a happy tune. But the song froze on her lips when she remembered that there might be a confrontation between Dakota and the Earl of Saffron today.

She dashed to the window and saw that a heavy fog had rolled in from the ocean, blanketing the land in its misty darkness. Breanna breathed a sigh of relief. Surely there would be no conflict on a day such as this. As the gray mass swirled toward land, she had the feeling she was being swallowed up in its depth. Tears hovered just behind her eyes, although she could not have said why.

Dakota moved up the stairs at Weatherford Hall, calling to John. When his startled cousin came out of his bedroom into the hallway, he looked at Dakota questioning.

"John, how much authority do I have to settle disputes concerning Weatherford Village and the village at Saffron?"

John was reflective for a moment. "Unlimited power," he said with assurance. "Your grandfather doesn't concern himself with what goes on here."

"That's what I wanted to hear."

Before John could ask what Dakota was talking about, his cousin had moved quickly down the stairs and disappeared out the front door. John shrugged his shoulders and went back to bed, thinking Dakota must want to thatch another tenant's roof.

With a curl to his lips, the Earl of Saffron read the note the messenger had just delivered to him from the Viscount of Remington. Crushing it in his hand, he swore aloud.

"Damn that young upstart. If he thinks he can intimidate me, he is mistaken. I will not be harassed by him. For generations the Saffrons have lived in the shadow of the great Remingtons of Weatherford Hall. It felt good to take their villagers and bend them to my will. I will not lose the advantage I have over them just because Lord Dakota Remington threatens me."

Lady Rye Saffron glanced up from her letter writing. "Whatever are you talking about, Martin? What does the note say?"

"It says, my dear sister, that he, the Viscount of Remington, will be fishing the waters that we have claimed as our own. He hints that if I don't like it, I will know where to find him."

Her laughter was mocking. "Your nose is out of joint because Dakota Remington is *her* son. It still pains you that Holden Remington took the lovely Cilia from you, doesn't it?"

"Little you know about it. You weren't even born when they were married."

She smiled maliciously. "Do you think his lordship is aware that the feud you have perpetrated over the years is your small-minded way of getting even with the Remingtons because Holden Remington married the woman you fancied for your wife?"

Martin's dark eyes narrowed. He picked up a whip from the end table and slapped the pearl handle across his palm. "It doesn't matter. I will make sure the son knows I detest his father before I squeeze the life out of him. It's a pity death claimed Holden Remington before I could avenge our honor."

"*Our* honor?" Rye questioned. "As you pointed out, I was not even born when Holden Remington whisked your lady love away, so my honor is not involved."

"You have enjoyed the benefits we have reaped from dominating the fishing trade in this area," her brother reminded her.

She glanced down at her three-year-old gown. "Not so you would notice, Martin. We barely have money to keep this house up, let alone keep clothing on our backs." Her eyes narrowed. "That's what really bothers you, isn't it? You live next door to wealth beyond anything you can imagine, and it galls you that we are in the thralls of poverty."

Martin had been so deep in thought that he had not heard his sister's goading. "I will bring this young pup to his knees and make him crawl in the dust. Before I'm done, he will beg me to kill him just to put him out of his agony."

Rye laughed bitterly. "You should watch out, brother. It may be he that gains the advantage over you." She tormented him further. "You have told me repeatedly that the lovely Cilia had green eyes. Can it be that the young Remington reminds you of her . . . hmm?"

Martin's eyes flashed angrily. "Don't provoke me, Rye. If anything happens to me, you will surely find yourself out in the street."

"Why not allow the feud to die? I would like to get to know Dakota Remington better."

"And his wife?" Martin asked acidly.

"A wife has never stood in my way before. I doubt if this one would either. I have heard this marriage was arranged by the old Marquess, so I doubt it is a love match."

Martin's eyes became secretive. "If I cannot gain the advantage today, perhaps you are the lovely tool I will use to bring Cillia's son to his knees."

"No one uses me, brother dear. If I decide to go after the Viscount of Remington, it won't be because of some old grudge you carry against his mother and father." Her eyes sparkled with fire. "No, I will go after him because he's a man." She turned her eyes on her brother. "A real man, Martin. Not one who is eaten up with bitterness and revenge."

"Don't get too interested in him, Rye. He may not be around too long."

"You play your game, Martin, and I'll play mine. We'll see who gets what they want."

Martin laughed. "It was obvious that you were panting after him, but as I saw it, he didn't appear all that interested in you."

Rye's eyes glowed with an inner light. "We shall see . . . we shall indeed see."

Dakota climbed into a small boat, knowing the gauntlet had been thrown down and he now had to wait for the Earl of Saffron to pick it up. The trap had been baited and all was in readiness.

Dakota had instructed his men on what they were to do. By now, he knew they were ready to board their boats, waiting to launch an attack as soon as the signal was given.

With the dependable Levi leading the fishermen, Dakota knew he had left nothing to chance.

Alone, Dakota rowed the fishing boat away from the shore. The small craft rocked back and forth with each restless wave that splashed against it. Dakota had stripped down to his breechcloth, knowing he would be swimming under water and his clothes would only hamper him.

The pale yellow brightness of the sun gave off an unearthly glow as Dakota settled down to wait for his adversary.

Will Simonton had given him an ancient horn that had been left behind by some fair-haired Viking marauders in some long ago, bygone raid. When Dakota blew on the horn, it would be the signal for Levi and the others to spring into action.

Moments hung in the air with timeless insignificance. Dakota found himself counting the number of waves that slapped against his small craft. That the foe would come, he had little doubt. He had nerves of iron and was willing to patiently wait for his challenge to be met.

Dakota's keen hearing picked up the sound of muffled oars slapping against the water. The fog had lifted somewhat, and he could see ten feet in every direction. He waited, biding his time until the sound came closer, then he raised the horn and gave a mighty blast.

Tossing the fishing nets overboard, Dakota waited for the boats to come into view. Like phantom ships, they came out of the fog. First one, two, six, eleven he counted, and each manned by six men.

He smiled and waved to them as if he were greeting old friends. "The fishing's good this afternoon. I suspect the fog has brought the fish to the surface."

Dakota glanced past each man until he eyes locked with the Earl's. Martin Saffron's face was murderous, and Dakota wondered how a man with his responsibilities allowed himself to be caught up in this pathetic, vindictive squabble.

"Why don't you all join me, Lord Saffron?" Dakota baited. "It's lonesome out here all alone—I could use the company."

"Don't play games with me, Remington. We both know that I am here at your invitation," the Earl shouted.

"It's not too late to talk about this like gentlemen," Dakota answered, stalling for time. He knew it was only moments away from a confrontation. He glanced just behind the Earl's boat and saw Levi's head bob up out of the water. Dakota smiled to himself, knowing his lordship was about to take a swim.

Dakota had chosen the strongest swimmers from his village to lead the attack. He watched them swimming near the foe, knowing the moments the boats were overturned, pandemonium would break out.

When the first boat was overturned, Dakota dove under the water. Bullets were whizzing all about him as he surfaced near the Earl's boat and watched the man splash into the water when Levi tipped his boat over.

Yells and screams could be heard as boat after boat met the same fate. When all the Earl's men were in the water, Dakota saw that many of them couldn't swim. His men had been instructed to help those that could not swim, because he did not want one single life lost here today.

Dakota swam to where he had seen the Earl of Saffron fall into the water. The Earl cursed loudly, and then the man called out in a frightened voice, "I can't swim. Help me!" He went under, sputtering and cursing.

Dakota dove under the water and dragged the submerged man to the surface. Martin was fighting to catch his breath and flailing his arms, dragging Dakota under with him. With superior strength, Dakota pulled the man to the surface. Trying to avoid the man's thrashing arms, Dakota delivered a hard punch to the frantic man's jaw. He was grateful when the Earl fell unconscious, making the rescue far less hazardous for them both.

"Destroy all enemy boats save one," Dakota called to Levi. "Find the *Annie,* and bring her to shore undamaged."

As luck would have it, by the time Dakota reached shore with the unconscious Earl, the fog had completely lifted, and it was easy to see the chaos that was taking place.

As his men dragged the half-drowned men from Saffron Village onto shore, Dakota stood up and called out to them.

"Listen and hear me, men of Saffron. We could have allowed all of you to drown today, but that is not our way. Know in your hearts that if any of you ever trespasses on our fishing waters again, we will not be so lenient. Take warning, and stay in your own waters."

Dakota turned to one of the Earl's men and pointed to Martin Saffron, who was still unconscious. "Take your lord home, and when he regains consciousness, give him this message. Tell him that I will no longer tolerate his aggressive attitudes. Leave my villagers in peace, and we'll leave you alone."

"What about our boats?" one of the younger fishermen of Saffron asked.

"Count them as the losses of war, because they have all been destroyed. My men agreed that it was far better to destroy your boats than to take your lives." He glanced around him. "Are all you men of Saffron accounted for?"

The youth who had asked about the boats took a quick count and nodded. "We are."

"Then go home, and remember this day as long as you live. Tell your children and your grandchildren that the fishermen from Weatherford counted coup on you today."

"What is that?" the youth asked.

Dakota smiled. "Counting coup is an American Indian war game where the bravest prove themselves worthy by touching, and not slaying, their enemies."

The men from Saffron stared with respect at the near-naked Viscount of Remington, counting themselves fortunate that they still lived. The coldness in Lord Remington's green eyes clearly told them that they could very easily have lost their lives today.

It was a pathetic group of men that gathered up their conquered lord and moved in the direction of their village. Defeat was written on their faces, but they had learned a valuable lesson that day. None of them were anxious to meet this young Viscount in the heat of battle.

A shout went up from Dakota's men, and soon the women and children joined the victors.

Dakota watched the enemy move away, knowing they had suffered a defeat that would take them years to recover from. There was no joy in his heart at the victory, only sadness that men, whether white or Indian, should prey upon their brothers.

Dakota was quickly surrounded with happy villagers, whose faces gleamed with pride.

"Your lordship did it! You showed them what for," Hubert Clowes called out.

"Yes, *we* showed them," Dakota agreed, "because we stood together. I don't think you will have trouble from those fishermen for a long time to come."

Shouts went up as the villagers cheered their lord.

Dakota smiled as he watched Will Simonton lovingly trace the name of the *Annie* with a bony finger. The smile of gratitude and respect the old fisherman bestowed upon Dakota said more than mere words.

There was deference mixed with admiration on all the men's faces.

Dakota moved among them, accepting a clap on the

back, a handshake, and nods from those who were too shy to come forward. He held up his hand, asking for silence because he felt there was more to be said.

"The time for grievances is past. Put your bitterness behind you, and resurrect your pride in your fishing trade. Do not harshly chastise your neighbors from Saffron, because by winning today, you can afford to be generous toward them."

Like children, the villagers listened to the young Viscount's words, finding them just and merciful. In silence, they watched Dakota mount his horse and ride away beside his friend, Levi.

For many generations to come, the villagers and their descendants would talk of this day's victory and of the young lord who led them in their fight.

Chapter Twenty

It had been three weeks since the confrontation with the Earl and his villagers. Word came from Weatherford Village that the fishermen were once again fishing their waters, thus bringing prosperity back to their families.

Levi had told Breanna some of what had transpired that eventful day, since Dakota seemed reluctant to discuss the incident with her. She was awed by her husband's understanding of the villagers' plight, and his quick solution to their problem.

The last time she and Dakota had ridden into Weatherford Village, Breanna had been aware that the atmosphere had changed. It was as if the village had been reborn. Men were mending their nets and repairing their boats, making ready to set out to sea, while the women and children joyously went about their daily tasks.

The villagers had rallied around Dakota and Breanna, welcoming them with loud cheers and smiles. The pride Breanna saw on the women's faces was echoed on her own. It was a moment she was never to forget.

Breanna and Dakota still resided at the hunting lodge, which she secretly thought of as their honeymoon cottage. She dreaded the day they would return to Weatherford Hall, because at the lodge she had her husband all to herself.

Much of their days were spent in search of knowledge. Dakota had infected her with his unquenchable hunger for learning. The floor in their bedroom was littered with books that he had brought from the library at Weatherford Hall. She would often find him bent over some thick tome, engrossed in whatever he was reading.

Breanna loved the times Dakota would discuss with her what he had read in a certain book and encourage her to express her opinion. Often, he would put his books aside and take her in his arms. She liked those times most of all.

Her swimming lessons had become a nightly ritual. She would wait anxiously for the servants to depart for the day so she and Dakota could swim together. By now, she prided herself on being an able swimmer.

At night, Dakota would take her in his arms,

and she would surrender to his passionate love-making. Happiness bloomed in her heart, to nurture and grow as her love for this man deepened.

The only dark cloud on Breanna's horizon was the fact that Dakota had never said he loved her.

There were moments when Breanna could feel a gap between them, and she wondered if it was because he was remembering the dead Indian maiden, Running Dear.

Dakota had gone hunting with Levi, and Breanna found time heavy on her hands, so she decided to go for a walk in the woods.

Removing her heavy crinoline and ruffled petticoats so they would not hinder her progress, she pulled her white shawl about her shoulders. As she moved down the path at the back of the lodge, her footsteps quickened.

Fall was in the air, and the leaves had turned to brilliant reds and warm yellows, and the musty smell of damp undergrowth filled Breanna's senses. As she walked along, she felt in tune with nature. A chattering magpie on a high branch and a precocious squirrel who scampered up a tree trunk both caught her attention. She was startled when a deer darted in front of her. The magnificent animal bounded through the air with a gracefulness that left Breanna staring in awe.

She had little time to think before someone who

was in pursuit of the animal leaped from behind a wide oak tree and knocked her to the ground.

"Breanna," Dakota asked with concern, "are you injured?"

She shook her head, while he steadied her on her feet.

"No, I am but winded—" She stared down at his moccasins, before lifting her gaze to his face. In shocked confusion, she saw that his chest was bare and that he wore buckskin breeches. Around his dark hair, he wore a leather-beaded headband.

Breanna stared at her husband in disbelief. When her eyes locked with his, she saw amusement in the green depths.

"I was in pursuit of an animal deer, and instead, I find a human 'dear' has become my quarry."

Her confusion did not lessen. She was accustomed to Dakota looking like lord of the manor. This man was not her husband; this was someone she did not know. She took a hesitant step backward. "Your . . . I don't know . . ."

He looked at her sadly, understanding her bewilderment.

"I'm afraid this is the real me, Breanna," he explained. "The man you have come to know as your husband is merely what others expect me to be."

"I don't understand, Dakota."

He looked at her proudly. "I have lived my life

253

as an Indian, and I have told you before that I make no apologies to anyone for the man I am—least of all, my own wife."

Breanna's eyes moved down his tanned chest, to the beaded belt he wore about his waist.

"I ask no apology of you, Dakota," she flared, her chin raised defiantly. "I was merely taken by surprise."

He reached out and gripped her shoulders. "Look at me, Breanna, so you will know this about me. For all of my life, I have lived, thought, and breathed as an Arapaho. With the exception of Levi, and Murphy, the man who ran a trading post, and an occasional white trapper that happened into my village, I knew no white men. I have learned to ride a horse with a saddle—though I have to confess I would still rather ride bareback—I have learned to eat my meat with a fork, but I do not think it makes me a better person, and it does not mean that the Indian heart beating within me has become white."

"I thought you had left your Indian ways behind when you came to England, Dakota."

He took a deep breath and reached for her, pulling her into the crook of his arm. "Breanna, I have always prided myself on being able to achieve anything I put my mind to. When I decided to come to England, I already had a good command of the language, and I could read and write English. But had you known me only a few short months ago, you would have called me a savage." He smiled slightly. "In fact, I believe you did call me that on one occasion."

"Now that I know you, I would never think that," she said, only slightly mollified.

"Forgive me, Breanna. Knowing you as I do, I should never have accused you of prejudice. I do so humbly ask your pardon. You will have to understand that inside I am the same man I was before John smoothed off my rough edges. Underneath the finely tailored clothing I wear, I am still an Arapaho warrior."

She reached up and touched his cheek. "I accept your apology, and I accept you for what you are. Dakota," she said earnestly, "I am your wife, and I like the man you are."

"Like?"

"Yes, I . . ." she stammered, unwilling to tell him that her feelings for him went far deeper. "We haven't known one another very long, Dakota . . ."

His laughter was warm. "Not long, but intimately, Breanna." His eyes darkened as he gazed at her lovely face. "Very intimately."

The tone of his voice, the passion that made his green eyes sparkle, the touch of his hand, all played a part in making Breanna tremble with frenzied delight. When he turned her to face him, bringing her body to fit tightly against him, she surrendered completely to his embrace.

They stood together while the setting sun painted the glorious autumn colors with a purple hue. Breanna felt the invisible bond that tied her to Dakota. He might not love her, but he could not deny the passion that he felt for her.

As Breanna's eyes moved over her husband's handsome face, she could not imagine any woman not being moved by this man. She watched, fascinated, as the bonds of civilization were stripped from him and he picked her up in his arms.

"I will show you how an Indian makes love to his woman," he whispered thickly in her ear.

He carried her off the path to a secluded glen and gently placed her down on a bed of soft leaves. Her world tilted crazily as he lay beside her, his hot lips playing with her silken lashes, while his wonderful hands moved slowly across her heaving breasts.

"Surely not here?" she asked only halfheartedly.

"Yes, here."

"But what about Levi?" she reminded him.

Laughter lit Dakota's eyes. "Let him find his own woman."

There was no chance for her to protest because his assault on her soft lips left her breathless and drained her of all opposition.

With expert ease he disrobed her, all the while kissing her to silence any further objection she might make.

Like brilliant patterns from a kaleidoscope, the

ACCEPT YOUR FREE GIFT AND EXPERIENCE MORE OF THE PASSION AND ADVENTURE YOU LIKE IN A HISTORICAL ROMANCE

Zebra Romances are the finest novels of their kind and are written with the adult woman in mind. All of our books are written by authors who really know how to weave tales of romantic adventure in the historical settings you love.

Because our readers tell us these books sell out very fast in the stores, Zebra has made arrangements for you to receive at home the four newest titles published each month. You'll never miss a title and home delivery is so convenient. With your first shipment we'll even send you a FREE Zebra Historical Romance as our gift just for trying our home subscription service. No obligation.

BIG SAVINGS AND FREE HOME DELIVERY

Each month, the Zebra Home Subscription Service will send you the four newest titles as soon as they are published. (We ship these books to our subscribers even before we send them to the stores.) You may preview them *Free* for 10 days. If you like them as much as we think you will, you'll pay just $3.50 each and *save $1.80 each month* off the cover price. *AND you'll also get FREE HOME DELIVERY.* There is never a charge for shipping, handling or postage and there is no minimum you must buy. If you decide not to keep any shipment, simply return it within 10 days, no questions asked, and owe nothing.

autumn leaves drifted down around them. But the beauty of nature was lost on the two lovers, who were only aware of one another. When Breanna looked into Dakota's face she saw a yearning that took her breath away and made her want to be closer, oh so much closer to him. He held her so tightly that she could feel the hammering of his heartbeat against her naked breasts.

Dakota cupped one hand behind Breanna's head to cushion her against the hard ground, making her aware of what a gentle and considerate lover he was.

Like the merging of land and sky, like the coming together of sea and shore, Dakota's and Breanna's bodies entwined, their hearts straining to become as one.

With gentle strokes, Dakota lifted Breanna to a world of passion — a world where she was lost to reality — a world where he was dominant and she submissive. As she looked deeply into his green eyes, she felt as though he was breathing for the both of them. This man whom she had not invited into her life was taking over and becoming her life. She knew she was in danger of losing her identity, but at the moment it did not matter. Nothing mattered but the wild sensations that robbed her of her strength and made her body tremble with anticipation.

Dakota's lips circled her ear and she heard his whispered words. "Would that I could always hold you as I now do, Breanna. At this moment you are completely in my power and you are mine."

"Yes," she agreed breathlessly, unwilling and unable to deny his power over her. "Yes, I am yours."

Breanna could feel the building tension within her body and she grasped Dakota's shoulders, wishing she could become a part of him. With a shuddering release, she felt herself floating back to earth and back to reality.

After the storm of passion subsided, Dakota still held her in his arms. They were both bound by the beauty that surrounded them.

"This is truly paradise." A wicked gleam brightened his green eyes. "You and paradise too. How fortunate can a man be?"

Breanna felt great sadness when the day came for her and Dakota to leave the hunting lodge.

She stood on the steps of Weatherford Hall, feeling as if she had been transported to another world. She would miss the intimacy and closeness she had shared with Dakota at the hunting lodge.

She tried to shake off the premonition that hung over her like a dark cloud, warning her that her happiness would be short-lived.

John greeted Dakota and Breanna warmly. With a wide smile, he kissed Breanna on the cheek. "At last, an end to my boredom," he said. "I have had enough of playing the country gentleman, and am ready for a diversion."

Dakota raised his eyebrow. "I did not expect you to be here, since Levi informed me you had gone off to London."

"London is a bore when one is without funds," John said with a slow shake of his head. "My financial circumstances force me to rely on your hospitality once more."

"I take it you have lost the money you won from the Henley brothers?"

John turned his pockets inside out to show Dakota they were empty. "I had a run of bad luck."

"I am always glad to see you, John," Dakota said. "Besides, I owe you a debt that cannot be repaid."

John laughed, his eyes dancing. "There you are wrong. I am sure I will think of a way."

Breanna excused herself and moved toward the stairs, knowing the two men must have things to discuss.

Both Dakota and John watched her move gracefully up the stairs.

"That is one beautiful woman, Dakota. You are a fortunate devil."

"You were saying," Dakota reminded him, not wanting to discuss his wife with anyone, including John. He was finding he was jealous of other men's attentions to Breanna, even faithful John's.

"Actually, I was only jesting about being

strapped. I have come for a very different reason. I fear I have some rather disheartening news."

"Grandfather? He's not dead, is he?"

"No, not dead yet, but he is sinking fast, and the doctor believes death is imminent. He slipped into unconsciousness before I left." John saw the stricken look on Dakota's face. "I am truly sorry, cousin, but your grandfather is an old man, and he has been ill for a long time."

Death had claimed so many of the people Dakota had loved. Even though he didn't know his grandfather well, he still felt a great sadness in his heart.

"Did my grandfather have any final instructions for me? Did he say what I was to do?" Dakota asked.

"No, he said nothing."

Once more, Dakota felt as if death had set him adrift. He knew that his grandfather's passing would place more responsibilities upon his shoulders and add invisible bonds which would tie him even more securely to England.

"I must go to London at once," Dakota decided, moving quickly out of the room in search of Baxley.

Breanna stood on the high cliff, looking down at the panoramic view of the Atlantic Ocean. The distant square sails of a ship reminded her of how limited her world had always been. She wondered if the ship might be bound for her husband's birthplace, America. Breanna sighed inwardly, wishing she could one day visit the land of Dakota's birth. She hoped the day would never come when he would want to return without her.

She heard soft footsteps and turned to see Dakota approaching. When he reached her side, he enclosed her in his arms.

"I watched you for a time, although you were unaware of it. I found myself jealous of your thoughts, for I was sure they were not of me."

She nestled her head against his shoulder. "As a matter of fact, I was thinking of you in a way. I was trying to imagine what America is like."

"What in particular were you imagining?"

She gazed up at him pensively. "I was wondering if you ever get lonesome to return to your country. I know you said the day might come when you would want to return."

She saw his jaw tighten. "Where is my country, Breanna? Is it this land of my father, or the land of my birth? Sometimes I don't know where I belong."

Breanna had never seen him like this, and she was surprised that he was allowing her this brief look into his mind.

"I wish I could help you find out, Dakota."

He smiled down at her. "You have already helped me more than you can imagine. If I had never come to England, I would never have known you, and that would be a great loss."

Breanna looked in the distance to the tall ship that had almost disappeared against the backdrop of the sky of azure blue.

Dakota was watching her face for some reaction. He could not know that her heart was drumming and her pulse was racing.

"Do you realize that I would still be living with my brother if . . . I had not married you, Dakota? I would not have wanted to miss knowing you either."

Hugging her to him, Dakota laughed, and she was glad to see he was in a lighter mood. "All Englishmen must be blind if they would allow a woman as lovely as you to remain unmarried."

"Do you think me beautiful?"

His eyes moved over her creamy skin to rest on her head, which was more golden than red in the sunlight. "Yes, you are extremely beautiful." He placed his finger over her lips. "My heart is filled with your loveliness."

A quick intake of breath tightened her throat. She searched his eyes, wanting him to say he loved her, but the words were never uttered. Dakota released her and glanced back toward the house, reminded of his reason for seeking her out.

"John has brought me the tragic news that my grandfather is gravely ill. I wanted to tell you that I am leaving for London immediately."

"Oh, Dakota, I am so sorry about your grandfather." She placed a hand on his arm, somehow feeling his pain and confusion, though he tried to hide it from her. "May I go with you?"

"No, it is better if you remain here," he said, wanting her with him but realizing he must travel quickly. "I have asked Levi to stay here and keep you company and see to your needs."

Breanna lifted her cool gaze to his face. Her heart was aching at the thought of being parted from him. She wanted to beg him to take her with him, but instead she smiled weakly. "When will you return?"

"I cannot say. Much depends on my grandfather."

She shrugged, trying to make light of her heartache. "Who will give me swimming lessons? Surely not Levi?"

Dakota's green eyes lit with an inner fire, and his jaw clamped down in an angry line. "You will allow no one to swim with you but me."

She was surprised at his sudden anger. "No, of course not, I was merely jesting."

He leveled his breathing. "I should think I will return within a fortnight," he said stiffly. His eyes moved over her as if he wanted to burn the vision of her into his mind. "Is that a riding habit you are wearing?" he asked, allowing his glance to sweep her wine-colored gown.

"Yes, it is."

"So you are going riding?"

"Yes, I thought I would."

He frowned. "Make sure you have either Levi or Frazier accompany you. I still remember the last time you took a fall, and I don't want you going alone. Promise me so I will not worry about you."

"I promise," she agreed, touched by his concern. She dared to hope he was going to miss her just a bit.

He raised her gloved hand to his lips. "I will think of you standing here waiting for my return, my Breanna."

Without a word, he dropped her hand and turned away. She resisted the urge to call him back. Why did she have this recurring feeling that something was about to happen that would tear her and Dakota apart?

Breanna watched Dakota disappear down the hill, wondering about this man who had swept through her life like a strong cleansing wind. When Dakota had first come to Weatherford Hall, he had appeared to be vulnerable and unsure of himself. But with each passing day, Breanna had watched him gain more confidence, while she had become less sure of herself. She wondered if she would ever hold his heart.

With a last look toward the horizon, she turned and made her way back toward the house. It was a beautiful autumn day, and she looked forward to taking Joya for a run. She would stay busy so she wouldn't miss Dakota so desperately.

Breanna refused to dwell on the lonely days and nights that yawned ahead of her.

Chapter Twenty-one

John stood near the foot of the bed while Dakota stood at his grandfather's side, staring down
at the aged, withered visage, wondering what his
grandfather had been like as a young man. All the
evidence pointed to his being a hard, cold man,
but had it always been so?

The doctor motioned to Dakota and John. "May
I speak to you both in the study?" he asked in a
whisper.

John and Dakota had followed the doctor to the
small study across the hallway from the Marquess's
bedchamber. Dakota waited for the doctor to
speak, knowing in his heart that his grandfather
could not live long in his wasted state.

The doctor, whose back was stooped and whose
eyes were dimmed with age, spoke in hushed
tones.

"I fear, my lord," the elderly doctor began, "that

your grandfather will not last out the night. It's a wonder that he has lasted this long. But if you don't mind my saying so, my lord, your grandfather was always a recalcitrant man. You see, I have been his doctor for forty years, and over that time we have become friends, so I speak from insight into his character."

"I never knew my grandfather. Was he always so stern?"

"No, not he. I would say your father's death made him bitter and uncaring. His lordship's goal in life was to have his line continue. Perhaps one day when you have been the Marquess for a long time, you will better be able to understand him."

The doctor excused himself and returned to the Marquess's bedside.

Deep in thought, Dakota frowned. The thought of being the bearer of the his grandfather's title made him tremble inside. "I have no wish to become the Marquess."

John knew what Dakota was feeling. "You will make a fine Marquess. You have already proven this by the way you handled the incident in Weatherford Village."

"I do not want the responsibility. And I don't intend to be forced into it."

John jammed his hands into his pockets, his eyes clouded with anger. "Damn it, Dakota, you owe it to future generations and to past ancestors. Whether you like it or not, you are about to become the head of the Remington family, and the rightful heir of the titles and properties."

Dakota had never known John to be so angry, and certainly not with him. "I am surprised that you feel so strongly about this, John."

"Just because I often wear the face of the jester does not mean I cannot feel as deeply about family pride and honor as the next person. Are you aware of what would happen to the title of Marquess of Weatherford if you refuse it?"

"No, suppose you tell me."

"The title will pass to Freddy Remington, a man in his fifties who still lives with his mother and takes orders from her. Cousin Freddy will not care for the villagers at Weatherford, and I don't care for Cousin Freddy. Besides, he has no one to succeed him. The title will stop with him."

Dakota's eyes grew cold. "That would leave you in a rather tight place, wouldn't it, John."

The two cousins stared at one another with anger.

Finally Dakota spoke. "I do not believe it is proper to talk about the title when the man who holds it is not yet dead," Dakota said, his anger deepening. I am surprised that you are not more sensitive toward your great-uncle, John."

"Regardless of what you think of me, I have always had the family's best interests at heart, Dakota. But in this, neither my great-uncle nor you matter. The title must endure."

John moved to the door, his jerky motions showing he was still incensed. "Now, if your lordship will excuse me, I will take my leave."

"Where are you going?" Dakota asked, knowing John had every reason to be angry with him.

"Out of London. I have no wish to be near you at the moment. You have things to consider, and a future to decide. It is hoped that you make the right decision."

The hansom cab pulled up in front of the Remington townhouse. Rye Saffron stepped out and sent the driver on his way, hoping no one of importance had seen her arrive by public transportation. Her lips curled in a snarl when she remembered the humiliation she had felt when her brother had been forced to sell their horses and carriages because he could not afford to maintain a stable. Then, last year, the London house and its furnishings had to be auctioned off to pay debts.

She would never have dared come to this house had she not heard that the old Marquess was near death. Her heart was beating so fast that she tried to quell it by pressing her hand against her chest. Hers was a daring plan, but if it worked, she would never have to worry about money again.

After running a nervous hand down her emerald green gown, she rapped on the door. Almost at once, the door was opened and the housekeeper looked down her thin nose at Rye.

"Whom do you wish to see, madam?" Mrs. Crowder asked in a stilted voice.

Rye had never liked it when a servant acted too high-handed. In her brother's house, the servants knew their places, and she dealt harshly with insubordination. She decided this haughty woman needed to know her place.

"I am Lady Rye Saffron. Be so kind as to inform the Viscount that I am here to see him."

Mrs. Crowder had never met the Earl of Saffron's sister, but she had heard enough about her to know she was no longer accepted in polite society. "Was his lordship expecting you this morning?" the housekeeper inquired, refusing to budge from in front of the door.

Rye's eyes narrowed at the insufferable woman. "Just tell him I am here," she demanded. "He will receive me."

She pushed past the housekeeper, who was determined to stand watchdog. "Tell his lordship that I will be waiting for him in here," she announced, stepping into the first room she came to.

Mrs. Crowder drew herself up with as much dignity as she could manage. "His lordship is having breakfast. I'll see if he will receive you, my lady."

Rye smiled to herself as the woman sailed down the hallway like an avenging angel. After the servant disappeared, Rye moved around the salon, overwhelmed by its grandeur. She had forgotten that there were still people who lived graciously. The gilded ceilings, the ocher-colored walls, the Chippendale chairs with silk coverings, all lent charm to the decor. Heavy silver candlesticks joined forces with the crystal chandeliers to lend their light to the room.

Rye moved in front of a heavy gilded mirror and studied her reflection. Removing the green bonnet which matched her gown, she patted her dark hair into place. That she was beautiful, Rye never doubted, and she could be at her best when trying to entice a man. She had come to the Remington townhouse today with the express purpose of becoming Lord Dakota Remington's mistress!

She had been in London for over a week and had heard the gossip that was circulating about the charm and good looks of the Viscount of Remington. It was said that every noble family in London was courting his friendship, but Rye wanted more than his friendship. Of course, the Viscount had refused all social invitations because his grandfather was dying.

Rye smiled, showing her teeth. It would seem that Dakota Remington was about to become the Marquess of Weatherford, one of the wealthiest and most powerful men in England.

Rye intended to share in his good fortune. She

had her eye on a charming little house in Bradford Square. She had a particular liking for emeralds, and she wanted very much to be a patroness of the fine arts. All this, and more, would be at her fingertips if she could but use her beauty to ensnare the handsome Viscount.

She had sensed that day they had first met in her brother's house that the Viscount had been attracted to her. It wasn't anything he had said, it was more of a feeling—she had seen it in his eyes. Rye went over in her mind the story she intended to tell the Viscount to gain his sympathy. Oh, it would be a terrible tale of woe. She would say that she was—

Dakota had entered the room so quietly that Rye was not aware of his presence until he spoke, dragging her mind out of her daydreams.

"I was told you wished to see me, my lady?"

She turned toward Dakota gracefully, making sure he had a good view of her creamy breasts and delicately arched neck. She lowered her eyes in the pretense of maidenly coyness. "I came at once to express my condolences for your grandfather."

"My grandfather is not yet . . . dead, so your condolences are premature."

His green gaze sent thrills echoing through Rye's body.

"I am sorry to have disturbed you, my lord, but you see . . ." For effect, her voice caught in her

272

throat, and she dabbed at her eyes as though wiping away tears. ". . . I had a most unfortunate incident happen to me."

Rye grasped the edge of a table, as if she were too weak to stand. "I hope you will not hold my brother's mistakes against me. I just didn't have anyone to turn to. Since we are neighbors of sorts, I hoped you would help me."

Dakota saw the woman sway, and he caught her about the waist. "Let me summon the housekeeper to assist you, my lady," he said with concern etched on his face.

"No, just help me to the sofa," she said weakly, not wanting the stern-faced housekeeper to spoil her plans.

After Dakota had her comfortably settled, he pulled up a stool to sit beside her.

"Please continue, my lady, if you are able. What has happened to cause you such distress?"

She stared into his eyes beseechingly. "While on my way to London, I was put upon by footpads. They took my money, smashed my trunks, and littered the road with my clothing."

Again she dabbed at her eyes, knowing the look of concern in the Viscount's green eyes was genuine.

"Was not your brother with you?"

"No, Martin and I had a disagreement, and he forced me to leave my home." She looked at Dakota through long silken lashes. "I have no money, and nowhere to stay. I knew when we met at my brother's house that you were a true gentleman, so I came to you."

Dakota felt pity for the woman's misfortune. Also, he was reminded of her resemblance to Running Deer. "You will stay here, of course, Lady Rye. As for your wardrobe, do not concern yourself, you shall have it replenished."

Rye was speechless for the moment. Surely he hadn't meant that she would stay here with him—not under his own roof! He must be aware of how that would set tongues to wagging. She hid a triumphant smile behind her handkerchief, then she looked at him dolefully. "But, my lord, people will talk if I remain here. And besides, I cannot buy a new wardrobe. I have no money."

"I care not about gossip," Dakota replied, walking to the bellpull to ring for the housekeeper. "And I shall pay for replacing your wardrobe," he assured her.

Mrs. Crowder entered the salon almost immediately, her hands clasped tightly in front of her, and her face drawn up in a dour frown.

"The Lady Rye Saffron will be my guest for a few days, Mrs. Crowder. See that she is made comfortable in one of the upstairs bedrooms."

Rye watched the woman's face redden with indignation. The housekeeper pursed her thin lips as if she was about to say something but thought better of it. "In which room do you wish me to install the . . . lady, my lord?"

"I leave that in your capable hands, Mrs. Crowder. I am sure I can trust you to see that she is made comfortable."

Rye gave the housekeeper a spiteful glance that was lost on Dakota. She had come here hoping to become a mistress, but instead found herself installed in the family house. It was too good to be true, and she intended to make the most of it.

She linked her arm through Dakota's and smiled up at him. "Will you go with me tomorrow when I shop for a new wardrobe?" she asked for the housekeeper's benefit. "After all, if you are buying the gowns, you should be able to help select them."

Dakota looked into brown eyes and was again reminded of Running Deer. Perhaps if he aided this woman in her plight, he would then be able to put Running Deer's ghost to rest. "I know nothing about women's apparel," he said.

Rye gave Dakota the practiced look that had induced many gentlemen in the past to do her bidding. She had never aspired so high before, however, and that gave her pause for thought.

Her eyes were soft, her smile seductive, promising much. "Please come with me. I shall need a man's opinion."

Rye turned spiteful eyes on the now steaming Mrs. Crowder. "And as I said, it will be your money that pays for them."

Dakota was unaccustomed to scheming women,

and he did not see the trap that was being so cleverly laid for him. All he saw was a woman who resembled Running Deer, and she was in trouble, and it was within his power to help her.

He saw no harm in accompanying her to the shops. Perhaps she could help him select a gift worthy to take back to Breanna. "Yes, I shall go with you," he answered. Although he did not relish spending a day shopping for women's apparel, it was little enough to do for the poor distraught woman.

Dakota did not see the proud jerk of his housekeeper's chin, or the outrage and indignation in her little black eyes. "I have duties to attend to, my lord," she said, moving toward the door. "I will send the upstairs maid to show Lady Saffron to her room."

Dakota did not know that the battle lines had been drawn between these two women. He was unaware that Mrs. Crowder had in no uncertain terms sent Rye the message that she would not personally lower herself to wait upon the Earl of Saffron's sister. That humiliating task would be performed by one of the underlings.

Rye would like to have protested the housekeeper's insolence, but she was not yet sure of the woman's status in the house. She would wait and bide her time.

A gleam came to her eyes as she thought of what the future might hold for her. Was it possible that the Viscount was unhappy with his lady? She had heard that his wife was comely, but perhaps she did not suit his taste.

Rye smiled to herself. She would endeavor to be everything this exceptional man wanted in a woman. Just for a moment, she entertained the thought that she might one day become the Marchioness of Weatherford!

For Breanna, time passed slowly. She had not heard from Dakota since his departure four weeks earlier, but then she hadn't expected to. She had hoped he would be home by now and wondered what could be keeping him in London.

During Dakota's absence, she had come to know Levi even better. He was a dear old man, and she developed a great affection for him.

Breanna worked her hands into her gloves as she descended the stairs. The weather had turned cold, and there was a light fog, but that would not deter her from riding Joya. She was walking past the sitting room when she heard her maid, Etta, talking to Polly, one of the downstairs maids.

Breanna paused in the doorway with the intention of telling Etta to lay her lavender gown out for dinner.

The two maids had their backs to Breanna and were not aware of her presence.

Etta's voice was raised in anger. "I never would

have thought it of his lordship, seeing as how thoughtful he's been to Lady Breanna."

"Well," Polly speculated, "that's a man for you. A woman gives them everything, and they end up breaking her heart."

"It makes my teeth ache to tell my sweet lady what's going on behind her back," Etta stated loyally.

"But you promised you wouldn't say anything," Polly protested. "If Mrs. Hopkins finds out I read her mail, she'll have me dismissed without a reference!"

"I won't say anything," Etta promised. "But only because I don't want to see her ladyship hurt. Tell me again about the letter," she urged.

Breanna stood as if frozen. She didn't want to eavesdrop, yet she couldn't leave. She had to know what Dakota had done that had caused the servants to gossip in corners.

"Well, I had to read the letter in a hurry, fearing Mrs. Hopkins would catch me," Polly continued, "but I got the gist of it. It was from the London housekeeper, Mrs. Crowder. I met her once when the old Marquess had several of us go to London when they remodeled the house there. She's a stern one, not given to gossip. I gathered from the letter she was angry and indignant at what's going on right under her nose. She wrote that she had even considered telling his lordship she would resign her post if he didn't send that woman packing. She says his lordship has bought Lady Rye Saffron jewels and clothing and has installed her in one of bedrooms at the townhouse."

Etta looked distressed. "But that's monstrous. It would be shocking for his lordship to bring any woman into his house, but the sister of a sworn enemy is unspeakable."

Polly nodded indignantly. "I can tell you right now that Lady Rye Saffron is no lady, if you understand what I'm saying. I've also heard that she is beautiful and has high aspirations. It will be hard for our sweet Viscountess to compete with her kind of woman, because they use all sorts of seductive powers on a man."

"But how could his lordship prefer that woman to our lady?"

Breanna did not know that Levi had been standing behind her in the hallway and that, like her, he had overheard everything the two maids had been discussing. She stayed to hear no more. Quietly she moved down the hallway and out the front door.

Feeling numb, she stood on the steps, trying to find some reason for what she had just overheard. She knew this wasn't merely servants' gossip, not if it had driven the dour, but loyal, Mrs. Crowder to the brink of relinquishing her post.

Breanna had to get away from the house so she could think this through. So deep was her hurt that she felt like a wounded animal that needed to be alone to heal its wounds. Her footsteps took her in the direction of the stable.

Frazier tipped his cap and smiled at Breanna, unaware that she was upset. "Joya has been waiting for you, my lady. She's sure getting spoiled, thinking you will give her your attention every day."

Breanna did not smile at the dear little man as was her custom. "I will not require you to accompany me this morning, Frazier," she said as he helped her mount.

"But, my lady, his lordship said that—"

"Never mind that. I will be riding alone today."

Frazier scratched his head as he watched Breanna ride in the direction of the hunting lodge, thinking she had been disturbed about something.

Breanna dismounted at the hunting lodge and looped Joya's reins through the hitching post. With a heavy heart, she walked down the steep trail that led to the beach. She felt as if her whole world had caved in. Had she had been forsaken? Surely there was some mistake. Dakota was too honorable to blatantly and openly take a mistress. Of course, she had heard of men having mistresses, but never would a gentleman allow his mistress to reside in his own home. Her heart felt as if it had been trampled. She could not bear to think of Dakota holding another woman in his arms as he had once held her.

As Breanna stared out at the ocean, she remembered the happy times she and Dakota had spent at the hunting lodge. Glancing up the cliff, she felt the rain on her face as it mingled with her tears. She remembered the beautiful night Dakota had truly made her his wife. Had he grown tired of her already?

She sat down on a rock and watched the restless waves wash to shore. Like flowers of remembrance pressed between the pages of a book, Breanna allowed her mind drift back to the happy times she had dwelled here in this paradise with her husband. Now those memories were soiled, besmirched, and she had only been living in a fool's paradise.

Dakota could not have cared for her at all or he would never have taken a mistress so soon after their marriage.

It started to rain harder, and she walked along the beach, weighed down with unhappiness. It didn't matter that the rain had soaked her to the skin. Nothing mattered anymore.

In a daze, Breanna glanced up and realized she had walked all the way to the caves. With a heavy heart, she retraced her steps. She had faced trouble before, and she would do it again, but oh, it did hurt so terribly.

Breanna looked up and saw the sun was getting low on the horizon. She had not realized she had been here so long. She remembered that Joya was still saddled and chided herself for neglecting her horse.

When Breanna reached the cliff top, she was surprised to find Levi sitting on the steps of the hunting lodge, whittling on a piece of wood. She was grateful to see that the dear old man had unsaddled Joya for her.

He stood up and handed her a wooden horse he'd been whittling, then watched her examine the delicate woodwork. "You about ready to go home?" he asked. "You are soaked clear through and are sure to catch your death."

"How long have you been waiting here?" she wanted to know.

"About three hours. When you didn't come home, I knew where to find you." His wise old eyes locked into hers, and she saw they were filled with compassion.

"You know, don't you, Levi?"

He didn't pretend to misunderstand her. "I don't know nothing, and you don't either, Breanna. You only know what you overheard."

"How do you know what I overheard?"

"If you hadn't been so upset, you'd have looked behind you and seen me standing there. I'd have followed you right away, but I thought you might need time to sort things out in your mind. Knowing you were of above normal intelligence, I figured you'd realize that what you heard was nothing but a lot of misinformation."

"You don't believe Dakota took that woman for

282

his mistress?"

"No, I don't. I know Dakota a might better then most people, and he would never do what he stands accused of doing. He's about the most noble and honorable man I have ever met."

Breanna felt hope stir to life in her heart. "You don't believe what Mrs. Crowder wrote in her letter?"

"I don't think the London housekeeper deliberately tried to mislead Mrs. Hopkins. She just got her facts all wrong."

Breanna turned and gazed out to sea. "There is one way to find out, Levi."

"Yeah, I thought you might be wanting to go to London. I don't suppose there's any way I can talk you out of it?"

"No, but you can come with me if you like. I would like your company."

"I'll go with you." He closed his knife blade and poked it in his pocket. "When we get to London, you'll see that Dakota hasn't betrayed you."

Breanna looked at the hunter with tear-brimmed eyes. "I hope you are right, Levi. Oh, I do hope you are right."

He lifted Breanna's saddle from the hitching rail and plopped it on Joya's back. "Let's get back to the big house, and you can decide what you want to do after you have eaten. It isn't good for you to make a decision of such importance on an empty stomach, Breanna."

For the first time in hours, Breanna smiled. "Perhaps, but I can almost assure you that I will be leaving for London early in the morning. No one wants to prove the gossip false more than I."

Chapter Twenty-two

John had spent the last month at a friend's estate outside London. His anger had cooled, and he realized he had been too harsh on Dakota. Hoping to make amends with his cousin, he returned to the townhouse.

After inquiring about his great-uncle and finding his condition had not changed, John handed his hat to the butler. He stood in the entryway, puzzled by the sound of a woman's laughter coming from the salon.

When he entered the salon, John was astonished to find Lady Rye within. He had met Rye Saffron on several occasions, but she had never been the slightest bit interested in him, since he was light in the pockets, so their acquaintance had been a limited one. He had often observed her, however, while she was flirting and beguiling young gentlemen until they made fools of themselves over her.

He wondered what Lady Rye was doing here with Dakota since the Remingtons and Saffrons were known enemies.

"Good evening, cousin," John said, moving casually into the room. "I have been told that my uncle's condition has not changed. I see how you have been entertaining yourself while I have been away."

Dakota was seated near the window and Rye had pulled up the stool to sit at his feet. Gowned in bright yellow velvet, Rye was beautiful, John had to admit, though a little too dark for his taste.

Dakota came to his feet with a relieved look on his face. "John, I am glad you have returned. Do you know Lady Rye Saffron?"

John could see the irritation in Rye's dark eyes, and he assumed that she was displeased by his intrusion. He bowed stiffly to her. "Indeed I do. How are you, Rye? It's always good to cross your path," he said out of politeness.

"I haven't seen you in some time, John, but then I suppose we don't frequent the same establishments," she replied, trying to cover up the animosity she felt because of his ill-timed interruption. "I had no idea that you were staying in London." She smiled maliciously. "Have you found some wealthy widow to take you in?"

He ignored her barb. "I take it you don't know

that Dakota and I are cousins."

Rye sprang to her feet. "I had no notion the two of you were related." Anger was quickly covered up with a sly smile. "How nice for you to have a relative you can depend on to shelter you in your need."

"Yes, pity you don't have someone yourself."

Dakota could sense the strain between John and Rye and he wondered at the reason for their sharp words. He had been in the woman's company for two weeks, and he was glad John had returned because he was beginning to find her tiresome. In truth, he didn't know what to do about the lady.

"John, Lady Rye was robbed on her way to London, so she is staying with us until she can make arrangements to return home," he explained, wondering why the look his cousin gave him made him feel as if he had done something wrong.

John's face whitened, and he quickly glanced at Rye. "Can this be true?"

"I can assure you it is," she said smoothly.

He turned back to Dakota. "Where is Breanna?"

"She's still in the country, John. You know I didn't intend to bring her here."

"I don't think you are aware that by allowing an unmarried woman to stay under your roof, you have committed a terrible breach in etiquette, Dakota."

Dakota looked puzzled. "But she had no place to go, and her clothing had all been ruined."

John's eyes gleamed as he turned to Rye. "Let me guess, Dakota. You generously offered to replace the lady's clothing and allowed her to stay here?"

"Yes," Dakota admitted. "How can it be wrong to help a friend in trouble?"

Rye smirked. "Yes, John, how can that be wrong? After all," she said, tossing her head, "Dakota seems to take in all sort of strays, does he not?"

John slowly shook his head, blaming himself for deserting Dakota when he needed him most. "This is unthinkable, and you know it, Rye. Dakota doesn't know what consequences can result from this action, but you do. Why in heaven's name did you allow this to happen?"

Rye was clever enough to realize John Donegal could be a real threat to her plan. She saw indecision in Dakota's eyes and decided to play on his sympathies once more. Dabbing at her eyes with a handkerchief, she sobbed. "How can you be so cruel, John Donegal? I have nowhere to go. Would you have your cousin toss me out in the street?"

"That will not happen," Dakota said, unable to stand the sight of the woman's tears. "If anything is amiss, I take full responsibility, John."

John looked from one to the other in disbelief. "Dakota, I don't think you know what is going on here. Have you considered Breanna in this? What will she say if she should learn that you have a woman staying here with you?"

"Breanna would not want me to turn away someone who is in need. And I believe she will have trust in me."

Rye's eyes darkened. She was beginning to feel frustrated because Dakota had not, as yet, taken her to his bed. Even though she had tried to bring him around, he had cleverly sidestepped her every move. Now that his cousin was here, her task could prove even more difficult. "I do not want to cause any trouble," she sniffed. "I will pack my belongings and leave at once." She knew Dakota well enough by now to realize he would not allow her to go like this.

"You will do no such thing," Dakota stated. "You are welcome to remain here for as long as you deem it necessary." He glanced at his cousin. "My grandfather's solicitor is waiting for me in the study, John. I will expect you to apologize to Lady Rye before I return."

John did not miss the satisfied gleam that passed over Rye's face as she watched Dakota leave the room. "What game are you playing, Rye?" he demanded. "What do you hope to gain by insinuating yourself in my cousin's life?"

She brushed a delicate finger over the heavy silver candlestick. "We all do what we must to survive, John. You should know about that. Haven't you attached yourself to your wealthy cousin?"

"Not in the way your think, Rye. My main pur-

289

pose in being with Dakota is to protect him from unscrupulous people who will try to take advantage of his generous nature," he said pointedly. "You have no future here, because he will never turn to you, Rye."

"How can you be sure?" she purred. "I take heart in the fact that he left his bride so soon after meeting her."

"Don't take comfort in that thought, because you would only be deluding yourself. Breanna is a *lady*, and you don't have a chance in hell of replacing her in Dakota's affections."

"Oh, so the *lady* has a champion in you. How gallant. Does Dakota know how you feel about his wife? Perhaps you would like me to end up with Dakota, so you would be free to have his wife."

John could see the spiteful and malicious glint reflected in Rye's eyes, and he recognized the danger she might represent to Dakota. "I would not mind if Dakota bedded you as he would any whore, but you wouldn't be satisfied with that, would you?"

"I believe we understand one another."

A slow smile played on John's lips. "How old are you, Rye? Thirty? Thirty-five? You are beautiful, but your age is just beginning to show in your face. I suppose you could attribute the slight lines at your mouth and around your eyes to the kind of life you lead."

Rye was not amused by John's observations. "I

suppose you are trying to make a point?" she gritted out.

"Yes, I am. Have you seen the Lady Breanna?"

"No." Rye smiled. "It would seem her husband prefers to keep her in the country and away from prying eyes. Perhaps she is a shy little bird."

John moved to the sideboard and poured himself a glass of brandy. He paused before bringing it to his lips. "I don't think that's Dakota's reason for not bringing Breanna to London, Rye. You pointed out a moment ago that I might be interested in the Viscountess, and you weren't far from wrong. If she weren't married to my cousin, I would be the first to plight her my troth. You see, she has youth, beauty, and innocence on her side. If you want my opinion, Dakota is one fortunate bastard. No, he will not be interested in you, Rye."

She shoved him out of the way and poured herself a liberal amount of brandy and downed it, coughing to catch her breath. "We shall just see about that, John Donegal. We shall just see."

Now John laughed. "I believe I note a touch of frustration in your voice. Can it be that Dakota has spurned your attempts to get him into bed?" John saw her eyes flash with anger. "No, it's more than that, isn't it? He doesn't even know you are offering yourself to him." Seeing he had hit on the truth, John's laughter filled the room. "Give up, Rye. Take what spoils you derived from your association with Dakota and leave."

Rye's face became distorted with anger. "I'll see you in hell first, John."

His laughter was now amused. "Very likely, Rye. Very likely."

She took another sip of brandy, and John saw something more in her eyes. "You love him, Rye," he said in an astonished voice. "You love my cousin." There was something akin to pity in his eyes now. "You can never have him. He is far above you, and he is everything you and I can never be. He believes in honesty and is capable of feeling deeply about the woman he loves. You mistook his generosity to you as something more. I pity you, Rye, because he is as far out of reach for you as Breanna is for me. Leave them alone and allow them to find happiness together."

She spun around, her crinoline swaying with the violent motion. "How magnanimous of you to sacrifice your love for the sake of honor. I assure you I am not motivated by the same sentiments. No, I will have Dakota one way or another. And he *is* interested in me, you shall see!"

John was weary of the conversation. This woman was like a viper in the house, and he intended to stand guardian so she couldn't spread her poison. It wasn't likely he could convince Dakota to throw the woman out, but perhaps he could explain that any gossip about him and Rye would hurt Breanna. He had to persuade Dakota to give the woman money and send her on her way before any real harm was done, if it wasn't already too late.

He only hoped it wouldn't be necessary for him to pretend to woo Lady Rye. There was only so much one should be expected to do for the sake of the family honor.

It was dark when the carriage bearing Breanna and Levi pulled up to the front door of the townhouse. Levi helped Breanna up the steps and pushed open the door for her to enter.

As Levi helped Breanna remove her velvet cape, Mrs. Crowder appeared. "My lady," she said in astonishment. "We were not told to expect you." The housekeeper's voice held a warmth that Breanna had not heard before.

"Good evening, Mrs. Crowder, is my husband in?"

"Yes, my lady." The elder woman looked as if she would like to bar Breanna's path — in truth she wanted to shield the Viscountess from any unpleasantness.

Breanna could tell by the housekeeper's expression that she was upset about something.

"His lordship is dining with . . . friends. Allow me . . . to announce you, my lady."

"That won't be necessary, Mrs. Crowder. I would like to surprise my husband," Breanna said as she moved past the housekeeper toward the formal dining room, Levi following close behind her.

Before she pushed open the door, Breanna heard a woman's laughter. Drawing on her courage, she opened the door and moved into the room.

Silence fell heavily as three pairs of eyes studied Breanna. Her eyes moved first over her husband's face. Was that the warmth of welcome she saw in his eyes? She nodded at John, and he came to his feet to stand beside her.

"Breanna," John said, moving closer to her, wanting to protect her. "What . . . when did you arrive?"

"Just now," Breanna answered. She noticed that the woman dressed in a ruby-red gown was lovely beyond belief. She had a certain sophistication that Breanna knew she would never be able to achieve.

Sitting to Dakota's right, the woman suddenly leaned closer to him, showing a generous amount of her bosom and laying a delicate hand possessively on Dakota's.

Pain ripped through Breanna's heart, and she swayed toward John. Levi stood on Breanna's other side, casting a startled glance at Dakota.

With a courage Breanna did not know she possessed, she proudly raised her chin. "Dakota, will you not present me to your guest?"

Dakota brushed Rye's hand off and stood up. His joy at seeing Breanna was tempered by the feeling of strong undertones in the room. John had made him understand this afternoon that it was not accepted in polite society for Rye to reside under his roof, and that Breanna would be hurt if word of this reached her ears.

Dakota, realizing he had committed a faux pas, had decided to ask Rye to leave in the morning. John had been right when he said Breanna would be hurt. He could see her pain, and it became his pain. The one person in the world he would never want to hurt was his beloved Breanna.

John, thinking to save the situation, intervened. "Breanna, may I present a friend of mine, Lady Rye Saffron. Dakota so graciously invited us to dine with him."

Breanna looked into John's honest blue eyes and saw that the lie came hard to him. With dignity, she turned to Rye. "I believe we are neighbors in Cornwall, Lady Rye. Are we also neighbors here in London?" Breanna prayed that the gossip had been wrong. Let the lady deny her suspicions and exonerate Dakota.

Dakota, who stood watching silently as if he were only a bystander, still had not welcomed his wife.

Rye's eyes moved over Lady Breanna Remington, noting the perfection of her youthful skin, the shining mane of hair that looked like strands of gold. She saw youth and innocence, a loveliness that came from within. Jealousy ate at her heart, and her lips curled up in a snarl. "No, I am not your neighbor, I have been staying here." She smiled smugly. "Dakota, when you asked me to help you select a gift for your wife, I didn't realize she was so fair. Had I known, I would have steered you away from emeralds and had you purchase a strand of pearls like the ones you gave me."

"Breanna," John broke in, hoping to save the situation, though it was deteriorating by the minute. "Why don't we all sit down and dine."

John's eyes met Levi's. "Why don't you first take Breanna to Mrs. Crowder so she can freshen up after her journey. We shall wait for you."

Breanna wasn't listening to John; she was staring at her husband in disbelief. "No," she said at last. "I can see I have intruded. I won't be staying."

Dakota moved slowly across the room, taking Breanna's cold hand in his. "You should have let me know you were coming, Breanna."

She refused to allow the tears behind her eyes to fall. "Yes, apparently I should have." She glanced at Lady Rye, and lowered her voice so only Dakota could hear. "Your lady friend is very lovely. However, you have made a grave mistake in bringing her into this house." Breanna whirled around, her chin high, her shoulders back. Pride was the only weapon she had to save her dignity. "Good evening to you all," she whispered through trembling lips.

The room was silent as Breanna moved out the door. Dakota stood, confused, while Levi gave him an angry glare.

"I told Breanna it wasn't true," he said accusingly. "I never had reason to be shamed by you until now." Turning away, Levi went dashing after Breanna.

John's eyes bore into Rye's. "You deliberately allowed Breanna to draw the wrong conclusions." With anger burning in his eyes, he, too, raced after Breanna.

John found her in the entryway slipping into her cape, Levi trying to talk her out of leaving. "Breanna, I know why Dakota is being nice to that woman. When I saw her just now, I was struck by how closely she resembles Running Deer, an Arapaho Indian maiden that was a good friend of Dakota's."

Breanna's head snapped up. "I know about her. She was . . . she . . . Dakota loved Running Deer!"

"Breanna, I want to talk to you," John interrupted, forcefully pulling her into the salon. When she looked up at him, he saw the tears trailing down her cheek, and his heart melted. "It's not what you think. I know it looks bad, but on my word, I swear to you that Dakota is innocent in this. Dakota's only crime is having a generous nature. This woman has used him to her own end, and he hasn't even looked at her as a woman. I promise you this."

She wanted to believe him. "Why has he bought her pearls?" she questioned.

John took a deep breath, glancing at Levi for guidance. The hunter shrugged to intimate that John was on his own.

"Breanna, Rye Saffron is every bit as devious as her brother, perhaps even more so. She appealed to Dakota's kindness by telling him she had nothing to wear and nowhere to stay. I swear to you, Dakota is only guilty of being uninformed of the consequences of aiding a lady he believed to be in distress."

Oh, she wanted so desperately to believe John. After all, had not Dakota pointed out to her on numerous occasions that he was unfamiliar with English customs. Could this be an innocent mistake on his part? "Are you telling the truth, John?" she asked hopefully.

"I swear to you, I am."

"Perhaps I should hear Dakota's side," she conceded.

"If you walk away now, Rye will have accomplished what she set out to do."

"Which is?"

"I admit she has designs on Dakota. You don't want her to win, do you, Breanna?"

"No," Breanna replied, handing her cape to John. "Wait here, I want to talk to my husband."

Dakota was trying to sort out the events in his

mind. He knew something was terribly wrong, but he was having trouble pinpointing the problem.

"Shouldn't you go running after your wife, too, Dakota?" Rye said, coming to her feet and tossing her napkin on the table. "My, my, the little wife has so many defenders, does she not?"

Dakota stared at Rye, and for the first time saw her for what she was. "I offered you my hospitality, and you have returned it with half-truths. You have deliberately allowed my wife to think something had happened between you and me."

Rye could see she was losing her only chance to win Dakota. "I love you," she cried, throwing herself into his arms. "I love you so desperately." To her amazement she meant it. For the first time in Rye Saffron's life, she loved a man.

Dakota stood rigid as Rye sprinkled kisses over his face. Feeling like a man who has been made a fool of, he grasped her waist with the intention of pushing her away. That was when he heard the gasp and glanced up at the door to see Breanna standing there, a look of disbelief on her face.

"I—I—" She turned and fled, feeling as if she had received a deathblow to her heart. Running past Levi, she pushed open the front door and ran into the night.

With Levi and John in close pursuit, Breanna dashed around a corner and pressed her body against a building. She didn't want to face anyone at the moment. She was too devastated. Her worst fears had been realized — whether it was because the woman reminded Dakota of his dead Running Deer, or for whatever the reason, it was apparent that he loved Rye Saffron.

Chapter Twenty-three

Breanna felt as if she had walked for hours. Tired, cold, and completely disheartened, she realized she was in a less than fashionable neighborhood and she was lost!

She huddled behind a tree, hoping to block the icy wind that battered her body and stung her face. Her hands were numb with cold, and she could hardly flex her fingers.

If only she hadn't left her cloak behind when she dashed out of the house, she thought miserably. The fog was damp and shrouded the landscape, making it impossible for Breanna to see where she was going. She didn't know where to go or what to do.

She was so cold, but she refused to return to the Weatherford townhouse. If only she had money. She glanced down at her hand where her mother's diamond ring rested. No, she couldn't sell her mother's ring.

She knew Levi and John would still be searching for her; perhaps Dakota had even joined them in their search. She had no desire to see any of them. Feeling more alone than she had ever felt in her life, Breanna knew she had to take a positive action.

With a chill shaking her slight body, she moved quickly past a small park. Suddenly, she heard the sound of footsteps behind her, and she froze with fear. Suppose it was a footpad? Or worse still, what if it was Dakota?

Breanna paused beneath a pale yellow streetlight that did little to dispel the gloom. Quickly moving into the shadows, she still carried a vision of Dakota holding that woman in his arms. How could he so brazenly flaunt his mistress in her face? She didn't want to think about Dakota, but her memories of that awful event were engraved on her mind, and the pain she felt over being betrayed would not be denied.

The footsteps behind her were drawing closer, and she started to run. With her breath coming out in frosted puffs, Breanna stumbled and caught herself before she fell. She dashed toward the cobblestone street, trying to escape whoever was pursuing her.

Breanna did not hear the carriage that loomed out of the fog. Too late she saw the faint glare of coach lights and the rearing horses. A silent scream built up inside her, but it was never heard as she was knocked to the cobblestones, unconscious.

Miraculously, her body rolled out of the path of the horses' flying hooves.

His Grace, Stephen Glendon, Duke of Clandannon, braced his sister, Mary, as the carriage swerved and came to a teetering halt. "What in the deuce has happened?" he called to the driver, who was fighting to bring the horses under control.

"I'm not sure, your grace. I think we hit something."

"Well, get down and see," the Duke said in an irritated voice. "I don't intend to sit here all night."

Stephen Glendon stared at his sister with a worried frown on his face. She had been ailing for several months, and lately her health seemed to have deteriorated to the point that he feared for her life. He had planned this night at the theater to get her out of the house. Since she lost her young husband three years ago, she seemed to have given up on living. He couldn't interest her in anything.

Stephen noticed how pale Mary looked beneath the carriage lights. "Are you all right, my dear?" he asked.

She glanced out the window. "Don't worry about me, Stephen, I'm fine."

The driver came up to the window. "Your grace, I think you had better come quick. We hit a woman!"

Stephen shoved the door open and jumped to the ground. In the dim light given off by the lantern, he could tell very little about the poor wretch. Bending down, he determined she was only unconscious and not dead because he could feel her warm breath against his hand.

Taking quick action, the Duke gathered her up in his arms and moved back to the carriage. "Bill, get going, but drive carefully. We don't want to have another mishap. We need a doctor as soon as possible because we don't know the extent of this woman's injuries."

Lady Mary gasped when she saw her brother lay the unconscious woman on the seat opposite her. With pain in her heart for the poor unfortunate person, she took her lap robe and placed it over the woman. "Are you sure she isn't—"

"No, she's not dead yet," her brother assured her.

As the carriage jerked forward, Stephen stared down at the red-gold hair that spilled across the green leather seat. The woman's face was covered with blood, so it was impossible to tell what she looked like.

"Oh, please tell the driver to hurry," Lady Mary cried, burying her face against her brother's chest. "Suppose she dies, will it be our fault?"

"We cannot go any faster, Mary, it's too dangerous." His arms closed around her slight body. "I had meant this to be a happy evening for you, my

304

dear." He felt her tremble. "All will be done to ensure the woman will live," he said with more confidence than he actually felt.

"Who do you suppose she is?" Mary asked, taking a peek at the body.

"I am sure when she is able, she will enlighten us on that point."

"What do you think she was doing out so late at night, and in this weather?"

The Duke frowned. "That, too, will be answered in time, if she lives."

Mary's eyes were beseeching. "She just has to live, Stephen. I could not bear it otherwise. There is too much death and sorrow in this world as it is."

The carriage came to a stop before a fashionable gray brick house. The Duke carried Breanna inside, waving away the startled footman who attempted to take her from him.

Curious servants gathered in the hallway as the Duke barked out orders. He sent Bill to fetch a doctor, while he carried his burden to an upstairs bedroom.

Breanna awoke and turned her head toward the only pinnacle of light in the room. In the dim candle glow, she saw a woman who was unknown to her, sleeping in a chair. A moan escaped Breanna's lips when she touched her throbbing head and found it had been bandaged. When she tried to move, her whole body was racked with pain.

"Don't move," the young woman called out, coming to her feet and standing over Breanna. "You have been injured, and the doctor wants you to lie as still as possible." She lightly touched Breanna's hand and found her patient was finally warm and the terrible chills were gone.

"Try not to worry," Lady Mary told her. "The doctor assured me you are suffering from no more than cuts and bruises. I feel you were very fortunate."

Breanna was totally confused. "Where am I, and who are you?"

Lady Mary dropped down near Breanna, testing the sling the doctor had tied about her right arm. "I am Lady Mary Snow. Do you remember being run down by my brother's carriage?"

Breanna was thoughtful for a moment. "No, I don't remember that at all."

"My brother and I were returning from the theater. It was so foggy that poor Bill, our driver, couldn't see where he was going. You dashed out in front of the horses and were knocked unconscious."

"I . . . hurt," Breanna said through dry lips.

"The doctor left a bottle of laudanum, should your pain become too great. Shall I give you a dose?"

"I . . . no, I have never liked the feeling of being drugged." Breanna was quiet for a moment before she spoke in a bewildered voice. "Now, how did I know that, when I cannot even remember my name?"

Lady Mary placed a comforting hand on Breanna's. "Don't fret about anything tonight. Just try and go to sleep. I will stay beside you in case you need anything."

Somehow Breanna found Lady Mary's voice soothing. Her eyes fluttered shut, and she fell into a troubled sleep.

A bright sunlight streamed into the room when Breanna opened her eyes. She blinked, trying to adjust her sight to the brightness. She allowed her eyes to wander over the room. The walls were white with blue trim, and yellow curtains hung at the windows and a lemon yellow rug covered the floor. Breanna was lying in an elaborately carved four-poster bed. The fireplace was glowing with a cheerful fire. This room reflected the owners' good taste.

"So, ma'am, you are awake." A cheerful maid in a stiff black uniform and white apron poked her head around the door. "I have your breakfast if you be hungry."

"I don't seem to be hungry," Breanna replied. "I don't feel like I could swallow a morsel."

Lady Mary came sailing into the room and took

the tray from the servant, dismissing her with a nod. "But you must eat, or else you will never build up your strength," she insisted.

The thought of food did not appeal to Breanna, and she wished her head would stop pounding. When Lady Mary placed the tray on a low table, Breanna turned her head away. "I don't want to eat."

Lady Mary placed a supporting arm behind Breanna's shoulders. "Hold on to me and I'll help you sit up. You might find it painful at first, but the doctor says it's for the best."

Breanna gripped Lady Mary's hands and gritted her teeth, wishing the room would stop spinning.

With a cheerful smile, Lady Mary plumped up the pillows and helped Breanna settle weakly against them.

"Now, since your right arm is in a sling, I will feed you." She dipped a spoon into thick cream and drew out a plump strawberry. "You are right-handed, aren't you?" she asked, holding the spoon to Breanna's lips.

"I . . . don't know for sure. I think so."

Breanna took the strawberry in her mouth, finding it delicious.

Lady Mary waited until Breanna chewed and swallowed before she spoke again. "Have you remembered your name, or anything about yourself?"

Breanna stopped chewing. "It's strange, but I do remember some things, but they are all shadowy,

and it makes my head ache to think about them."
She tried to move and moaned from the pain it
caused her. "Yes, I know my name. I believe I am
called Breanna."

"That is a lovely and unusual name. Can you
recall your surname?"

"Yes, I think so . . . no, it's gone now. I remember . . . running from something or someone." She
looked distressed. "It's all so mixed up. I cannot
always tell the real from the unreal."

"Don't try to rush it, and do not worry. I feel
sure that very soon all of your memory will return."

Breanna observed Lady Mary. She had a fragile
bone structure, and her complexion was pale. Her
hair was light blond, and her soft eyes were hazel.

"Is this your home?" Breanna wanted to know.

"No, it's my brother's home. I am . . . a widow."

Breanna read a deep sadness in Lady Mary's
eyes. "I am so sorry. I should not be intruding on
your sorrow."

"No, no. I have been widowed these past three
years. My Tom and I . . . he is very difficult to
forget. Everyone keeps telling me that I should put
him out of my mind, and my brother, Stephen,
worries about me like a mother hen. I am just not
ready to put Tom aside."

Breanna leaned against the bed poster, allowing
the smoothness of the cherry wood to cool her
face. "Then don't. He was a part of your life, and

apparently you loved him a great deal. Examine the memories you have of your Tom, and think about the good times you had together. While you remember him, he will never truly be dead to you. One day, you will just wake up and realize that he is a beautiful memory, and when you think of him, you will smile."

"Oh, Breanna, you are the first person who has ever understood how I feel. I loved Tom, and I don't want to let him go. At times I just don't want to go on without him."

"You must not talk like that, because you also have an obligation to the living. I'm sure it would hurt your brother to hear you talk thus. Just remember, if anything happened to you, your beautiful memories of Tom would die with you."

"I never thought of it that way." She poked another strawberry at Breanna. "Is it possible that you also lost a husband? You seem to know what I have been going through."

"No, I don't think so," she said, looking down at her diamond ring. "When I examine my grief, it seems to come from the loss of a mother and father."

When Lady Mary offered Breanna another strawberry, Breanna refused with the shake of her head. She did, however, accept the cup of spiced tea that Lady Mary insisted she drink.

All morning, Lady Mary bustled around Breanna, brushing her hair, straightening her bed, and anticipating her every need. In the afternoon, she sat beside Breanna while she slept. Then when she awoke, Lady Mary read her amusing excerpts from *The Times*.

When Breanna fell asleep again, Lady Mary tiptoed out of the room. Glancing at the hall clock, she saw that she was late for dinner. Patting her hair into place, she entered the dining room to find her brother already seated at the head of the table, an amused smile on his face.

Stephen noticed the rosy glow on his sister's face. He had not seen her this happy in a very long time. "Well, Mary, have you done all that was possible to make our patient comfortable?"

"Yes, and she is an extraordinary person."

The maid entered and set Lady Mary's plate on the table. After the servant had gone, Lady Mary continued. "As I have already told you, she doesn't remember very much about herself. But Dr. Mathers believes she will be completely recovered in a few days."

"So, she still can't remember who she is?" Stephen asked skeptically.

Mary took a bite of fish and shook her head. "No, no yet. She thinks she may have been running away from something or someone."

Stephen watched his sister eat with relish, something she hadn't done since her husband's death.

"We know nothing about this woman, Mary. You realize she could be an undesirable, don't you? Or perhaps even a criminal."

"No, she isn't capable of any wrongdoing!" Mary adamantly defended her charge. "You have not seen her or talked to her as I have, or you would not make that statement. She is well born, and extremely kind and thoughtful. She understands about my feelings for Tom." Mary's eyes were tear-bright. "Breanna has helped me begin to accept Tom's death, and in time, I believe I shall be able to put his ghost to rest."

Stephen could hardly believe the transformation that had come over his sister in only one day. Her eyes sparkled, her cheeks had color in them, and she was chattering endlessly. He laughed, feeling the weight from years of concern for his Mary's health lift from his shoulders. "I don't care what the woman has done or how debased her life may prove to be. She has been good for you, and I will be eternally grateful to her."

Mary leaned forward and placed her hand on her brother's. "See her and talk to her, Stephen, then you will know that she is a lady. We have to help her."

He chuckled in amusement. "I will do all I can to help your lost lady. If she finds it acceptable, I will talk with her tonight to see if we can begin to unravel the mystery of her past." His grip tightened on Mary's hand. "I merely feel it would be remiss of me if I didn't point out to you that she might prove to be other than the angelic picture you have painted of her in your mind."

Mary lifted her wineglass and held it out to her brother. "Talk to her, and you will come to the same conclusion as I. Breanna is very special."

Breanna had agreed to receive Lady Mary's brother, Stephen, in her bedroom. Now that the hour approached, however, she felt nervous about the meeting.

Lady Mary, sensing Breanna's apprehension, spoke to her encouragingly while tying the pink bow on the dressing gown she had given her. "No need to be frightened, Breanna, Stephen is harmless, especially when he's talking to a pretty woman. You see, he is my twin, so I know him very well."

"Am I pretty?" Breanna questioned.

"My dear, yes." Lady Mary laughingly grabbed up the hand mirror from the dressing table and held it in front of Breanna. "Here, judge for yourself."

Breanna stared at the face of a stranger, noting the color of her eyes and hair. "Who am I?" she asked with terror in her voice.

Lady Mary felt her heart go out to the beautiful lost Breanna. "My brother will help you find out who you are," she said with assurance. "When

313

Stephen sets his mind to a task, he always sees it through to a successful conclusion."

At that moment, a soft rap sounded on the door, and Lady Mary swept across the room to admit her brother. Breanna stared at the tall man who towered above his delicate twin sister. His eyes were hazel like Mary's, and his hair was the same color, but where her features were soft, his were finely chiseled. He was dressed in buff-colored trousers and calf-high riding boots. His eyes were alert, and Breanna had the distinct feeling that the Duke was a powerful force to reckon with.

Mary led Stephen forward. "Breanna, this is my brother, Stephen, Duke of Clandannon. Stephen, our guest, Breanna."

The Duke stared at the most beautiful woman he had ever seen. Her lovely delicate face was framed by riotous red-gold curls. The fear in her golden eyes cut at his heart. He could not bear the thought that his horses had run down this lovely angel. He had came here tonight with the intention of exposing the woman should her loss of memory prove to be a trick. Now, all he could think of was how beautiful and angelic she was.

"Has my sister made you comfortable?" He paused, smiling. "I hope you will not think it improper if I call you Breanna, since we do not know your surname."

"I don't think it would be improper at all, Your Grace, and I am feeling much better, thank you."

Stephen took note of her manner of speech, the cultured tone, the upper-class pronunciation, and he immediately realized that she was of the aristocracy.

He seated himself in the chair beside her bed, while Mary stood beside him. "Can you remember nothing else about your past, Breanna?"

"Several times today, I have had a vision of a place, but it quickly disappears. It seems a great house, perhaps a palace beside the ocean."

Stephen was thoughtful for a moment. "Do you recall anything else? Mary says you thought you had been running away from something. Can you remember what?"

"No." She looked into compassionate eyes. "I have been remembering something, but I don't know how it relates to me. The name Kenton . . . Fielding Kenton."

The Duke's eyes brightened. "I know of a Lord Fielding Kenton. He used to game at my club some years back. I had heard that he retired to his country estate. I wonder if this could be the man?"

"Do you feel this man might be your husband?" Lady Mary asked.

"No, I don't think so. But I cannot say for certain."

The Duke stood up. "Well, Breanna, we have something to go on now. I will see what I can do to help you find your past." He held his hand out to her, and she placed her hand in his warm clasp.

"Your only task will be to rest and grow stronger."

She smiled up at him. "How can I ever thank you and Lady Mary for your kindness to me. I am sorry to have to rely on your hospitality, but I seem to have little choice in the matter."

"Nonsense. You must consider our house as your own. Since you are starting to remember people and places of your past, I feel you will get your complete memory back any day. The doctor does not think your loss of memory is caused entirely by the accident. He believes there might be something in your past that you are avoiding."

Breanna's eyes grew round and frightened. "What if I am a despicable person and have committed some horrendous crime? I could be a thief or . . . worse!"

He laughed softly, while turning her hands over and seeing no callouses. "Nay, Breanna, you have not the hands of a thief. These are the hands of a high-born lady." Stephen glanced into eyes so deep he felt as if he were drowning. "Trust me in this, Breanna. I am a good judge of character, and my intuition tells me that you are what you seem, a sweet innocent."

Mary smiled as she moved to the bed and motioned for Breanna to lie down. She could easily see that Stephen was captivated by their guest, as she knew he would be. Pulling the covers up to Breanna's chin, she turned to Stephen. "My patient has had enough excitement for one day. Let us leave so she can sleep."

Through tear-filled eyes, Breanna watched the brother and sister depart. Why did she feel as if she were being swallowed by some deep, dark void? Were there things in her past that she did not want to remember? What if the Duke was wrong, and she was a criminal?

Closing her eyes, she willed her mind to be a blank. She didn't want to think about anything. She just wanted to sleep and keep on forgetting.

Chapter Twenty-four

Dakota rushed up the steps and into the house. For three days he had executed an exhaustive search for Breanna without success. He was frantic, wondering what had happened to her, and his burden was twofold, since his grandfather had taken a turn for the worse.

On entering the sitting room, he found John and Levi lounging in chairs, both mud-spattered and exhausted. The dejected looks on both their faces told Dakota their search had been as fruitless as his.

"Where can she be?" Dakota asked, sinking wearily into a chair. His eyes were metal-bright, and his face was a veil of misery.

"There isn't any way to track her here in this town, like on the prairies," Levi observed, feeling completely defeated.

"It doesn't seem possible that she could have eluded all three of us." John's eyes were hard as he looked at Dakota. "Just what did Breanna see when she went back into the dining room to talk to you that made her run away?"

Dakota's eyes were dull. "She saw Rye Saffron in my arms." Bitterness laced his tone.

"Damn you!" John roared, coming out of his seat. "I gave Breanna my word of honor that you hadn't touched that woman."

"I never touched Rye Saffron. I didn't even like her," Dakota admitted angrily. "I merely felt pity for her."

John paced the floor. "I warned you this could happen, but you think you are so damn noble and insisted you knew what you were doing. Incidentally, where is the lady in question at this moment? I hope you have had the good sense to send her away."

Dakota did not like John's tone of voice and his own voice was cold as he replied. "I do not need you to point out the errors of my ways. I am now well aware that Rye Saffron was not truthful with me."

Dakota's shoulders slumped in defeat. He did not know how to deal with deceit and dishonesty. "I was told that the lady left of her own accord. I am sure she realized it was the wise thing to do."

His jaw tightened in anger. "She is fortunate that my mind was filled with concern for Breanna, or I would have thrown her out."

"Well," Levi chimed in, "the way I see it, a man's got a right to be a fool once in his life. That is, if he learns something from the experience."

Dakota stood up and walked to the window. The morning mist dispelled the night shadows, and a bright sun promised a cloudless day, but he felt a chill in his heart.

He was frantic to find his love. What if something had happened to her? He battled between fearing for her life and wanting to punish her for putting him through this hell. He had to find her—he just had to! He prayed that nothing had happened to Breanna. There was no light in the world without her; there was only this deep empty void.

"The messenger you sent to Weatherford Hall returned an hour ago. Breanna has not been there," John said in a lethargic voice, his anger melting away.

Dakota was bone-weary, but he would not rest until he had found Breanna. "Let's go," he said wearily. "If today brings no success, I may consider going to the authorities as you suggested, John. Today the messenger that we sent to see if she was with her brother should return."

Fielding Kenton stood at the door of the Duke

of Clandannon's London house, waiting for someone to answer his knock. It took only moments for a butler to open the door and bow stiffly to Fielding.

"I am Lord Kenton to see His Grace," Fielding announced.

"Yes, my lord. I was told to take you to His Grace the moment you arrived."

Fielding was still puzzling over the strange letter he had received from the Duke. It had urged him to come here in all haste on a matter of the utmost urgency and delicacy.

As the butler announced him, Fielding stood in the presence of the Duke, still at a loss as to why he had been summoned. He did not like this man.

"Lord Kenton," the Duke said, coming across the room to meet him. "Thank you for responding so quickly. I am indeed glad that you are here."

"I came, your Grace, because you said in your note that it was urgent, though I have not the slightest notion why there should be any urgent business between the two of us. Pray enlighten me."

The Duke offered Fielding a chair, and then seated himself. "I have a story to tell you that you may find extraordinary. Four nights ago, while my sister and myself were coming home from the theater, a young woman dashed out in front of our carriage and my driver could not avoid hitting her. While she did not sustain any lasting injuries, she has lost most of her memory. She remembers only her first name and a few other details."

Fielding was puzzled. "I don't see what this has to do with me."

The Duke eyed the young man, wondering what connection he would have with Breanna, and why she should remember his name when she remembered little else. He intended to proceed cautiously in the event that this was the man Breanna had been fleeing from.

"Have you no notion of the woman I am speaking of?" Stephen asked, watching Fielding's eyes in case he should be untruthful.

"No, you have me totally confused."

"Let me ask you a few questions, so I might know where you stand in this matter."

Completely at a loss, Fielding nodded. "I would be glad to be of service to you, if I can."

"Have you a wife?"

"Of course."

"May I ask her name and have a brief description of her?"

"I don't see—"

"Please bear with me. This is important."

"Very well, my wife's name is Sophie, and she has brown hair and gray eyes."

Stephen breathed a sigh of relief. He was glad Breanna was not married to this man; he hoped she was not married to anyone. He frowned, wondering what the association could be between

Breanna and the Earl of Kenton. "This may sound a little indelicate, but do you have a mistress residing in London?"

Fielding smiled. "Your Grace's question is in poor taste and somewhat rude."

"Even so, will you answer for me?"

Fielding smiled slightly. "No, I have no mistress here, or anywhere. Does that answer your question?"

Stephen frowned. If Breanna was neither wife nor mistress to Fielding, then who was she? "Can there be any other female in your life that is important to you?"

Fielding sat forward, lacing his fingers together. "Is it possible that you think the woman you hit is in some way connected with me? I can assure you that is not the case."

"How then do you account for the fact that yours is the only name she remembers from her past?"

Fielding shook his head. "I cannot imagine. Suppose we turn the tables and you tell me this woman's name and describe her to me."

Stephen was reluctant to reveal Breanna's name until he found out what the connection was between her and this man. "I find myself in a dilemma, Lord Kenton. You see, the lady feels that she was being pursued by someone. I hesitate to say her name, lest that someone was you."

"You said this happened four nights ago? It

could not have been me pursuing her. I have not left Kenton these last three weeks."

Suddenly the golden eyes that Stephen gazed into reminded him of Breanna's. With hope in his heart, he formed his next question. "Do you know a woman who has golden eyes, very much like your own?"

"I . . . yes." He sprung to his feet. "Dear God, Breanna! Is the woman named Breanna?"

"Yes, she called herself Breanna. You do know her then?"

"Take me to her at once. She is my sister!"

Breanna's eyes were closed while she listened to Lady Mary read verses of poetry. When she heard a knock, Lady Mary laid her book aside and opened the door. Seeing her brother and a stranger standing in the hallway, her eyes were questioning.

"Mary," Stephen said in a whisper so Breanna would not overhear, "this is Lord Fielding Kenton. He's Breanna's brother."

Her face flooded with relief. "Oh, thank goodness. Breanna will be so pleased." Mary glanced back and saw that Breanna's eyes were closed. "She's resting now. Do you want to disturb her?"

"Yes, she has a right to see her brother," Stephen answered.

Fielding gently pushed Mary aside and moved

over to the bed. His eyes were filled with misery as he saw the bandage about his sister's forehead and the bruises and scratches on her face.

Dropping down to his knees, he took his sister's hand in his. "Breanna, dear, it's me, Fielding. Wake up."

Her eyes fluttered open, and for a moment golden eyes stared into golden eyes. At first her eyes were puzzled, then the light of recognition registered there. "Fielding?" She softly touched his face. "Is it really you?"

He laid her limp hand against his cheek. "I can assure you it is I, Breanna. What happened to bring you to such a circumstance?"

"I don't know, Fielding." She tried to sit up, but the pain in her head halted the movement. "I cannot remember."

"Where is your husband?" Fielding asked with anger in his voice.

Like a whirling pattern of bright lights, Breanna felt the room spinning around. As she clutched her brother's hand, the events of that horrible night unfolded before her eyes. She was not aware that she was sobbing as Fielding held her in his arms.

Lady Mary bent over her with a concerned look on her face, while the Duke stood by helplessly.

"Oh, Fielding, why did you make me marry him? Why?" she sobbed.

Fielding had been weighed down with guilt, and seeing his sister in such a state increased that feeling. "It's all my fault, Breanna. I will see that everything is put to rights." He rocked her back and forth. "Don't cry, honey, I'll take care of you from here on out. You'll go home with me, and Sophie will nurse you back to health."

John entered the sitting room to find Dakota standing at the window. When Dakota turned around, his face was a mask of frustration and misery. "There has still been no word, John. How can a woman disappear without anyone seeing her?"

"This just came by messenger. It's a note from her brother," John said, handing Dakota the sealed envelope.

Dakota ripped open the letter and began to read aloud.

" 'Sir, I have the obligation to inform you that my sister, Breanna, is well and in my custody—' " Dakota glanced quickly up at John with relief flooding through his whole body. Happiness shone in his eyes as he shouted, "She has been found! She's alive!"

John moved to Dakota's side and glanced at the letter. "Go on, read the letter," he urged.

" 'Since through your neglect, my sister became injured, I will ask that you do not try to see her. However, I will call on you this afternoon, so you can give me an accounting of the events of the

326

night my sister ran away from you.' It's signed, Lord Kenton," Dakota finished, crushing the letter in his fist. "What does he mean she was injured? Not he, or any man, can keep me away from Breanna. She is my wife."

John was thoughtful for a moment. "He says he will be calling on you. Since we don't know where to find him, we can do nothing but wait for him to come to us. We will just have to wait to find out about Breanna's condition. At least we know she is safe."

"Yes, she is safe," Dakota agreed, hiding his pain so John would not know how he felt inside. "I do not care if this man is Breanna's brother, he will not keep her from—"

Before Dakota could finish what he was saying, Mrs. Crowder entered the room. "Begging your pardon, my lord, but I thought you would want to know, Lord Kenton has asked to see you."

"Show him in," Dakota said, glancing at John. "We shall soon know where to find Breanna."

Fielding rushed into the room, his eyes going first to John, whom he recognized, and then to Dakota. "I assume you are my sister's husband?"

Dakota bowed, detesting the polite, gentlemanly customs that bound the English to false courtesy. What he really wanted to do was rip this man apart and make him tell him where to find Breanna. Instead he answered, "I have that honor. You said in your note that Breanna had been injured. Is she well? What happened?"

"No thanks to you, my sister will suffer no long-term injuries as the result of her accident."

"What accident?" Dakota demanded.

"She was hit by a carriage, but—"

Dakota grabbed Fielding by the shirtfront and jerked him forward. "Do not play games with me. Is Breanna all right?"

"Yes," Fielding answered, prying Dakota's hands loose and extracting himself from the iron grip. "I have come to tell you what I think of you. I have been called many things in my life, and most of them have been true, but I have never mistreated my wife, and I will not stand by while you mistreat my sister."

"For a man who sold his sister to another without knowing if she would be ill used, your concern is hypocritical." Dakota stared at the man with cold eyes. "I can see where you might think I have mistreated your sister, but it was all a misunderstanding. Breanna was mistaken in her assumption that I cared about Lady Rye."

"I don't know what your quarrel was with my sister, because she will not talk about it. I only know she has been hurt, and she needs love and understanding to heal. She apparently will get neither from you."

Dakota's eyes blazed with anger. John, seeing this, moved between the two men, knowing that Breanna's brother was treading on dangerous ground if he provoked Dakota too far.

"You know me, Fielding, and I have to back up my cousin's story. Breanna thought Dakota had taken Lady Rye Saffron for his mistress, which is not true at all."

Fielding looked into John's eyes, knowing and respecting him as a truthful man. "Were you present the night of my sister's accident?"

"I was. And Dakota is being truthful with you; there were misunderstandings all the way around that night."

"Suppose you tell me what happened then."

It was a cold, dreary morning, and a heavy rain was falling. Breanna felt well enough to get up and dress. Lady Mary had told her that Dakota was coming to take her home today. Mrs. Crowder had sent over some of Breanna's own clothing, and she was now dressed in a mint-green tea gown. Her eyes were anxious as she sat beside Lady Mary in the morning room, her hands tensely clasped in her lap, her eyes wide with uncertainty.

"Mary, I hope I am doing the right thing. My brother thinks I should go back to my husband. He assures me that I misinterpreted the events that occurred the night I ran out of the house. But I just don't know."

Lady Mary set her sewing aside. Her heart was heavy at the thought that Breanna would be leaving. "Do you remember everything, Breanna?"

"Yes, everything. Some things I wish I had never remembered."

Mary's eyes softened. "Do you want to talk about it?"

"No, I cannot."

"How do you feel about your husband?" Mary asked, remembering how she had loved her Tom.

"I don't know. I begin to think that I loved Dakota. Now I'm not so sure." Breanna turned her golden eyes on her new friend. "Oh, Mary, I am so mixed up and I feel so numb inside."

Lady Mary shook her head sadly. "I cannot advise you in matters of the heart, Breanna. You will have to be the one to decide your own future."

"Wrong," Stephen said, coming around from behind Breanna and kneeling down in front of her. "If you decide you do not want to go home with your husband, then you don't have to. You will always have a home with Mary and myself."

Stephen watched the firelight bring life to Breanna's red-gold hair. "Your brother informed me of the circumstances under which you married your husband, and I am appalled. You do not have to go back to that man, Breanna."

Breanna saw the kindness in Stephen's eyes, and she thought he was perhaps the dearest man she had ever known. "Thank you, Your Grace, and while I appreciate everything you have done for me, I cannot stay here."

He took her hand, wishing he could tell her how his heart was filled with love for her. But he realized that to confess to that love at this time would only serve to further confuse her life. "I beg you to call me Stephen. And I do not intend to lose contact with you, Breanna. You must always consider Mary and me as your friends. If ever you are in trouble, let me be the first to know."

"I will, Stephen," she whispered, brushing a tear from her cheek. Breanna had never had friends before. She knew being parted from her two dear friends was going to be very painful. "Where is my brother?" she asked, wondering why Fielding wasn't there to lend his support to her when she came face-to-face with Dakota.

Stephen's lips hardened into a thin line. He could not understand himself why Fielding had deserted his sister, so how was he going to explain it to her? "Your brother asked me to offer you his best wishes and to tell you he had pressing business that needed his attention at home."

"He . . . didn't even tell me good-bye."

"It seems not."

Breanna leaned back in her chair. Fielding had been so kind and caring when he arrived yesterday. She had thought he had changed, but he hadn't really. He would always be weak and would sidestep any kind of unpleasant confrontation. "It doesn't matter," she said, knowing that it mattered very much.

Breanna tensed when she heard the butler announce Dakota and John. She watched Stephen draw himself up to his full height as Dakota approached. Her eyes looked into those of her husband, and as always, she could not tell what he was thinking.

He acknowledged the introduction to Stephen and Mary with a nod of his head, his eyes always on Breanna.

"Are you well enough to travel?" Dakota asked, his eyes moving across Breanna's face. Inside his heart was crying out to her, but this did not show. He wanted to go down on his knees and hold her to him, to beg her to believe in his innocence—while another part of him rebelled because she had not had faith in him.

"I am well enough," Breanna answered, allowing Stephen to help her to her feet. "Please tell me first the condition of your grandfather."

"He is no different," Dakota answered, his voice cold and without feeling.

Lady Mary reached out toward the handsome young Viscount. "Please take the greatest care of Breanna," she pleaded. "She has been very ill."

"We shall be very aware of her health," John spoke up, feeling the undertones in this room. He saw the naked love shining in the Duke's eyes when they rested on Breanna. "Rest assured Breanna will receive every consideration."

Stephen stood eye-to-eye with Dakota. "Does

your cousin speak for you?"

Dakota did not miss the way the Duke's hand rested possessively on Breanna's arm, and he wanted to tear her away from the man. "No man speaks for me. I will take my wife home now."

Stephen turned Breanna to him and whispered next to her ear. "Why couldn't I have met you first?"

She glanced into his eyes in confusion. Turning away to hide the tears that threatened to fall, she knelt before Mary. "Please take care of yourself. Get out more and see friends. I expect you to come to visit me as soon as possible."

"I shall, Breanna. Remember, you will be missed by both my brother and myself."

Turning quickly toward the door, Breanna held her hand out to John because she could not bear to have Dakota touch her.

Dakota saw this, and turned to Mary. "I owe you and your brother my thanks for taking such good care of my wife."

"Just see that you do the same," Stephen warned.

Dakota's eyes met Stephen's in mortal combat. Today was not the time to settle what was between them, but both men knew that day was not far off.

Mary and Stephen watched as Breanna departed with her husband and his cousin. The brother and sister felt the silence of the now empty room.

"Shall we ever see her again, Stephen?" Mary asked, feeling as if she had lost her best friend.

"Yes, we shall," he stated with assurance.

Mary's eyes followed her brother as he moved restlessly about the room. Finally, he sat down by Mary, where a trace of Breanna's perfume still lingered in the air.

"Mary, I have no notion of what Breanna has gone through, or indeed may be going through now as we speak. But I intend to find out. I do not know if her husband is guilty of misusing her, or if he was a victim of circumstances."

"You care for Breanna a great deal, don't you, Stephen?"

"I could easily care too much," he admitted. "I finally understand how you felt about Tom, and why it has been so difficult for you to put his memory aside."

"But, Stephen," she reminded him sadly, "Breanna is married to someone else. You must put her out of your mind. There is no future for you and her together."

"I have never coveted another man's wife before, and I am not sure how to deal with this. One thing is for certain, I plan to call on her husband very soon. I am still not convinced that Breanna wanted to go with him."

Mary placed her hand on her brother's. "Let it alone, Stephen, because I could tell that Breanna loves her husband a great deal."

A spasm of pain crossed his face. "Nevertheless, I shall call on the Viscount of Remington to satisfy my mind that Breanna is being treated well."

Chapter Twenty-five

John helped Breanna into the coach and tucked a
lap robe about her, while Dakota remained distant
and cold. The coach ride to the townhouse was
long and uncomfortable for Breanna. She did not
once look at Dakota, but she could feel his eyes
burning into her, watching her every move.

When they reached the house, Mrs. Crowder
hurried Breanna off to bed, clucking over her like a
mother hen. As Breanna lay in the strange bedroom, she tried to make some reason out of her
life. Tired from the day's ordeal, she closed her
eyes and drifted off to sleep.

She did not hear Dakota when he entered her
bedroom. She was not aware that he stood over her
for a very long time, just watching her sleep. She
did not hear him when he turned and walked quietly out of the room.

* * *

336

The next morning, Breanna had just climbed out of bed and was pulling on her dressing gown when she heard a knock on her door. Diving back into bed, she pulled the covers over her, calling out for whoever it was to enter. She had known Dakota would pay her a visit, but she had hoped he would not come so soon.

He stood tall and proud, his face a mask that revealed nothing of what he was feeling. "May I sit down and talk to you for a moment?" he asked politely.

She nodded, indicating the gray silk-covered chair. "I have been expecting you," she said dully.

He saw the faint trace of bruises on her face and felt her pain. "Are you recovered from the accident?" he wanted to know.

"I feel stronger with each passing day." She met his eyes and saw such misery there that she wanted to cry out. Was he innocent? No, she had seen that woman in Dakota's arms with her own eyes. She turned her eyes away, not wanting to forgive him.

"How is your grandfather this morning?"

"There has been no change."

"I'm sorry, Dakota."

"Breanna, I just want to say this, and then I will never mention it again. I am sorry about this misunderstanding between us. My mistake was one of judgment, and not one of immorality. I wish that you had trusted me. The next time there is a disagreement between us, I hope we can talk about it, and you won't go running off into the night."

Breanna's anger could no longer be contained, and the words spilled out of her mouth. "But I saw that woman in your arms. You brought her under this roof, bought her clothing, gave her jewels. What did you expect me to think?"

"I did not bring her here, I merely allowed her to stay. I know now that was a mistake. But I did not take the woman to my bed. I did not desire her." His jade green eyes burned with conviction. "No woman has ever tempted me like the one with the face of an angel and the temper of the devil."

"Me?"

A slight smile curved his lips. "Who else could it be?"

She was not ready to believe him. The hurt and disillusionment were still burning inside her. "You have a strange way of showing your affection, Dakota."

"I did nothing wrong."

"I find I am weary, Dakota. Will you leave me now?"

He stood up, knowing he was losing her and there was nothing he could do about it. Pain throbbed in his voice. "Will I see you tomorrow? Perhaps you would like to take a ride in the carriage?"

"No, I will just want to rest for a few more days." Her eyes were lusterless as she turned to the wall.

Dakota stood over Breanna for a moment, wishing he had the words to tell her how he felt about her. If only he could make her understand how his world had stopped when he could not find her. He reached toward her with a trembling hand, then drew back, quietly leaving the room.

Dakota entered the library to find John and Levi talking over a glass of brandy. "How is Breanna feeling today, Dakota?" Levi inquired.

Dakota removed his coat and tossed it over the back of a chair, then ripped his cravat from his neck, tossing it aside. "I don't know anything about women, least of all my own wife. But I have more pressing things on my mind at the moment."

Levi and John exchanged glances. "Is it your grandfather?" John asked. The pressure of not knowing from day-to-day, or minute-to-minute, when the old Marquess would take his final breath was taking its toll on everyone's nerves.

"No, it is not my grandfather."

"I suspect you are only upset because Breanna did not trust you," John offered. "After she comes around, you will sing a different tune."

Levi, who knew Dakota better than John did, realized that something deeper was troubling him. "What has happened?" the hunter asked.

"I'm going home, Levi," Dakota stated flatly. "I

have to."

"I assume you mean back to Weatherford Hall?" John said, knowing that Dakota was taking his grandfather's imminent death hard. "You cannot leave until . . . my great-uncle has gone. It would not be the proper thing to do."

"I will be saddened to leave my grandfather, but I have to go home to America. Something happened that requires my attention."

The color drained from John's face. "But what about your grandfather? What about Breanna? You cannot expect her to go with you, and you can't desert her."

"Breanna is free to do as she chooses. She has always known this. As for my grandfather, God will choose for him."

"Has something happened?" Levi asked again, knowing Dakota's decision to return to America was not merely a whim. There was something definitely wrong.

Dakota picked up his coat and pulled a letter from the inside pocket. "This came today. It's from Murphy at the trading post, Levi."

"What's he got to say?"

"I cannot credit what he says is true. Black Otter is not dead. He escaped the same night we left the Arapaho village. He and several young warriors are wreaking havoc on the white settlers, as well as striking at Indian villages. Murphy writes that Black Otter has turned renegade—he is killing without mercy. He says if something isn't done, the soldiers will be brought in to hunt him down, and that would cause a real bloodbath. Murphy thinks I am the only one who can stop Black Otter."

"Yes, I reckon he's right," Levi admitted. "Chances are, Black Otter expects you to come back. Hell no, he *knows* you'll come back. That's why he's doing this."

Hatred burned in Dakota's eyes. "Black Otter said we would meet again, and it will come to pass."

"Have both of you lost your minds?" John asked. "I can't believe you are standing here discussing some Indian who is no longer your problem. Let the Americans deal with him. Your life is here."

"That's where you are wrong," Dakota said. "Black Otter will not cease being my problem until one or both of us are dead!"

"Good day," a clipped voice called out from the doorway, drawing the three men's attention. "I persuaded your housekeeper to allow me to announce myself. I hope I'm not interrupting anything," the Duke of Clandannon said.

Dakota's eyes narrowed as he stared into the Duke's cold eyes. "Would it matter if you were?" Dakota asked pointedly.

"No, not really," Stephen replied. He nodded to John before his eyes moved on to the white-headed man. "You must be Levi Gunther," he concluded. "Breanna has told me many things about you."

341

"Yep, that's who I am, but who are you?" Levi asked, certain he already knew who the man was, and knowing that if it was Breanna's newest champion, there was certain to be trouble ahead. That was all they needed.

"This is His Grace, the Duke of Clandannon," John said to Levi, knowing that Dakota did not feel inclined to make the introduction.

Stephen nodded politely. "I am pleased to meet you, Levi. Breanna spoke highly of you."

"Now that the flowery compliments have been handed out," Dakota said curtly, "what is your business here?"

Again the two men's eyes locked.

"Actually I have come to inquire into your wife's health. I trust Breanna is faring well."

"Yes, she is."

"I wonder if I might see her, just to assure myself that she is well."

Dakota's eyes narrowed. "No, you cannot."

Stephen shrugged. "Can I assume that you would have no objections to my sister calling on Breanna? You see, we both care for her and want to be assured that she has not suffered from her . . . ordeal."

"Your sister is always welcome to call. If you require nothing further, we will bid you a good day."

John's jaws fell open at Dakota's display of jealousy. "If your grace will follow me, I'll show you the way out," he said, trying to save the situation. He could see that the Duke was overly interested in Dakota's wife, and it was apparent that Dakota knew it too.

Stephen bowed. "You can expect my sister to call tomorrow."

The look on Dakota's face was murderous as the Duke followed John out of the room.

Levi thought it was just as well that the Duke was leaving. "Well, if that don't beat all. Am I mistaken, or was that man a mite too interested in Breanna's welfare?"

Dakota glared at Levi. "You were not mistaken. There seem to be too many gentlemen interested in my wife."

For two days Breanna had remained in her bedroom. She was beginning to feel lonely and cut off from everything. She vacillated between wishing Dakota would come to see her and fearing that he might. At last, unable to stand the confinement of her room any longer, she decided to take her courage in hand and go downstairs. After all, she reasoned, she couldn't hide in her room for the rest of her life. She had to face Dakota sooner or later.

Breanna encountered no one on the way downstairs. Looking into the sitting room, she found no one there either.

When she entered the library, she was almost

glad it was empty. A cheery fire blazed in the fireplace, and various titles of books beckoned to her.

Breanna thought of how well read Dakota was. In the past, he had shared much of his wondrous knowledge with her. He had challenged her mind, and awakened in her a craving for knowledge. Unlike other men, he did not believe books had been printed for men alone. Now she decided she would read on her own, hoping Dakota would be pleased.

Selecting a book about mysterious India, she dropped down on a window seat and began to read. Fascinating pictures of an ancient culture unfolded for her on the pages of the book. She was so engrossed in what she was reading that she had not heard Dakota and John enter the room. She looked up only when John's angry voice reached her ears.

"Dammit, Dakota, you can't just walk away from your responsibilities here in England. You can't leave your grandfather when he is dying. And what about the other people here who depend on you?"

"We have talked this to death, John. And if you see my duties as important, why don't you take care of them?"

"Now you are starting to sound like your grandfather. He never considered others when they stood in the way of something he wanted. You know how long he neglected the villagers in Weatherford."

"I have responsibilities in America also, John. I was hoping you would stay with my grandfather until . . . the end. Then go to Weatherford Hall and watch over the villagers for me. I will give you leave to make decisions in my absence."

Breanna drew in her breath. Was Dakota planning to leave her? The book she had been reading dropped from her lap and landed with a thud, catching both men's attention. Her eyes sought Dakota's as she stood up and walked slowly toward him. "You are going away?" she asked.

"Yes. I hadn't meant to tell you in this way, but I am going back to America."

John watched Breanna's face whiten. He felt it was time to leave them alone. Neither of them heard him when he excused himself and left the room.

"You once told me that you might return to America, Dakota. I had begun to believe you felt at home in England."

"I would hasten to tell you that in all probability I shall one day return to England, Breanna. I realize I cannot just walk away from my duties."

"Your duties to whom? Me, or the villagers at Weatherford?"

"Both, Breanna."

She felt as if someone had stabbed at her heart with a knife. "Are you leaving because of the trouble between the two of us?"

His jaw set in a firm line. "No, I would never want to leave with this misunderstanding between us if I didn't feel compelled to go. There are many things in my mind that are unclear. I do not want

345

you to think this is a cowardly act and I am running away. Know instead that I have a larger responsibility elsewhere."

"I do not understand. Will you return to the Arapaho village?"

"I don't know. Perhaps." He hesitated to tell her his real reason for leaving. "I cannot even tell you when I will be free to return."

Now Breanna was confused. "Will you not tell me why you are going? I want to understand."

"I cannot, Breanna."

Suddenly she couldn't stand the thought of being parted from him. He might not love her, but he was her husband. "Take me with you," she cried, all pretense of indifference stripped from her. "Don't leave me behind," she pleaded, grabbing his arm and holding on to him with desperation.

Dakota could not believe his ears. Under other circumstances he would be overjoyed that she wanted to be with him. He had thought she would be happy to see him leave. He looked into her eyes, trying to read the truth in the golden depths. The pain of leaving her would be great, but he could not take her with him—it was too dangerous.

"Why would you consider going to America, Breanna?"

She could not tell him that her life would cease to have any meaning with him gone. Instead, she told him a half-truth. "You have told me so much about your America. I want to see it for myself."

346

"It is impossible, Breanna. The journey will be difficult. You have not been brought up to endure hardships such as the ones I will encounter once I leave civilization as you know it. Besides," he reminded her, "you have been ill and will need time to recover."

"When do you leave?"

"Within the week."

"I will be well by then, Dakota. Your father took your mother to America, and conditions then were much worse than they are now."

"Yes, my father took my mother, and you know what happened to them. Had he left her safely in England, they might both be alive today."

Breanna heard the bitterness in Dakota's voice.

"I am strong, Dakota. If you take me with you, I will not once complain. I promise you."

In many ways she reminded him of a little girl. He could feel himself weakening. Perhaps if she were to see where he had come from, she would better be able to realize the person he was.

"No, Breanna," he said regretfully, "and that is my final word. If I took you, there would be times when you would curse me for allowing you to come along. Will you stay here and look after my grandfather? The family is what he lived for. Do not allow him to die without a member of the family at his bedside. Will you do this for me, Breanna?"

She felt the pain of tears behind her eyes and turned away. "Yes, I will do this for you." She hurried from the room, fearing she would cry in front of him.

As night settled over London, dark clouds gathered in the east. Breanna felt restless, as she always did when a storm was brewing, and she paced the floor.

Dakota had been in his grandfather's room all day, and she dared not disturb him. She knew it would do no good to keep begging him to take her with him, for he would never relent.

The servants had gone to bed hours ago, and Breanna was caught up in the silence of the house.

Streaks of lightning flashed across the sky, and the double doors flew open from a gust of wind, fanning the candles until they flickered and went out. Breanna used the light from the fireplace to guide her across the room. Icy wind and rain pelted her face and body, and she had to clamp her teeth together to keep them from chattering, but she finally managed to close the doors and bolt them.

It wasn't a sound that alerted her to the fact that she wasn't alone in the room; it was more a feeling. When she turned around, a flash of lightning revealed Dakota's face.

Breanna caught her breath at the sight of intense longing she saw in his eyes. Were the thunder and lightning reminding him of that first stormy night they had come together in a uniting fire that had threatened to consume them both?

She wasn't aware that she had moved, but she must have, because she found herself locked in Dakota's arms. A whimper escaped her throat as his warm lips nuzzled the lobe of her ear.

"I have wanted this for so long," he murmured. "I thought you would never allow me to touch you again. I am glad you willingly came into my arms."

She glanced at him questioningly. Had she come to him? "Dakota, I . . . wasn't . . ."

"Shhh," he whispered as he framed her face with his hands. "Have the servants gone to bed?"

"Yes," she said breathlessly.

He lifted her in his arms and carried her across the room. "You are wet and will become ill if you don't get out of these clothes."

Breanna leaned her head against his shoulder and closed her eyes as he took the stairs with ease. The thundering of his heart matched the racing of her pulse.

Dakota walked past the bedroom she had been using and carried her to his. On entering the room, he did not bother to light a candle.

Placing Breanna on her feet, he began the slow process of undressing her. Each movement he made left her trembling, not with cold, but with wild anticipation. The troubles of yesterday did not matter—tomorrow did not exist—there was only now, and the desire that burned between them that would not be denied.

Breanna felt a coldness creep into her body as Dakota removed the last article of damp clothing. In the darkness, she felt something soft and warm enclose her body and knew that he had wrapped her in a blanket. With soft motions, he began rubbing her dry. Her knees went weak when his hand slipped across her breasts. Moments later, she felt his tongue encircle her nipple. Then she felt him lift her into his arms.

The storm intensified, with lightning and thunder charging the night sky and rain pelting the roof. A flash of lightning revealed Dakota's hard, muscled body as well as the heart-wrenching longing in his green eyes.

"Breanna," he breathed. "You are like a cleansing wind; you sweep through my body, leaving nothing untouched. Like a fire, you ignite a flame in my heart. I am overwhelmed by you, consumed by you. You are as much a part of me as the heart that pumps blood to my body."

This was not the first time Dakota had compared her to the wind. His beautiful words went around and around in her mind, heightening her feelings to a fevered pitch. Her body was on fire, and she gravitated toward the virile body that promised joy beyond endurance, fulfillment that would leave her breathless. His arms were a comforting heaven, his lips invoked burning desire. With every nerve in her body, she was conscious of Dakota.

With gentle control, he brought her fully against him. "I burn for you, Breanna. Can it be that you have missed this also?"

"Yes, I admit it."

"Give me something to take with me when I leave, something I can remember when I can no longer see you or touch you."

Tears wet her cheeks as she clutched him to her, wanting to hold on to him so he would never want to leave her.

His hands were working magic on her body, and she became his to command. "Sweet Breanna," he said, smothering her lips with a fevered kiss.

She was mindless, and unable to do more than press her lips against his. With a groan, he rolled her over, murmuring her name over and over.

Breanna was lost in a world that had no beginning and no end. As Dakota pressed against her soft body, she was burning with a fire that raged out of control.

She did not see Dakota's eyes fill with pain or the anguished twist to his lips. Dakota knew he could rule Breanna's body with a touch of his hand, but would he ever rule her heart?

Her heart was what he craved above all else.

He sank into her and sensuously pulled back, repeating the motion until it reached fever-ridden heights. When Breanna's body erupted in total satisfaction, he crushed her to him, knowing he held a part of her that no man would ever have. He had made joy sing in her blood, and she had given her whole being to him in the moment of her surrender.

Breanna felt her body relax, and Dakota rolled over and pulled her into his arms. For a moment, while the tide of passion ebbed, Breanna was content to lay his arms. But suddenly she remembered the picture of Rye Saffron in Dakota's arms and it tore at her heart.

"Dakota," she said, hating herself for needing to know. "How can I know that you did not . . . make love to Lady Rye Saffron?"

He was quiet for a moment. When he spoke, his voice was hardly above a whisper. "I have rarely had my word challenged, but you do not yet know that I am an honorable man. I have already told you once that I did not lie with that woman. What else can I say to convince you?"

"I saw her—"

"You saw what she wanted you to see. I never liked the woman, but at first I believed she was destitute and needed help. I did not know what her deceitfulness would cost me."

"What did it cost you, Dakota?" she asked, remembering the pearl necklace and the extravagant gown the woman had been wearing.

"It cost me your trust, Breanna, it almost cost me you." He hugged her tightly. "And it could have cost you your life."

Breanna had decided that her husband was either

the kindest man she had ever known, or the most devious. "I want to believe in you, Dakota, but I know what I saw."

"Until you learn to trust me, Breanna, there can be no real substance between us." He sat up and moved off the bed. "I will always hope the time will come when you will come to me with more in your heart than questions."

She could hear him pulling on his clothing. Why did she have the feeling she had wounded him deeply? But surely it was he who had betrayed her?

"Breanna, I have several letters to send out. You needn't worry that I will disturb you again tonight."

She heard the door open and close. With a heavy sigh, she wondered if she would ever know this complicated man she had married.

That night Breanna slept very little. What she didn't know was that her husband slept not at all.

Dakota paced back and forth, damning the circumstances that had burdened him with the knowledge of two different cultures, making him at war with himself. If he were an Arapaho, he would go to the woman he loved and bend her to his will. But his English side cautioned him to be patient with Breanna.

It was almost dawn when he went to his grandfather's room. Nodding, he indicated that the nurse should leave them alone.

Dakota seated himself on the edge of the bed, wishing this man who held on to life by the thinnest thread would give him some sign, some insight on what to do.

He held the old man's hand, which was hot and dry to the touch.

"I have to go away, Grandfather. It is not my wish to leave you alone at this time. I have to think you would understand that I owe something to the people who raised me. I did not ask to be your grandson, nor do I want to take your place as head of this family. If God wills it so, I will return. If I do, I will take it as a sign that I should take my place as Marquess in your stead."

There was no sign that the Marquess had heard. Dakota gently tucked the hand under the coverlet, looking for the last time upon the face of his grandfather.

With a heavy heart and a much-troubled mind, he left the bedchamber, silently closing the door behind him.

Chapter Twenty-six

Breanna was up before daybreak because Dakota would be leaving early this morning, and after what had passed between them the night before, she wasn't sure he would seek her out to tell her good-bye.

She hurriedly dressed in a cream-colored gown and twisted her hair into a knot, securing it to the top of her head. Pinching her cheeks to add color, she dashed downstairs, hoping she would be in time to share breakfast with her husband.

Hearing voices in the small dining room that was just off the kitchen, she pushed the door open and entered. Dakota, John, and Levi all came politely to their feet.

John smiled at Breanna and pulled out a chair for her to be seated. "You are up early," he commented.

She seated herself, noticing that Dakota hadn't spoken to her. "It's a lovely morning for travel," she murmured incoherently.

Levi tossed his napkin on the table and stood up, thinking it was time to give Dakota and Breanna a chance to be alone. "Me and John will be waiting for you out front," he told Dakota, "but there's no need to hurry."

"Wait," Breanna said, getting up and moving quickly over to stand beside the old hunter. "I just wanted to tell you that I will miss you, Levi. I feel that you are a great part of this family."

Levi saw tears swimming in her eyes and, on a crazy impulse, enfolded her in his arms. "I have been honored to know you, Breanna. You are one of the finest ladies I have ever met, and I will also miss you."

She rested her cheek against Levi's rough face and whispered so only he could hear. "Take care of him, Levi. Don't allow anything to happen to him."

The hunter nodded and released her. "No long faces today, Breanna, and don't you fret. Before you get to missing us, you'll look up one day and there we'll be."

Breanna turned to Dakota, who still had not spoken. "I shall keep busy, Levi."

John stifled a make-believe yawn, while ambling out of the room. "I will not miss either of you. The life you live has played havoc with my peaceful existence," he said over his shoulder. "I yearn for a quiet life."

Suddenly Breanna and Dakota were alone. He

walked slowly to her side, pulling her into his arms. "I shall count every day we are apart, dearest heart," he murmured in her ear. "If God its will, and circumstances permit it, I will soon return to hold you in my arms once more."

He raised his head, his green eyes probing her golden ones. "I will take the memory of last night with me and keep it in my heart always."

"Don't talk like that, Dakota." Desperation laced Breanna's words. "You make it sound as if you won't be coming back."

"Breanna, as long as there is breath in my body, I will return to you, for my desire for you is great."

She longed to hear him say he loved her and not that he merely desired her. "I will await your return."

"You will be with my grandfather as long as he needs you?"

"Yes, I will stay with him until the end," she assured him.

"Should you need anything, look to John, and he will lend you his support."

"I shall, Dakota."

His eyes moved over her face, taking in every soft curve, the blush of her cheek, the tears in her eyes. He wanted to imprint her likeness on his heart to sustain him through the days ahead. To leave her was to tear his heart out.

With his thumb, he wiped away her trailing tears, knowing he would always remember how her golden eyes glistened with sorrow at his leaving. Tenderly he kissed her lips. "An Indian does not like a lengthy good-bye, Breanna. It is enough to say I will think of you every day." He then abruptly turned away and left the room.

Dakota did not look back, so therefore, he did not see the beseeching hand Breanna held out to him.

She wanted to run after him, to once again beg him to take her with him. She felt as if a part of herself had been torn apart.

Calling on all her strength and willpower, Breanna moved down the hallway and into the salon. Pulling the pleated draperies aside, she watched Dakota and Levi get into the carriage. John stood on the steps, waving good-bye.

Leaning her cheek against the soft velvet draperies, Breanna allowed herself to cry out her misery. The silence of the house crept into her heart, as she watched the coach pull away and disappear down the tree-lined driveway.

Loneliness hung heavily in the room, and she was overcome by the silence. After allowing time to compose herself, Breanna made her way slowly up the stairs to sit with the Marquess so she would be fulfilling her promise to Dakota.

The old Marquess died that night without ever regaining consciousness.

Breanna and the doctor were with him when he breathed his last ragged breath. She cried, not out of affection for the Marquess, because he had not been a lovable man, but because he was Dakota's grandfather, so therefore worthy of her grief.

The Marquess's body had been prepared so he could be transported to Weatherford Hall, where he would be interred in the family crypt with generations of Remingtons.

It was a dreary day. Breanna and John stood beside the graveside, surrounded by the servants from Weatherford Hall, while the village vicar spoke glowing words about the old Marquess.

Tears blinded Breanna's eyes as she thought about the sad old man who had so few people who mourned his passing.

John stood stiffly at her side, and Breanna could tell by his eyes that he was sad at his uncle's passing. She understood how he felt, because the Marquess had been head of the family.

As a flock of ravens winged their way through the darkened heavens, gloom hung heavily in the air. John put his arms around Breanna and led her back toward the house, while the servants disbursed, going their separate ways.

As Breanna and John walked slowly along, John reflected on the Marquess's life. "My uncle was a forceful man, and he almost always got his way. But oddly enough, I respected him and I shall miss him," John said sadly. "He was the last of a proud breed of

Remington men with his kind of thinking. He always put the survival of the family name above all else, never weighing the consequences or how it would affect any individual family members."

"I did not have the chance to know him very well," Breanna replied. "But I have to say in all honesty that in our few meetings, I did not gain an affection for him."

"He was not the kind of man who encouraged affection. I wonder how different he would have been if Holden and Cillia had lived."

"Many things would have been different if they had lived," Breanna speculated. "Dakota would have been raised here in England and . . . oh, well, that did not happen. Tell me about Dakota's parents," Breanna urged, wanting something to take her mind off the sad old man who had lived his life without true affection.

By now, they had reached the steps of the house and John steered Breanna to the library.

She walked over to the desk and stared up at the portrait of Holden and Cillia. "They look like they belonged together," Breanna said, noting the green eyes of the woman—green eyes that she had passed on to her son.

"They were very much in love. I was young, but I always felt good just being around them. They laughed a lot, and made the people around them laugh also. I can remember being devastated when we received word that they had died so tragically."

John walked over to the desk and opened the drawer, pulling out Holden's journal. "Have you read the last entry my cousin made in his journal before he died?"

"No, I haven't," Breanna said, sitting down in the chair and allowing her eyes to move over the yellowed pages of the journal. Tears blinded her as she read:

On this day, the first day of November, in the year of Our Lord, 1833, Cillia died, delivering our child while I was away. It is my belief that the child lives and has been taken by Indians. It is my hope that every effort will be made to find the baby so it can be sent to my father in England. It is my wish that my wife and I be buried in a common grave so we might spend eternity together.

"Even after all this time, it is so tragic," she said, wiping her eyes on a linen handkerchief. "It must be wonderful to have such a love as Dakota's father had for his mother."

John could only stare at Dakota's beautiful wife, thinking how exceptional she was. He would always have a special place for her in his heart. But she must never know how he felt, or he might lose her friendship, for John knew that Breanna belonged to Dakota.

"You realize that one or the other of us will have

361

to leave today for the townhouse in London, Breanna. If we stay under the same roof, it won't take gossiping tongues long to draw the wrong conclusion."

Breanna rose and stood beneath the portraits, unmindful of John's concern for her reputation. "Cillia never allowed her husband to go anywhere without her, did she, John?"

"No, never. I recall Holden once commented to me that since their marriage, he and Cillia had never spent one night apart." John looked at her suspiciously. "What makes you ask, Breanna?"

Baxley chose that moment to enter the room, carrying a tray. "Mrs. Hopkins thought you might like your tea served in here, my lady."

"Baxley," Breanna said, still staring at the portrait of Cillia, "you knew my husband's mother and father very well. Would Lord Holden have considered going to America without his wife?"

"No, my lady, never!"

Breanna's eyes took on a glow, as she turned to face both men. "Then Dakota should not have gone without me."

John shook his head, knowing by the gleam in Breanna's eyes that trouble was coming. "I know there is a bee in your bonnet, Breanna. What are you thinking?"

She raised her chin with defiance etched on her face. "I am going to join my husband in America."

"No, you are not," John said emphatically. "Where

Dakota is going is no place for a lady."

"Be that as it may, I am going. I will take a page of courage from Cillia's book. I promised Dakota I would stay with his grandfather as long as he needed me, and I have fulfilled that promise. There is no longer anything to keep me here."

John turned to Baxley, hoping to enlist the valet in his argument. "You went to America with my cousins, Baxley. Tell her ladyship it would be impossible for her to go."

The old retainer's eyes danced with excitement. "I would never presume to tell the new Marchioness what to do, sir."

For the first time Breanna realized that on the old Marquess's death, Dakota had become the Marquess of Weatherford. "See, John, Baxley doesn't believe that my joining Dakota is a bad notion."

Baxley smiled broadly. "If your ladyship will allow it, I will be honored to accompany you. I know a lot about the land and would be of great help to your ladyship."

John threw up his hands. "I think you are both mad. Dakota would not approve of your going to America."

"You cannot know that, John," Breanna said, her mind already filled with preparations for the voyage.

"I will not be a party to such a scheme," John stated, disconcerted by the far-off gleam in Breanna's eyes.

"With or without you, John, I am going. My

363

mind is made up."

Seeing the determination in Breanna's eyes, and knowing he would do anything she asked of him, regardless of the consequences, he conceded. "I will accompany you if you persist in this madness, but you will have to explain it to Dakota when we see him."

Breanna, in her glee, threw her arms around John. "You won't regret it, John, I can promise you." She smiled at Baxley. "Make all the arrangements, because I want to leave as soon as possible. My husband has already had a week's head start on us."

The *Phoenix* was a steam-powered merchant ship that could make the voyage between London and New York in less than three weeks. John had told Breanna that they might even reach New York ahead of Dakota and Levi, since the two men had been forced to sail on a frigate, which could take four to five weeks to cross the Atlantic, depending on the wind.

The *Phoenix* had set sail from London on a cold, dreary morning and had been under way for a week. As they neared the end of the voyage, the weather had changed from cold damp fog to clear days and warm breezes. Even though it was late autumn, the weather was so warm that Breanna had exchanged her heavy wool cape for a light shawl.

John's cabin was located on one side of hers, while Baxley's was on the other, and both men had appointed themselves her faithful watchdogs.

In her weaker moments, she wondered if Dakota would be angry with her for her impulsiveness, but she pushed those concerns aside, having convinced herself that she was doing the right thing. Besides, it was too late to be concerned now. She was on her way to America to join Dakota, and there was no turning back.

Breanna felt her heart lighten and her cares melt away in the heady salt air. With the wind in her hair and a warm sun on her face, she stood on deck, feeling exuberant and alive. No longer would she have to dream about sailing away to some far-off land; it was a reality.

"America," she said aloud, loving the way it lingered on her tongue. In her mind she pictured America as wild and unpredictable as her husband.

John joined Breanna on deck. "Pipe dreaming, or fanciful wishing?" he queried.

She gave him one of her warmest smiles. "Actually, I was wondering about America. I know you have been there. What's it like?"

He leaned his arm on the top railing and propped a booted foot on the bottom rail. "I didn't see much of it."

"Have you been to the Arapaho land?" she wanted to know.

"No, just New York. I found it damp, humid, and

the mosquitoes were intolerable."

Her eyes were shining with excitement. "I cannot wait to go ashore. I'm looking forward to seeing my first Indian."

John's lips curled into a smile. "I hate to be the one to point this out to you, Breanna, but the whole time I spent in New York, Dakota was the only Indian I saw."

She missed the amusement in his voice. "Oh, John, I mean a real Indian. Dakota was only raised by the Arapaho war chief, he's not really one of them."

John glanced into her face, and something akin to pain throbbed in his heart. She was the loveliest creature he had ever seen, and again he reminded himself that she belonged to his cousin. "I have a feeling that when you see Dakota, it will take some of the enthusiasm out of you. To say he is not going to be happy is putting it mildly."

"Dakota may not like it at first, but when I assure him that I will not be a burden to him or slow him down, he will accept it," she said confidently.

"You say you would like to see a real Indian, but have you ever considered that a 'real' Indian might want to slit your pretty throat?"

She only laughed. "Oh, John, you have always been one for dramatics."

"My God," John said, throwing his hands up. "You think you are going on a Sunday picnic."

She smiled at him. "I only know that I am going

366

to be with my husband." There was no longer any doubt in her mind that she loved the man she had married. She no longer fought against the emotions that ruled her heart and dominated her thinking. She longed for the time when she would see him again.

It was a bright Wednesday morning, without a cloud in the sky, when the cry came from the watch. "Land ho."

Excitement ran through the passengers who clambered to the railing, straining to catch their first sight of America.

Brenna stood beside John and Baxley, expectancy in her eyes.

"We'll sleep on American soil tonight," John said. "Heaven help me when we face Dakota, because he is going to want to rip my head off for allowing you to come."

"I shall tell him you had no choice in the matter. He will be grateful you came along to protect me. Besides," she said, conceding that Dakota might be a little upset, "let him vent his anger on me."

"Oh, I shall, because you have better powers of persuasion with him than I."

Happiness brightened her smile. "Do you think Dakota and Levi will still be in New York?"

"I would think so, Breanna."

She linked her arm through John's, catching sight

367

of a tiny speck of land in the distance. "I can hardly wait, John. I have dreamed of this moment!"

John offered Breanna his spyglass. "Use this for your first glimpse of America," he said, helping her adjust the lens to fit her eyes.

"I see it," she cried happily. "Just think, I am about to set foot on American soil."

"I hope you won't feel disillusioned, Breanna. It isn't much by English standards.

Breanna handed John back his spyglass and gave him an impish smile. "You are such a snob, John. I want to see the mountains and rivers and prairies."

He smiled down at her. "Who has been filling your pretty head with such romantic notions? It sounds like Levi talking."

"Yes, Levi and Dakota. I will even be glad to see Levi. I have missed him."

John stared at the shoreline, knowing he would have to face Dakota's wrath. He glanced down at Breanna and saw the happy glow on her face. It didn't matter what trouble came his way, because he would do anything Breanna asked of him.

Chapter Twenty-seven

As the hired carriage rattled over the cobblestone streets, Breanna's spirits were dampened, not only by the mist that had rolled in and hung in the air, cloaking her view of New York, but also because now that she had arrived, she feared Dakota would be angry with her.

John and Baxley sat silently across from her, neither of them inclined to talk. Breanna knew that both men were wondering what Dakota's reaction would be when he discovered they had followed him to America.

In the glow of the carriage lamp, she glanced at John. "I see no reason to allow the gloomy weather to keep us from enjoying our first day in America."

"There's nothing to see," John said, pulling his hat low over his forehead.

Glancing up to catch Baxley's eyes, she saw understanding there. "Begging your pardon, my lady, but this fog could clear within a moment's notice."

"I did so want to see New York," she said wistfully. Glancing out the window, Breanna could see nothing past damp mist, and could hear nothing but the sound of muted horses' hooves.

"You will probably see more of this city than you want to before we leave," John observed with his usual cynicism for anything American. His eyes caught Baxley's. "You are sure that the frigate his lordship sailed on has docked?"

"Yes, sir. I was told they tied up yesterday."

"How long do you think Dakota will remain in New York?" Breanna asked.

"I should think it will take at least three days to gather what supplies and equipment they will need for the journey, my lady. This is Wednesday. . . . I would expect his lordship to leave by Friday."

"We should have no trouble finding them if they stay at the same hotel as before," John stated.

"I should think they would, sir."

The rest of the ride was covered in silence. Breanna thought it strange that three people who were about to embark on a great adventure found little to say to one another. Her head was filled with questions she wanted to ask Baxley since he had been to the wilderness, but now was not the time to ask them.

Breanna's heart was thumping against her ribs. Soon she would see Dakota. Let him be angry with her for coming, let him tell her how irresponsible her actions were, but please, she prayed, oh, please, let him be happy to see me.

When they reached the hotel, John steered Breanna inside while Baxley made inquiries at the front desk, his voice carrying to Breanna.

"Have you a Lord Remington registered here, sir?" Baxley asked, with his stiff English accent.

The desk clerk peeped over his glasses, studying his ledger. "No, but I have a Dakota Remington."

"That would be him, sir. Would you please tell me his lordship's room number?"

John glanced at Breanna. "Well, dear girl, the fat's in the fire now. Do you want to take ship home?"

She gave him a half-smile. "Certainly not," she replied, exuding more confidence than she actually felt.

By now Baxley had rejoined them, dangling the key from his fingers. "If your ladyship will allow me, I will see you settled into his lordship's room. After that, I'll have your trunks sent up."

"Is his lordship in?" she asked.

"No, my lady. Not at this time. The man behind the desk informed me that his lordship and Mr. Gunther had gone out early this morning and have not yet returned."

Breanna had been waiting for Dakota for over an hour. For the hundredth time, she looked at the green and white furnishings, wondering what could be keeping her husband. She removed her bonnet

371

and draped it over the bedpost, realizing she might have made a mistake in coming here. Suppose Dakota insisted she go right back to England?

Moving over to Dakota's trunk, she picked up a blue shirt that she found there and held it up to her face because it made her feel close to him. She loved him desperately and was so anxious to see him.

Another hour passed and still Dakota had not come. John had knocked on the door earlier to see if Breanna wanted to go to the dining room for dinner, but she sent him away.

The mist was still heavy and she could see nothing as darkness fell over the town.

It had been a long day and Breanna was weary. She thought she would just lie down for a moment and rest, but when her head touched the pillow, she relaxed into the soft mattress and was soon asleep.

Dakota stood in his darkened room; his keen hearing picked up the sound of soft breathing. He knew there was another presence in the room. He moved, catlike, across the floor, staying in the shadows. He heard the breathing coming from the bed and unsheathed his knife. Silently he reached out, his hand coming in contact with a woman's soft body!

Breanna felt the touch of a man's hand on her wrist, and she knew it was Dakota. Raising her arms, she slid them around his shoulders. She took advantage of his astonishment to press her lips against his.

He stiffened for a moment, and then the knife clattered to the floor. There could be no mistaking the soft scent of his wife's perfume that now enveloped him. "Breanna! Can it be you?"

"Yes," she whispered, her lips seeking his kiss.

Dakota felt the touch of her soft lips and felt himself surrender to the wonderment of holding the woman he loved. He had ached for her since sailing from England. He had known he would miss her, but nothing had prepared him for the deep void that had engulfed him without her in his life.

A soft moan escaped his throat as he eased himself down on the bed beside her. "Breanna," he murmured, "my Breanna."

It felt so good to be crushed against his hard body. "I was afraid you would be angry with me for coming."

She felt his body tense as reason returned. "You said you would stay with my grandfather."

She sat up, pushing her tumbled hair out of her face. "I stayed with him until he was buried, Dakota. Your grandfather died without ever regaining consciousness. The doctor said he did not suffer. It saddens me to inform you that you are now the Marquess of Weatherford."

There was silence in the room as she reached out to him, feeling his pain. He pushed her away and stood up. Lighting a lamp, he waited until the room was bathed in light before he looked at her.

There was no warmth in his voice when he spoke. "Why are you here, Breanna?"

"I came because . . . I am your wife and I did not want to be separated from you."

His eyes blazed. "It was a foolish thing for you to do. Where I must go, you cannot go—what I must do, I must do alone. I will expect you to take the first ship back to England."

"No, I want to be with you," she pleaded.

"Where is your maid?" His voice was cold. "Have you a woman to attend you?"

"No, I did not bring Etta with me."

His eyes darkened. "Surely you did not come alone, did you?"

She hesitated. "No, but I want you to know it was entirely my idea to come. John tried to talk me out of it, and when he failed to change my mind, he and Baxley accompanied me."

Dakota's jaw tightened. "You traveled with only John and Baxley as your companions?"

"Yes, but I—"

"Had you been an Indian woman, you would not have dared insult your husband in this way."

She came off the bed and stood before him, her eyes wide and innocent. "I am not an Indian, and you cannot ever forgive me for that, can you? If I thought it would make a difference, I would paint my skin and wear my hair in braids. Look at me, Dakota. I am as you see me. If I displease you, then say so."

He had never seen her behave in this manner before, and he had never known she would go to such great lengths to please him. Dare he hope that she had missed him and had come to be with him? Did she not know how beautiful she was with her hair tumbling down about her face and her breasts heaving from her labored breathing.

"I do not want you other than you are, Breanna. But neither am I pleased by your actions. What am I to do with you?"

"Take me with you."

"I cannot."

"Cillia wouldn't have allowed Holden to go anywhere without her; Baxley told me this."

"And you know what happened to them," he reminded her.

"Yes, but they were together."

He took a hesitating step toward her. "Dare I hope that you really want to be with me, or are you merely looking for adventure?"

Now was the time to tell him that she loved him, she thought. Why did she hesitate? Could he not see that she wanted to be with him? "You and Levi have talked so much about America I wanted to see it for myself."

His voice was dull. "You have gone to the extreme."

She moved closer to him and caught his arm. "Take me with you."

His resolve softened. It was not in him to deny her anything she wanted. "You have no notion of the hardships you will face, Breanna."

"I promise that if you will allow me to go with you, I will do exactly as you say. I will not be a burden, Dakota. You have my word on this."

He studied her face. "I remember the first day we met, you assured me that you always kept your word."

"I do, I do," she said eagerly.

He took in a deep breath. "All right, Breanna. But only as far as Murphy's Trading Post, and only if you will follow my orders and do exactly what I say. You will not have preferential treatment just because you are a woman; is that understood?"

She could not hide her joy. "I understand, and I will follow your orders, I promise."

He found her trunk at the foot of the bed and and threw open the lid, tossing gowns and petticoats onto the bed. "None of these are suitable for where we are going."

"I did not know what kind of clothing to bring, and we left too quickly to have others made up," she answered, gathering up an armload of gowns and placing them back in the trunk. Happiness shone in her golden eyes. He was going to take her with him!

Dakota stepped back from her, angry with himself for not insisting she return to England. He wanted to strip her clothing off and take her to his bed, but his outrage at her behavior tightened his resolve and made him want to strike out at her, to wound her.

"I hope you will be comfortable here. I will stay with Levi, whose room is just next door. Should you need anything, call out and we will hear you."

"But—"

He turned away and moved out the door, leaving her confused. Dakota had agreed that she could go with him, but he did not want to share a room with her.

Dakota pushed the door open to John's room and angrily faced his cousin. "Why did you bring Breanna here?" he demanded.

John was sitting in a chair with his booted feet propped on the bed. "I have been wondering that myself. What in the hell could have possessed me to agree to this foolery?"

"I cannot believe you disregarded her safety in bringing her here. And now I have agreed to take her with me, and where I am going is no place for a woman."

John came to his feet, a smile on his face. "So, she persuaded you to allow her to go with you. If you cannot deny her slightest wish, how do you expect me to?"

Dakota's eyes darkened. "You love her." It was not a question, but a statement of fact.

John became serious. "You have nothing to fear from me, Dakota. Whatever you know of me, you

377

know I place honor and family above all else."

"That is no answer, John. Do you love my wife?"

"Don't we all?"

Dakota's eyes narrowed, and John shivered at the coldness he saw there. "I trusted you, John."

"You still can. If I had not accompanied her, she would have come alone. Think about that, Dakota. And I'll tell you something else. If you allow Breanna to go with you into the wilderness, then I am going, too. I intend to see that she comes to no harm."

"You are not invited."

John shrugged, knowing his and Dakota's friendship hung in the balance. "I will always honor you as head of the family, Dakota." Then he smiled faintly. "Besides, even if I did covet your wife, she would never consider dishonoring you."

Dakota stared at him. He had never admired a man more than John, but now jealousy made Dakota suspect his cousin's motives. "I will not stop you from coming with us, John. I have always wondered what kind of man you are. The wilderness has a way of testing a man and making him face his true self. I wonder if you are up to that?"

John stared long and hard at Dakota. "Do not think because I laugh at life that I cannot be called upon to take it seriously. I have not dishonored you in any way. You are my friend, and I would not betray you. Breanna does not even know that I love her, nor will she ever know unless you tell her."

Dakota turned away, wrenching the door open. "I would hate to have to kill you, John." With that, he softly closed the door behind him.

Chapter Twenty-eight

The next morning Dakota appeared at Breanna's door and escorted her downstairs to the dining room. He was silent and brooding, contributing little to the conversation, while her nervousness made her patter on.

"I was astounded by how quickly the steamship made the voyage to America. John says the sailing ships will soon be a thing of the past."

Dakota gave no hint that he had heard her. "I have important business to attend to this afternoon. Can you manage alone? I will not see you until sometime this evening."

Disappointment showed in her eyes. "Yes, I can manage, but I had hoped you would show me New York."

"Breanna, I am unfamiliar with New York, so I would be of little use to you. You were aware when you came here that it was not for pleasure. If you cannot accept that, then I suggest you go back to England on the first possible ship."

She was hurt by his cold words, and further wounded that he should suggest that she leave. "I told you if you would allow me to go with you, that I would not be a bother to you," she said bravely, refusing to allow him to see how hurt she was.

For a moment she thought his eyes softened, but his voice was cold and emotionless when he spoke. "I will ask Levi to entertain you today. John will go with me," he said, watching for her reaction.

"I am sure Levi has things he would rather do. He doesn't need to entertain me," Breanna said, not wanting to be treated like a child.

"Nevertheless, he will accompany you."

When Dakota escorted Breanna back to her room and abruptly left her, she stood silently long after the door had closed behind him. Finally she moved to the window, her heart aching but her eyes dry.

She watched as the swirling mist thinned, offering her a better view of the city. Her eyes moved across the cobblestone streets, past the rooftops, where in the distance she could see the spire of a church.

Breanna was struck by a feeling of newness. This was a young nation, exciting and teeming with ideals of freedom. The people bustling along looked no different from anyone she would have met on a London street. She felt a kinship with these Americans, perhaps because her husband still considered this his country.

Some of the excitement had gone out of Breanna, and she dreaded the thought of remaining alone in this small room. She loved Levi, but was not overjoyed by the prospect of spending the day with him. She had so wanted to be with Dakota. Why hadn't he asked her to go with him?

There was a rap on the door, and she crossed the room to find Levi in the hallway. She had to smile at the dear old man. He was dressed in fresh white shirt and stiff neckerchief, and his hair was still wet where he had slicked it down with water. His marvelous eyes were dancing. "It's good to see you, Breanna. I'm yours to command today."

She decided to throw off her gloom, and responded to his invitation by offering him her hand. "I am most delighted to see you also, Levi, and I want to see America through your eyes," she announced fervently.

The smile on his face told Breanna that Levi was pleased.

Levi took Breanna on a carriage ride through a park and then along the bay. They had lunch from a street vendor, then drank tea in a wonderful little shop that specialized in herbal teas.

She had to laugh at Levi as he sat in the tea shop uncomfortably balancing the dainty teacup in his hand. She could tell he had gone to great lengths to please her, even to having tea in an environment that made him squirm. She listened attentively as he told her funny stories and explained the history behind many of the New York landmarks they had seen.

When they stood before a white arched building, Levi removed his hat with a look of reverence on his face. "This is Federal Hall," he explained. "In this building George Washington became our first President. They wanted to make him King, but he would have none of it. My father fought for him and swore there was no better man to serve under."

"I know a little about your General Washington," she smiled. "Of course from the English point of view, he was more scalawag and upstart than hero."

Levi grinned. "I can see as how you might feel that way. But to us in America, Washington is the symbol of our freedom. We could use someone like him now because I fear civil war is about to rip this nation apart. I wouldn't want to see that happen."

"Isn't that what happened when America fought against England? Was that not considered civil war?"

"Not in a sense. You see, we never have felt English, but we was born feeling American."

"Any war is devastating, isn't it?"

"Yes it is. Especially when it is brother against brother," he said, thinking about Dakota and Black Otter. "It's a bad thing when a brother is forced to slay a brother."

Breanna stared at the building where this country

had made George Washington its first leader. "I don't know about such things, Levi. I would think with what this country has gone through to gain its freedom, the Americans would not risk losing it all by fighting among themselves."

"You would think so, wouldn't you? Now," he said, his eyes brightening, "I have exhausted my knowledge of New York. Are you ready to go back to the hotel? There's a storm coming up, and we may not make it back before it hits."

Breanna had been enjoying herself so much, she hadn't realized that dark clouds were gathering over the city, bringing with them a premature darkness. A lamplighter treaded along, lighting the streetlights to disburse some of the gloom.

"Yes, I am ready, and I thank you for a most enjoyable day." She found she meant it. What would she have done without him today? she wondered.

Levi helped Breanna into the carriage before he spoke. "You mustn't mind Dakota's preoccupation at the moment. He has things on his mind that have nothing to do with you. He has to see them through to the end."

She stared out the window. "I had always thought a husband and wife shared everything. Why will he not tell me what is bothering him?"

"Not ever having been married myself, I cannot answer that for you. But you know by now that Dakota is not like other men. There is something in his past that is calling him back. If you understand this, and don't ask him too many questions, you will save you both a lot of grief."

Breanna's eyes were flaming when she faced Levi. "Well, I do not understand, but I gave Dakota my word that I would do as I was told. However, I can tell you this, Levi, when I have fulfilled that obligation, I intend to demand that Dakota supply me some answers."

By the time they reached the hotel, heavy drops of rain were falling from the dark sky. Breanna rushed into the hotel and thanked Levi for a wonderful afternoon before going upstairs to see if Dakota had returned.

When she found the room empty, she sat in the darkness, listening to the rain pelting the window. Her spirits were at low ebb, and she was hurt that Dakota would not share with her whatever was troubling him.

After she ate a solitary meal in her room, Breanna dressed for bed and crawled under the covers. She ended her second day in America without saying good night to her husband.

With the sound of the intensifying storm in the background, Breanna drifted off to sleep, remembering other storms when Dakota had held her in his arms and had made passionate love to her.

* * *

Breanna was awakened from a sound sleep when Dakota slipped into bed beside her and pulled her into his arms. At first she fought against the hands that ran over her body, pulling her ever closer to his heat. But little by little, Dakota gained the advantage, and she turned her head to find the mouth that teased her ear. Burning heat ran through her veins as his lips settled on hers in a kiss that left her weak and breathless.

"I didn't think I would see you tonight," she said in a voice that was too throaty to be accusing.

"Shhh," he whispered. "I will always want to be with you, sweet, sweet Breanna."

Dakota could feel the tremor that went through Breanna, and he ran soothing hands across her hips and up her back. His lips explored the curve of her cheek, the delicate arch of her brow, the lobe of her ear.

"I tried to stay away from you, but I couldn't." His voice sounded as if that confession had been forced from him.

Somewhere in the deep recesses of her mind, Breanna knew she should not submit so easily to Dakota. She should tell him how angry she was for being neglected all day, but when his lips traveled down her neck, to sensuously enclose the tip of her breast, she could only moan with urgent longing.

With a fluid movement, Dakota rolled to his back, bringing her on top of him. She was mindless with need as he moved her forward and buried himself deeply within her. His emerald gaze moved over her face noting the fever-bright passion that gleamed in the golden depths. Breanna felt her heart stop beating as his lips settled on hers, and when his kiss deepened, she could only quiver in his arms. For a moment she felt as if she was suffocating and dragged her mouth away from his so she could take in a deep gulp of air.

"What are you doing to me," she questioned breathlessly as his fingers trailed a blazing path down her back and across her hips. With a forward lunge he deepened inside of her.

"I am proving to you . . . or perhaps myself that I still have some control over you."

As he started a slow rhythmic motion, she tossed her head from side to side. "I admit that you are in control, my lord."

His eyes flickered. "Oh no, my lady, it is you who rule me."

She gasped with a quick intake of breath as his smooth motions robbed her of speech. Again and again he plunged into her body, bringing her to the brink of total surrender. He took Breanna on a sensuous journey where soft murmured words made her soar through the dark storm clouds to break through to the brilliant sun above.

At last when their bodies found the quivering satisfaction they both craved, Dakota held Breanna to him. They lay locked in each other's arms until at last Dakota spoke.

"Levi said he took you to see the town today."

"Yes. Where did you go?"

His hand ran soothingly up her arm. "For one thing I had some gowns made for you."

She raised her head, her eyes still softened from his lovemaking. "You did?"

His fingers trailed down her arm and he gloried in the softness of her skin. "Mm-hmm. I found a shop that could make what I wanted for you in one day's time."

Her curiosity was piqued and she raised up on her elbow to look into his face. It was difficult to imagine Dakota shopping for women's apparel. "What kind of gowns?"

"As I told you, the clothing you brought with you is unsuitable for where we are going. I had the woman make skirts for you that are slit so you can ride astraddle. It would not be advisable for you to ride sidesaddle."

Joy sang in her heart. She like the thought that he had been concerned for her comfort. "When can I see the gowns?"

"They will be delivered tomorrow."

Breanna laid her cheek against his chest, listening to the drumming of his heart. How deeply she loved this man, and how tightly she wanted to hold on to him. But she had the feeling no woman could hold on to Dakota. He was restless. And he was fighting a battle of his own somewhere in his mind. Until he won that battle, no one would get close to him.

"Go to sleep," he whispered. "There are not too many more days that you can enjoy a comfortable bed."

"I want to sleep under the stars and listen to the sound of the coyote," she said fancifully.

He smiled against her face. "Who has been filling your head with such whimsical ideas?"

"Levi."

"Yes, I thought so. I'd be willing to bet that he failed to tell you that a bedroll is lumpy and hard, and those coyotes can keep you awake all night with their mating call."

"Mating call?"

"Yes," he murmured against her ear. "Yes, mating call, like my heart is calling to you at this moment."

She knew deep inside that the soft words he whispered to her tonight would disappear with the appearance of the morning sun, and he would again become the cold indifferent stranger. She asked herself why she allowed him to take her body and give so little of himself in return. Because, fool, she answered herself, you love him with your heart and soul, and you will take anything he has to offer.

Breanna felt the blood run hot through her body as his hands once again awoke a need in her that he would soon satisfy.

She forgot that Dakota had neglected her all day. All she could think about was his tongue teasing her naked breasts, and his hands touching her where it brought the most pleasure.

"Dakota," she said in a throaty voice. "I want to talk to you. I have questio—"

"No talk," he murmured against her lips, silencing her voice in the most sensuous way.

She clung to him, knowing at this moment he belonged to her alone. Tomorrow she would lose him again, but that was tomorrow, and this was now.

Chapter Twenty-nine

Although it was late October, the weather was unseasonably hot. Those who professed to know, the tillers of soil and the trappers from the mountains, predicted the warm weather would continue.

Breanna, John, and Levi made their way through the dusty streets of Indianapolis to the hotel. Dakota had left them as soon as the train had pulled into the station, saying he would join them later.

By now, Breanna was growing accustomed to Dakota's silent brooding, but it took much of the joy away from her adventure. She glanced around at the frontier town, feeling the excitement that charged the air. As John helped her from the buggy that had transported them from the train depot, she stepped onto the plank walkway in front of the hotel.

Instead of going in, John took Breanna's arm. "That sign on the shop down the street says they have tea. Suppose we have a cup before getting settled into the hotel? I haven't had a decent cup of tea since we left London."

Breanna nodded. "I could use a cup of tea just now. Levi, would you like to come with us?"

"Not me. As you know, I don't care for your tea. I'll just make arrangements for our rooms and wait for Dakota."

The tea turned out to be bitter and too strong, but Breanna savored every drop. She and John were seated by the window, watching the local population going about their daily lives.

"I have yet to see my first Indian," she said, watching a young woman, not much older than herself, scurrying by and trying to keep her seven children in line.

John, with his elbows propped on the table, rested his chin on his clasped hands. "I cannot imagine why you would want to."

"Perhaps I am fascinated by the Arapaho, since Dakota was raised by that tribe."

"As I see it, you will be a lot better off if we pass this trek without meeting any Indians. I don't favor having my scalp lifted."

Breanna glanced up at that moment and saw Dakota enter the shop; his face was a mask of fury. He must have seen her and John through the window, but why was he mad? she wondered.

John continued to express his views on the Indians, unaware that Dakota stood just behind him. "I have little doubt that the Indian has no love for us either."

Dakota spoke up. "Most Indians would be right in their disregard for the white man, for they have lied to them and betrayed them." Dakota's eyes bored into John's, making his comment personal.

Unaware of the cause of Dakota's anger, Breanna stood up, placing her hand on his arm. "John has just been warning me about the perils we may face with the Indians . . ." Her voice trailed off. "You would know more about that than . . ." She felt the arm beneath her fingers tense and harden. She could feel anger between Dakota and John, but she did not know the reason for it.

Dakota's emerald eyes glinted. "Was he? I am not aware that John is an expert on Indians."

John's hands balled into fists. "I am forced to bow to your superior, firsthand knowledge of the savages."

Tension filled the air like the crack of electricity. Breanna was stunned into silence as Dakota took her arm and pulled her out of the shop. She was embarrassed for herself and embarrassed that Dakota would treat John with such rudeness.

When they were outside, Dakota turned turbulent green eyes on her, and she shrank from him.

"I will not have you flaunt yourself in front of my cousin, Breanna. An Indian wife would never act with such total disregard for her husband's honor."

Breanna's temper smoldered. "Nothing I have done would besmirch your honor," she returned, her tone even. "First of all, as you have pointed out on numerous occasions, I am not an Indian. Secondly, I was not flaunting myself, as you so rudely put it. And thirdly—"

His hand closed over her shoulders, and he led her toward the hotel. "It was a mistake to allow you to come along. If I had the means, I would send you back to England today."

"I will not go," she declared, her breasts heaving and her curly mane swirling about her like shimmering gold. She jerked her hand free of his, unmindful of the curious stares they received from the passersby.

Breanna was soon to discover that Dakota had once again placed them in separate rooms. Today she had been angry and humiliated, but most of all she had been hurt by Dakota's coldness and false accusations. She wondered where this would all end.

Nature was lavish with her foliage as giant trees dipped their branches into the mirror-bright Missouri River. The cable-drawn barge that was taking them across the river was loaded with horses, pack animals, men, and supplies.

Dakota had hired two other men to accompany them. Since Breanna was along, he didn't want to take any chances with her safety.

With some unknown herbal plant scenting the hot breeze that touched her face, Breanna closed her eyes, wanting to remember this moment always.

This was America as she had imagined it—a primitive wilderness with trees that were too dense to hack your way through—a lovely land which was a vast incubator for the wildlife it supported.

Breanna was dressed in the clothing that Dakota had purchased for her. Levi had told her that Dakota's mother had worn similar apparel. It was made of black broadcloth, and although it was divided, it was so full that it fell together to resemble a skirt. She could hardly wait to ride astride a horse like a man. Even though it might be unconventional, no one here would mind.

She tried to visualize how Cillia Remington must have felt as she accompanied her husband to this wild and beautiful land. Had she gazed on the same landscape and felt the exultation of the warm sun on her face?

Breanna's eyes moved to her husband, who had stripped off his coat and was rolling up his sleeves. She watched how the muscles rippled across his back and the way the wind feathered through his dark hair, which now almost reached his shoulders. She was aware that she was slowly, bit by bit, losing him. The farther they got from civilization, the more he retreated within himself.

Breanna glanced at Baxley, noting the eagerness in his eyes. The valet was in his element, she thought. Her eyes moved on to John, who was swatting at a persistent fly that was pestering him, and he gave Breanna a glance that clearly asked: *What am I doing here?*

She was aware that John and Dakota were still angry with one another, but she didn't know what to do about the situation or what had set it off.

Luther, one of the Americans Dakota had hired, was a huge man with coffee-colored hair, who always seemed to be smiling. The other man was named Inman and was slender. A startling thing about him was that one of his eyes was blue, while the other one was brown.

Breanna smiled gratefully at Luther as he dusted off a barrel with his neckerchief and offered her a seat. She had found these American men gallant and respectful. They never spoke directly to her, but she would often be the recipient of their kind consideration.

When the barge bumped against the opposite shore, John helped Breanna up the bank. "I want to talk to you alone," he whispered.

She glanced quickly into his eyes. "Why alone?"

"I can't talk to you now. Later."

She was curious as to why John would want to see her alone, but she soon dismissed it from her mind, because the sun was warm, the birds were singing, and she was caught up in the loveliness of her surroundings.

Dakota was leading several horses off the barge. He handed Breanna the reins of a buckskin mare. "Is this one mine?" she asked, running her hand over the sleek neck.

"Yes. The care and upkeep of this horse will fall to you. You will be given no special consideration just because you are a woman," he told her pointedly.

She raised her chin, stung by the coldness in his voice. "I have not thus far asked for special consideration, nor do I intend to."

His eyes drifted to the nearby woods, which to the untrained eye seemed impregnable. "See that you don't."

She was hurt and angry that Dakota should treat her in such an overbearing manner. She watched him lead his mount forward, and she yanked on the reins of her horse so she could follow him.

Dakota had never allowed her to feel close to him, but now he had shut her out completely. She must have been a fool to come along on this journey, she thought, fighting against tears. She would show him that she didn't need anyone's help. She would give him no reason to criticize her.

Breanna watched everyone else mount and, for the first time, noticed the hard leather saddle on her own horse. She puzzled for a moment on how to mount the horse.

Glancing out of the corner of her eye, she watched Levi slip his foot into the stirrup and throw his leg over his horse. Drawing in her breath, she likewise poked her boot into the stirrup, but at that moment her horse took it in its head to spin around in a circle, and Breanna had to hold on tightly to the reins to keep from falling off.

Her heart was pounding, and she could see herself being flung beneath the horses' hooves. Knowing that Dakota and the others were probably watching her, she gritted her teeth and forced her leg over the horse's back. When she was firmly planted in the saddle, she gripped the reins and pulled back hard, bringing the prancing mare under her control.

Breanna became aware that she was the center of attention, so she nudged the horse in the flanks with the heel of her boot and rode to the front of the column where Levi waited.

"Good girl," the hunter said under his breath. "You showed that husband of yours, and I have a feeling before this is over, we will all have learned a thing or two from you. This will be an adventure you will one day tell your grandchildren about."

"I don't know, Levi," she said in a voice that was choked with emotion. "If it becomes too much for me, there is no one to blame but myself. As Dakota is so fond of reminding me, I asked to come along."

"Then why not show him what you are made of."

Breanna smiled at his logic. "Just watch me, Levi. I intend to." She pushed her troubles to the back of her mind, deciding that nothing was going to keep her from enjoying this glorious adventure, not even Dakota.

Her excitement mounted. Tonight would be her first night to sleep under the stars. Of course, they would actually be sleeping in tents, she thought, but that would prove a blessing if it rained.

She noticed Dakota had ridden on ahead, disappearing into the woods. She tried not to think about him, but it was impossible to get him out of her thoughts.

By noon, they had moved away from the river, following a trail that had been beaten into the ground by the iron rims of countless covered wagons on their westward journey, a trail that would remain for centuries to come as a testament to the men and women who had sold their meager belongings and pinned their hopes and dreams on finding a new life in the West. She imagined the fragile women, their eyes bright, their sights on a better life. She almost envied those countless, faceless women who had been allowed to stand by their men through hardship and even death.

She was so lost in thought she had not realized that John had ridden up beside her until he spoke. "It's hard to imagine there is supposed to be a paradise at the end of those wagon ruts, is it not?"

"I assume you are speaking of the Oregon Territory?" she answered.

"Yes, Oregon and California."

"You have to admit these people have courage to set out against almost impossible odds. Levi has told me how their graves litter the prairies."

"If you ask me, it's a lesson in futility. If they feel compelled to take the westward trek, they would be better served going around the Horn."

Levi pulled his wide-brimmed hat lower to shade his eyes. "Most of them don't have the price of a ticket on a sailing ship. They barely have money enough to see them across the wilderness as it is. The westward trek is only beginning. The time will come when there will be a great migration across this country. Then the Indian will have cause to complain in earnest."

Breanna's eyes were big and round. "I can easily imagine what compels a person to want to seek the unknown, to hope for a better life, John."

"I am still wondering why I agreed to come along. I must be losing my mind," John said, shaking his head. I could have gone back to England, or awaited your return in New York."

Levi smiled to himself as he drew in his mount and fell back to ride with Baxley. John talked as if he was bored with life, but the hunter surmised that if danger came, John would be a good man to count on.

Now that they had left civilization behind, John had become increasingly troubled. He knew the reason why Dakota was driving himself so hard, but he wondered if Dakota had considered the danger it would present to Breanna.

John nudged his horse closer to Breanna. "We can talk now, Breanna," he said urgently. "I think you need to turn back. Dakota should never have allowed you to come with him this far, and if he doesn't consider your safety, I must."

She stared at him in surprise. "But why? What do you know that you aren't saying?"

"That's not important," he said evasively, watching her expression. "Just trust me in this, and promise me you will tell Dakota you want to return to England."

"No, I will not do that, John, not unless you give me a good reason."

John sighed. "Isn't it enough to tell you that my reasons are sound?"

"No, not when you are asking me to leave my husband."

"Damn it, Breanna, wake up. Dakota is not here to pass pleasantries with his Arapahos. He has come to kill a man!"

Breanna turned to John, her face ashen. "No, John! Dakota wouldn't . . . he isn't . . . no!"

"I can assure you it's true. I hadn't meant to tell you, but I have to make you listen to reason. I thought before you got this far you would decide to turn back on your own."

"No, what you are saying is unthinkable," she replied in an unconvincing voice. Had Dakota ever killed a man? She couldn't bear to think that the hands that caressed her so tenderly may have committed murder.

"I intend to talk to Dakota about this," she said, gazing up at the sun, which had become unbearably hot. She tied her hat firmly under her chin, feeling the perspiration that ran down her neck, plastering

her blouse to her skin. Was it possible that John
was right?

Chapter Thirty

Night covered the land. The camp had been set up, the tents raised, and still Dakota had not made an appearance. Breanna was just outside the ring of light given off by the campfire, feeding and watering her horse. Although John and Levi had offered to tend her mare, she had refused their help. She set her jaw firmly as she removed a burr from the mare's tail, only to have the sharp barb stick into her.

Crying out in pain, she found the burr deeply embedded in her finger. She had not heard the silent figure that emerged from the trees just behind her, and she was startled when a hand landed on her shoulder. Spinning around, she saw Dakota. Like a child who has been hurt and needed sympathy, she held her finger out to him.

A soft smile curved his lips as he gently removed the burr and raised her finger to his lips, kissing the wound. "Sweet little girl," he said, pulling her into his arms. "You have a brute for a husband."

She closed her eyes, allowing his soothing hands to move up and down her back.

"I watered and fed my horse," she said. "Of course, Levi did help me with the saddle, it's quite heavy."

He shook with silent laughter. "Oh, Breanna, what am I going to do with you?"

She moved away from him. "Why do you say that? I did not ask for Levi's help."

"No?"

"No."

"Come," he said, leading her toward one of the tents. "You have had a long day."

When they entered the tent, Dakota lit a lantern, and in the warm glow he saw that two cots had been set up, and a buffalo hide had been thrown on the floor. "Baxley is a wonder. He can even make a tent look like home," Dakota observed. His eyes softened as they rested on Breanna's face.

"I want to say something to you, and when I am finished, I hope you will understand about me." He took her hand and seated her on one of the cots. "Not many husbands and wives start their lives together as strangers as you and I have. I understand how difficult this has been for you. I have not always known how to please you, and I admit I have made many mistakes. Now that we are in America, you see me as I really am, with all pretense stripped away. You may not like me this way, but this is who I am."

"I have always wanted you to be yourself, Dakota."

"You don't know the real me."

"I would like to."

He dropped down on his knees beside her and took her hand in his. "Breanna, there are many things that I cannot tell you. You will just have to know that I am doing something that I have to do. Until I have accomplished that, I cannot call my life my own."

She remembered what John had told her today. "Can you not tell me what is driving you, Dakota?"

"No."

She looked into his green eyes so she would know the truth. "Have you come here to kill a man?"

She saw his eyes dilate. "Yes," he admitted.

"But that's barbaric! Have you killed before?"

"Yes." His eyes hardened. "But I will not discuss this with you, and you have no right to ask it of me."

"But I do ask. How can you so coldly plot a man's death?"

His dark brows knitted. "I will say no more. But after this is all over, if you feel you cannot stay with me, I will not hesitate to set you free."

She caught her breath, unable to think about a life without Dakota. Was he issuing her a warning? "I have always known you were troubled about something, Dakota. Like me, you had no say in this marriage. And like you, I will allow you to have your freedom if that is what you wish."

A serious expression transformed his face. "I think we begin to understand each other today."

He towered above her, and she stared up at him. "Dakota, I want to ask you about John. What happened between the two of you? I can tell that there is something wrong, and I don't like to see this rift between you."

His eyes glistened with an inner green fire. "Have you ever observed a herd of wild horses, Breanna?"

"No, not wild horses."

"Then perhaps I should explain to you about the stallions." His voice deepened. "Two stallions cannot coexist in the same herd. When the beautiful mare is desired by both stallions, they will battle, sometimes to the death! The mare goes to the strongest and most able."

"I don't understand. Are you comparing me to a horse? Are you saying that John is interested in me?" She shook her head. "No, you are wrong. He has always been my friend and a perfect gentleman with me. I don't know what I would have done without him. John admires you so much. Think of all he has done for you."

Dakota moved forward and gripped her arms, bringing her to her feet. "You are an innocent if you believe that John only wants friendship from you. I am telling you for your own good that it would be a mistake to encourage him, Breanna."

She tossed her head and glared at him. "How

dare you suggest that I am encouraging John! You have your facts turned around. It was you who practiced deceit, not me."

His jaw clamped tightly together, his temper stretched to the limit. "If you are referring to Rye Saffron, think what you will. However, I should point out you are walking a dangerous path, Breanna. You can push a man only so far, even a man like me."

"You are hateful, and I don't like you very well at the moment," she whispered, turning her back on him. "Just leave me alone!"

"If that is your wish," he said in a hard voice. "As I said, we are beginning to understand each other. As for your John, I would prefer you not be alone with him. Levi will look to your needs."

Breanna turned to face him, a slow anger building inside her. "How dare you think you can order me about. As for John, you do him an injustice. And as for Levi looking after me, aren't you fortunate that you have him to take the burden of me off your hands?"

Dakota looked as if he would like to say more, but clamped his jaw tightly together.

Through angry tears, she watched him leave, fighting the urge to run after him. She hurled herself onto the cot and buried her head beneath a blanket. Even though he left her angry, bruised, and humiliated, she still ached to feel his strong arms around her. Why did she feel like losing herself to the misery of tears?

For two days, Breanna's spirit was dampened. Dakota did not come near her or speak to her. Each day·Levi would ride at her side, but he made no comment about the trouble between her and Dakota. Evidently something had been said to John, because he did not try to approach her.

Breanna held her breath every time Dakota rode near her, but he didn't look in her direction, and he did not come to her tent at night. If the others noticed anything was wrong between them, they were too polite to comment.

Being young and spirited, Breanna could not remain angry forever. On a warm·cloudless day, she decided to throw off her gloom, and she set her chin stubbornly. She was not hurting anyone but herself by acting like a hurt child. With a determined lift of her shoulders, she mounted her horse, urging it to the front of the column to ride beside Levi. By now, she was accustomed to Dakota riding off alone and not returning until long after dark. She didn't know what he did with his time, and she did not ask.

All morning the travelers rode along the tracks left by wagon trains, but in late afternoon, Levi guided them off the rutted trail, heading due north. "This is the last of any kind of civilization you will see for some time," he told Breanna. "From here on out, if you meet someone, they will either be a hunter, a trapper, or an Indian."

"When will I see my first Indian, Levi?" she inquired, glancing at the cedar and juniper trees with their stubby shapes, growing along the steep cliff walls.

"Chances are, an Indian will see you, but you may not see him. We are now in Sioux country, and they are not inclined to be too friendly toward the white man."

"Are they dangerous?"

"Not to me, and not to you, since you are with me."

"Oh."

They rode past high buttes of sandstone, some of which the wind had carved into sculptural forms, almost as if the hand of man had lent art to their shape.

After they rode for several hours, the arid buttes gave way to soft, rolling grassy plains, and Breanna saw her first herd of buffalo.

She stared in wonder at the shaggy beasts which aimlessly grazed on the sun-dappled grassland.

John rode up beside Breanna, staring at the strange sight. Their eyes met at last, and he smiled as if to tell her he wanted only to be her friend.

Breanna smiled back at him in understanding.

"Well," John observed. "I suppose I am one of a handful of Englishmen who have seen a herd of buffalo in their own environment. Think of the stories I can tell at the club in London."

"It is truly amazing," she agreed, drinking in the animals' rugged beauty.

"Let's be riding on," Levi said. "Where you find the buffalo, the Sioux will not be far away."

"But you said they were friendly to you," Breanna reminded him.

"And so they are, but I try not to test them too often."

Levi seemed to read the land, and he knew exactly where he was going. It was almost dark when he held up his hand, indicating that they would make camp on the bank of the small river.

After Breanna had fed and watered her horse, she entered her tent to find that, as usual, Baxley had laid clean clothing on her cot.

The heat was oppressive, and the cool river was so inviting that Breanna had to take advantage of it.

As the dying rays of the golden sun painted the scene a tranquil hue, she found a secluded spot where she could bathe. Breanna slipped out of her clothing, grabbed up a bar of soap, and waded into the water, thinking how gloriously refreshing the water felt to her hot, tired body. She was lathering her long hair when she heard the sound of an owl. Peeping through the soapy lather that burned her eyes and nearly blinded her view, she remembered Levi telling her that Indians often imitated bird and animal sounds.

Breanna discounted the fear that prickled her spine. She was just being nervous, she told herself, washing the soap from her hair and diving beneath the water. As she came up through the water, she felt a hand clamp over her mouth and stared in horror at a hideously painted face. Breanna finally saw her first Indian!

She felt her whole body come alive with fear, and she fought against the rough hands that tightened about her waist. She bit at the hand that threatened to cut off her breathing, but the man was just too strong for her. He was dragging her out of the water, and there was nothing she could do to save herself.

She saw they were only a short way from the riverbank, and she fought wildly to keep her naked body from being exposed to the man. Kicking and twisting, she tried to gain her freedom, but to no avail.

The Indian said something to her, which she did not understand, but she understood the knife he planted at the base of her throat. A sob was building up inside, and she felt her body tremble with fear so strong it made her stomach churn. Would this man ravish her, or merely kill her? she wondered.

Just then, she glanced over the Indian's shoulder and relief flooded her eyes. It was Dakota come to rescue her!

He said something to her tormenter, but the In-

411

dian merely tightened his grip on her and touched the knife to her throat.

Again Dakota spoke, and this time the Indian's eyes widened. "Dakota?" the man asked. That much she did understand.

The two men conversed back and forth, and finally with a quick glance at Breanna, the Indian released her.

She plunged facedown in the river, too happy to be free to worry about the mouthful of river water she swallowed. When Breanna finally caught her breath, she saw that the Indian had vanished, melting away in the bushes.

Dakota quickly handed Breanna her clothing, while he placed his knife back in its sheath. "Get dressed," he ordered, his eyes alert to any signs that the Indian might return.

She pulled her gown over her head, but her hands trembled too badly for her to fasten it.

Dakota picked her up in his arms and carried her out of the river. Setting Breanna on her feet, he turned her around and fastened her gown.

"You will not do this again. Do you understand?"

She was still too frightened to disagree with him. "Yes. I only wanted to—"

"Do I have your word that you will not go off alone to bathe," he pressed.

"Yes, yes."

He lifted her in his arms once more and carried her back toward camp.

Levi was at the campfire, supervising the coffee, when he saw Breanna and Dakota emerge from the bushes. "Breanna, I thought you were resting in your tent," the hunter said, looking first at her wet hair and then at Dakota's angry expression.

"Come with me, Levi," Dakota ordered, making his way into Breanna's tent.

Once inside, Breanna felt her legs could not hold her any longer, and she sank down on the cot.

"You can guess what she was doing," Dakota said to Levi.

"Yep, it appears she went bathing."

"You were supposed to keep an eye on her. I hold you responsible for what happened."

"It wasn't his fault," Breanna said, only to have both men look at her with silencing glances.

"What happened?" Levi wanted to know.

"My wife was leisurely taking a bath while a Sioux warrior decided she would make a pretty decoration to his lodge."

"Ah. I hope you didn't have to kill him to persuade him otherwise. I wouldn't want to have to deal with the whole Sioux Nation, just because one of them took a fancy to Breanna."

"He was a young warrior, and apparently he had heard of me. He released her with little hesitation." He turned to Breanna, though his words were for Levi. "From here on out, one of us will be with her at all times."

"Yes, that's good reasoning." Levi glanced back at

Breanna. "Are you hurt in any way?"

She was grateful that at least he cared enough to ask if she had been injured by the brute who had attacked her. "I was merely frightened."

"And rightly you should have been," Levi announced, ambling out of the tent.

For a moment Breanna and Dakota stared at one another, then he knelt down beside her and slipped her feet into her soft leather shoes he had picked up by the stream. "I don't have to tell you how serious this could have been, Breanna."

"I know," she said, tears brightening her golden eyes. "I was so frightened."

He gathered her close, pressing his cheek tightly against hers. "Don't ever do that again. I don't know what I would do if anything happened to you."

She pressed her body against him and felt his quick intake of breath. Seeing the flame in his eyes, she shook her head, knowing the others were just outside the tent.

"Surely not here," she whispered through trembling lips.

His emerald gaze deepened with desire. "Yes, Breanna, here. No one will come in," he murmured in her ear.

Dakota blew out the lantern and velvet twilight filtered through the slit in the tent, washing the surroundings in its soft light. Dakota held Breanna to him, wishing he could absorb her into his body, to make her his so completely that no man would dare look on her with longing. She was his and his alone. Couldn't she see that?

When his eyes moved over her fragile features, he saw the light of surrender in her eyes, and the breath became trapped within his body.

Breanna was burning with a slow fire. As Dakota would remove an article of her clothing, he would kiss her, touch her in a certain way that made her want to melt against him. Masterfully, he maneuvered her to a mindless world where she was riding the tide of passion.

Dakota lowered her onto the buffalo hide that served as a rug, and joined her there. She surrendered to him completely when he slid his hard naked body up the length of her soft curves. She gasped, rolling her head from side to side. His lips were hot against her breasts, his hands touching magical places that brought a gasp from her lips and caused her to tingle all over.

Caught within an emotion she could not control, Breanna slid her fingers into his midnight-colored hair, pressing her lips against his in total surrender.

When he slid into her, she bit her lip and arched to meet him. The dark passion that glowed in Dakota's eyes caught at her heart. Wild emotions encased her whole being as she rose and sank, rose and sank, in tune with his fluid motion. She trembled in his arms, her mind and body as one with him.

Breanna realized that this man was her life and she would be lost and adrift without him.

A tremor shook Dakota's body in reaction to his final deep thrust, and he held Breanna tightly to him, his pleasure heightened because he felt an answering tremor from her body. Rolling over, he carried her with him. "You are mine," he breathed, kissing her eyelids, her cheek, her neck, her lips.

"Yes," she whispered. "Yes." Not willing to let him go, she clung to him, kissing his shoulder, nuzzling his neck, brazenly rubbing her breasts against his chest. She felt his renewed desire swell against her thigh, and she looked at him with uncertainty.

With deep laughter, Dakota rolled her over, his knees between her thighs. "You are asking for it, Breanna, and I will go to great lengths to please my lady and give her what she wants."

This time he took her in a swirl of passion. She gave him joy that sang through his body, and he had the satisfaction of knowing she was completely his while he was making love to her.

Through a drifting haze, Breanna lay curled up beside him on the cot, feeling contented and secure in Dakota's warm embrace.

He watched her eyes drift shut, and moments later he knew she was asleep. Dakota felt her even breathing while he reflected on their situation. Would Breanna ever reach out for the love that burned within him like a fire out of control? He ached to speak of his love, for it needed to be confessed, but he dared not. Now was not the time to make promises he did not know if he could keep. He could make her body react to his lovemaking, but he wondered if he had ever touched her heart.

Pressing his lips against her closed eyelids, Dakota felt love throb through his body. He wanted to hold Breanna and protect her, keeping her from all harm.

He lay awake, wanting to touch her, to hold her forever. He was jealous of every smile she bestowed upon another man. Tonight belonged to him alone, but with the appearance of the morning sun, he would have to let her go. He was a man with a purpose, and he could not allow himself to think about a future with Breanna or he would lose his concentration. He would need all his cunning when he finally faced Black Otter.

Chapter Thirty-one

When Breanna awoke, it was still dark, yet she could hear sounds that alerted her to the fact that the men were breaking camp. Remembering the night before, she reached out to touch Dakota, only to find he was already gone.

Sitting up, she hurriedly dressed and ran a brush through her hair before twisting it up and tying her bonnet beneath her chin.

As she stepped outside, Inman smiled and wished her a good morning before he began disassembling her tent. She found Levi by the campfire and walked over to him, while her eyes searched for Dakota.

Baxley poured Breanna a cup of coffee, a brew that she had been forced to drink out of necessity. She thought how good a cup of tea would taste.

"Where is Dakota?" she asked, shaking her head

to refuse Baxley's offer of food.

Levi piled dirt on the campfire and watched it sputter and go out. "He's about somewhere. Like as not, he's having a look-see."

Breanna noticed that Levi had abandoned his usual attire in favor of buckskin trousers and shirt. She had to admit he looked more at ease in his buckskins.

John came out of his tent and stumbled toward the coffee pot. "I detest this brew, but it does go a long way toward bringing me back to life in the mornings."

Breanna smiled as she took a final swallow of her coffee. "I agree with you. I was just wishing for a cup of tea."

John looked Breanna over. "I heard about your experience last night. Are you all right?"

"Yes. Everything is intact except for my dignity."

"You would have lost a good deal more than your dignity if Dakota hadn't come along when he did," Levi informed her.

Breanna shivered, remembering the incident.

The sun was just coming up over the tall pine trees when Breanna saw the lone rider coming toward camp. Since the blinding sun was in her eyes, she couldn't tell who it was. As he rode down a gully and up the other side into her view, she gasped. It was Dakota! But he was different.

Like Levi, Dakota wore buckskin trousers, but his chest was bare, and he wore a knife in the leather sheath about his waist. Around his dark hair he wore a leather headband. He looked so like an Indian that Breanna held her breath.

Breanna knew she was staring, but she couldn't help it. She remembered the one other time she had seen him dressed this way—the fringed trousers, the moccasins, the leather headband. She stared in wonder at the bear-claw necklace he wore about his neck.

As her eyes met his, she saw indifference there. It appeared as if civilization had been stripped from him, and when he rode into camp, he dismounted with ease and agility, moving with a panther-like grace, the muscles on his back rippling with each movement he made.

"I'll be damned," John said, forgetting Breanna's presence as he stared at his cousin. "I had forgotten how much you can resemble an Indian when you are dressed like this."

"I am an Indian," Dakota said, turning away and directing the hired men as they loaded the packhorses.

Breanna had hoped that after last night there would be some sign of affection from Dakota when they met today, but her hopes were soon dashed. He didn't even acknowledge her presence. She would have spoken to him, but it was apparent that his mind was on whatever it was that had been driving him these past few weeks.

In less than an hour everyone was mounted and

the column moved out. It did not escape Breanna's notice that the men were watchful and alert. When Dakota did not ride off as was his usual habit, but stayed at the head of the column, she realized he was being cautious because of her encounter with the Sioux warrior the day before. What she did not know was Dakota and Levi were concerned lest the Sioux warrior change his mind and decide to recapture Breanna with the help of others from his tribe.

All day they rode north with the hot sun beating down on them. Breanna felt exhausted, and every bone in her body seemed to ache. The only reprieve came when they dismounted to rest the horses. She was careful not to complain, however, and pushed herself beyond endurance so she could prove to her husband that she could keep up with him.

She pulled her bonnet low over her forehead, hoping the sun would not burn her delicate skin. She kept her eyes on Dakota's rigid back, wondering what was going on in his mind. She longed for a look, a kind word, anything that would tell her he knew she was alive.

It was late in the afternoon, and they were riding through a canyon with steep inclines on both sides. The limestone walls were painted with a rosy glow from the setting sun, and Breanna was awed by the beauty. This land was such a contrast, with its mountain peaks, valleys, and prairies. She halted her mount to glance up at the boulders overhead, which seemed almost suspended on the cliff side. She was so engrossed in what she was witnessing that she did not notice that everyone else had ridden on ahead.

With a smile on her lips, she cupped her hands and yelled out, "Hello." The echo of her own voice reverberated back to her. "Hello . . . hello . . . hello."

She was so engrossed in the beauty around her, and she did not know that the slightest noise could easily start a rock slide. At first she did not see the danger because only loose sand and pebbles slid down the slope.

When Dakota heard Breanna's voice, he whirled his mount around, realizing that her echo had set off a landslide. Now larger rocks and earth were breaking loose, and when Dakota saw Breanna right beneath the slide, he spurred into action. Kicking his horse in the flanks, he raced forward while the others watched in horror, sure he would lose his race against time and Breanna would be crushed to death!

By now Breanna was aware of the danger, but she couldn't seem to react. Thinking she would surely be crushed and buried alive, her eyes sought Dakota.

Her horse, panicked by the landslide, wheeled

around, pitched, and sent Breanna flying through the air. Free of her rider, the mare made it to safety.

Breanna felt herself rolling and sliding down the slope. Her body twisted like a rag doll as she was slammed against the rock face of the canyon.

It had all happened so fast, but in an instant Breanna knew she was going to die. In a haze of pain, she saw Dakota racing toward her, but she knew he would never make it in time.

The roar of the landslide was now deafening as it gained strength, sweeping scrub oaks and boulders in its path. She closed her eyes, not wanting to see the final moments of impact.

Breanna felt a rock smash against her left shoulder, and she waited for another impact, but it didn't come. Instead, strong arms went around her waist and she was yanked from the jaws of death as Dakota pulled her up on his horse.

He whirled his horse out of the way just in time to avoid the falling debris. Breanna's body trembled with relief as she buried her face against Dakota's chest and he pressed her tightly against him. He had saved her, she was alive!

When Dakota lifted her down into Levi's waiting arms, she cried out in pain and grabbed her shoulder. They were quickly surrounded by the other men, who were anxious to see that Breanna had not been harmed.

It was Levi who pronounced that Breanna's

shoulder had been dislocated.

Dakota ordered the men to make camp. Breanna was placed near the fire, her back braced against a boulder, while a tent was quickly erected under Dakota's supervision.

John was seated beside Breanna, and he poured a glass of the wine and held it out to her. She was in so much pain that she didn't realize John was talking to take her mind off what was to come. "Here, drink this," he ordered. "I brought three bottles with me, and this is the last of the lot. I doubt there will be anywhere I can purchase good wine in this forsaken country."

When she tried to settle herself more comfortably, she cried out in pain. "I don't want to drink wine, John," she said, wiping away the beads of perspiration that gathered on her brow. "Save it for yourself."

His eyes were sympathetic. "I would advise you to drink as much of this as quickly as you can, Breanna."

She glanced from him to where the tent was now erected and several lanterns were being lit. "Why? What . . . is going to happen to me?"

He shoved the glass in her hand. "Drink up."

"Is he going to hurt me?"

"Breanna, if your shoulder is not properly tended, you will suffer with it all your life. Now drink the wine," he said kindly.

She nodded and quickly drained the glass, then

held it out, indicating she wanted John to refill it. "Will it hurt?" she wanted to know.

"Not if you drink enough of this," he assured her.

That was all Breanna needed to hear. After the third glass, her head was swimming and the pain in her shoulder had dulled a bit. She even managed to smile at Dakota when he lifted her in his arms and carried her into the tent. She saw that several lanterns lit the interior.

When Dakota placed her on the cot, Levi moved to one side and John knelt at her head, while Baxley held a lantern so Dakota could see.

Dakota's hands moved over her shoulder tentatively, touching the place where the bone was dislocated.

Levi saw Dakota hesitate. "Do you want me to do it?"

Dakota glanced down at Breanna, feeling guilty for what he was about to do, because she was looking at him so trustingly. "No," he said grimly, "I will do it myself."

"She drank almost half a bottle of wine, and that should take the edge off the pain," John said.

Breanna gritted her teeth. Even with the wine dulling her mind, she could still feel the pain.

John placed his hands on either side of Breanna's head, while Levi braced her arm. "Don't watch them," John said encouragingly, trying to take her mind off what was about to happen. "Think about

Weatherford Hall. Try to imagine yourself in the library, watching as the waves are spraying against the windows."

Breanna swallowed convulsively. She was trying to imagine the picture John had painted, but the reality of her pain throbbed in her mind. She wasn't expecting it to happen so suddenly, and she screamed out in pain when Dakota jerked her arm sharply. She was sure she had felt the bone move back into place. Blackness closed in on her, and she fought to hold it at bay.

John dabbed at her face with a damp cloth while Levi made a sling and slipped Breanna's arm into it.

Dakota spoke to her, his voice seeming to come to her from a long way off. "It's over, Breanna," he assured her. "You can rest now."

Suddenly the heat from the lanterns became too much for Breanna and she tried to sit up. "I cannot breathe in here. I need air," she said, looking beseechingly at Dakota.

Gently he lifted her into his arms and carried her out into the night air. She rested her head against his shoulder, wishing the ache in her own shoulder would go away.

John handed her another glass of wine, and after she drank it, the pain lessened.

The Americans looked on with concern, their eyes kind with understanding. One of them pulled out his old battered guitar and began strumming a tune. His voice was high and sweet as he began singing an old Irish ballad, his gift to Breanna.

"Do you want me to carry you in now, Breanna?" Dakota asked.

"No, I want to hear the music." Suddenly she felt giddy and lightheaded. "I want to dance."

John smiled, while Dakota frowned. "Don't worry, cousin," John told him. "That's the wine talking. Chances are she will not even remember in the morning."

"Put me down, Dakota," Breanna insisted. "I want to dance."

Dakota gave John a heated glance. "You did this to her," he said accusingly.

"Yes, and because I did, she was able to bear the pain."

Angrily, Dakota turned away, carrying Breanna into the tent. When they were inside, she became aware that Dakota was silent. When he set her on her feet, she swayed and then covered her mouth with her hand, suppressing a giggle. "As my brother would say, I'm in my cups." She backed up to Dakota, and feeling frivolous, she spoke with a slurred imitation of a Cockney accent. "Unhook my gown, will ya, ducks? There's a good chap. I suppose you will have to cut the gown, but no matter."

Dakota had never seen Breanna like this, and he was not amused.

He unhooked her gown and then carefully removed her injured arm from the sleeve and tied the sling back in place.

Breanna stepped out of her petticoats and kicked them aside, leaving her dressed only in her chemise. With her hand over her mouth, she eased herself back on the cot, her head spinning drunkenly. When Dakota sat down beside her, she tightly clasped his hand, wishing the world would right itself.

"Why do you not have a glass of wine tonight?" she asked, noting the dark look of displeasure on his face. "It will make you feel better."

"I do not drink wine. As an Indian, I never understood why the white man indulges in false stimulation when it tastes so foul."

She sat up and made a face at him. "Oh, so you are an Indian now, are you, my lord? I know what is wrong with you. You never learned how to have fun," she mocked, giggling at her daring statement.

"I did not have fun watching while you were almost crushed to death today. I did not enjoy the fact that I had to cause you pain so you would not lose the use of your arm."

With a forwardness that came from the wine, she walked her fingers up his arm to his bare chest and brazenly ran her hand over the mat of black hair that covered his chest. "But I know how to make you enjoy yourself," she said, leaning forward with parted lips.

Dakota didn't want her this way. He wanted to

push her away, but the sparkle in her golden eyes drew him to her, while the softness of her caress held him spellbound.

Gently taking her in his arms, very aware of her injured shoulder, he held her so tightly she could scarcely speak, but she didn't care. She moved forward and caught his bottom lip with her teeth and nipped playfully at it.

With a muttered oath, he grabbed her chemise and ripped it down the front, exposing her body to his gaze. In a frenzy, he disposed of his own confining clothing, but he was tender when he pulled his wife under him.

"You asked for this, Breanna," he said in a thick voice. He spread her legs and gently plunged into her, driving against her again and again, trying to expel the demon that had hold of him. His lips bruised hers with savage kisses.

When he tasted the saltiness of her tears, Dakota softened his movements. Ashamed of his brutality, he started to withdraw, but she touched his cheek.

"Love me, Dakota," she whispered in a pleading voice. "Please love me."

With an unquenchable ache in his heart, he used her body, while allowing her to use his. He did not like the taste of wine on her lips, and he mistakenly interpreted her cry for love as a sign that he was hurting her, so he gentled his motions even more.

The only sound in the night, besides the wind rippling against the canvas tent, was Breanna's soft breathing.

Dakota held his sleeping wife in his arms, loving her with all his heart. He realized his fear for her today had caused him to speak sharply to her, when all he really wanted to do was hold her, assuring himself that she was alive. Here in the darkness, he also admitted to himself that he had wronged John. How could he be angry with John, when he admired the very beauty that Dakota admired in Breanna.

"I love you, my heart," he whispered against her ear. "I am only alive when you are with me."

Breanna smiled in her sleep, unaware that her husband had just confessed his love for her. She did not see the look of pain in his eyes that was brought on by the knowledge that they must soon be parted.

Dakota now realized he could no longer keep her with him. Today she had almost been killed by the landslide, and yesterday she had almost been abducted by the Sioux warrior. There was no telling what new danger tomorrow would bring.

He thought of Black Otter, and what he must do. It was tearing at him because he was being forced to go against his promise to his father. But Black Otter had to be stopped.

Dakota rested his lips against Breanna's temple.

Black Otter was nearby. He could feel it. He knew Levi would have posted a guard, but still he would sleep lightly. When Black Otter learned that Dakota had returned, it would only be a matter of time before they met in battle — and one of them would die!

Chapter Thirty-two

Breanna awoke with sunlight streaming into the tent. When she tried to move, pain reminded her of her injured shoulder. When she turned her head, her stomach churned and she felt as if she was going to be sick.

"Ohhh," she moaned, knowing the amount of wine she had consumed the night before had made her nauseous and made the inside of her mouth feel like straw.

"Good morning, my lady," Baxley's voice called out just outside her tent. "I have your morning coffee."

"I don't want any coffee," she called out weakly.

"Very good, my lady. Will you require anything to eat?"

She clamped her hand over her mouth. "No, nothing."

"Can I come in?" Levi called out. "I need to talk to you."

Breanna pulled the covers over her and called for him to enter.

When Levi stepped inside, his eyes were wide with concern. "You're feeling rough this morning, aren't you?" he asked.

"Oh, Levi, I don't know which is the worse, my shoulder or the symptoms of too much wine."

He propped his foot on a camp stool. "I suspect you will battle both of them for most of the morning. If you want my advice, I'd say don't move about too much until the sickness leaves."

"I won't have any trouble doing just that. I couldn't move if my life depended on it."

"I don't suppose you want any coffee?"

She clamped her hand over her mouth. "Please, don't say that word."

"Dakota wanted me to tell you that he had to leave you."

"He's not here?"

"No. He left about midnight. When you are feeling up to it, I'm suppose to take you to Murphy's Trading Post to await Dakota's return."

Breanna felt hurt and betrayed. "Why didn't he tell me himself?"

"You should know by now that he doesn't like good-byes."

Breanna closed her eyes, but not before a tear rolled down her cheek. "Can you tell me where

433

he's gone?"

Levi's eyes grew sad. "I think it's time someone told you something. I'm going to take it upon myself to do just that."

"I know he's come to kill a man, Levi. He admitted that much to me."

"Did he tell you who the man is?"

"No."

"He is being forced to face his brother, Black Otter, and it's tearing him apart on the inside. You will have to understand that the two of them grew up together. There was a time when they were very close, until the time Black Otter became jealous of Dakota."

Fear for Dakota tightened her nerves. "But why? I do not understand."

Levi looked inward, searching his mind. "Actually, it goes back a long way. Did Dakota ever tell you how he got that scar on his chest?"

"He said something about a bear."

"Yes, but did he tell you that he battled that bear when he was ten years old, with nothing but a hunting knife, to save his mother and Running Deer?"

"No, he did not," she admitted.

"That's just like him, he's never been one to brag. He almost lost his life fighting that bear. He was honored by his father and the whole Arapaho tribe, and Black Otter was shamed that day because he acted like a coward. That's when things

434

began to go wrong between them."

"Did both of them love Running Deer?"

Levi hesitated. "That's not for me to say. But it was Black Otter who killed Running Deer in a jealous rage, and she died in Dakota's arms."

Breanna felt her heart ache at the picture Levi drew. "How tragic," she said. Breanna now thought she knew why Dakota could not love her—he loved a dead woman. "Why must Dakota be the one who faces Black Otter? Is there no law to punish him for his crime?"

"Not any law as you know it. However, Black Otter was supposed to die for slaying Running Deer, but he escaped. He has been terrorizing the countryside, making sure word got back to Murphy so he would pass it on to Dakota."

Breanna gasped. "He wanted Dakota to come back?"

"Yes, Black Otter is eaten up with jealousy and anger. He will not be satisfied until either he or Dakota is dead."

Breanna tried to rise, but pain prevented it. "Why didn't you go with Dakota, Levi? He needs you."

"Because where he goes, he must go alone—what he has to do, he must do alone."

"I am frightened for him, Levi. Can he defeat this Black Otter?"

"Dakota is stronger and braver, but Black Otter is cunning and deceitful. When they come to-

435

gether, to most folks' thinking, both white and Indian, it will be like good battling evil."

"You didn't answer my question. Can Dakota defeat Black Otter?"

Levi looked her in the eye. "I can only hope—that's all any of us can do. As his wife, I thought you should know how things are."

Helpless tears rolled down Breanna's cheeks; she feared for the man she loved. "I wish I could help him, Levi."

"You can't, though. None of us can."

She rolled her head from side to side. "How will I be able to exist, not knowing if he is alive or dead?"

"You will live each day one at a time, because he would expect it of you."

Her eyes were swimming with tears. "He is the most wonderful man I know."

"You love him a lot, don't you?"

"Yes, but he doesn't seem to want my love."

Levi stood up. "I'll tell you something you aren't going to believe. Dakota doesn't believe that you love him."

"That's because I have tried very hard to disguise my feelings."

Levi shook his head, wondering why neither of them was aware of the other's feelings when it was so apparent to everyone else. "I've said enough for one day. Try to get some rest. Tomorrow, if you're feeling up to it, we'll go on to Murphy's Trading

Post."

Breanna rode beside John and Baxley, wishing they would soon reach the trading post. They had been riding since early morning, and according to Levi, they would arrive before sundown. Her shoulder was aching, and she just wanted a soft bed where she could lie down.

When they topped a rise, she looked down at the green valley which was surrounded by mountains and green pine forests. The land around Murphy's Trading Post had been cleared of trees, and a stockade wall built around a fort-like structure. Breanna saw the tepees outside the walls, and glanced at Levi questioningly.

"They would be Sioux," he told her. "Murphy is a friend to them, and most always you will find whole families of the tribe camped nearby."

As they descended into the valley, Breanna wondered if there was anywhere so beautiful. When they reached the gates, she encountered her first glimpse of Indian women and children. She smiled at the dark-eyed children, who stared at her with equal curiosity.

Murphy turned out to be a wiry little Irishman, whose beard was as red as his shaggy head. His eyes sparkled with welcome as he approached Levi. "I never thought to lay eyes on you again, Levi Gunther. I thought some English woman would wrap you up and take you home with her."

"Nope, they didn't seem inclined to take me in."

Murphy glanced at Breanna with curiosity. "Breanna, this Irishman is a friend and longtime acquaintance," said Levi. "Murphy, this is Lady Breanna, Dakota's wife, and John Donegal, Dakota's cousin."

Murphy's eyes widened in appreciation. "I welcome you, my lady," he said respectfully. "We've been expecting you for over a week. My missus has made everything ready for you. She has been buzzing around like a bee, happy to be welcoming another white woman."

After Levi helped Breanna dismount, she smiled at the Irishman. "How did you know we were coming, Mr. Murphy?"

He scratched his red beard. "We have ways of knowing everything out here. Sometimes our lives depend on it. Our sources are very reliable, too. We had even heard that Dakota's woman was very beautiful. A certain Sioux warrior couldn't say enough about your charms."

Breanna's face reddened, and Levi gave Murphy a warning glance.

The redhead cleared his throat and moved on to another subject. "Black Otter knows that Dakota has returned. He was here day before yesterday. Killed a Sioux woman and an old man. His way of leaving his calling card, I guess."

Breanna's eyes widened with fear. "Will Dakota

know about this?"

"He knows," Levi assured her.

Breanna was seated beneath a wide oak tree, having tea with Henrietta Murphy, while John and Baxley made a tour of the fort with Mr. Murphy. The last anyone had seen of Levi, he was conversing with a Sioux warrior.

Henrietta was a woman in her early forties with soft gray hair that waved around her face, and there were permanent laugh lines that fanned out around her blue eyes. She had come to this country twenty years ago with her father, who had worked for the London Fur Company. She had met and married Murphy, and she told Breanna that she had never regretted it for a moment.

Henrietta saw the worried frown that etched Breanna's lovely face, and she noted the way her guest absently traced the handle of the porcelain tea cup. "Does your shoulder pain you, my lady?" the woman asked solicitously.

"No, it's much better, thank you."

"Then you are worried about Dakota, aren't you, my lady?" the older woman asked in her soft English accent.

The golden eyes that Breanna raised to Henrietta were troubled. "Yes, I am. It's difficult for me to sit here, drinking tea and acting as if nothing is amiss, all the while knowing that my husband is in

439

danger."

"I know your Dakota. I've known him since he was but a boy. Levi used to order books for him to read, and they would be shipped to us here. Your husband is something of a legend in these parts, my lady. He is revered by the Arapaho. The tales of his valor and strength lose nothing in the telling. I would put my mind at rest if I were you. Dakota . . . er . . . I mean, his lordship, can take care of himself."

"Mrs. Murphy, I see no sense in standing on ceremony. Please call me Breanna." She looked to the older woman to allay her fears for Dakota. "Tell me what you have heard about Dakota."

"Well," Henrietta said reflectively. "It was known by everyone that Dakota was the pride of his father. Two Moons was an extraordinary man who believed in honor."

"Dakota has not told me very much about his Indian father. I do know that he respected him a great deal."

"Yes. Two Moons was a powerful war chief, and his name is still honored among his people. It was plain to everyone that he favored Dakota over his own son, and perhaps therein lay the tragedy. As a young man, Dakota was well loved and excelled in everything he attempted. But Black Otter was treacherous and unlovable. As he grew to manhood, his hatred and anger became directed toward Dakota."

440

"I cannot understand how anyone could hate my husband. He is a remarkable man."

"That would be one of the reasons Black Otter hates him. Of course, Black Otter hates everyone now, and he has murdered and pillaged Indian villages as well as white settlements to revenge the wrongs that he thinks have been done to him. Black Otter did much of this so Dakota would hear about his deeds and be forced to return. His whole reason for living is to see Dakota dead."

"But why?" Breanna asked with growing uneasiness.

"I cannot say, but it is said by the Arapaho that the day will come when the two brothers will face one another, and one of them must die."

Breanna trembled with fear. "I do not understand why Dakota has allowed Black Otter to pull him back. He is tormented, and I have seen this thing tearing him apart inside."

The older woman pursed her lips. "He feels responsible for Black Otter's actions. You will have to understand that he looks on Black Otter as his own brother. Black Otter knows that Dakota promised their dying father that blood would not flow between them. He also knows that forcing Dakota to break his word to Two Moons would be the greatest revenge of all. Can you see now why Dakota is tormented?"

Breanna closed her eyes, aching deep inside for the man she loved. "Yes, I can see. I see no way out for Dakota."

"If he slays his brother, he will have broken his word to his father. If he does nothing, he will feel as if he were betraying the Arapaho, for they are the ones who will pay for Black Otter's rampages. The soldiers blame all the Arapaho for the raids, and Washington has threatened to send troops to corral Black Otter. If that happens, innocent Arapaho men, women, and children will die."

Breanna felt tears gathering in her eyes. How would this ever reach a happy conclusion? Even if Dakota won, he would never be able to forget he had slain his brother and broken a vow he had made to his Indian father. Now she could understand the torment he had been living with. Oh, how she wished she had known earlier. Perhaps she could have been more of a comfort to him.

Suddenly Breanna felt someone staring at her, and she glanced up to see the silhouette of a man lurking near the corner of the house. She drew in her breath as the man moved forward and she saw he was an Indian!

Dark eyes swept over her face as the near-naked warrior boldly approached.

"Wh—who is that?" Breanna asked, fearing it might be Black Otter.

Henrietta smiled and came to her feet. "You do not need to fear this Arapaho warrior, Breanna. He is Dakota's boyhood friend, Shadow Walker."

The Indian now stood before Breanna, his dark

eyes moving over her curiously. With a smile, he said something she did not understand, but Mrs. Murphy translated for her.

"Shadow Walker wishes to say that Dakota's woman is fair of face, and he finds the color of your hair pleasing to his eyes." Mrs. Murphy laughed. "You will find the young warriors of the Arapaho have flowery words when talking to a pretty woman."

"Please tell him that I am pleased to know Dakota's friend, and ask him if he has seen my husband."

While Henrietta translated, Breanna watched the dark face, noting how intently he was listening. After he had answered, Henrietta turned back to Breanna. "Yes, he has been with Dakota. That's why he's here. It seems Dakota sent him to look after you."

"But why?"

The older woman spoke to Shadow Walker. When she met Breanna's eyes, her expression was troubled. "Shadow Walker says Dakota fears Black Otter may try to get at him through you."

The color drained out of Breanna's face, but Henrietta hastened to assure her that she would be safe in this fortress.

For two long days, Breanna waited for some word of Dakota, but she heard nothing. Fear for Dakota's safety became her constant companion. Tense and near tears, she now stood at the window of her small bedroom, glancing out the stockade gate. It seemed to her that the whole world had paused, waiting . . . waiting. . . .

She saw Shadow Walker leaning against the stockade wall, his eyes alert, his hand resting on his knife. He was never far away from her. Even though Breanna knew John and Levi were also keeping an eye on her, she drew comfort from Shadow Walker's presence because Dakota had sent him to watch over her.

With Shadow Walker following a few paces behind, Breanna walked around the compound, hoping she would be tired enough to fall asleep that night.

When she heard shouting and saw Levi, Murphy, Baxley, and the Americans riding out the gates at breakneck speed, she was confused. John joined her near the gate, and they both watched the men disappear.

"What is wrong?" Breanna asked.

"One of the Sioux informed Mr. Murphy that the small settlement nearby was in flames," John said grimly. What he did not tell Breanna was that if it was true, they would probably be too late to be of any use to the settlers.

"You did not wish to go with them?"

"No, I'm going to stay near you. I don't like the sound of this."

"Surely you do not think that . . . Black Otter is somehow involved?"

"Who can say?" John replied as he and Breanna watched the compound gates close and the man who worked for Murphy slide the heavy bolt into place. The man then climbed upon the scaffold, where he proceeded to stand watch.

One would have thought, to glance at Shadow Walker, that he viewed all this activity with bored indifference, but not if one looked into his eyes. He was very aware of everything that went on around him. When Breanna, John, and Henrietta sat beneath the oak tree, trying to find relief from the heat, Shadow Dancer positioned himself nearby.

"I am not too sure I trust that Indian," John said suspiciously.

"Oh, you can trust Shadow Walker, and be glad that he's here," Henrietta exclaimed. "Dakota must have thought so too, or else he wouldn't have sent him."

"When do you think the men will return?" Breanna asked.

"I don't know." Henrietta's eyes met John's. "It depends on what they find."

Breanna waited in her bedroom for Levi's return. When darkness deepened across the land, the flames from the north could be seen glowing

445

against the ebony sky. Hours passed, and still Levi and the others did not return. John had finally given up waiting for them and had gone to his quarters to retire for the night.

Breanna sat on the bed, tracing a pattern of the patchwork quilt with her finger, unable to sleep. There was such a silence that it was almost deafening.

Even the Sioux who had camped outside the compound had folded their tepees, loaded them on pack horses, and ridden away. It was as if they knew trouble was coming and did not want to be a part of it.

She lay back, thinking only to rest. Her mind was so troubled, and her body so weary, that she soon drifted off to sleep.

Breanna was awakened by a feeling of deep dread. The candle had gone out, and the room was in total darkness. Hearing one of the plank boards squeak, she froze in terror. Someone was in the room with her!

Easing herself up to a sitting position, she swung her legs off the side of the bed. She thought about calling out for help, but her throat had closed off. Suddenly she was grabbed with a viselike grip.

A hurtful hand clamped over her mouth, cutting off her breathing. A guttural voice whispered orders in her ear, orders she did not understand. She did not have to be told that Black Otter was her tormenter! Dear, God, was he going to kill her?

He violently jerked her to her feet, and she could feel the prickle of a knife at her spine.

Whimpering sounds were blocked in her throat. When Black Otter's hand moved away from her mouth, Breanna took a deep gulp of air, just before he tied a cloth over her mouth so tightly it cut into her skin.

Rough hands bound her hands and she was half dragged, half carried, toward the open window.

Breanna wondered what had happened to Shadow Walker, and why he had not come to her rescue, when her captor pulled her across a prone body and she saw that it was Dakota's friend. There was a knife sticking out of his back.

Anguished sobs were building from deep inside Breanna, and she was so frightened she could not move.

Pain exploded inside her head when Black Otter struck her with a hard object and she fell unconscious.

Breanna was not aware when Black Otter picked her up and slung her over his shoulder. Staying in the shadows of the compound, he left through an opening he had made earlier.

As Black Otter mounted his horse and rode away with Dakota's woman, he felt alive for the first time in months. Dakota would suffer much to get this woman back. Black Otter would play with him, torment him, and then when the time was right, he would kill this woman right before Dakota's eyes.

Yes, revenge would be long and sweet.

Chapter Thirty-three

Shadow Walker felt his strength waning as he dragged himself across the compound. He knew he had lost a lot of blood, and weakness threatened to render him unconscious. He had to get help for Dakota's woman! Dakota had trusted him to keep her safe and he had failed. His shame hurt him almost as badly as his wound. With his last ounce of strength, he crawled to the door of the man who was Dakota's white cousin. With his last effort, Shadow Walker rapped on the door, then gave in to the darkness that claimed him.

John had been unable to sleep, and he heard the noise at the door. Thinking it might be Levi returning, he quickly lit a candle and opened the door.

Seeing the body of Shadow Walker, and knowing what it must mean, John quickly sounded the alarm while he ran toward Breanna's quarters. When he reached Breanna's door, he flung it open and called out to her.

449

Advancing into the room, John shuddered with mounting dread. When he fumbled around, found the candle, and lit it, he discovered his worst fears had been realized—the room was empty. There on the bed, among the rumpled covers, was a broken lance.

Henrietta burst into the room, her long braid trailing down her back, her breath coming out in gasps. When she saw the lance, she whitened. "Black Otter has been here. He has Breanna!" she cried.

John closed his eyes, blaming himself. What could he have done differently to protect her? More importantly, what could he do to get her back? He didn't know the country, nor was he able to track anyone. "Have the others returned yet?" he asked.

"No. Our man is tending Shadow Walker. We hope he will recover with the right . . ." Her voice trailed off and tears filled her eyes. "What can we do about Breanna?"

At that moment they heard riders entering the stockade and Murphy's voice called out.

"Thank God," John said, running out of the room. "Keep in the saddle!" he yelled. "Black Otter has taken Breanna."

"That bastard," Levi spat out gruffly. "He set that fire so he would draw us off. I'm mad as hell that I fell for the oldest trick known to man."

"I didn't think he would come into my compound to take Dakota's wife," Murphy said angrily. "Let's

450

get going before he's too far ahead. I sure as hell don't want to be the one to tell Dakota his woman is missing."

"We can't track him in the dark," Levi reasoned. "The best we can do until daylight is go in different directions and hope one of us finds some sign of them."

Everyone agreed this would be the best way. Luther, Inman, and Baxley would ride to the north, while Levi and John would cover the south. Murphy and his man took the west. "What about the east?" John asked.

"We can discount that direction. Black Otter would not be welcome on Sioux land," Levi explained.

In a thunder of horses' hooves, the riders disbursed in different directions. Each had little hope they would find Breanna.

Dakota came down the gully at a dead gallop. Wheeling around, he reigned in his horse. Slowly dismounting, he saw in the distance three men spread-eagled with wooden stakes.

Cocking his rifle, he approached them cautiously, wary of a trap. Taking cover behind a bush, he crept slowly forward.

When he was near enough, he saw that it was Baxley, Luther, and Inman who had been staked out. It was obvious that Inman was dead, because his one blue and his one brown eye were blank, staring at nothing—seeing nothing.

Dakota quickly examined Baxley and Luther, finding to his relief that they still lived. Their faces, however, were blistered from the sun, their lips cracked, their clothes in tatters, their tongues parched and swollen from their piercing thirst.

Dakota cut the two men loose and reached for his canteen. As cool water washed the sand from Baxley's throat, he opened his eyes and smiled ever so slightly. "Begging your pardon, my lord, but we could not find her."

"Find who?" Dakota cried, fearing he already knew the answer.

"Her ladyship," Baxley gasped. "That devil, Black Otter, came right into the compound and took her, my lord."

Dakota tried to beat down his rising alarm. He had to keep a clear head if he was going to find Breanna. "How did this happen to you, Baxley?"

"Mr. Gunther had us all ride in different directions to search for her ladyship. We were put upon by three Indians, my lord. They didn't seem intent on killing us as much as they seemed to want to torture us."

Luther rubbed cool water from Dakota's canteen over his face before he spoke. "One of them gave me a message to give you," the American said weakly. "He said to tell you that you will find—let me see if I have this right—you will find whom you seek at the place where a bear almost ended your life. He said Black Otter wanted you to know that what happened to us here will happen to your woman there."

Dakota tensed. His eyes became narrow slits, cold and piercing. "When did Black Otter take Breanna?"

"Last night . . . or was it two nights ago. I can't be sure how long we have been here," Luther told him.

Dakota's face paled beneath his tan, and he couldn't bear to think of his Breanna being in Black Otter's hands. "If I leave you the water, can you bury Inman and make it back to the trading post on your own?"

"Yes, my lord. You don't worry about us. Just find her ladyship," Baxley said, dragging himself to an upright position to show that he was capable of standing alone.

Dakota's face was unreadable, his eyes cold, as he turned away to meet his destiny and save his woman.

Baxley and Luther watched Dakota ride away, each knowing he would not like to be in Black Otter's shoes once Dakota caught up with him.

Dakota spurred his horse on relentlessly, sparing neither himself nor the animal. He knew where Black Otter would be waiting for him. He only hoped he would be in time to save his beloved!

* * *

When Breanna regained consciousness, it was morning. She found herself on a galloping horse, being held in place by the Indian who had abducted her. She was still bound and gagged, and her head ached where Black Otter had struck her. She stared up into black eyes that were filled with hate.

Black Otter's dark hair was encircled with a raw-hide band. He wore a yellow buckskin vest. He was haughty and insolent, and Breanna had the feeling that this man would end her life abruptly if she gave him the slightest provocation. She wondered why he had not already done so.

She remembered Levi saying that an Indian respects bravery, and she hoped she would not shame Dakota by acting the coward, but she was so very frightened.

The Indian halted his horse and tossed Breanna to the ground. For a moment she could not move because the pain was too great. When she did finally try to move, the Indian yanked on the leather rope and sent her tumbling to the ground once more. It was clear to her that the Indian meant to humble her, but he would never succeed, she vowed as she stood up, her golden eyes defying him.

Black Otter jerked at the rope to assert his power over her, and once more she tumbled to the ground. He dragged her over to a tree and bound her tightly to it.

Breanna wanted to cry because of the pain and

humiliation this hateful man was putting her through, but she was determined not to give him the satisfaction.

When he unsheathed his knife, she closed her eyes, expecting to feel it plunge into her heart. She was relieved when he merely cut the cloth that was bound around her mouth.

"I know who you are, Black Otter," she spat out. "You have killed Shadow Walker."

If he understood her words, he did not show it. He turned away from her, took his horse's reins, and bounded on its back. When he rode away, Breanna felt momentary relief, until she realized that if he didn't return, she would die anyway. She would never be able to loosen the leather thongs he had used to tie her to the tree. Her mouth was so dry, she would probably die from thirst before anyone could rescue her.

In total desperation, she leaned her head back against the tree trunk and cried bitter tears. What did it matter if she gave in to tears? No one would see her.

Time passed slowly, and Breanna finally fell asleep, thinking it was better to lose herself in sleep for a time than to be awake in a living nightmare.

Dakota's face was haggard as he removed his rifle from his dead horse's carcass. The poor animal was covered with lather, and flecks of bloody foam covered its mouth. He had never in his life ridden a horse to its death. Two Moons had taught him that an Arapaho warrior always took care of his horse before seeing to his own needs.

In desperation, Dakota looked around. How would he ever reach Breanna before Black Otter harmed her? On foot it would take two days to reach the valley where he had encountered the bear as a young boy.

Shouldering his rifle, he started off in a run. He had to try. Hatred burned in his heart for his brother. Now he would not hesitate to take Black Otter's life. He had made a fatal mistake; he had taken the one person that Dakota loved above all else.

In his tortured mind, he could see Breanna's smile. He remembered so clearly how her golden eyes would soften when he was making love to her. The sound of her laughter played on his ears, and he ached to hold her, to protect her from Black Otter's evil.

He had been running for about an hour—pushing himself beyond human endurance. He had to go—had to save Breanna. When he at last felt his strength drained, and his breath coming out in short gasps, he cursed the human body that had its limitations. When he finally stopped to lean against a tree to catch his breath, despair overwhelmed him. It was futile; he would never reach Breanna in time.

Suddenly Dakota heard the sound of a rider, and he ducked behind a bush. With his rifle cocked, he waited for whoever it was to ride into sight. Relief washed over him when he recognized Levi.

The hunter pulled up his mount and called out. "If I'd a been Black Otter, I'd have picked you off an hour ago. You left a trail any blundering fool could follow—killed your horse, did you?"

Dakota grabbed the reins from Levi's hand. "I will take your horse. I have to get to Breanna."

Levi obligingly slid to the ground. "Do you know where Black Otter's taken her?"

Dakota tossed his rifle to Levi, since there was already one in the saddle holster. "Yes. He waits for me at the place where I encountered the bear."

Levi glanced into Dakota's eyes. "Take heart, he may not have harmed her yet. He will probably keep her safe until you arrive. I wish I could go with you; I'd like to kill that bastard myself."

"You cannot come with me, Levi. This I must do alone. I can promise you this, if he has harmed Breanna, he will die a painful death."

"Be careful. He knows you are coming. He will have had time to prepare for you."

Dakota's eyes narrowed. "Nothing can stop me from slaying him now. Not even the promise I made our father."

Breanna woke with a start when Black Otter untied her from the tree and jerked her to her feet. She fought against him, and he slapped her with his open palm. "It would take very little to make me kill you, white woman."

"You speak English?" she said, stating the obvious. Testing her cut lip, she found it was bleeding. "Dakota will find you, Black Otter. There is nowhere you can hide that he will not seek you out."

His dark eyes moved over her, and he found her pleasing. Her hair, which tumbled about her face, was a golden color he had never before seen. He was astonished to see that her eyes were also a golden color. "I have made sure Dakota can find me. I want him to suffer before I kill him."

Breanna felt her heart skip a beat. "That's why you took me. You are using me to draw him to you."

Black Otter gripped her chin and pushed her hair out of her face. "I think he will be in torment, wondering what I am doing to you. I think Dakota must love you very much."

"You are wrong. Dakota does not love me. He . . . still loves Running Deer."

"Do not take me for a fool, white woman. Dakota never loved Running Deer. I loved her, but he did not. It is because of him that she is dead. It is only right that I take his woman's life in exchange."

Breanna felt her courage slipping. "It was not Dakota who killed Running Deer. It was you."

"It is because she wanted him and turned her

458

face away from me that she is dead. You should look to your own safety, white woman. It does not bother me to kill a woman."

"I do not fear you," she said in an attempt of bravado. "Neither does my husband fear you."

Black Otter's dark eyes flinched, and she knew she had struck a nerve.

"My husband is a brave man, and he will never be defeated by a coward like you."

His face was murderous as he raised his fist to strike her.

Breanna willed herself not to flinch away, and stared at him with impudence. "Yes, a coward would hit a woman."

To Breanna's surprise, Black Otter did not strike her. She felt relieved until she discovered he had a far worse punishment in store for her.

He led her down a slope where he had driven four stakes in the ground. She tried to jerk away from him when he pushed her down to her knees, but she was helpless against his strength as he pushed her hands over her head and tied her wrists to the stakes. She tried to twist away from him when he grabbed her leg and secured her ankle to another stake. This was repeated with her other ankle, and soon Breanna could not move.

"What are you going to do?" she asked, fear rising in her throat like bile.

"I am using you as bait, white woman. You will not be so pretty once the sun has cooked your skin."

459

He grabbed her gown and ripped it down the front, exposing her lacy chemise.

"No," he said, running brutal hands over her white shoulders and pushing her chemise down to expose her breasts. "I do not think Dakota will find you so desirable when your skin cracks and dries up like leather."

She cried out when he ripped her gown the rest of the way and threw it aside, leaving only her chemise to cover her body.

Now, in her near-naked state, Breanna could no longer hide her tears. She cried for herself, but most of all she cried for Dakota because he was being lured into a trap. She thought it very likely that she would be the instrument of his death, and there was nothing she could do to prevent it.

Chapter Thirty-four

Dakota silently jumped from Levi's horse and slapped it on the rump, sending it galloping back the way he had come. He knew that on foot, he was still an hour from his destination, but it would be foolish to ride any farther since it would only alert Black Otter he was coming.

Dakota was on familiar ground now, for this was the land where he had walked in childhood, and he knew every hill and tree. He found an old familiar trail but avoided it, choosing instead to stay within the cover of the trees. Cautiously, he made his way forward, keeping the Wind River to his right and the mountains to his back.

Dakota's eyes were burning, and there was fear in his heart for the woman he loved. He blamed himself because she had fallen into Black Otter's hands.

He had been selfish, thinking more of himself than her by allowing her to come with him instead of insisting that she return to England. He had known the danger she would face, and still he had agreed to bring her along because he had wanted her with him. Even when he had been angry with her, he had found joy just in knowing she was nearby.

Breanna felt the heat of the sun on her face. Her throat was dry and she was so thirsty. She tried to remember the times when Dakota had taught her to swim, and to imagine that she was now immersed in cool sea water. But the burning heat from the sun made it impossible to imagine for very long because reality was the hot, scorching sun overhead.

Breanna could feel her strength waning. A groan escaped her lips, and she weakly jerked against the leather thongs that bound her to the stakes. With defeat reflecting in her eyes, she realized she could not free herself.

Red-hot heat was broiling her delicate skin, and she imagined this was the way it would feel to be cooked alive.

Breanna knew Dakota would come for her, but he might arrive too late to save her. She wished she had the means of warning Dakota that he would be falling into Black Otter's trap. A shuddering sob escaped her lips. Today might be the last day of life for her and her love, for Black Otter was cunning and devious, and he had planned well, leaving nothing to chance.

For some reason, Breanna's fevered mind remembered the words of Dakota's father when he had written in his journal that he wanted to be buried with his beloved Cillia so they might spend eternity together. If she and Dakota were both to die today, she wondered if some kind soul would place them in a common grave so they might spend eternity together.

Breanna rolled her head back and forth, knowing she wasn't thinking clearly, and that she must fight against the delirium that clouded her mind, distorting everything with a feeling of unreality.

The sun was a red-hot ball of fire in the sky, and it was drawing every ounce of strength from her body.

"Dakota," she whispered, "if only I could look upon your face once more before I die. I want to tell you that I love you." Her voice sounded weak even to her own ears.

Breanna heard movement to the right of her, and she painfully turned to see Black Otter crouch down as if he was listening to something. By the excited gleam in his dark eyes, she realized Dakota must be nearby!

She considered calling out to warn Dakota about the trap, but then she quickly thought better of it. If Black Otter had not bound her mouth to keep her silent, he must want her to call out to Dakota. She bit her trembling lip, vowing to remain silent. She would not help Black Otter capture Dakota.

At that moment Black Otter confirmed her suspicions. He slunk over to Brenna and whispered up to her in a sharp voice, "Call to your man to help you, white woman. He is near and will rush to save you," he taunted.

"No," she moaned, "never."

Dakota flattened his body on the ground and parted the thick bush so he could get a better view of what lay ahead.

With a shuddered intake of breath, he saw Breanna, her half-naked body blistering beneath the scorching sun, her arms and legs stretched tightly between four stakes. Anger such as he had never known shook his body, and hatred for his brother coiled like a snake inside him. Black Otter would pay for doing this to his woman!

Dakota had to fight against the urge to run to Breanna and cut her loose and hold her protectively in his arms, for he knew that was exactly what Black Otter expected of him. He watched Breanna lick her dry lips, knowing he had to act quickly. Already her body was burned from the sun, and he couldn't be sure how much longer she could endure the heat.

Dakota allowed his eyes to move over each bush and tree, his ears alert to any sound that would give away Black Otter's hiding place. At last his eyes settled on the slope just beyond Breanna. He remembered leaping down that very slope as a boy, to face the bear that was charging his mother and Running Deer. Suddenly he knew that was where Black Otter waited for him.

Dakota glanced up at the sun, knowing he would have a better chance to free Breanna under the cover of night. He gauged that there were still three hours until sunset—too long to wait—Breanna would never last that long—he had to act now.

Slowly rising to a kneeling position, Dakota gripped his rifle in one hand. In complete silence, he stood up, unsheathing his knife with the other. It flashed through his mind that much of his life had been played out on this spot. Perhaps this was even where his life would end.

Black Otter could feel Dakota's presence, and his dark eyes narrowed with hatred. Soon he would have Dakota's blood on his knife, but first he would torture him, make him cry out for mercy, humble him into the dust.

The renegade warrior hugged the sides of the incline, knowing the time to act was now. The same man had trained them both, so he knew how Dakota was thinking. He would never give his presence away, so Black Otter would just have to draw him out into the open.

Black Otter slowly moved up the incline. When he raised his head, he knew he would already be in Dakota's view, so he rolled forward to keep low. Coming to his knees beside Dakota's woman, he drew his knife.

Breanna's eyes were closed, but they opened slowly as she felt the Indian beside her once more. "No," she murmured weakly, as he pressed the knife at her throat. He yelled out something, and the only word she understood was "Dakota." Was Dakota here? she wondered, feeling as if the hot sun had muddled her mind.

"I know you are here, Dakota," Black Otter called out in the tongue of the Arapaho. "Come forward so you can watch your woman die."

Dakota watched helplessly as Black Otter ran his knife blade down Breanna's neck. His mind would not accept the thought of Black Otter touching his wife. But he could not allow himself to think about that. If his mind was not clear, he would never defeat Black Otter. He needed his concentration if he was going to free Breanna.

"Come out of hiding, Dakota. If you don't, I will plunge this knife into your woman's heart."

Dakota came to his feet and moved out into the open. He was some thirty paces from Breanna, and he knew he could never cover that distance before his brother would make good his threat to end her life.

Dakota's eyes were on his wife as he spoke, pain tearing at his heart. "Leave her out of this, Black Otter. She has nothing to do with our feud."

Black Otter laughed maliciously. "Oh, no, my brother, I cannot do that. This woman will be the means of my revenge." To demonstrate his point, Black Otter ran the knife blade across Breanna's shoulder and sliced through the last remaining material that covered her breasts.

While Dakota watched helplessly, Black Otter ran the knife blade around Breanna's nipples, first one, then the other.

"This woman is beautiful for a white woman. I can only imagine how you must care for her. Shall I carve a scar on her, to match the one the bear gave you?"

"Black Otter," Dakota said, gnashing his teeth. "If you harm her, I will kill you!"

Black Otter's eyes gleamed with something akin to madness. "You are in no position to issue threats, Dakota. Throw the rifle down and toss your knife aside, or I will kill her now." As proof of his intentions, Black Otter's knife pierced Breanna's skin, slicing across her shoulder to the swell of her breast, while her blood stained the tip of his blade.

Breanna groaned in pain and turned her face to Dakota. Although she could not understand Black Otter's words, she could tell by his tone of voice that he was goading Dakota.

"Don't let him degrade you because of me, Dakota," she pleaded, knowing what a proud man her husband was. "Do whatever you have to do. I . . . am not afraid to die."

Dakota felt a sensation so unfamiliar to him that it took his breath away. His eyes burned with unshed tears, and his pride was great for this woman whom his grandfather had chosen to be his wife. He had always known she was extraordinary, but until now, he had not known how courageous she was.

"Do not despair, Breanna, for my love for you is great. If I cannot free you, then I will walk with your spirit this day," he promised her.

Dakota did not realize that he had spoken in Arapaho and Breanna had not understood his declaration of love.

"Very touching," Black Otter hissed. "But when I am finished with you both, there will be only enough left of you to scatter to the four winds."

"You may kill us, Black Otter, but in doing so, you go against our father's wishes and condemn yourself in a way that will one day destroy you."

"I do not have to listen to you, white man, because Two Moons was not your father, he was mine. The time for your walk in the spirit world is near, and I will never have to think of you again. Enough talk. Throw down your weapons, or I will slay your woman now!"

"No, do not touch her," Dakota said, tossing down his rifle and knife in defeat. Black Otter had found the only way in which he could hurt him—through Breanna. Too late, Dakota realized he had made a mistake in allowing Black Otter to see how much he cherished his wife.

Breanna moaned, knowing if she had not insisted

on following Dakota to America, then he would not be burdened with her welfare and could have fought Black Otter on his own terms. Now he had no weapons to defend himself with and it was all her fault. She wanted to tell him she was sorry, but the words stuck in her parched throat.

As she watched Dakota standing before his enemy, stripped of his pride and humbled because of her, she wished desperately that there was some way she could help him.

Breanna was confused when Black Otter sliced through her bonds, freeing her arms and legs. He roughly grabbed her about the waist and hauled her to her feet. Breanna felt like a rag doll with no substance, and she had to hold on to the Indian to stand upright.

Black Otter's laughter was ugly to her ears. "You are a fool, Dakota. Look behind you and you will see one of my warriors, who only waits for my command to kill you. I have you now, Dakota. You will never save this woman!"

Breanna saw the pain and indecision on Dakota's face, and she knew Black Otter was once again taunting him. In a haze of pain, she saw the other warrior with his rifle aimed at Dakota, and she knew her husband was facing impossible odds. "Do not allow Black Otter to . . . humble you because of me," she cried past the dryness in her mouth. "Do what you must."

"Do not talk, woman," Black Otter commanded,

shaking Breanna as if she were indeed a rag doll.

Suddenly Dakota needed to know if Black Otter had ravished his wife. He would never be able to bear the pain if Breanna had been forced to suffer that degradation. "What have you done to her?" Dakota asked in a warning voice.

Black Otter's eyes gleamed. He was enjoying himself because he had Dakota where he had always wanted him. "I have done nothing to this woman . . . yet. But after you are dead," he shrugged, "who knows?" His eyes gleamed at the pain he saw on Dakota's face. "Of course, I may decide to be merciful and kill her first," he taunted, "so you can watch."

Black Otter was so caught up in toying with Dakota that he allowed his eyes to rake the half-naked white woman. That was when Dakota saw the knife which Black Otter held at Breanna's throat waver, and he knew now was the time to charge his enemy.

Leaping through the air, Dakota felt a hot burning in his shoulder, and he realized that he had been shot by Black Otter's warrior. But that did not stop him or slow him down as, maddened with anger, he caught Black Otter off guard, knocking both him and Breanna to the ground.

Breanna rolled down the incline and landed with a thud at the bottom, while Dakota and Black Otter were caught in a death struggle.

The two men fought for possession of Black Otter's knife. Both men were straining, their muscles tense and trembling as the knife blade moved from Dakota's throat, back to Black Otter's throat — wavering, varying, changing directions several times.

Dakota knew the helplessness of his situation. Even if he should overcome Black Otter, there would still be the other Indian to deal with, and his strength was waning fast. What would become of Brenna should he die?

He had overestimated Black Otter's bravery. He should have known his brother would not stand alone, for he was too much of a coward.

Dakota had gained the advantage, and he now rolled Black Otter over and straddled him. With a strength that came from his love for Breanna, he grabbed his brother's wrist, wrenching the knife from his grasp.

As Black Otter's eyes widened in fright, Dakota's finger's tightened around the hilt. "Now *you* die, Black Otter. May you walk in darkness this night, for your treacherous soul is not worthy to walk in sunlight."

"Kill him!" Black Otter called out to his companion. "Do it now!"

"Your friend can't help you, Black Otter, he's otherwise engaged." Levi's welcome voice spoke up from behind them. "Do what you have to, Dakota, me and John have this buck under our aim."

Dakota shook his head to fight off the dizziness that came from his loss of blood. Breathing a sigh of relief because Levi was there to take care of

Breanna, he felt renewed strength.

Dakota's hand tightened on the knife. "There is no help for you, Black Otter," he hissed. "Now you are at my mercy."

"Kill me then," Black Otter spat. "If you have forgotten what our father asked of you, take my life and let my blood stain your hands."

Dakota hesitated. He had every reason to kill Black Otter, but why was it so difficult to drive the knife into his treacherous heart? Black Otter's hands had been stained with the blood of hundreds of victims, why could Dakota not end his life?

Dakota yelled out in his frustration, burying the knife in the ground only inches from Black Otter's head. "You deserve to die, but I cannot be the one to take your life."

Dakota stood up and staggered backward. "I cannot go against my father's wishes. I will take you to the village and let the Arapaho decide your punishment."

No one saw Black Otter until it was too late. He grabbed the knife from where Dakota had left it and leaped agilely to his feet. Taking aim, his eyes gleamed as he visualized Dakota's death.

Dakota turned, knowing he was helpless to prevent his brother from throwing the knife. He waited for the impact, but heard instead the sound of a rifle.

No one had seen Breanna crawl up the slope or take the rifle Dakota had thrown down earlier.

There was not time to take aim, so she pointed the gun at Black Otter and squeezed the trigger.

Dakota saw the confused look on Black Otter's face and the red stain on his chest.

Slowly, Black Otter crumpled to the ground, his eyes begging for an explanation—it wasn't supposed to happen this way. He was not the one who should die.

Dakota turned to see Breanna throw the rifle to the ground. "I am not sorry that I killed him," she said, falling to her knees. "I would do it again, if . . ." Weakness overcame her, and she fell forward, lost in the oblivion of darkness.

Dakota rushed to Breanna, gathering the most precious person in his life up in his arms.

John came forward, removing his coat and handing it to Dakota so he could cover Breanna's nakedness. "Allow me to carry her for you," he offered, knowing Dakota was weak from loss of blood and was swaying on his feet unsteadily.

"No," Dakota growled, his eyes daring anyone to try to take her from him. "I will carry my wife to the Arapaho village, where the medicine woman will tend her wounds."

Dakota did not look at Black Otter's dead body as he carried Breanna toward the Wind River.

When John would have followed him, Levi's words stopped him. "Leave him be. What he does now, he does without our help. He will find a warm welcome waiting for him in the Arapaho village, with those who care about him."

"But they both need attention, Levi," John protested.

"Nothing happens here that the Arapaho don't know about. They will get all the help they need in the village. I'm sure word has already spread that Black Otter is dead. There will be a cry of welcome for Dakota and Breanna when they arrive."

Chapter Thirty-five

Night was stirring as Breanna awakened. At first she was oblivious to her surroundings because all she could think about was the pain that covered every inch of her body, making her feel as though she were on fire.

Gentle hands were rubbing soothing, cool liquid on Breanna's face. In her hazy state of mind, Breanna was able to make out dark Indian eyes — but they were not hostile as Black Otter's had been, they were kind and concerned.

The old medicine woman had stripped Breanna's remaining clothing away, and was now applying a healing mixture to her entire body. When that was accomplished, the woman placed damp cloths across Breanna.

The medicine woman turned at last to Dakota. "I have done all I can for your wife. She will need to be kept in the dark until the sun goes around twice, then I believe she will begin to heal."

"Will she fully recover, Cloud Woman?"

"Yes, her wounds are not so serious as that bullet you have in your back."

"Will there be scarring?" Dakota wanted to know, unconcerned with his own wound.

"No. I do not think so. The mixture of herbs I used on her should prevent any scarring. Of course, I believe there will be a slight scar where Black Otter cut her with his knife. Knowing that devil, I would say she is fortunate to be alive. Now all I can do for her is keep the cloths damp and give her plenty to drink."

The old woman looked at Dakota, who had refused to have his wounds treated until Breanna had been taken care of. "Now that I have seen to your woman's needs, I will remove that bullet from you."

Dakota knelt down beside Breanna, his anger still burning for what Black Otter had done to her. Taking her limp hand in his, he ached because of the pain she was going through. "You saved my life, beloved Breanna, proving you are brave and strong. You will heal, and soon your spirit will soar with mine through the clouds and we shall love one another forever."

Breanna moaned, unaware that her husband had again declared his love for her, because again he had spoken to her in the Arapaho language.

"I will no longer wait to take that bullet out, Dakota, while you make pretty speeches to your

476

woman," Cloud Woman informed him. "I will do it now."

Dakota leaned back on the buffalo robe, too weak to protest any longer. He knew he had lost a lot of blood and that the bullet was very deeply imbedded.

Breanna huddled near the cook-fire. She smiled at the old medicine woman who had been tending her for the last week. Already the places where Breanna's skin had been sunburned had healed, and the only signs of her ordeal were a slight scar from the knife wound and a golden tint to her skin.

Since the medicine woman did not speak English, she and Breanna communicated through gestures.

Breanna felt uncomfortable dressed in the buckskin gown that fell to her ankles.

Dakota had been in to see her several times, but as her strength returned, he seemed to become more silent, and she began to feel he resented her because she had taken the life of his Indian brother.

The tepee flap was pushed aside, when Dakota entered. Breanna pulled the soft fur robe about her, feeling uncomfortable under Dakota's intense scrutiny.

The medicine woman gave Breanna a toothy grin and ambled out of the tepee, leaving Dakota and Breanna alone.

Dakota wore buckskins, and Breanna noticed for

the first time that he was allowing his hair to grow longer. She wondered if that was a sign that he intended to remain in America.

There was an uncomfortable silence before Breanna was courageous enough to speak. "Does your wound still pain you, Dakota?" she inquired.

"No, it is all but healed." His eyes swept her face. "I am told that you are recovered sufficiently to make the journey back to England." He dropped a bundle of clothing down beside her. "Levi, John, and Baxley arrived this morning. Baxley sent you some of your clothing; the rest are on the packhorse. You will go with them when they leave this afternoon."

Her heart stopped beating. "You will not be coming with us?"

Regretfully, he shook his head. "I cannot leave at this time. Black Otter did much damage to the Arapaho, and I must see that the army understands that my brother's raids in no way involved this village."

She wanted him to take her in his arms, to assure her that he would come to her in England. Breanna knew him well enough by now to realize that he would not leave while the Arapaho needed him. Now that she had been in this village and seen the love and respect the people directed at Dakota, she could better understand his feelings for them.

She wondered if these were to be their final moments together—if indeed she was looking upon his face for the last time. "Will you ever return to England?" she asked at last, fearing to hear the truth.

"I would like to tell you yes, but there is still much for me to do here. I have it within my power to make life easier for my people, and I intend to see that they have everything they need."

Breanna realized that nothing she could say would change his mind. "I have been wondering about your friend, Shadow Walker, who was injured the night Black Otter abducted me. Is he recovered? Did John or Levi tell you his condition?"

"Shadow Walker's injuries were serious, but he is recovering at Murphy's Trading Post. He will be well enough to return to the village in a few days."

"Dakota, I have something to say to you. I have the feeling the death of Black Otter stands between the two of us. I have to be honest with you, if the circumstances were the same, I would do it again. You have never said so, but I have to know if you blame me for his death."

Dakota sat down beside her, wanting and needing to touch her, to crush her in his arms, but if he did that, he would weaken and never allow her to leave. This time, he had to consider Breanna's safety above his own needs.

"Breanna, what you did was the bravest, noblest act I have ever seen, and you saved my life. It was strange, but at the moment I could have taken Black Otter's life, I found the promise I made my father stayed my hand."

Her golden eyes became misty. "I am glad you did not have to kill him, because I know now that you could never have lived with the guilt of a promise broken. Strangely enough, I feel no guilt at all for what I was forced to do."

He smiled and touched her cheek tenderly. "When one is brave, there need be no guilt."

Pushing his love for her to the back of his mind, he hardened his heart. With lowered lashes concealing the love that shone in his green eyes, he stood up and helped her to her feet. "I will leave you to dress. When you are ready, I will send Levi for you." He glanced at the buckskin gown she wore. "You were not meant to wear rough leather clothing against your soft body. You should wear only silks and satins."

"What you are saying is that I do not belong here with you."

"I am saying you belong in England."

Breanna's eyes traveled over his tall form. He looked so at ease dressed as an Indian. "I cannot say the same about you. I can see now that you have a life here, Dakota. You talk about staying to help the Arapaho; is it not possible that this is where you want to be?"

"What do you mean?"

"I mean, do you feel you belong here?"

"This is where I was born and grew to manhood. A part of me will always feel at home here."

Breanna had the unsettling feeling that she might

never see him again. This Dakota was a man she did not know. He was an Indian, and she could feel him slipping away from her. Did this land, this people, have a prior claim on him? Would she have the courage to leave him when the time came?

Breanna had too much pride to make a scene. If she never saw Dakota again, she wanted him to remember her leaving with dignity and not hanging on him, begging him to keep her with him.

"I will dress now," she said in a resigned voice, turning away and dismissing him. "I will send word when I am ready to leave."

Dakota could feel Breanna's coldness in the depths of his heart. It appeared to him that she could not leave fast enough to suit her.

"Breanna, it has to be this way. Winter is coming on, and I fear you would not survive the cruel winters of this land. Always in the back of my mind lurks the vision of how my white mother died. I do not want this to happen to you."

Without turning around, she spoke. "I have not asked you if I can stay," she reminded him.

"No, you haven't," he agreed.

Breanna did not hear him leave, but when she turned around, he was gone. Now that she was alone, she could allow the tears to fall, and they fell in a great flood down her cheeks.

As last, exhausted and spent, she dried her eyes. Removing the buckskin gown and moccasins, she dressed in her own gown and boots, which went a long way in fortifying her for the task that lay ahead.

The America she had longed to see had become her rival for Dakota's affections. How do I compete with a whole tribe of people? she asked herself. You don't, her mind answered.

Breanna moved through the village beside Levi, looking neither to her left nor her right. The Arapaho people had been kind to take her in, especially the old medicine woman, who had nursed her back to health and shared her tepee with her. But Breanna would not be sorry to leave. This was not her world — but the world that had taken Dakota from her.

A young Indian woman stepped into their path, and Breanna looked into soft brown eyes and a lovely face with high cheek bones and midnight-black hair. The girl said something to Levi which Breanna did not understand. The hunter then turned to Breanna and translated.

"Breanna, this is Running Deer's sister. She is also the wife of Shadow Walker. She wishes me to tell you that her dead sister's spirit can rest now that you have killed her murderer, and that Running Deer will know peace because Dakota has found happiness with you."

Breanna stared long and hard at the Indian woman, not in the least comforted by her words.

"Tell her, Levi," she finally replied, "that I send my greetings to her husband, Shadow Walker, and I shall be eternally grateful for his sacrifice on my behalf."

Without waiting for Levi to translate, Breanna nodded politely to the Indian woman and stepped around her. She did not want to be reminded of Dakota's dead love—certainly not at this time. She would need all her courage and strength to ride out of Dakota's life today, for she might never see him again.

When Breanna reached the horses, Baxley greeted her with a smile and took her bundle, securing it to the packhorse.

Dakota stopped talking to John and turned to her. With a firm grip on her waist, he lifted her into the saddle and handed her the reins.

Was this how it would end—coldly and impersonally? she wondered.

His eyes caught and held her glance. "Breanna, it is not my wish to say our good-byes in this public manner, but it is better so."

Her voice was cold. "No need to explain, Dakota. I understand."

His hand closed around her hand that held the reins. "Do you?"

"Yes, I think so."

"I doubt that you do, Breanna. There is so much that is unsaid between us."

She stared at the Wind River, unable to look at

483

Dakota any longer. "I will agree with you on that. But sometimes good-bye is the only thing left to say."

Knowing that if she didn't leave soon, or if he uttered another word to her, she would fling herself into his arms, Breanna set her shoulders and nudged her mount forward.

"Good-bye, Dakota."

John, Levi, and Baxley fell in beside her, and they rode slowly out of the village.

Breanna could feel Dakota's eyes on her, but she did not look around. When she reached the river, she fought the overwhelming urge to ride back to him. Instead, she kicked her heel into her horse's flanks, making the animal plunge into the river.

She bacame aware that several Arapaho warriors plunged into the river just behind them. She looked at Levi questioningly.

"The Arapaho will ride for several days with us, to assure our safety," he explained.

When Breanna rode up the opposite bank of the river, she looked back just long enough to see Dakota standing on the far shore. He raised his hand in a silent salute, and she responded in kind.

"I don't like the way you two parted," Levi observed.

"It was the only way it could end, Levi."

"Something isn't right here, Breanna."

"Nothing will ever be right again," she said tearfully.

"Dakota would have come with us if you had asked it of him."

"I chose not to pressure him. I had the means to tie Dakota to me, and I chose not to use it. I do not want him unless he comes to me of his own accord."

Breanna urged her mount into a gallop, and Levi had to ride hard to catch her.

"What are you saying?" Levi asked when he finally drew even with her.

"I am saying that I am with child, and I didn't tell Dakota because he would feel obligated to come with me."

Levi looked at her with softened eyes. "If I was a good friend to Dakota, I'd ride back and tell him right now. A man has the right to know when he is going to become a father."

"Promise me that you will keep my secret, Levi. As I said, I do not want Dakota unless he returns to me of his own free will."

Levi shrugged. "Seems like a man should be smart enough to know when he is going to be a father without someone else having to spell it out for him," he said, deciding not to interfere.

Levi was reflective, remembering how Lady Cillia Remington had given birth to Dakota no more than two days' ride from this spot. The old hunter was determined to get Breanna out of this wilderness as quickly as possible, and back to England with all haste. He did not want her child to be born here and risk Breanna suffering from the same fate that had cost Lady Cillia her life.

Winter would soon be upon them, but Levi would drive them hard until he got her back to civilization, to England.

Chapter Thirty-six

Cornwall

Breanna walked along the beach below the hunting lodge, feeling the spring sunshine on her face. Time seemed to pass slowly here where the ever-restless waves had been pounding the cliffs for untold centuries. It somehow made her feel insignificant, as if she were only a pebble on the beach, no more than a passing thought in the blinking of time.

Breanna often came here to the beach. Perhaps it was because she had been so happy here with Dakota. Or perhaps because she could daydream here and imagine that Dakota walked beside her.

Slanting her straw bonnet down over her forehead to protect her skin, Breanna heard someone calling out to her, and she glanced up the cliff to see Levi waving at her.

"Come on down," she called. "You can keep me company."

The old hunter made his way down to her.

Levi saw the tent-like structure that had been erected to protect the baby from the sun and wind. Pausing, he looked inside.

"How's the little one today, Breanna?"

Breanna smiled. "Healthy and growing."

"You know, he's about the best-looking baby I ever saw."

"On behalf of my son, Lord Holden Remington, Viscount of Remington, I thank you."

"That's a mighty big title for such a little mite."

"Yes, it is, but he will one day bring pride and honor to the name."

"Little Holden looks a lot like his father," Levi observed.

Breanna sat down on the quilt beside her son and lifted him in her arms. "Yes, that has not escaped my notice."

Levi reached out and lightly smoothed the black hair on the infant's head. "I was thinking that little Holden will be two months old tomorrow. It doesn't seem that we've had him that long. He sure has brightened up my life."

Breanna smiled. "I am surprised you remembered the exact date. I had not thought about it."

He gave her a lopsided grin. "I never forget important dates, and I consider little Holden's birth one of the most important."

She placed the baby in Levi's arms and watched the happy smile on his face.

"I feel like I have a stake in this baby," Levi said. "Wasn't it me and John who walked the floor while you were giving birth to him?"

"Yes, it was, my dear friend. I don't know what I would have done these past six months if it hadn't been for you and John."

"I got a letter from John today. He says London is not the same without you and me there. But it seems he is courting a wealthy widow, and he thinks she might have marriage on her mind."

Breanna laughed. "How does he feel about that?"

Levi shrugged. "He didn't say."

Breanna placed her cool cheek against Levi's rough one. "I don't know what I would have done without you, Levi. You are so dear to me."

His eyes became misty, and he cleared his throat before he spoke. "I'm right fond of you too, Breanna." He felt the baby's little fist close around his finger and smiled down at the child. "I got me a real family."

"Yes, but one of us is missing," she reminded him.

Levi saw the sadness in her eyes, and it brought an ache to his heart. "I would have thought Dakota would be back by now. But don't you fret none. One day you'll look up, and there he'll be."

"I have cautioned myself not to hope, Levi. I have a feeling that Dakota is where he wants to be. And I am not one to take rejection without being affected by it. Even if Dakota does return. I will not readily receive him. A woman likes to feel as if she is important in her husband's life, and not someone he can so easily cast aside."

"I haven't a thing to say in his defense, Breanna. But had you allowed me to send word to him that he had a son, he would have come home immediately."

"Yes, he would return for a son, but not for me."

Levi shook his head. He could no longer make excuses for Dakota. "It's not my place to convince you of Dakota's feelings; you already know what a fine man he is."

"That has never been in question. If you are going to tell me how noble and honest he is, do not bother — we are all agreed on that point."

Levi knew it was time to change the subject. "I heard a bit of gossip today that you might find amusing."

Breanna laughed. "Why, Levi, I have never known you to be interested in wagging tongues."

"No, but this is different. It's about Lady Rye Saffron."

Breanna knitted her brow. "What's she done, run off with the crown jewels, or perhaps Prince Albert, the Queen's husband?"

Levi chuckled. "Now, Breanna, animosity does not become you."

"No, but it gives me the greatest pleasure. What have you heard about that woman, Levi?" she asked, curious in spite of herself.

"Well, word has it that she's gone off with this married Russian nobleman, who has taken her to Russia with him. It seems that her brother was so enraged at her escapade that he took to his bed, swearing she had disgraced him for the last time."

"How did you hear this?"

"From the most reliable source, of course. I overheard the servants talking."

Breanna smiled. "Yes, a most reliable source." Suddenly her eyes turned sad, and Levi knew she was remembering the day she had overheard the servants gossiping about Dakota and Rye Saffron. "You don't still believe anything happened between Dakota and that woman, do you?"

"No, I know nothing happened between them," she admitted. "As you said, Dakota is an honorable man."

Levi handed the baby back to Breanna and stood up, knowing she probably needed to be alone. "I'm going back to the big house. Do you want me to take little Holden with me?"

"No. I'll bring him home after a while. I like to have him with me."

Levi climbed the cliff, wondering why Dakota had

not returned and hoping he wouldn't stay away too long. Breanna was not the kind of woman who should be neglected. She was too headstrong, too independent, and she had too much pride.

Levi was coming from the stable when he heard the sound of an approaching rider. As he walked toward the house, his face lit up with happiness when he saw Dakota dismount. Rushing forward, the old hunter grabbed Dakota's arm and shook it so hard he almost wrung it off.

"I'm glad you decided to come home, Dakota."

Dakota smiled. "I'm home to stay, Levi. I had many things to attend to before I could leave, else I would have come sooner."

His green eyes moved to the house, searchingly. "Where is Breanna?"

"Did you expect her to just be sitting around, waiting for you?" the hunter asked accusingly.

"You of all people should know I could not return until everything was settled with Arapaho."

"You have done right by them, it's now time to do right by Breanna."

"Don't rush me, Levi," Dakota said. "I know better than you what my obligations are."

Levi's heart softened, and he wondered if Dakota knew about the baby. "Did you stop at the London house?"

492

"No, my ship docked at Plymouth and I came directly here."

"You will find Breanna at the hunting lodge. I just left her, and she was walking on the beach."

"How is she, Levi?"

"Why don't you go and find that out for yourself."

Breanna kissed the soft cheek of her sleeping son, loving him in the very depths of her heart. She had convinced herself that this child might be the only part of Dakota she would ever have.

Placing the baby in the shade of the tent, she stood up, her eyes tracing the far horizon. Loneliness settled on her shoulders as she once more remembered how happy she had been here with Dakota. Was this to be the extent of her life, drawing on borrowed memories from yesterday?

Dakota's eyes ran hungrily over his wife as she walked along the deserted beach. How he had ached for her. His life had been an empty void without her. Even though he could not see her face from this distance, he could feel her loneliness like a knife in his own heart.

His footsteps were noiseless as he hurried down the cliff toward her, his heartbeat racing, his eyes shining with anticipation.

Breanna felt another's presence so strongly that she whirled around, her heart drumming, her pulse pounding. When she saw Dakota striding toward her, her hands balled into fists and her nails cut into her palms from the tight grip she was keeping on herself.

She fought against the need to run into her husband's arms, to feel him hold her and tell her that he wanted her in his life.

Her eyes ran over him, noting his hair had been neatly trimmed and that he wore no headband. His buckskins had been exchanged for gray trousers and a powder-blue waistcoat. The sleeves of his white shirt had been carelessly rolled up and revealed his tanned, muscled arms.

All this she saw in the flickering of a second, and she wondered if it was symbolic. Had he, of his own free will, traded his old way of life for a life here in England? No one had ordered his return. Dared she hope that he was here because it was his choice?

Dakota halted an arm's length away from Breanna. There was something different about her, he thought, a new maturity. If possible, she was even more beautiful than he remembered. He saw in her golden eyes skepticism and a certain amount of accusation, which he knew that he deserved.

"How are you, Breanna?" He hadn't meant to say that; he had rehearsed in his mind how he would rush to her, take her in his arms, and declare his love for her openly and proudly.

"I am faring well, Dakota. I do not have to ask about you. You appear to be well."

He tried to lessen the tension between them by smiling. "I see you still prefer the hunting lodge to the big house."

"I am not living at the hunting lodge. I just like to come here sometimes . . . to . . . because it is secluded and I can think more clearly."

His eyes drew her gaze. "Do you think of me while you are here?"

"Yes," she admitted.

"Dare I hope that you have pleasant thoughts of me?"

Her eyes dulled. "You have no right to ask that of me, Dakota. Why didn't you just stay in America? That seems to be where you are the happiest."

He reached out and took a wisp of red-gold hair and tucked it behind her ear. "I have missed you, Breanna," he whispered, pain lacing his words.

"Did you? I find that difficult to believe. One would have thought there was plenty to distract you from England . . . and me."

Dakota wanted to take her, shake her, make her understand how he needed her. He wanted to tell her about the empty months when he had thought he could not get through another day without seeing her, holding her in his arms, making passionate love to her. He wanted to force Breanna to admit that she had missed him also.

At that moment, Dakota heard a faint sound like an infant crying, and he swung around, looking about until he located where the sound was coming from. He saw the makeshift tent flapping in the gentle breeze, and surmised the child was there.

Breanna moved in the direction of the tent, and Dakota fell into step beside her. "Is that a servant's baby?" He looked about him, as if trying to locate the infant's mother.

Breanna did not bother to answer him as she went down on her knees and lifted her son in her arms.

Dakota dropped down beside her, resenting the intrusion of the child. There was so much he wanted to say to Breanna, and he wanted to say it now before he lost his nerve.

Breanna cooed softly to the child and immediately the crying stopped.

"Here," she said, thrusting the child at Dakota. "Hold him while I shake the sand from the blanket."

"No, I do not know anything about babies," he admitted, horrified when she placed the child in his arms against his protest. He held the child awkwardly at first, then finally he pulled it closer to his body so he could support it. When the child's head bobbed, Dakota's hold tightened and the baby started to cry.

"Give the baby back to its mother, Breanna. I want to be alone with you. There is so much I want to say to you."

Anger sparked to life within her golden eyes. "You have not asked me the child's name, Dakota."

He glanced down at the round little face, thinking offhandedly that it was a beautiful child, but feeling little interest in it otherwise.

"Tell me the child's name if you must. But then come with me to the hunting lodge. I want to be alone with you, Breanna."

"The baby that you seem so anxious to abandon is named Holden Remington. He is the new Viscount of Remington."

Dakota's throat was working convulsively as he realized the significance of what she was telling him. Now he looked at the child searchingly, and he could scarcely breathe when he saw the green eyes, so like his own, staring back at him.

Dakota glanced up at Breanna, his eyes filled with misery. "My son?"

"Yes, my lord. Your son," she told him proudly.

Tremendous emotions shook Dakota as he picked up one of the tiny hands and held it in his. "My . . . son," he said in a voice filled with wonder. "How can this be?"

Breanna stood, hands on hips, legs spread apart, and anger gleaming in her eyes. "I could tell you the 'how' of it, my lord, but I believe you already know that. Oh, you are very adept at wooing a woman into your bed, but you care little for the consequences."

"Breanna," he asked, dismissing her sarcasm and trying to take in all she was telling him, "did you know you were with child when you left the Arapaho village?"

The proud tilt of her head gave no hint to the trembling that was going on inside her. "If you are talking about when you sent me away, yes, I knew."

"Why didn't you tell me? You know I would never have allowed you leave without me had I known you were with child."

"I knew that, Dakota. That's why I chose not to enlighten you."

There was now anger in his eyes. "Why, Breanna? I had a right to know."

"Because, if you had decided to come with me, I wanted it to be because you wanted to, and not from some misplaced duty you might have felt."

He cupped the baby's soft head in the palm of his hand, awed that anyone so small could belong to him. Dakota was overcome with a strong love and protectiveness. This little person was someone who had been created by him and Breanna. It softened his heart to think she had carried his seed within her body.

Breanna was watching the different emotions that chased across Dakota's handsome face. She felt tears stir in her eyes when he lifted his son and held him against his face, planting a soft kiss on the baby's hand.

There was no denying that Dakota was moved by his child. Still Breanna wanted to strike out at him, to make him pay for not being with her when she had brought their son into the world.

"May I assume that this is the first child you have fathered, my lord?"

His jaw tightened, and his eyes narrowed in on her. "Yes, you may make that assumption."

"Hello," Levi called out, making his way down the cliff. "I've come to take the baby, seeing as how the two of you have things to talk over."

"Never mind, Levi," Breanna stormed. "I am going with you."

Dakota stood up and placed the child in Levi's arms. "No, she's not. You take the baby with you. Breanna and I may, or may not, be back to the house tonight."

Levi nodded and smiled, satisfied. He knew when Dakota got that gleam in his eyes, he made things happen. Poor Breanna was about to meet with an immovable force. The hunter chuckled to himself as he climbed the cliff, the young Viscount Remington in his arms. All Breanna needed was for Dakota to quit acting as if he was afraid of her rejection of him, and to make her see things his way.

Levi knew that Breanna was a strong woman and

she needed an even stronger man to rule her, one who loved her and would cherish her as Dakota would if she would only give him the chance.

Levi glanced down at his precious burden. "Well, little one, it seems you are going to belong to a happy family after all."

Chapter Thirty-seven

Breanna watched Levi depart with a feeling of panic. She did not want to be alone with Dakota. She was afraid she would allow him to see too much of what she was feeling, and she had to protect herself from being hurt again.

Dakota took her trembling hand in his, his eyes soft and pleading. "Breanna, will you ever be able to forgive me for not being with you when our son was born?"

She shrugged, pretending indifference, all the while watching the way his hair gleamed, black and thick in the sun.

"It was of no great significance. You did not know I was with child, so, therefore, you are excused."

He looked at her, puzzled. "No, I'm not. At least not in your mind. Will you tell me all that you are thinking and feeling so I can tell you what is in my heart?"

She faced him with a stiff, proud tilt to her head.

"No. Your questions are easy, my lord, but my answers would be more complicated."

"I have time to listen."

She pulled her hand from his grasp and walked to the water's edge. "Since I have known you, Dakota, I have had to compete with your memory of a dead Indian girl, the whole of the Arapaho tribe, and your reluctance to let me be a part of your life. I am not condemning you, I am merely stating facts. I really have no reason to condemn you for anything. You did not choose to be my husband, so I should not have expected you to act the part."

Breanna could feel him behind her. The warmth of his breath teased her hair, and she felt a weakness shake her body.

"You have every right to expect just that," he said. "Would you feel more tied to me if we went through a proper ceremony? I know if my grandfather had not become ill, he would have insisted we have the ceremony. Of course, I do not need some rites to make me feel married to you, Breanna."

She turned around. "I believe the time for that has passed. It would not seem proper since we have a son."

"If that is your wish. I am willing to do whatever it takes to make you happy."

"Does this mean you will be staying in England?"

"I have no intentions of ever leaving unless you drive me away." He smiled. "Even then, I doubt if you would be rid of me."

Now she searched his eyes, daring to hope. "Are you saying you have cut your ties in America?"

"I have settled the problems caused by Black Otter. The Arapaho have been exonerated from any blame in the raids he perpetrated. I am now free of any obligation I may have owed them. In my heart I know Two Moons would say this to me if he were alive."

Dakota reached for her, and Breanna reluctantly allowed him to pull her into his arms. "I have no further ties there. My life is here, with you and our son. My life and my love are here," he said softly, his arms tightening about her.

She jerked her head up, a tremendous splintering of her defenses crumbling to let in hope. "Your . . . love?"

He smiled, and there was a wealth of feeling in his green eyes. "Yes, my dearest love," he said thickly. "How could you even question how I feel about you?"

"I thought . . . Running Deer . . . I . . . you love me?" she choked out.

Laughter shook him as he pulled her back into his arms. "I never loved Running Deer. I admit there was a time when I thought I might love her, but that was nothing compared to this aching need I feel for you. All I can think about now is the sparkle of your golden eyes or the way your beautiful hair frames your face."

Tears swam in her golden eyes. "Oh, Dakota, I never—"

He placed his finger on her lips. "How could you not know that I love you? It seems everyone else knew it."

She was still not convinced, and being female, she asked, "When did you . . ."

His eyes moved over each feature of her face as if he was becoming reacquainted with them. "I can tell you the exact moment I fell in love with a beautiful fiery woman who set my blood boiling and wrapped herself around my heart so tightly I could scarcely think of anything else."

"When?" she asked again.

"The first day I saw you. You were unconscious on the ground, and when I lifted your head onto my lap and you opened your golden eyes, my heart was no longer mine."

"But I didn't know."

"I realize that, because I took the greatest pains to keep you from finding out. You couldn't know that first night, as I waited for you to come downstairs, I was actually considering leaving rather than facing you. I had heard the unflattering things you said about your husband, and I feared you would not accept me. But I stayed. Already it was too late for me, Breanna, because I had to have you."

She reached out and touched his face. "Oh, my dearest love, that day when I regained consciousness, I was so disturbed by the feelings a handsome

504

stranger had brought to life within me. I found myself telling you things I would never have told anyone else." She smiled. "When I discovered you were my husband, I was horrified because of what I had said, but I was also glad you were the man to whom I had been married."

He raised her hand to his lips and kissed the soft palm, while his eyes darkened with something akin to passion. "We had to go a long way to find each other, Breanna, and I never want us to be parted again."

"Dakota, there is something that has been bothering me. Can you ever forget that it was I who killed your Indian brother?"

He pressed his rough face against her satin-smooth cheek. "I will never forget that you cared enough for me to take up a gun and shoot a man. I know what that cost you, since you had never before taken a human life."

Her aching fingers reached around him, and he lifted her into his arms, carrying her up the cliff toward the hunting lodge.

"Where do you take me, my lord?" she asked almost coyly.

His eyes flamed with an inner light. "I am taking you to my bed, my lady, and I may keep you there the rest of the day and on into the night."

Breanna threw back her head, feeling as if her heart would take flight. No one had a right to be this happy, she thought as he pressed hot kisses on her throat.

Dakota entered the hunting lodge and carried Breanna to the bedroom that the two of them had occupied the first time he had made love to her.

He placed her on the bed and stood staring down at her, loving the way her red-gold hair fanned out around her. Driven with burning desire for her, he first wanted to feast his eyes on her beauty.

"Is there a chance that I can seduce you into loving me, my lady?" he asked sincerely.

She held her arms up to him, feeling a thrill go through her body as his deep voice stirred her desire to life. "There is a very great chance, my lord."

Dakota enclosed Breanna in his arms while he bruised her lips with hungry kisses, heightening their sensations.

"I love you, my Breanna," he murmured. "Never be where I cannot reach out and touch you. I need you in my life."

Breanna closed her eyes tightly as his weight drove her into the soft bed. Loving him as she did, her lips sought his sensuous mouth.

When at last Dakota raised his head and he stared into her eyes, Breanna tried to speak of her deep feelings, but her voice came out in a deep throaty sigh.

Dakota understood what she was feeling, because he was caught up with the essence of her, and it reached to the depths of his whole being.

"I will stay with you for eternity, my love," he

assured her, chasing away any remaining doubts she might have.

Breanna could not have said why, but at that moment she thought of Holden and Cillia, and she smiled. She hoped wherever the two lovers were, they would know that they had a son of whom they could be proud.

Fleetingly, she thought about the Arapaho war chief, Two Moons, and gave him credit for shaping Dakota into the man he was today.

Happiness fused the lovers together, as the distant pounding of the surf was drowned out by the murmured words of everlasting love.

FIERY ROMANCE
From Zebra Books

AUTUMN'S FURY   (1763, $3.95)
by Emma Merritt

Lone Wolf had known many women, but none had captured his heart the way Catherine had . . . with her he felt a hunger he hadn't experienced with any of the maidens of his own tribe. He would make Catherine his captive, his slave of love — until she would willingly surrender to the magic of AUTUMN'S FURY.

PASSION'S PARADISE   (1618, $3.75)
by Sonya T. Pelton

When she is kidnapped by the cruel, captivating Captain Ty, fair-haired Angel Sherwood fears not for her life, but for her honor! Yet she can't help but be warmed by his manly touch, and secretly longs for PASSION'S PARADISE.

LOVE'S ELUSIVE FLAME   (1836, $3.75)
by Phoebe Conn

Golden-haired Flame was determined to find the man of her dreams even if it took forever, but she didn't have long to wait once she met the handsome rogue Joaquin. He made her respond to his ardent kisses and caresses . . . but if he wanted her completely, she would have to be his only woman — she wouldn't settle for anything less. Joaquin had always taken women as he wanted . . . but none of them was Flame. Only one night of wanton esctasy just wasn't enough — once he was touched by LOVE'S ELUSIVE FLAME.

SAVAGE SPLENDOR   (1855, $3.95)
by Constance O'Banyon

By day Mara questioned her decision to remain in her husband's world. But by night, when Tajarez crushed her in his strong, muscular arms, taking her to the peaks of rapture, she knew she could never live without him.

SATIN SURRENDER   (1861, $3.95)
by Carol Finch

Dante Folwer found innocent Erica Bennett in his bed in the most fashionable whorehouse in New Orleans. Expecting a woman of experience, Dante instead stole the innocence of the most magnificent creature he'd ever seen. He would forever make her succumb to . . . SATIN SURRENDER.

Available wherever paperbacks are sold, or order direct from the Publisher. Send cover price plus 50¢ per copy for mailing and handling to Zebra Books, Dept. 2502 475 Park Avenue South, New York, N.Y. 10016. Residents of New York, New Jersey and Pennsylvania must include sales tax. DO NOT SEND CASH.

LOVE'S BRIGHTEST STARS SHINE
WITH ZEBRA BOOKS!

CATALINA'S CARESS   (2202, $3.95)
by Sylvie F. Sommerfield
Catalina Carrington was determined to buy her riverboat back from the handsome gambler who'd beaten her brother at cards. But when dashing Marc Copeland named his price—three days as his mistress—Catalina swore she'd never meet his terms . . . even as she imagined the rapture a night in his arms would bring!

BELOVED EMBRACE   (2135, $3.95)
by Cassie Edwards
Leana Rutherford was terrified when the ship carrying her family from New York to Texas was attacked by savage pirates. But when she gazed upon the bold sea-bandit Brandon Seton, Leana longed to share the ecstasy she was sure sure his passionate caress would ignite!

ELUSIVE SWAN   (2061, $3.95)
by Sylvie F. Sommerfield
Just one glance from the handsome stranger in the dockside tavern in boisterous St. Augustine made Arianne tremble with excitement. But the innocent young woman was already running from one man . . . and no matter how fiercely the flames of desire burned within her, Arianne dared not submit to another!

MOONLIT MAGIC   (1941, $3.95)
by Sylvie F. Sommerfield
When she found the slick railroad negotiator Trace Cord trespassing on her property and bathing in her river, innocent Jenny Graham could barely contain her rage. But when she saw how the setting sun gilded Trace's magnificent physique, Jenny's seething fury was transformed into burning desire!

Available wherever paperbacks are sold, or order direct from the Publisher. Send cover price plus 50¢ per copy for mailing and handling to Zebra Books, Dept. 2502, 475 Park Avenue South, New York, N.Y. 10016. Residents of New York, New Jersey and Pennsylvania must include sales tax. DO NOT SEND CASH.